YEARS IN THE MAKING

RIGHT PLACE, RIGHT TIME BOOK 2

MEGAN MCSPADDEN

For Grandpa, a man who, loved quietly, laughed loudly and lived simply.

Tash, a friend I miss every day.

Jen, I'll cheer extra hard for the Blue Jays for you, even when they suck!

CONTENT WARNINGS

Aneurysms
Death of a parent (off-page but described, not gory)
Car accident

PLAYLIST

You're All I Need To Get By - Emilia Jones, Ferdia Walsh-Peelo

Terrified - Vincent Lima

Peer Pressure - James Bay, Julia Michaels

Years In The Making - Arkells

Save Me - Noah Kahan

Don't Let Me - Morningsiders

My Repair - Sons Of The East

In A Perfect World - Dean Lewis, Julia Michaels

Broken - Jonah Kagen

Lost at Sea - Loyalties, Vincent Lima

Good Grief - Bastille

Against All Odds - Phil Collins

Turn - E The Wombats

Mountain Sound - Of Monsters and Men

Carried Me With You - Brandi Carlile

Before You Go - Lewis Capaldi

Gloria - The Lumineers

Hear Me Now - Bad Wolves, DIAMANTE
If You Only Knew - Shinedown
Sound of Madness - Shinedown
Meet You At The Light - Desiree Dawson
Passenger - Noah Kahan
I'll Follow You - Shinedown
I Won't Give Up - Jason Mraz
Dear Agony - Breaking Benjamin
Place to Hide - O.A.R.
Two of Us - Mike Edel
Maroon - Taylor Swift
All Eyes on You - James New
Slipped Away - Avril Lavigne
My Home - Myles Smith
Locksmith - Sadie Jean
Wanted Dead or Alive - Bon Jovi
Evenings with Family - Vincent Lima

Available on Spotify

CANADIANISM GLOSSARY

Bunkie - a small one room cabin often used for guests at cottages

Gravol - anti-nausea medication

Shoppers - Pharmacy like CVS or Boots

Muskoka chair - slopped back deck chair, similar to an Adirondack chair

Klick - a kilometer

Swedish Berries - like Swedish Fish but shaped like berries

Coles Notes - student guide for literature. (Like Sparknotes/Cliffsnotes)

Kitty-corner - seems regional, catty-corner/caddy-corner, diagonally opposite someone/something.

PROLOGUE

December
Nellie

This is not me, I think as I pull Teddy's mouth back to mine. *I don't make out with virtual strangers after ten minutes of knowing them,* I scold myself, leaning in as his hand slides under my shirt to palm my breast. *I certainly don't make out with men in open areas where anyone can see us,* I remind myself as I reach down and pull my sweater up and over my head, tossing it to the side.

Somehow, Teddy walking me out to my car has resulted in one hell of a make-out session. First against the door and now in my driver's seat. I should be in it alone, already on the road. But he's the one sitting while I'm straddling his lap, topless, breathless, and senseless.

What the actual fuck is happening right now?

Of course, Teddy is not exactly a stranger. I met him years ago, on a train, in another life. My mind keeps trying to pull me back there, but I'm desperate to keep it in the present. So I focus on where his body is pressed against mine. How his breath and mine seem one and the same, how his grip is like a vice, holding me as if he is afraid I'll disappear again. But it wasn't me who disappeared. One day he was there, and the next—poof, gone. I'd spent years acting out what I'd say to him if he ever walked back into my life, and then one day I just... stopped thinking about him. I let myself finally move on from the guy who won my heart only to smash it with two words and no further explanation.

This was not a scenario I'd ever thought about. Not a single one involved his lips on mine, his teeth grazing my neck, his hand squeezing my breast, and his arousal blatantly pressed beneath me. When I rock my hips, he lets out a hiss and his hands move to my ass, driving me harder against him. The Teddy I knew over a decade ago was sweet and gentle, always the one to slow down the urgency that would build in us. This Teddy is desperate and a little rough. I tell myself I hate it, but the truth is, I fucking love it. More than that, I *need* it. I've spent twelve years hating this man and he has the nerve to walk back into my life and immediately get under my clothes.

"Goddammit, I missed you, LG," he says breathlessly, and that's it, that's the cold bucket of water I needed ten minutes ago.

I pull back, untangle myself from him, grab my sweater from the passenger seat, and practically fall out of the car as I struggle to dress myself. When I look back, I know he knows what's coming. He tips his head back against the headrest, trying to catch his breath.

"Yeah. That was—"

"Something that will never happen again," I say with conviction.

He doesn't respond right away, just watches me until the sadness from earlier replaces the hope in those pale blue eyes and he slides from the car. *Yes,* I think, *it sucks, doesn't it? This feeling of not being wanted.*

I set my jaw and square my shoulders. "Nothing has changed, Teddy. You're still the guy who made me fall for you that summer and then fucked off without so much as a goodbye, and I'm the girl who stupidly thought you'd come back to me." I push past him to get behind the wheel, then grab his coat off the passenger seat and throw it at him. When I turn to face him again, his expression is void of emotion, void of the guy I used to know.

"Bye, Teddy." I slam the door shut, put the car in reverse, and head towards home. Despite the urge, I manage to get to the main road without looking in my rearview mirror.

Twelve years, and the only guy I've ever loved shows up working for my best friend's soulmate. And within minutes of seeing him again, he had the audacity to give me an explanation that would have saved me years of pain.

If I thought the universe had been looking out for me all those years ago on that train, then it was definitely fucking with me now.

THEN

ONE

NELLIE

12 Years Ago, April

I've made a terrible mistake, I think as yet another half-drunk person decked out in a baseball hat and jersey slams into my side. If I had bothered to use my brain, I'd have checked the baseball schedule before arranging a time for my parents to pick me up from the station. I can never remember how early in the year the season starts. Hell, I would have walked from Toronto all the way home. It would have taken me until tomorrow afternoon, but at least I wouldn't have to deal with this buffoonery.

As the train pulls in, people ignore the yellow line on the edge of the platform. The yellow line you're supposed to stay behind to lower your risk of dying by getting hit the very train you're waiting to board.

People have now surrounded me, and my hope of securing a place to sit slips away. When the door opens, I'm jostled violently as people catch themselves on my backpack and kick my suitcase this way and that.

"Don't mind me," I call out. "I enjoy being invisible." I'm

hoping I sound as bitchy as I feel but probably not. I've been told that I'm too easygoing, and even when I'm miffed about something, it takes a great deal of effort to get my true feelings across. A chronic people-pleaser, that's me.

I feel hands on my shoulders and immediately stop breathing, but those hands keep me in place as another person rams into me.

"Not invisible." A voice comes from behind me. "Just too nice." His hands leave my shoulders, and he steps to my right. I look over just in time for him to gesture towards the train. "After you."

He steps on after me and is forced to stop just inside the door as I block the way forward. Sure enough, every seat is taken and three people are sitting on the stairs, blocking the way to the second level. It looks like I'll be standing at the entrance for the next little while. I take a step to the side and pull my backpack to my front and my suitcase as close as possible, and let out a sigh as my back hits the flimsy train wall.

Mr. Chivalrous leans against the wall to my right on the other side of the door. He looks completely unbothered by the entire situation. His long legs are crossed at the ankles, and his attention is on his phone. I use his distraction as an opportunity to study him. He's tall and lanky with dark brown hair that curls below the base of his cap. It's hard to tell his age, but I'd guess somewhere around my own, early twenties. I'm staring at the crest on his jersey when I feel that telltale tingle of being watched. When I glance up I see that he's looking back at me, eyebrows disappearing under the rim of his hat. I smile shyly and immediately look away, but not before he sees my entire face turn bright red.

We spend the rest of the time between leaving the station and the first stop, exchanging not-so-subtle glances. I catch him looking at the tattoo behind my right ear, and he catches me staring at his hands. He has a ring on his one index finger, a thick silver band, and when he's not texting, he's spinning it with his thumb. I can almost feel those hands on my shoulders still. The comforting weight of them keeping me firmly in place while people pushed by. Then that voice, smooth and deep, letting me know that at least one person sees me

Right before the first stop is announced, people begin to gather at the door and block my view of my seatless buddy. The sudden disappointment at not being able to see him shocks me. Perhaps I just prefer looking at him to staring down at my feet or my reflection in the window across from me.

After people disembark, I notice he's gone, and my heart sinks a little. I must just be tired or ashamed that I didn't thank him for being kind when everyone else just pushed by. But then I hear the same voice from earlier.

"Hey. I snagged you a seat." And sure enough, when I look over, he's sitting in a section of four seats, three of which are empty.

"Thank you," I say sitting kitty-corner to him. "And thanks for earlier."

He smiles over at me shaking his head. "No need to thank me." He's got pretty nice teeth, although his canines are so pointy I can't help wondering if he's ever made someone bleed when kissing them. *Don't think of him kissing anyone, Nellie, I* scold my wandering mind. I force myself to wonder what I'd do if I had teeth like that. For starters, I'd be a vampire or some kind of faerie character every Halloween. When people asked me where I got the teeth, I'd say my mom and dad gave them to me and probably laugh maniacally.

For three more stops, we sit quietly pretending not to look at each other. But as the train empties even more, it feels weird to be sitting this close to someone without headphones and not talking.

"How was the game?" I ask, slipping my cardigan off. I don't know if the train is hot or if this guy is having some kind of physical effect on me, but I do know that the extra layer is now totally unnecessary.

I see his eyes follow my actions and then stick to my arm. "It was good. They won so can't complain. Are you a fan?" he asks, tilting his chin towards the blue jay in flight on my inner forearm.

I wince. "No, not really. I'm not a sports girl."

"So just a bird girl then?" His eyes land on the black swallow on my wrist.

"My dad's an ornithologist, and birds are kind of our thing."

"That's someone who studies birds right?"

"Excellent deductive reasoning," I say approvingly.

"Is that what you're in school for?"

"How do you know I'm in school for anything?"

He points at my suitcase. "It's the end of the school year, you look around my age, and you've got a suitcase without any airline tags. Also"—he nods down at my backpack—"there's an Ossington University pin on your backpack."

"Right..." I say slowly looking down at my case and then back up at him. He's smiling again with one eyebrow quirked, waiting for my answer. "No, but my major is equally nerdy."

"Geology?"

I shake my head.

"Elvish?"

"Elvish? I don't think that's a thing."

"Oh, it's definitely a thing. There's a course at Ossington."

"No, there's not," I reply in disbelief because I would know.

"There is. I nearly took it," he claims, almost proudly.

"Why didn't you?"

He leans in, smirking. "Too nerdy," he says quietly, a wide

smile replacing the smirk. "Nah, I didn't have room for it in my schedule."

"Well, clearly I'm not majoring in Elvish if I didn't even know there was a course on it." I straighten primly, trying to ignore what that smile does to me. Trying desperately to not think about what those teeth would feel like against my tongue.

He studies me for a beat. His hand with the ring pinching his bottom lip, keeping my attention right where I'm trying not to look. "I'm not sure I can think of anything as nerdy as those three things."

"I'm a library sciences major."

"So you can be a..."

"Librarian."

He looks taken aback. "I don't mean to be rude, but you need a degree to be a librarian?"

"What is it that you think librarians do?" I ask with a slight tilt of my head.

"Tell people to be quiet and stamp books."

"Yes, well, there *is* a proper way to shush people," I say with a straight face. "I need two credits in Shushing to get my degree. It's basically a language course in Library Science."

He leans back and crosses one ankle over his knee. "I don't fully believe you, but I also had no idea that librarians needed a degree so I'm not confident in my assumption."

"Stick with your gut. It's not a course. The goal is to be an information professional."

"Like a professional know-it-all?" He offers a crooked grin, and if I had been standing, I'm pretty sure my legs would have given out.

"Well, that sounds like someone who would be the most unpopular person in the room."

"Sorry, I don't mean it negatively," he amends. "I'm just trying to understand what it is you study then. Like, do you just learn everything? Is it something you need additional schooling for?"

"A master's is pretty much necessary. But I'll have loads of job opportunities. It's not just libraries, it's working for corporations, media, law..." I could go on, really delve into my courses and career opportunities, but I don't want to talk about me anymore. "What about you? What kept your schedule too busy for Elvish?"

"Environmental Science." He blushes when he says it. He's hot, chivalrous, and is interested in the natural world? Be still my nerdy heart.

"Ah, so you can be a professional environment know-it-all?"

He shrugs. "I don't know, it was just a major that appealed to me, and having a degree can't hurt, right?"

"So you're not passionate about it?"

"I mean, I am, in a way. I like nature, being outdoors, and knowing things about being outdoors. I just don't really know what I'm going to do with the degree. Probably something with trees. I like being in the forest. Ask me in a couple of months."

"Shall we meet on the train to discuss in two months?"

"I was thinking maybe you'd give me your number... or I could give you mine."

This catches me off guard, and the lie slips out before I can stop it. "I'm not sure my boyfriend would like that."

He blanches. "Shit, sorry, I shouldn't have assumed. I mean, look at you." He says it so softly I'm not even sure I hear him correctly.

"It's fine. I'm flattered. Do you regret saving me a seat now?"

"Nope." He shakes his head without breaking eye contact. "I had no ulterior motive before we started talking."

"What stop is yours?"

"Wellington. You?" So close, only a twenty-minute drive from me.

"Stewardsville."

"You from there?"

"No..." I debate lying about where I'm from, but decide he doesn't seem like the type of guy who's going to track me down. Not that that kind of guy is going to be wearing some kind of identifier. "Comrie."

"Ugh, so you've gotta take the bus the rest of the way home?"

"Thankfully no. My parents are meeting me in Stewardsville. My dad would drive to the ends of the earth as long as he didn't have to go through Toronto. So I get as far from the city as I can via train. That way he avoids the city and I avoid a bus. It's a win-win."

"Solid arrangement. Did you go to Centennial?"

"I did. Did you go to Wellington High?"

"Sure did. Do you know Spencer Caldwell?"

"He may be a distant relation of mine."

"No shit. He ended my high school baseball career by hitting me with a line drive."

Awkward. "Did I mention he's a distant relation?"

"You did, yes."

"So did you have grand dreams of playing for the hometown team before my distantly related cousin ended your promising career?"

"Nah." He shakes his head, laughing softly. It's a nice soothing sound in this somewhat chaotic environment. "I was a mediocre pitcher just trying to get through high school with a decent number of extracurriculars."

"What else did you do? Maybe you know someone who ended my debating career or something."

"I don't think we had a debate team."

"We didn't either, but I wish we did. All those American shows with debate teams made me so jealous."

"I would have been terrible. I'm too much of a pushover. I was in the orchestra, if you can believe it."

"Oh?" My mind immediately tries to guess what instrument he played. He has long fingers which would come in handy for many things—I mean, instruments. "Cello?"

"Think smaller."

"Violin?"

He smiles and nods.

"Huh."

"What, don't I look like a violin player?"

"I'm not sure anyone wearing a baseball hat, jersey, and jeans has ever looked like one."

"You know I can take these things off, right?" I feel my face heat again. "Like I have other clothes."

"Well, I figured. Do you still play?"

"Occasionally. Makes my mom smile so I'll play for her sometimes."

Why the hell did I tell him I have a boyfriend?

"You don't play for you?"

"Okay, once in a while I'll play for myself too. I have to practice, after all. I'd hate to subject her to a wrong note."

"You're a good son." I offer a small smile, and he returns it.

"I hope so." He looks out the window, and I see his brows furrow slightly in the reflection. "How about you?" he asks, turning back to me, his face relaxed again. "Play any instruments?"

"Ha! I have no aptitude for music. Hitting the play button is as close as I get to it."

"Well, we can't all be good at everything, or life would be boring."

"True. I read a lot."

"How else are you supposed to know everything if you don't read?" he jokes. "What do you like reading?"

"Historical fiction and fantasy, mostly."

"Those do not seem like two genres that go together."

"I don't know. They both kind of take the reader out of the real world. I mean, historical fiction is the real world, I guess, but I tend to read books set before the end of World War Two. So it seems otherworldly sometimes."

"I don't read much, but I do like it when I do. My dad's a big spy novel guy and is always recommending his latest to me. They don't really appeal to me, though."

"What about them don't you like?"

"I don't know." His forehead scrunches up in thought. "It's like someone gave an author a checklist of manly things and said, 'Include all this stuff, and men will read the book.' It feels so forced."

"You could say the same thing for some romance. But it's definitely not all the books, so maybe there is one out there you'd enjoy. I mean, the nice thing about books is that there is something for everyone. Some people want a very formulaic story, and there's nothing wrong with that. While others, like yourself it would seem, need something a bit more out of left field."

"Look at you with the baseball term," he says proudly.

"Hard to avoid when it's part of everyday vernacular."

His eyes widen and that crooked grin appears. "Vernacular, nice word. Okay, question. If you were to recommend two authors for me to check out, one in each genre, who would you suggest?"

I think for a minute. "Kate Culliver for historical fiction. And... Maira Sahni's series The Forest of Despair. You can't go wrong with either."

He pulls out his phone and taps away, probably typing "This girl is a nerd."

The next stop is announced, and I feel myself panic as he stands. "You know, I don't think my boyfriend would mind if I gave you my number to talk about books." He looks down at me in a way that makes me think he sees through my lie.

"I'll only use it for book purposes, scout's honor." He holds up his fingers in a salute and hands me his phone.

"I think that's the Girl Guide's salute." I laugh as I type out my number and add "Library Girl" into the name field before handing it back.

He looks down at me, and for a minute I don't think he's going to say anything. But then his lips tilt to the side in a crooked grin. "It was nice to meet you, Library Girl."

"You too, Enviro Guy." And then I watch as he steps off the train and waves back. I have the sudden urge to stick my head out the door and yell that I'm single, but instead I watch as he disappears down the platform, barely noticing the jerk of the train as it starts towards its final stop.

Five minutes later my phone pings with an unknown number.

UNKNOWN

Thanks for the book recs, LG.

I can feel the heat of the blush as it spreads across my face, and I add him as a contact under Enviro Guy.

Anytime, EG.

TWO

TEDDY

The minute my stop was announced, I wanted to conveniently forget it was mine and stay on with her. But I also didn't want to be that guy, the guy who doesn't seem to hear the "I've got a boyfriend" part of the conversation. My older brother would have stayed on. Will likes to say that anyone is fair game if they don't have a ring on their finger. That's how Will has gotten himself punched in the face more than once. Unfortunately, no one has knocked any sense into him yet.

I'm fine with another friend. I'm good at making friends. Making someone more than a friend on the other hand? That I'm not so good at. My twin sister Zoe says it's because I'm too nice and no woman wants a nice guy at my age. It's not like I'm out there looking for the one—I just graduated from university, and I kind of want to sort my shit out before I begin the search for love or have it fall into my lap...or sit across from me on a busy train. Tonight, I was just trying to show her there was at least one person who saw her. She didn't strike me as timid, more so unable to put herself before others. Something admirable in some areas of life and a hindrance in others. Like getting onto a train before it leaves, for instance.

I wasn't going to send her a text so quickly, but I didn't even make it to my car before I fired one off. Just so she can have my number, I told myself. Now I'm sitting here staring at her reply wondering what it was about her that drew me in in the first place. Her dark auburn hair was piled up on her head, held back with a pair of glasses—not sunglasses, glasses-glasses. Like she'd pushed them up and then forgot about them. Dark blue eyes, full lips, and a smile that made me not want to be such a nice guy, or maybe just not any nice guy, but *her* nice guy. But then she said she had a boyfriend. I enjoyed talking to her, though, and I genuinely wanted her book recommendations. And hey, in the end, I did get her number.

When I get home my sister is in the living room, watching one of her reality shows while her girlfriend, Gaby, is sound asleep with her head in her lap. Our old lab, Morris, is curled up at her feet. None of this is an uncommon sight.

"Good game?" Zoe whispers when she sees me.

"Yeah, it was alright," I say, slipping my shoes off and walking to the kitchen. I'm taking down a glass when I hear her slippers sliding on the tile.

"Mom has a cold." She's not whispering anymore, but her voice is softer than usual, like she's worried.

"If it's just a cold, she'll be okay, Zo," I try to reassure her.

"It's the cough I'm worried about."

I put my glass down and turn to face her. "How bad is it?"

"It sounds like it's deep in her lungs. Dad wanted to take her to the hospital, but she was pretty insistent that she was okay."

"We need to trust her. She's not a baby," I say as I turn and open the fridge. "You and Dad worry too much."

"I think it's Dad I worry the most for."

I stop mid-pour and turn back to her. "What do you mean?"

Zoe is twining her fingers and not looking at me. "I worry what will happen when his world is gone."

"Are you going somewhere? Am I? Hell, is Will? We're his world too, Zoe. Besides, Mom is fine, and she's going to be fine for a long time. She's way too stubborn to let a cold take her down. I guarantee she'll outlive us all just to prove a point."

"I hope you're right." Zoe smiles at me but it doesn't reach her eyes.

"I am," I say confidently. "Have a little faith, baby sister."

"You're three minutes older than me," she scoffs, throwing off the arm I've lovingly tossed around her shoulders. "Three. Minutes."

"It counts. If a runner beats another runner by three minutes, they're faster. I don't make the rules of time, Zoe."

"Maybe you were just faster." She punches my arm before heading back to the couch.

"Faster, older... it's all the same in the delivery room." That gets me not one but two middle fingers, and I laugh as I head towards the stairs.

I stop in front of my parents' door to listen for any signs of illness and only hear a faint cough come from within. It's not that I don't worry about my mom; I do. But I don't let it consume me the way Zoe and my dad do. I think part of me just believes that nothing is going to happen to my mom because Dad takes such good care of her. I shake my head at my ridiculous family as I take the stairs two at a time.

Zoe's door is ajar, and I stop outside it realizing that she has loads of books and maybe she has one by one of the authors LG recommended. Her room is immaculate—everything in its place, things organized by color or style, and her books by author. Sure enough, I find a book by Kate Culliver, grab it, and hurry off to my room. I sit back in my bed and flip the book to read the synopsis. I debate taking a picture and sending it to LG but decide that seems a bit desperate. I'll read it and then let her know what I think after.

"Teddy." I'm being jostled, but I'm unwilling to respond. "Teddy. Goddammit, you're supposed to be taking Mom to the dentist today." That has me bolting upright and then scrambling out of bed. "Is that my book?" I look back from my dresser to see Zoe reaching for her once-pristine book, slightly less pristine now. "Why do you have my book?"

"Ugh, a friend recommended the author," I say, tossing clean clothes onto my bed, hoping she will get the hint and leave. "I'll replace it."

She eyes me skeptically but leaves the book where it's twisted up near my pillow. "What friend?"

"Just a friend. Do you mind? I need to change."

"You don't have friends that read. Is it a girl?"

"The friend?"

"No, the reason you're getting dressed. Yes, dumbass, the friend."

"Yes, the friend is a girl." I see her face start to shift teasingly and rush on. "She is just a friend, not a girlfriend. Only one of us in this room has one of those."

"One of what?" Gaby asks, leaning against my door frame.

"Teddy borrowed one of my books based on the recommendation of a friend who happens to be a girl. And no doubt a friend I've never met before."

"Ooooh." Gabby's eyebrows jump. "Intriguing. Who's this friend then, Teddy?"

"For fuck's sake, you're perfect for each other. Get out so I can get dressed, please." Zoe manages to just make it into the hall before I slam the door, but I can hear them laughing as they head downstairs.

I'm sliding on socks when there's a knock on my door. "Yeah?"

"Just me." My dad opens the door and sticks his head into the room. "Making sure you're up and ready."

"Thanks to Zoe." I stifle a yawn. "How's Mom?"

"Better. The inhaler seems to have done its job. But still, just be extra aware of that today when you're out."

I know better than to tell my dad to chill, so I assure him that he has nothing to worry about. "I'll let the hygienist know too, just in case there are any issues."

He nods and follows me as I head to the bathroom. "I'm on shift tonight. Your brother said he'll handle dinner, but I've left some meatballs in the fridge to defrost in case he forgets."

"Is he still seeing that woman..." I stop to think as I squeeze toothpaste onto my brush. "Cat...s...t..."

"Patricia?"

"Oh wow, so not even in the same realm."

"I'm pretty sure Cat...s...t was two women ago."

"He's had more girlfriends in the last month than I have in my entire life." I shake my head and shove my toothbrush in my mouth.

Dad pats me on the back. "You're just more selective." I meet his eyes in the mirror and roll mine. Sure, that's it, I'm selective. "You don't need five a month, kid. You just need the right one, and you can't rush that." Then he turns and leaves me to aggressively brush my teeth in private.

It's not like I've never been in a relationship. It's just been hard with Mom. I apparently attract women who get freaked out that I have a parent who depends on me, a parent they can't communicate "normally" with if they come for dinner. I get it, it's not what everyone wants to sign up for—hell, if I had it my way I'm not sure I would either—but this is my reality, so if someone wants to be in my life, they need to get on board with that. Gaby had fit in immediately, and I'd be lying if I wasn't slightly envious of my sister. I mean, we're twins. Couldn't some of that luck rub off on my love life? Still, I'd rather have Mom here in this state than not here at all, and if that means me being single, so be it.

While Mom is in with the dentist, I sit in the waiting room reading. I'd fallen asleep with the book last night, too engrossed in it to recognize how tired I was. LG was right, though; the author's writing is fantastic, and I'm very much sold. I take my phone out and send a picture of the book to her.

> Turns out my sister is a fan. So far, I get why.

Her reply comes a minute later.

> **LIBRARY GIRL**
>
> Stick with me, Enviro Guy. I'll keep you up to your neck in good books.

I tell myself that I should leave it there, but my fingers don't get the message and reply.

> How's day one of summer vacation?

> Quiet.

> Is that a good thing?

> My roommates are party animals, so I am not mad about silence. At least for a few days. Ask me in a couple of months.

I know this is a joke, but I wouldn't hate another train trip with her. Even if it is platonic, I can't remember the last time I wanted to hang out with someone the way I'd like to hang out with her. My fingers are off and typing again before I can think about what I'm texting.

> Actually, would you like to go book shopping with me?

What the fuck am I doing?

> As friends, book shopping as friends.

I quickly add before she can respond. Although maybe she won't; maybe she's already deleted my number. When her reply comes, my entire body lights up.

That's my favorite kind of shopping. When?

I have no idea. I still can't believe she said yes. She must be really secure in her relationship, I hope I'm not setting myself up to follow in Will's idiotic footsteps and get punched. I rack my brain trying to remember Mom's appointments and dinner plans. I should be starting work next week so that shouldn't factor into it.

> Are you around tomorrow? I could drive up there.

This week is wide open and that would be ideal. Have you heard of Peregrine Books?

> I haven't but Google has!

Perfect. What time would be best for you?

Want to have coffee or lunch?

My funds are depleted from tuition and rent so the thought of buying a book *and* lunch makes me feel a bit nauseous.

Let's do coffee.

Perfect. How's 10 at Trojan Horse Cafe? It's down the road from Peregrine.

I'll see you there at 10.

I've just slipped my phone back into my pocket when Mom slowly comes into the room. I do my best to remove the goofy smile from my face. A smile I should not have while chatting with someone in a relationship. Mom grimaces and nods as I offer her my arm to steady her as we walk out of the office. On the drive home, I tell her I'm heading to Comrie tomorrow to meet a new friend. When I look over to make sure she hears me, her eyes are wide and a smile brightens half her face as though she can see right through the word friend.

I know I'm at an age where advice from my mom isn't always desirable, but I'd give anything to hear some from her right about now.

THREE

NELLIE

The Trojan Horse Cafe is the one place in town that serves anything more elaborate than drip coffee, and I'm such a regular when I'm home that whoever is behind the counter has my drink started before I'm through the door. It's one of the benefits of living in a small town, I guess.

I'm waiting for Enviro Guy, in one of the armchairs at the front of the cafe, hoping he shows up. I asked the barista to put EG's drink on my tab. I figure he drove here, so the least I can do is buy him a drink. My mind is going a mile a minute as I wait. I'm so unbelievably nervous about seeing him again. Will he be as nice as he was on the train? Does he really want to buy a book? The mental inquisition comes to an abrupt halt when I see him open the door and walk in, bringing the smell of the late spring blooms that decorate the street with him. He gives me a small wave and notices my drink at the same time. He points to the front and mouths that he'll be right back. I peek around the side of the chair, in time to see the barista pointing towards me and him giving me one of those "That wasn't necessary" looks.

He's not wearing a hat so his wavy dark hair on full display. It's the kind of hair I'd want to run my fingers through if I wasn't pretending to have a boyfriend. He's also taller than I remember, although I'm sitting down so maybe it's a matter of perspective more than anything.

"You didn't need to pay for my drink," he scolds, sitting down in the chair across from me. "But thank you," he tacks on with a smile.

"You drove all the way here, without me even asking, might I add." I smile back. "How was the drive?"

"Uneventful in just about every way." He takes the lid of his coffee cup and blows on the dark liquid.

"Just about every way?"

"Some woman dodged out in front of me just as I pulled onto the street here. She came out of nowhere."

"Ah." I nod sagely. "That would be Edith."

"Edith?"

"The town jaywalker."

He stares back at me. "Town jaywalker, huh? Is that a position one has to apply for or is it inherited, assumed…"

He's smiling again, and I try really hard not to look at those too-pointy canines, but I know I'm failing. I manage to pull my gaze from his teeth and drag my attention to the street. "Elected. She's run unopposed in the last four elections."

"And before that?"

"A guy named Albert Moyer held the position but died before the election."

"Did he get hit by a car?"

"Would you believe natural causes got him in the end?"

"Well, that's probably a better way to go." He chuckles and takes a sip of his coffee, his eyes flicking up to meet mine. The contrast between his pale blue eyes and his dark hair is utterly captivating.

"So what book do you want to pick up?" I ask, turning my attention back to my latte.

"The one I'm reading, actually." I look back up at him, confused. "I fell asleep with it last night, and it no longer meets my sister's exacting standards."

"Ah, she's one of those." I nod in understanding.

"One of what?"

"A reader that likes their books markless in every way. Someone who wants their books to appear like they've never been read."

"Yes, I guess that is the kind of reader she is."

"And what kind of reader are you?"

He shrugs. "The kind that borrows books without asking and then falls asleep with them." I can almost picture him falling asleep mid-chapter, those icy blue eyes growing heavier with each word, the book eventually falling from his grasp. I wonder what he sleeps in. He seems like a boxers and nothing else kind of guy.

He's giving me a strange look, probably because I've been staring at him thinking about him falling asleep in boxers. "Scandalous," I tease.

"Truly," he agrees. "So are we going to exchange names or just stick with these fun little nicknames?"

I desperately want to know his name, but I also really like the nicknames. "Nicknames for now, I think." He nods just as the cafe's owner walks in and sees me.

"Nellie! Home for the summer?"

EG immediately bursts out laughing.

I glare at him before turning my attention to Mr. Wilson. "I got home Tuesday night."

"Excellent! I'll let you get back to your..."—his eyes slide to EG— "morning."

As soon as he walks away, EG says, "I'm not sure I've ever seen something so perfectly timed in my entire life."

"Okay, so I guess real names it is."

He shakes his head. "Nah, I like you calling me EG."

It's almost flirty the way he says it, or maybe I just want it to be a little flirty. "I like you calling me LG." I pout.

Enviro Guy is making the kind of eye contact you make when you want someone to know you're the only one they care about in a room. "I'll still call you LG. No one else calls you that, right?" Okay, that *definitely* sounds flirty. I should be mad that he would do that after I told him I have a boyfriend—who doesn't exist—but still, it's the principle. And yet I'm ridiculously happy that this nice, attractive, intelligent guy seems happy about a nickname only he gets to use.

"Just you." I smile into my drink and break eye contact as my face begins to heat. "So you have a sister?" I pull myself together and decide to start getting to know this guy who I want flirting with me.

"A twin sister, actually. I've got an older brother as well. You?"

"I have an older sister. She lives in the Philippines with her husband. She's quite a bit older so I grew up feeling a bit like a spoiled only child."

"Why do I feel like you aren't spoiled at all?"

"Oh, I am. I've never been a brat, though, so maybe that's why."

He's looking at me as if scanning for signs of brattiness. "No, definitely not a brat." And now we're just sort of smiling at each other and I'm beginning to panic. The last time I panicked around him I told him I had a boyfriend, and I'm worried about what might come out next.

"So why does your sister live in the Philippines?" he asks,

finally breaking contact to look down into his cup and saving me from spewing some new deception.

"Her husband is a researcher at an endangered bird organization."

His eyes widen. "More bird people."

"Sylvia isn't a bird person at all. I'm still shocked she married one."

"Well, being interested in all the same things isn't a requirement for marriage." He shrugs.

"No, of course not," I rush to say. "It's more that she moved to the other side of the world for birds. It's funny, that's all."

"Have you been to visit her?"

"Yeah, we helped them when they first moved. My dad was so excited to get a tour of the facility. It's actually where I got my first tattoo."

His eyes grow wide. "You got a tattoo at a bird facility?"

"No, sorry. In the Philippines."

"What is it?" he asks, leaning forward slightly.

"It's a scale-feathered malkoha."

He nods. "Right, the famous scale-feathered malkoha, I know exactly what that is."

"Oh yeah?" I grin at him.

"Yeah, it's a bird from the malkoha family with these unique scale-shaped feathers."

"Nailed it," I say, not even bothering to hold back my laugh.

"So." He leans forward and sets his empty cup down on the table. "Where is it?"

It's on the inner part of my left upper arm and would be easy enough to show him. "On my body," I smirk back. *Rein it in, Nell, the boyfriend remember? The bullshit excuse you gave because this hot guy asked for your number after being nice to you, and you panicked.*

"Where on your body?" His eyes sweep over me quickly.

I try not to let myself imagine him searching for it. Those long fingers skimming across my body, hunting. "On my skin."

His eyes flick to mine, and he swallows before he looks at my arms. "On a limb?"

"Maybe." Heat spreads through my body. This feels like foreplay, which is wrong, very wrong.

He looks like he wants to keep going, but I'm afraid of where it would lead, of where I kind of want it to lead. I look down at his empty cup and then empty my own. "Should we go?"

He keeps looking at me, his lips twisting knowingly. "Yeah, let's go buy some books."

"Keep talking like that, and I may show you anything you want," I joke. Oh my god, what am I doing? I need to come clean. But this is nice, and what if I make it weird and he leaves?

To his credit he doesn't say anything inappropriate back, just stands and holds out his hand towards me. I take it, and he hauls me up. I desperately don't want to be one of those girls who swoon at how perfectly my hand fits into his, but goddammit it does. I don't have time to appreciate it, though, because once I'm up he lets go. Disappointment floods my entire body, and I'm once again upset that I started this relationship out with a big fat lie.

EG reaches down to pick up his empty cup and my mug and takes them to the garbage and dirty dishes area. Most guys our age would just leave them on the table. He really is just a nice guy who does nice guy shit.

"Shall we?" He gestures towards the door and follows me out the cafe.

TEDDY

I've caught myself just staring at her too many times. I'm fine with being just friends, I really am. But goddamn, she looks good in the jeans and white button-up she's rocking today. And I may have leaned a bit too hard into my desperation to know where that tattoo of the scale-feathered ma-something or other is located. She's not helping, though. She says she has a boyfriend, but then she also seems kind of flirty. Maybe that's just who she is. Maybe she's like this with everyone. Or maybe I just want her to be flirty and so that's how she's coming across.

Then there is the ridiculous tote slung over her shoulder that is not helping me keep my mind firmly in the friend zone. "Readers do it by the book." I stand beside her doing my best to look like I'm reading the back of a book when I'm wondering what exactly "it" implies.

"How does it sound..." She pauses, studying me. "Gavin?" She's pushed her glasses back onto her head so clearly they are just for reading.

"Ugh." I try to focus on the words in front of me. "I'm not sure," I mutter, placing it back on the shelf. "It's definitely one

I'll need to consider. And my name isn't Gavin." She lets out an adorable huff, and I secretly hope this is a game we get to play for a while.

"What's your favorite show?" she asks out of the blue.

"*The Office.*"

"Favorite band?"

"Shinedown."

"Greatest fear?"

"Heights."

"Your name?"

I level her with a look and slowly shake my head. Her mouth twists in frustration, and I let my gaze linger there for longer than I should.

"Favorite color?" she continues.

"Blue." Specifically the color of her eyes, but I keep that to myself.

"Original." She rolls her eyes. "Food?"

"Cauliflower."

"Seriously?"

I smirk down at her and shake my head. "What's your favorite show?"

"You haven't answered my last question."

"I will after you answer the ones you asked me."

"Fine. *Downton Abbey.*" She looks up at the ceiling in thought, "Favorite band changes, but right now, Of Monsters and Men. I can't stand blood. I adore green, specifically fresh sage leaf green. And nothing beats fresh-cut french fries from a chip truck with malt vinegar and too much ketchup."

"Those are very specific answers."

"Details matter, EG. Now spill."

"I don't have one." I shrug.

"Who doesn't have a favorite food?" She almost looks offended.

"Who doesn't have a favorite all-time band?" I fire back.

"Me."

"Well, there ya go."

"Well, are there foods you hate?"

I shrug again. "Not really, but I'm sure there is something out there I haven't tried yet. My family isn't exactly adventurous when it comes to food."

"Hmm." She reaches for another book in front of me at crotch level, and I jump back like I'm afraid she didn't see me and then she'll think I moved there. If she notices me acting like a complete weirdo, she doesn't acknowledge it. "Read this synopsis and let me know if it interests you." She hands it to me and walks away. Maybe she did notice.

I did come here to get a book, but my reading comprehension seems to have fucked off because the words are not making sense to me. I read it over three times and then take out my phone to record the title. I'll read about it online later. Maybe my brain will be cooperating by then. I slide it back into the spot Nellie had pulled it from and follow in the direction she went. She's in the nonfiction section flipping through a large book about birds.

"My dad's birthday is next month. Figured I'd get a jump on his gift."

"He doesn't have that one yet?"

She flips the book to the cover, her eyes narrowing through her glasses in concentration. "I'm 90% sure that he doesn't. But that's what gift receipts are for." She smiles up at me and winks, and I can't help but release a puff of a laugh.

"Did you just wink at me?"

She immediately looks embarrassed but laughs too. "Yeah, I don't know where that came from. Everyone needs a creepy friend. Do you have one of those yet, Steven?"

"I think I do now. And nope." I say, taking the book from

her to look through it myself. It's not what I'd look at and describe as easy reading. It has large and beautifully photographed images of birds, but the text is dense, like a textbook. "Doesn't your dad know all of this stuff yet?" I ask, handing it back to her.

She shrugs. "Possibly, but these are mainly South American birds. He's more of a North American raptor guy." I must look confused because she clarifies further. "As in birds of prey. So eagles, hawks, falcons, birds that you wouldn't want to be a small creature around."

I don't have the heart to tell her that I don't have a whole lot of interest in being around birds as a 6'2" creature so I just nod in understanding.

"Did that book not interest you?" she asks when she sees that my hands are empty.

"Sort of." I shrug. "I'm just trying to be good with my money. If they don't have the book for my sister, I'll consider it." I send a silent prayer into the universe that they do have the book for my sister.

"I wish I had your self-control in a bookstore." She laughs and leads me back to the historical fiction section, right to where Kate Culliver's books are.

There are only two, but one is the book I'm after. "That's her second." Nellie points to the lone book left on the shelf. "It's not exactly a series, but the characters from that book"— she points at the book I'm holding—"do make an appearance."

"Is it the type of book I'll want to start immediately?"

"I wasn't ready to leave the world when I was done." She gives me a sly smile. *She has a boyfriend,* I mentally chant.

"It feels a little like you're trying to bring me over to the dark side, LG."

"Who? Me?" She looks genuinely affronted. "I would never do that..." Her eyes narrow. "Matthew?"

I shake my head. "Nope. And your face says differently," I grumble as I reach for the second book. Before I can grab it though, she takes my hand and pulls it back. Goosebumps erupt across the surface of my body, and my eyes immediately go to where she's got my fingers in hers. A guy could get used to holding her hand. I'm sure her boyfriend is. Lucky bastard.

"Actually," she says, letting go of my hand, "I loaned out my copy to someone and never got it back. Do you mind if I get it for myself?" Do I mind? Hell no. I shake my head and watch as she grabs it and slips it next to the bird book.

I have the book I was looking for and she's got what she was looking for, but I am not ready to head home. "I was thinking I'd see if they had the other author you recommended, um..." I'm blanking on the name, but I had looked the books up and they did sound good, so at least I won't have to fake knowing what they're about. "Maria..."

"Maira." She laughs at my terrible memory for names. "Maira Sahni. Her books will be in the YA section. Follow me, sir." I've been called sir once before, and it did nothing to me. "Sir" out of Nellie's mouth has my entire body on high alert. Lord help me.

"Wait, YA?" I ask trailing behind.

"Young adult."

"Oh, are we considered young adults?"

"How old are you? Twenty..."

"Two."

"Well, technically no. We would be NA, new adult."

"What's the difference?"

"Ugh." I can see the blush spreading across her cheeks, like watercolor added to a drop of water. It's beautiful. "Usually NA has more mature themes."

"Such as?" I can put two and two together, but friends tease each other, right?

"Swearing, more gruesome deaths, um... sexual content."

"Maira's books are YA? So they lack swearing, gruesome deaths, and"—I lower my voice to a whisper and lean closer to her—"sexual content?"

Nellie glares at me in the most adorable way. "I'd classify her books as NA or even adult, but for some reason, they stuck her in YA. Still interested?"

"I was never not interested, LG, even if there was no swearing." I smile smugly and earn myself an epic eye roll.

I follow the rest of the way, wordlessly trying to figure out a way to prolong the time with her. When we get to the right section, she pulls back and squints at the shelf. She leans in a bit and brings her glasses down. Or rather, she tries to, but the nose piece gets stuck in her hair. "Shit," she says quietly.

"Let me." I reach out and gently pull them free and for some reason, I cannot explain why, other than my hand going rogue, I run my hand over where pieces of her dark auburn hair have been pulled out of place before tucking a stray strand behind her ear. Her breath hitches causing alarm bells to go off in my brain as we make eye contact. What the actual fuck is wrong with me? That was a very non-friend move on my part. "You should get one of those chain things." I mime taking glasses off and letting them hang around my neck.

"Really lean into the librarian look?" She adjusts her glasses and turns her attention back to the books. Her red cheeks do not go unnoticed.

"You could start a whole line for our generation." I gently nudge her with my elbow like a friend would do.

"I'll consider it," she says absentmindedly. "Here." She hands me *The Forest of Despair*, and I flip it over immediately to look at the price. It's significantly cheaper than the replacement book for my sister.

"Why is this book half the price of this book?" I ask, holding up the historical fiction.

She shrugs as she slides her glasses right back into her hair. "I have no idea. Everything about it seems like it should cost more, eh? I mean there are twice as many pages, the cover is embossed, it's a hardcover."

"I didn't expect to get a little lesson on the book industry while here, but I'm getting the impression that nothing makes sense."

"Ah, so you've learned something on this trip north. Time well spent." Her blue eyes sparkle up at me. Holy shit, I'm imagining sparkles now. At this rate I'll be driving home with giant cartoon hearts obscuring my vision.

I nod because if I open my mouth I'm going to say spending time with her was more than worth it. Everything else is just a bonus.

"All set, David?" she asks, nodding down at the two books in my hand.

"Yeah, I think so." I'm getting the second book. I shouldn't, but I am. I'll just forgo the after-game drinks tomorrow with my team. "And my name isn't David."

FIVE

NELLIE

As we approach the front counter, I stop dead when I see how dark it is outside. Shit. I'd checked several times, and yet there was no mistaking what that darkness foretold.

"What's wrong?" EG asks, coming up beside me.

"They didn't call for rain today."

His gaze follows mine. "You mean the weather people got it wrong? Shocking."

"No, it's just that I walked here and I'm in a white shirt and I didn't bring an umbrella because why would I when they said it was going to be a clear sky kinda day."

"It's not a problem, LG," he says calmly.

"Says the guy not wearing a white shirt and, well, not a woman."

"No, it's not a problem because I can give you a ride home."

"But it's the opposite way you're going," I whine and immediately hate myself for sounding like a spoiled brat. Twenty years old and fucking whining.

"Just think of it as another opportunity to ask me mundane questions." When I look up at him, he's smiling at me, but not his open-mouthed smile. This one is closed-lipped and serene. I don't know how he's managing it because usually that kind of smile would seem fake, but his is genuine. The kind of smile that would appear during a kiss. Nope, I need to stop that.

"I am good at those."

As we're paying, I try to get a look at the name on his credit card, but he's onto me and covers it as he slips it into the card reader. I'm determined to get the name out of him before we get to my house.

Big drops of rain begin to fall as we're about halfway to his car so we pick up our pace. Just as we jump in the sky opens.

"Maybe *that* was the most perfectly timed thing ever," he breathes out, turning his key in the ignition.

I buckle in and then slip my bag behind my seat. "It's so clean in here," I say, looking around.

"Were you expecting empty fast food bags and dead rats?" he asks, one eyebrow quirked.

"No!" I throw my hands up defensively. "Okay, maybe one or two burger wrappers, but no rats."

"I share the car with my sister, and she's a neat freak. If it was solely mine, there would probably be some empty water bottles at the very least." He shifts the car into gear and looks over at me expectantly.

"What?"

"Am I just driving around, or do you have directions for me?"

"Right, I've heard those help. We are going that way." I point straight ahead. "So you're already in a good position. Then you'll make a left at the first stop sign after the lights, onto Renfrew. Then—"

"Whoa!" he cuts in, laughing. "How about just letting me know the next direction after I've completed the one right before it?"

"As you wish," I say sweetly, and if I'm not mistaken his eyes darken ever so slightly. But when he blinks, they are the pale blue they had been before. "Okay, questions." I drum my hands on my knees, my mind suddenly blank. "Favorite dinosaur?"

He breathes out deeply, his eyes glued to the road. "A T-Rex. I think they were probably misunderstood."

"You think a tyrannosaurus was misunderstood? Was it the teeth and general build of a predator that gave it away?"

"We assume it was the bad guy, but how could we ever truly know? No one was there to record anything. I mean, I trust all the science behind fossils, but they don't tell us how they were behaviorally. They could have been amazing parents or scavengers, out there cleaning up dead things."

I stare at him, waiting for him to laugh, but he doesn't.

"I've got one," he says, briefly looking over at me and catching me staring.

"Shoot."

"What exactly do you want to do with your degree?"

I have to think for a minute because there are several paths I've considered taking. "Well, I do enjoy my job at our local library. Helping people find the perfect book and assisting with various children's programs. But I love the idea of working in the archives of some grand library."

"I'm not going to lie, that sounds dusty."

"Honestly, it would probably be the opposite of dusty. They keep old collections and documents in very specific rooms. Like a missile defense system against dust."

"Do they have places like that here?"

"Yeah, although things would obviously be far newer than, say, in places like Italy or the UK. I'd love to go work for a bit at the University of Edinburgh."

He nods, his eyes still on the road. "Would you want to live abroad for a long time, or would it just be short term?"

I shrug. "I don't really know. I haven't thought of it that hard. I've got two more years of my undergrad before I start my master's. I think I would go away with the intention of it being temporary, but you never know." He gives a single nod, and his face is a bit pinched. "Don't worry, there is plenty of time to become my best friend before I leave. Turn left here."

The rest of the drive is pretty uneventful, and the rain stops five minutes in. I find out a bit more about his family, although it seems like he's holding something back. I can't be upset about that, though; we've only just waded into the waters of friendship. I tell him about my part-time jobs, and he tells me about his spring and summer baseball leagues, including the one year they played snow baseball for three weeks. And while I try not to let my imagination wander, I can't help wondering what he looks like in his baseball uniform. Is he a socks-up-to-his-knees type? What color is his uniform? Because the idea of a blue jersey and white pants isn't the worst visual.

All too soon he's pulling into my driveway. I'm reaching around to grab my bag when I see the front door open out of the corner of my eye. When I turn around fully, I see my dad's old apprentice, John Keisman, standing on the bottom step, hands on his hips, squinting at the car. John is a few years older than me and is currently doing his master's in biology at Oxford. It's been more than eight months since I've seen him, and I feel a bubble of excitement rise through me.

I look at EG and then back at John before settling my eyes on EG again. He's looking at John too—actually, he's glaring at John, so I lightly touch his arm to get his attention.

"Thanks for today, it was a nice change from doing all that stuff on my own."

"Yeah." His attention drifts back to John, and I'm wondering if he thinks he's the boyfriend I do not have. I'm about to come clean, but he continues. "We, ah..." He rubs the back of his neck before looking back at me. "We should do it again sometime."

I fight the giant smile that's threatening to form. "I would love that." His eyes dip to my lips, and I fight the urge to lean into him. "Have a safe drive home, Thomas." I try one last name, earning another head shake before I exit the car and run at John who wraps me in a giant hug.

"I didn't know you were home," I squeal, barely noticing the sound of EG reversing out of the driveway.

"I'm not home for long." He pulls me back in for a side hug as we make our way to the house. "I'm here for my brother's wedding but had a free afternoon so figured I'd pop in to see your dad at the center for a bit."

"You know this isn't the center," I tease as we walk into the house.

"I was wondering why it was so quiet and didn't smell like a thousand pounds of bird shit. He sent me over for the box of mice in the garage freezer."

"Ah." Storage at the center is lacking so my dad keeps a lot of deliveries here until they have room. I'm just glad they got the extra freezer because the thought of opening the one in the kitchen and finding a box of dead mice is a surefire way to zap any kind of appetite.

"So who was the guy?"

"Just a friend," I say, setting my bag down on the coffee table before flinging myself down on the couch.

"Just a friend?" he asks not so subtly.

"Yes, Johnathan, he's just a friend. He thinks I have a boyfriend."

He cringes. "Does he think I'm that boyfriend?"

"I have no idea, but by the way he was looking at you, maybe." I shrug and cross my ankles on the table.

"Do you *want* him to think I'm your boyfriend?" he asks, sitting in the armchair across from me.

I glare at him. "No, I don't want him to think you're my boyfriend."

"Well, then." He sighs and leans back like he's never going to leave. "You'd better clear the air quickly. Unless of course you really do just want him to be your friend."

"We literally just met. I just want to get to know him right now." And that's the truth. Am I attracted to EG? Yes. Is he nice? Yes. Is he someone I could see dating? Also yes. But I don't know him yet, and I like to do my research before getting into anything serious.

John's hands go up. "Okay, okay, I was just curious. He did kind of look familiar, though."

"He went to Wellington High, he's two years older than me, played baseball..."

John's eyebrows go up. "You think telling me he plays baseball may help me place him?"

I laugh. John kind of looks like a jock, but I don't think I've ever met someone who has less interest in sports. "He also played the violin."

"Siblings?"

"A twin sister Zoe, and an older brother, Will."

He claps so suddenly that I nearly jump out of my skin. "Will Fletcher? I know him. Or I know of him, anyway. Biggest player north of Toronto. If his younger brother is anything like him, watch out." If I hadn't actually met EG, the warning in John's voice would make me wary.

"Don't worry, I'm not about to jump into bed with the guy. Like I said, we're just getting to know each other. He's nice, John. And people aren't their siblings." I give him a look that lets him know I'm not going to hold him responsible for the sins of his sister, who treated me like garbage after she found out I was becoming friends with her brother. Apparently, she thought I was gunning for her older brother when we worked together during the summers. Forget that I was only fifteen when we started working together, and he wasn't about to break the law. Still, she hated that we were friends, and that made life around her hell. "How is dear Lori, anyway?"

"Being her nightmarish self. You'd think she was the one getting married. Bridemaidzilla? Bridesmaidzilla?" He waves off his attempts to rework Bridezilla. "Whatever, she sucks."

"That she does. How is Oxford, smartypants?"

"It's, it's good." He smiles at me and rubs his hand over his beard, which is his tell.

"Who are they?" I ask, sitting up. "Spill."

"His name's Nigel, and he's in the same program." I can't help it and burst out laughing. "Wow, that's exactly the reaction I was hoping for."

"Oh my god, I'm sorry. It's just, could you have found someone with a more English name?"

He looks less than impressed at me as he mutters. "Probably."

"I'm sorry. Tell me more."

"I met him at a party his roommate was having, and I was maybe casually dating the roommate at the time."

"No way."

"Yeah, it was kind of awkward, to be honest. She was pissed at first, thought I was just using her to get to him. Then after she cooled off, we chatted and she admitted that she didn't feel any spark between us either."

"When was that?"

"Six months ago."

"Johnathan Lee Keisman, you've been seeing this guy for

six months and haven't said a word about him? There aren't even any pictures of the two of you on social media."

"He's not out to his family." Ah, that explains it then. John had come out to me at the end of our second summer working together. He'd also done it in the nerdiest way possible. He'd said, "*I think I'm like a Humboldt Penguin.*" I'd asked what made him say that, and then he'd just looked at me for a while until all the facts about Humboldt Penguins sorted themselves out in my mind. When my eyes went wide he just nodded. "*So you think... or you know?*" I asked. "*Well, I guess I know I'm not straight, other than that I don't really have a distinct label.*" And that was that. He had come out to my dad earlier in the week, but other than him, I was the only one who knew. John didn't know how our small conservative town would take it. In the end, no one seemed to care all that much, and his family embraced him just as they always had. Seeing John happy was high on my list of wants. While it took fifteen years for us to get to know each other, he'd become like a brother to me in the five since.

"You still could have told me."

"I know, I'm sorry. I think you'd like him, though."

"If you like him, I'm sure I would too. So he's not coming for the wedding?"

He smiles sadly and shakes his head. "Nah. Anyway—" He looks down at his watch. "I've gotta get those mice to your dad, and then I've got a suit fitting or I'm helping pick out fun socks for the groomsmen or something." He stands, and we walk out to the garage together.

"I think I'll give you a hug goodbye before you've got an arm full of deceased rodents."

"Good idea." He stops and holds his arms out wide.

He folds me into himself, and I mumble, "I'm happy for you, John."

"Give that guy a call or something and come clean if you want whatever it is between you to have a chance," he says, leveling me with a look that has me promising to do just that. And then he's gone, and I'm alone with my thoughts.

Lying about having a boyfriend hadn't felt that huge at first, but now as I sit back down on the couch, I can't help but think it was growing into something that could poison whatever chance I had with EG, even if it is purely friendship. And after spending the morning with him I can imagine being friends with him. I reach for my phone to lay it all bare when I see he's already texted me.

> Enviro Guy
>
> LG, I had a great time today. Thanks for putting up with me.
>
> EG, it was a hardship, but one I was able to endure easier than I had anticipated.
>
> I don't know if you'd be interested, but I've got a game tomorrow night in Sherman. Would you want to maybe come watch for a bit?
>
> Just for a bit?
>
> Well, you may get bored and want to leave. I would hate to hold you there against your will.
>
> Such a gentleman. What time?
>
> The game starts at 8. We'll be there around 7:30 for warmups.

By eight, both my parents would be home from work and I'd have a car. I would also be able to answer the socks up or socks down question that was no doubt going to plague my mind.

I'd like that!

Awesome. It's at the Sherman Lions Park, 30 Standford Dr. See ya tomorrow.

Looking forward to it!

I set my phone down and lean back again. Tomorrow. I can tell him tomorrow. In person is always better anyway.

SIX

TEDDY

Zoe surprises me by jumping into the passenger seat as I'm about to leave for the game. The minute the seatbelt clicks she throws her head back and sighs dramatically. "I hope you don't mind me coming with you. I need a fucking break from this place."

"You know I don't mind, ZoZo." I reverse out of the driveway and turn the music down, anticipating my sister needing to chat. Some may call it twin intuition, while others may just recognize it as knowing someone you've spent twenty-two years living with.

"I tried to convince Dad to come to your game tonight. Will said he'd come and hang out with Mom so he could go without worrying about her. If it wasn't such a late game, he could have brought her along."

My sister is the social butterfly of the family. She supposedly takes after our mom, but it's been a long time since my mom was someone else, and I think part of me has blocked that person because it's painful to recall what we had. Dad had been someone else too. He never would have missed a game, probably because he was the one coaching. He coached us all when we were little, in multiple sports too. I didn't appreciate how busy his life was until he had to take over for a lot of the things Mom did too, and he did it without complaint. But in doing so, he's become a shadow of who he'd once been.

"She's his entire world, Zoe. Remember?" I tease, glancing over at her briefly. Her mouth is set in a hard line while she glares out the windshield. "Sometimes I'm envious that by our age he had found his person."

She looks over, her face still set in a grimace I know all too well. "Well, maybe he needs to broaden his fucking world, Teddy. She's not going to be here forever, and what's he going to do then ?"

I shrug. "He'll figure it out. Besides, she's not going anywhere for a very long time." Zoe's expression changes to one I can only describe as pity before she turns and looks out her window. I'm the one who should be feeling pity for her if anything. Constantly living with this cloud of doom hanging overhead, always prepared for the worst.

"I'm just glad they had so many years together before we came along and everything went to shit."

Our parents met when they were twelve and thirteen. Mom was the new kid in town, and she and Dad became friends immediately. By the time Dad was seventeen, he had money socked away for a ring, and on Mom's eighteenth birthday, he proposed. He'd been scouted by a few pro baseball teams and offered spots at training camps, but Mom had dreams of university and a career as a teacher. So Dad put his dreams away and got a job at a plant that made plane engines. I have no idea if he regrets staying here, especially after things took a turn for the worst. I also don't know if I would ever do the same thing if given the choice. Follow a dream or stay for love. At this moment, I'd follow the dream without a second thought. But I don't have the love factor adding weight to the decision.

"Do you think he regrets it?"

"Regrets what?" Zoe asks, turning back to me.

"Not going pro and getting out of here."

I can feel her eyes boring into the side of my head and resist the urge to turn back to her. "No, not at all. And if he thought it for one second he'd probably internally combust from the guilt he'd feel for thinking it. I think Mom might, though."

"Might what? Regret him staying?"

"Yeah..." She pauses and takes a deep breath. "Sometimes it seems like she feels bad for him. Just the way she looks at him like she kept him from living his life then and even more now."

"It's not like Mom asked for any of this. All she wanted was Dad, and probably us. But she didn't ask for the rest of it. Who the hell would?"

I take Zoe's responding grunt as an agreement. I've always suspected Zoe resented our mother on occasion, and I think it eats at her a bit. Since she was twelve, she hasn't got to do the things with our mom like other girls her age. And it wasn't like our mom wasn't there—she just couldn't take Zoe shopping for a bra or give her advice about crushes or whatever else mothers and daughters do together. We learned earlier than most kids that life isn't fair, but sometimes I feel like Zoe's experience learning that was harsher than mine and Will's.

"Listen, my next game is on Saturday and it's midday, so maybe we can convince Dad to come then. Maybe even bring Mom along." I know the chances of either happening are slim, but it never hurts to put it out into the universe.

As I put the car into park, my gaze snags on an auburn ponytail as it gets caught in the breeze. "Shit," I say under my breath.

"What?" Zoe looks at me and follows my gaze. "Who's that?"

"Who's who?" I don't know how I'd forgotten I'd invited Nellie tonight. A busy day taking Mom to various appointments and reading probably had something to do with it.

"No one," I say quickly before getting out of the car and slamming the door. Zoe follows me to the trunk where I've stashed my gear and grabs it before I can. "Give me my stuff, Zoe," I say between clenched teeth.

"Not until you tell me who Red is." She swings the bag behind her back. I can easily get it from her but not without drawing attention to us.

"Just a friend, now give me my bag," I grumble, holding my hand out.

"Wait, is she the 'just a friend who reads'?" Zoe's face morphs into that of a villain who just caught the hero. My sister does sinister too well for my liking.

"Yes," I say, rolling my eyes, exasperated. "But she has a boyfriend, ergo, literally just a friend. Bag. Now." She hands the bag back to me, still smirking, and then walks beside me towards the stands without further comment. I am officially dreading how the rest of the night is going to go.

I dump my bag in the dugout and say hi to a few of my teammates, most of whom I haven't seen since last summer when we lost the championship game by one run in extra innings. My last memories of them are hazy at best, swimming beneath way too much alcohol.

"This is our year, boys."

"Excuse me?" Carol Lawrence calls out.

"This is our year, boys and girl," Dan Lawrence says again, slapping his wife's ass as he walks by. "Sorry, babe, habit."

"Well, you better break it soon, or it's going to be a very

long summer." She smiles sweetly at him despite the threat laced through those words.

"You should probably just say 'team,'" Jimmy Sung says as he laces his cleats. "Inclusive words are best for everyone."

"This is our year, team," Dan cries louder, and everyone whoops.

I sit beside Jimmy and lean in. "Not even an argument. Hell must have frozen over."

"We've had a lot of workshops during PA days lately, and they seem to be finally sinking in." Jimmy laughs and stands to begin stretches. Half the team are teachers at the local high school, and the other half, excluding me, teach at the elementary school. If someone here didn't teach me, they taught one of my siblings, or, like Jimmy, they were a student with me.

"How was your year, kid?" Carol asks, sitting next to me. Carol was my fifth-grade teacher, and it's taken me three summers of seeing her at games to drop "Mrs. Lawrence" when addressing her. It still feels wrong to call her Carol, however.

"Pretty good, no complaints."

"You're done now, right?"

I nod as I stand and begin to stretch. "Yeah, all done, officially free."

"What's the plan?" she asks.

"Um..." I loathe this question. I also secretly hate people who have everything planned out before school hands them a piece of paper. My eyes dart to where Nellie is sitting, and I amend my thought: I hate *almost* everyone who has everything planned. I admire Nellie for her goals. "I'm still weighing my options."

"Understandable. Things can't be easy with your mom."

I nod again, trying to ignore the annoyance I feel every time someone says something that sounds like pity. It's why I keep a lot to myself with people who aren't from here. I cannot stand to be pitied.

"I'm going to warm up my arm." I grab my mitt and a ball out of my bag and head out to the field. When I pass Nellie I look up to wave, but she's engrossed in a conversation with my sister. "Fucking great," I mutter to myself as Jimmy jogs by me, in his catcher's getup.

"Sorry, bud, Dev can't make it tonight so you're stuck with me," Jimmy calls as he gets into his catcher's stance.

"Oh, that wasn't directed at you, dude. Sorry."

"All good. Now give me the heat."

After a few pitches, I head back to the dugout where I stretch again, but only so I can peek over at Nellie. She's no longer talking to my sister; now her eyes are glued to me. I grin back and give a casual wave despite my heart feeling like it is trying to escape my chest. She tips her chin up in acknowledgment.

"Who's the hot redhead?" Jimmy asks.

"Um, a friend of Zoe's," I stammer with my attention on the glove in my hand.

"Looks like she wants to be a friend of yours." He laughs and knocks me with his elbow.

"She's got a boyfriend," I say, twirling my glove around.

"Huh... I'd hate to be that guy then."

"Why?"

"If my girlfriend was looking at other guys the way she's been looking at you, I'd be worried." And down goes my glove into the dirt.

SEVEN

NELLIE

EG is good. At least I think he's good—it's not a game I understand well. But the other team doesn't get many hits, and he looks good doing what he does. When he walked out of the dugout to warm up, I bit my lower lip so hard I was sure I'd make it bleed. Have baseball uniforms always looked that good? Or does it just look good because of the guy wearing it? Some of the players definitely have tighter pants, and some looked like they'd lose them without the belt. EG's fit snuggly but don't look too tight, and the socks pulled up to his knees did something to my brain that I was not prepared for. Why the hell is that such a good look?

"Who are you here with?" the woman next to me asks.

"Oh," I stammer, feeling panic creep in as I look back at EG. "Just a friend. The, uh, the pitcher."

She follows my line of sight. "He's not your boyfriend?"

"No!" I say, probably too quickly.

I look over to see she's wearing the smuggest grin. Her blue eyes slide to mine and that grin turns into a full-on smile, and that's when I see the teeth that are just a little bit too pointy. Shit, EG's twin sister has caught me ogling her brother.

"It's funny," she mumbles. "I didn't peg you as the type."

We'd talked for five minutes, I don't know how she'd be able to peg me as anything. "As what type?" I ask, letting my eyes wander to the field and settle back on EG just in time to see him finish another strikeout.

"The cheating type." I nearly give myself whiplash because of how fast my head swings back around. She fully laughs this time. "Ah, because you're not, are you?" I shake my head slowly. "So why does he think you have a boyfriend?"

I swallow and look back at the field. "Because I told him I did."

"Why?"

"Because he was a stranger on a train, and it just came out when he asked for my number."

She stares unblinking at me for a minute before her eyes narrow. "My brother, the guy in blue throwing the balls." She points to the field. "That guy... asked for your number?" She sounds genuinely shocked.

"Yeah. He sort of helped me at the station then saved me a seat, and we got talking and eventually he asked for my number, and 'I don't think my boyfriend would like that' sort of slipped out."

"So what now? You're just going to keep acting like you have a boyfriend while you attend his games to drool all over him?"

"I'm not drooling all over him," I say, sitting back and crossing my arms.

"Well, maybe not literally, but figuratively speaking, you sure as shit are."

I don't respond, just watch as he leaves the mound. When he glances up at me and smiles, I can't help but grin back.

"It's obvious you like each other. I mean, I don't know you from that chick with blue hair over there, but Teddy's never been the aggressive type when it comes to women. Apparently, my older brother and I got 100% of that gene, so if he asked for your number, that's not nothing."

Teddy. My eyes find him where he's lounging in the dugout.

"Zoe fucking Fletcher!" a voice calls from the end of the bleachers. "When the hell did you get home?"

"Mary-Anne Losani!" Zoe jumps up before turning back to me. "Tell him the truth, Red. He's a good guy. He deserves it." Then she leaps off the bleachers and into the other woman's arms, both of them shrieking like banshees.

The thing is, I had every intention of telling him, but now I'm not sure I want to. While I do want things to change, I also want to get to know him more as a friend. *You could just tell him that you know,* a little voice says at the back of my mind. That would be the mature thing to do. But what if he's mad that I lied, or he doesn't believe I may eventually want more?

As I'm having the most epic of internal battles, I catch EG, Teddy, looking at me again. He smiles, and everything goes quiet in my brain. It's like the time my parents took me snorkeling in Indonesia, the world quieting the second my head slipped below the surface. He's done that a lot since I met him, made my brain quiet down a bit. Dulled the constant thoughts racing through it. His ability to soothe and unnerve me at the same time is wild. My brain stills while my body comes alive.

Zoe climbs back up beside me to grab her bag and once again catches us staring at each other. "Can you let Teddy know I'm heading out with a friend?" she asks before putting her hand on my arm and squeezing a bit. "Just be honest with him."

Just be honest with him.

The game doesn't make it to the final inning. Apparently, there is something called a mercy rule, and Teddy's team scored so many runs that their opponents begged for the bleeding to stop. I'm glad it's over already for two reasons. First of all, it's getting chillier and I'm not dressed for it, and secondly, I'm starting to wonder if the people sharing the bench with me could feel me vibrating with nervousness through the metal seat. A totally normal way to feel while waiting to tell a friend that you lied about having a boyfriend.

After the teams shake hands and disappear back in their dugouts, I begin to count slowly, trying to give myself something else to focus on. He's walking towards me with his bag before I get to ten. There's something different about the way he's carrying himself tonight. He's almost got swagger, like someone who pitched a perfect game. At least that's what people were talking about around me; I still don't know the rules or all the terms. But I do know that I like the way he's walking my way. And if I hadn't already decided to come clean, I'd be making it now.

"I think you undersold your abilities when you said you were just okay," I say, slowly making my way down to where he's standing.

"Oh, well, in this league I'm a fucking superstar." He laughs, hauling his bag over his shoulder. My eyes go to the forearm holding the bag, and I try not to focus too hard on how his muscles and veins move beneath the skin. "Do you know where my sister went?" he asks, looking around.

"She said she was going out with a friend."

"I thought I heard Mary-Anne's voice."

"That is the name she said, so I guess you did." *This is going to be awkward*, I think as I've now greeted him and told him what Zoe asked me to. What more is there to say?

He's just standing there looking at me, and I'm doing my

best to not just throw myself at him or run away. Both seem like incredibly over-the-top reactions to a slightly uncomfortable silence. And then his hand is coming towards my face, and I all but stop breathing.

"Eyelash," he whispers, pulling his fingers back. I'm just starting to think that this is one of those ridiculously romantic moments that only exist on screen when he goes and flicks the lash off his finger.

"Did you just flick away my wish?" I ask.

He looks down at his fingers, then in the direction he flicked it as if he'll be able to find the discarded lash, then his head snaps back in my direction "Seriously?"

"You never know when one's going to come true, Teddy."

"There are like 300 of those dandelion things... Wait, did you just say Teddy?"

Oops, I hadn't meant to let that slip just yet. "Who's Teddy?" I ask, trying to play it off like I hadn't said it.

His eyes narrow at me, and he sighs. "Fucking Zoe," he curses up at the sky although the smile on his face softens the words a bit.

"Did she know I didn't know your name?"

"Until tonight she didn't even know you existed."

"Hmm." I tap my chin. "She knew about my boyfriend." His eyes go wide, and all the color seems to drain from his face as he looks anywhere but at me. *Lady up, Nell, tell him the truth.* I let him stew in his embarrassment for half a second longer before adding, "Who doesn't exist, by the way." And when he looks back at me, it's my turn to look everywhere but at him.

"As in, you broke up?" he asks.

I shake my head slowly. "There was no one to break up with."

"Why did you tell me you had one?" he asks quietly.

"You were a stranger asking for my number."

"You could have just said no."

"No doesn't always work. Hell, 'I'm seeing someone' doesn't always work either." He sits on the bottom bench, and I slowly lower myself down beside him. "If it helps, your acceptance of my answer made me feel bad for lying to you."

"Why didn't you tell me yesterday?" Because I'm twenty, dumb, and a bit freaked out by this cute guy who seems to want to just spend time with me even if that means he can't get in my pants? "Who was that guy at your house?"

"John's just a friend. He's been away at school in England, and I hadn't seen him in eight months."

"That definitely explains your enthusiasm, then." He sighs, and his shoulders hunch forward. "I wish you'd just told me, LG."

"Me too." I reach over and take his hand in both of mine. "You're just so damn nice, and I didn't know if it was an act or like... real."

He's looking at his hand in mine and squeezes my fingers gently. "My curse is that I'm a nice guy."

"I happen to like that you're a nice guy."

"Well, obviously we all want nice friends." My god, he sounds sad.

"Look, we just met. I like this new friendship, but I kind of also want to kiss you or let you kiss me or mutually agree to let our lips collide."

Those icy blues meet mine, hope and worry warring within. "I feel like there's another 'but' in there."

"But... I... it's just..." Good lord, I'm making such a mess of this.

"But you're not there yet."

"But I'm not there yet." I nod. "I *want* to be," I rush to add.

"It's okay, LG." He squeezes my hand again. "It's been

what... four days since we met? Would I like to kiss you? Hell yes. But I also have liked just talking to you and getting to know you as Nellie." Did his voice get deeper and smoother when he said my name? Fuck, now I really want to kiss him.

We sit there for a while, both just staring at our hands, still folded together.

"So, want to come to the bar? The team goes after every game."

I look at my watch. Nine thirty. "Yeah, I could come for a bit."

EIGHT

TEDDY

Deep blue eyes meeting mine over a glass of ginger ale. Laughs ending in a little snort. An impromptu lesson on how blue jays are both beneficial and the worst, and how she wishes we had loons nearby because their calls are her favorite sound. Those are the memories that echo in my mind as I open my eyes the morning after Nellie told me she wanted to kiss me but she wasn't ready. There was this strange sense of falling without ever hitting the ground when she said it. Elation and devastation had slammed into me at the exact same moment.

My head is pounding. Not from alcohol—I'd stuck with ginger ale along with her. The headache is probably from a lack of sleep and a hint of sexual frustration. It's definitely not something about to rupture, I repeat to myself over and over again. We stayed until last call, talking. After we left, we sat on the hood of my car and talked until the sun reminded us that a new day was beginning. I had every intention of spending time with my team, but when all was said and done, all I'd done was nod my hellos and goodbyes. Nellie had all my attention, and I didn't feel bad about it for one second. Not even now with my head pounding with some kind of happiness hangover.

By the time I get downstairs, I find my parents having a late breakfast in the kitchen.

"You got in late," Dad says, smiling at me and then sharing a knowing look with Mom.

I busy myself by grabbing coffee and hiding my face behind an open cupboard door. "Yeah, lots to catch up on with the team."

"Zoe said you played very well. Everyone in the crowd was pretty impressed from the sound of it." His attention is back on Mom who is struggling with a slice of tomato that's attempting to escape the toast it's sandwiched between.

My parents have a pretty steady morning routine. Coffee for Dad, orange juice for Mom, and always, without fail, a toasted tomato sandwich. Then they share the newspaper and go over all the news from near and far. The only difference between now and before I was twelve is that when they're done reading the paper, Mom doesn't head off to work. In a couple of months, Dad will be retired, and I'm sure they'll get up to all sorts once that happens. He's talked about buying a small cabin somewhere as a little retreat for them. Something he can fix up, no doubt with our help, but somewhere just for the two of them. I'll be happy to help. I can't think of anyone more deserving than my dad.

"Yeah, definitely not a bad way to start the season. You should come to the game on Saturday afternoon. Maybe I'll attempt to break my record from last year." Last summer, I threw five perfect games. It's not all that impressive when you take into account that 90% of those playing have only played baseball in gym class. There are only about seven people who play competitively, and three of the seven are pitchers. We aren't really known for our hitting.

"Maybe," Dad says noncommittally. That's better than an outright no, but I won't be getting my hopes up.

My phone buzzes in my pocket and I pull it out to see a text from my boss.

DALE

I've got you on the schedule starting Monday at 6 am. You good with that?

Yeah, that works. Thanks.

See you then.

Dale Kramer has employed me at his landscaping company for the last five summers. This is the first year I'll be tagging along with his tree team. I'm not sad about not spending the summer shoveling and mowing, but I have no idea what to expect. I won't be one of the people up in the trees; I'll be on the ground getting shit sorted and helping lug around branches and trunks. Thank fuck because I'm not great with heights. Still, it's something different, and I'm looking forward to it. Jimmy wasn't too pleased when I told him though.

"You'll fuck up your arm or your shoulder and won't be able to pitch," he'd said.

I'd shrugged because I'm not about to put beer league baseball above income. As much as I like it, I don't want to be living in my childhood bedroom for longer than I have to. Even if living here makes it easier to help Mom.

"Back to work Monday," I say, looking up at my parents. "Need me to do anything around here before then?" I know my dad is going to tell me to go spend time with my friends, maybe meet someone before I get busy with work. He says the same thing every year, and every year I putter around the house doing odd jobs he's been too distracted to complete. I see friends at night, but during the day, most of them are already working. But then I remember that Nellie said she wasn't starting work until next week too.

I pull my phone back out of my pocket, and just as I'm tapping on my message app, a notification from her pops up.

LIBRARY GIRL

You may be sick of me but feel like going for a hike today?

As if I'd get sick of you, I think to myself. I met her on Monday, and in less than a week I feel like I need a healthy dose of her to get through the day. Something warms in my chest as I realize she's the one initiating plans this time.

Sounds good. Where would you like to go?

I reread the text before I hit send. Does it sound too blasé? I don't want it to seem like I'm not jumping out of my skin in the best way at the thought of spending another minute with her.

Two hours later, we're walking down a secluded trail talking quietly. Nellie is identifying bird song, smiling brightly when it's a bird she likes a bit more than the others. If you'd asked me Monday morning if I gave a shit about birds, I'd have laughed and said absolutely not. A friend in high school had a budgie, and it used to freak me out swooping around his basement while we played video games. Now I'm hanging on every word about fucking birds. I'm even asking questions about them because Nellie's knowledge of the feathered demons is sexy as hell. Also sexy as hell are all the tattoos she has on display. She's dressed in athletic wear, a tight tank and leggings, and I've got a front-row seat to the art that sweeps across her upper body. Most are just black, but there are a few with splashes of color. The blue jay and cardinal both have muted accents of blue and red. I want to trace every single one with my finger—actually probably my tongue, but I'm desperately trying not to let my imagination go there.

I shouldn't be so focused on Nellie when it's a bit slick on the trail from the rain we had yesterday morning. The sun can't breach the canopy above enough to have it dried up already, but I'm not ready when I hit a particularly damp spot and feel my foot slip forward. Within half a second I find myself stuck in a desperate attempt to stay upright. My arms start to windmill, and my feet fight to gain purchase on the mud. Gravity wins though, and I'm on my ass a minute later.

"Oh my god." Nellie slides over to me, bending and holding her hand out. "Are you hurt?"

"Just my pride," I grumble, taking her hand and slowly getting back to my feet. When I look up she's red, desperately trying to hold in a laugh. "Oh go for it, let it out. I would." I stare down at her. All she needed was permission, and she's lost in a fit of wheezes and snorts. I'd fall a million more times if this was what the result was. Eventually, I'm laughing right along with her as I brush off my shorts.

When she gets control of herself, she looks mortified. "I'm so sorry for laughing."

"Why? I would have done the same thing if the roles were reversed."

"Oh, good to know."

"I am an equal opportunity laugher," I say seriously.

"How progressive of you," she purrs rather demurely as she reaches out, grabs my arm, and begins rubbing her fingers over a spot just above my elbow. I don't move, just let her do her thing while I stare helplessly. I wonder if she can feel how my skin buzzes beneath the touch of her fingertips or if she knows how fucking incredible she smells. Notes of coconut and something else overwhelm my senses, and I have to work hard at holding myself back from dropping my nose to the top of her head and breathing in.

When she looks up at me, her hands remain on my arm, and I don't look away. I want it to be very clear that I would like to kiss her. I want her to just go for it when she's ready, without any doubt that I want the very same thing. *Five days*, the little voice says, *it's only been five days, have some patience.* I swallow, and a small smile curves her lips. It's shy yet flirty, and very Nellie.

Her hands return to her sides, and she gestures up the trail with her head. "Come on, I want to get to the waterfall before noon."

I don't know how I have so much energy. I'm going on roughly three hours of sleep, but if she asked me to hike across the country right now, I'd tell her to lead the way. Even if my legs gave out from exhaustion, I'd fucking crawl after this woman. The feeling both thrills and terrifies me.

NINE

NELLIE

This would be the ultimate place for a first kiss. I am standing on a dry flat boulder at the base of the waterfall as soft mist cools my skin. I look back at the shore where Teddy is searching under rocks for salamanders. His degree is starting to kick in as he admires the nature around him. It's such a nerdy endeavor, and I love it.

Five days, I think to myself. I've kissed guys within five hours of meeting them; five days isn't too soon. But I don't just want to kiss Teddy. I want to kiss him and never stop. There's a piece of me that feels like he's *it*, and I don't want to rush into it or run from it. I want to explore this feeling a bit more. I'm not naive enough to think that we aren't in the honeymoon phase of this relationship, be it platonic or romantic. We haven't discovered those annoying habits people have. He could eat popcorn loudly during a movie or be rude to service people. Although he has given me no indication that he'd be rude to anyone.

When Teddy finally makes his way over, he stops on the rock beside mine, squinting up at the waterfall, and then he looks at me. No one has ever looked at me the way Teddy does, and it's complicating everything. I can't quite identify what it is between us because I've never felt it before, and even though I've never been in love, I can say with absolute certainty that this feeling isn't love. I wonder if it's the feeling of potential and anticipation, maybe a dash of hope in there. I told him outright that I want to kiss him and that I want him to kiss me but that I'm not ready. Then we talked all night long, and the first thing I thought when I woke up was how badly I wanted to talk all night long again. How desperately I want to see him under the sun and in the shadows of the trees as the sun moves across the sky. How the idea of waking up to his face sounds better than just about anything else because it means he's there with me. None of what I've felt this week feels like not being ready.

The boulder I'm on is large, and Teddy steps onto it with me. Now I'm standing on a rock in the middle of shallow gentle rapids fighting an internal battle I know I'm about to lose. But I've never been one to go down without a fight, even if the fight is half-assed at best.

The first sign of me breaking comes when I link the fingers of my right hand with the fingers of his left. He doesn't say a thing as we stand there, both watching the water cascade down the cliff in front of us. I don't say a thing when he raises our hands and presses a soft kiss to the back of mine. I feel his lips all the way down to my toes, washing away every ounce of reservation I have.

Fuck it, I think when we make eye contact. Except I must have said it out loud because his eyes widen a half second before my lips connect with his.

The sensation of his lips on my hand is nothing compared to what I'm feeling now. He drops my hand, and both of his hands cradle my head while mine are gripping the front of his T-shirt and pulling him into me. When I feel his tongue slide along the seam of my lips, I open without hesitation. Confetti cannons and champagne bottles are firing along the synapses in my brain and there's a voice screaming that this is what a first kiss should be like. I can't help but smile beneath his lips, and when he feels it, he slows his pace. I can feel his heart beating under my hands and his breath on my lips as he pulls back slightly.

"I guess that means you were ready?" He laughs as if he can't believe what just happened.

"More than ready." I lick my lips, wanting to taste him again. I'd never gotten the appeal of cinnamon gum until this very moment.

He nods down at me, his eyes boring into mine, full of hunger. He looks like a starving man who has been allowed to smell fresh bread but not given any to eat. "Four days wasn't enough, and five was almost too many."

"Like an avocado," I say, and we burst out laughing again.

The walk back to our cars is different, more handsy, more stops to make out against trees and rocks, more silence, more stolen looks that neither of us tries to hide. I still don't want to rush into things. I'm not going to be dragging him into the back of my car or planning sleepovers just yet.

"So," I begin as we reach my car and come to a stop, "today has been a lot." I can see panic start to take shape on his face, and I quickly add, "A good kind of a lot." I reach up and place my hand on his cheek to try and convey how I feel. "But I still want to work on getting to know each other. So um—"

"You want to take it slow. Just maybe with more kissing?" I don't know how he always seems to know what I need to hear or what I mean to say. He takes both my hands in his and slowly backs me into the side of my car. "I'll have you know, Nellie, that I am pretty okay with taking things slow." His lips drop to my jaw, and he kisses me lightly to my chin. Then his arms are caging me in and he's gazing down at me with a fierceness that causes the butterflies to escape my stomach and travel elsewhere. "Just as long as you know I won't be taking it slow or at any other speed with anyone else. It's just you, LG. Only you," he whispers before his lips meet mine again.

Just when I think I'm going to pass out from a lack of oxygen, Teddy stops and steps away abruptly. "Have a safe drive home." He turns and leaves me leaning against my car door, panting like I've just run a mile. I watch him walk across the lot to his car, and when he gets there, he turns around.

"Hey, LG," he yells.

"Yeah?"

"Wanna come to my game tomorrow? Maybe give me a good luck kiss?"

"I'll think about it." I smile stupidly back at him. I'm obviously going. Wild horses could not keep me away from that man.

I would have spent the whole day with him if I could have, but my father asked me to come into the raptor center for a bit today. I have no idea why, but I have a feeling it's to help get things ready for his summer interns. I just hope I can focus on the task at hand with the past hour on repeat in my memory. I try to concentrate on what the afternoon will bring instead of waterfalls and kisses. I know that if my dad sees me in this state, he'll know something is up. He's a romantic, and I have no trouble sharing my relationship status with him, but for now, I want to keep this for just me.

John greets me at the entrance when I arrive with a big hug and a gift bag.

"All the way from the streets of Oxford," he boasts with a big smile.

I tear the tissue paper from the top of the bag and laugh when I see six UK chocolate bars at the bottom. "Why do I get the feeling that you got these at the duty-free on the way home?"

"Because you know me better than anyone else." John throws his arm around my shoulder and leads me towards the offices. "Aren't you going to bust one open?"

I look into the bag and back at him. "I just brushed my teeth so I'll save one for later." I am not ready to erase the taste of Teddy quite yet.

"Cornelia!" My dad's voice booms through the office as we walk in. "Any Flakes in that bag, my dear?" He walks over and peeks in.

John leans into me. "Don't let him steal any of yours just because he has no self-control."

I shove the bag behind my back and glare at my dad. "I cannot believe you would dare to steal my chocolate when I know you got some of your own."

"Hey, I had to share with your chocoholic mother." Dad pouts.

"Oh, stop it. A middle-aged man pouting is up there with pineapple on pizza. Unacceptable."

"Hey, I like pineapple on pizza," John says, sounding hurt.

"I know you do." I gag.

"I have no problem taking that chocolate back, ya know." John tries to grab for the bag, but I twirl away before he reaches me.

"Okay, why am I here?" I huff, sitting at one of the empty desks and shoving the chocolate into a drawer that locks. I turn the key and then slip it into my pocket. Chocolate secured, for now at least.

"I've taken on a couple of extra interns this summer so..."

"And in your world, how many is a couple?" I interrupt, knowing full well that he doesn't mean two extras.

"My money is on four," John says, leaning back in his chair and grinning over at me.

"Spill, Dad."

He looks between John and me and rolls his eyes. "Four."

"Typical." John claps in triumph.

"I just need assistance with the packages, then you're free to leave." My dad is incredibly detail-oriented but somehow negligent at the same time. He'd likely have the right number of packages but not all would contain what they should. Between the three of us, all the interns would get what they needed.

"How many in total?"

"Seven," he says without looking up at me. He complained last year about the four he had under his wing, so I have no idea how he's going to handle seven.

When I look over at John, he's making a face that matches the concern I feel. "Are you going to be okay with that many, Doc?"

Dad shrugs. "I've got two extra sets of hands this year. Mind you, they are still green." He seems lost in thought like he hasn't thought about how he was going to manage. "It'll be fine." He waves off our concerns and stands. "Let's get started."

"I'll be right back," I say, jumping up and heading to the back room where injured birds are kept for observation. I give my hands a thorough wash then stop by the freezer to snag a cricket.

The cage I'm looking for is about halfway down the hall, and when I arrive in front of the one I want, I'm greeted by four high-pitched klee sounds. Mr. Fitzgibbons calls to me from the highest branch in his enclosure, his right leg wrapped in a bright green bandage. The little kestrel was born at the center and recently had a run-in with a stupid moment. At least that's what Dad's assistant referred to it as. No one knows what happened, but his leg was broken and now he's spending his days in the recovery ward.

"Hey Mr. Fitzgibbons," I coo, holding the cricket through the bars and watching as the little bird navigates his way down to me. "You seem to be getting better on one leg." I pull my phone out and suck my teeth to get his attention, then I snap a picture to send to Teddy.

> Meet my favorite raptor, Mr. Fitzgibbons.

He replies almost immediately.

ENVIRO GUY

> My favorite Raptor will forever and always be Vince Carter.

I respond with an eye-rolling emoji and slip my phone back into my pocket.

Mr. Fitzgibbons had arrived along with an egg mate and the mother about two years ago. Someone had surrendered them from what my dad believes was a falconry program gone wrong. Mr. Fitzgibbons will live at the center for the rest of his life while his mother and sibling have gone to other bird sanctuaries that work with public education. If I had more time, I'd be slipping on a glove and pulling him out for a snuggle, but in his state rushing is the wrong course of action. So I wiggle my fingers and blow him a little kiss goodbye before dashing to the presentation room where my Dad and John have started organizing things. That's where I find them in a heated argument about semantics, of all things.

"You can't just throw around 'a couple' when you mean twice that."

"Everyone knows a couple could mean more than two.

Besides, there are more important things that I keep up here." Dad taps his skull.

"If you told me that you were bringing a couple of people to my house, I'd prepare two extra meals. If you showed up with four extra people, I'd be short two meals. How can you remember every single fact about the fifty-three birds at the center, but you can't keep a couple and a few straight?"

"Should I..." I gesture behind me.

"No, it's fine, chickadee." My dad has called me that since the day they found out Mom was pregnant, but today there's an accompanying sigh of exhaustion attached to it.

"You know, Dad, you could head home, and John and I can finish up here."

He eyes both of us as though we've got something planned, like letting all the birds out of their enclosures. Which I've only threatened to do once so he doesn't have any grounds to suspect I'm about to do it now.

"Yeah, Doc, this isn't the first time we've done this. Go home and rest or mow the lawn or um..." He looks over at me, clearly out of suggestions.

"Take Mom out to that antique store she likes and then go out for dinner. Next week you're going to be way too busy to do any of that stuff." I know I've won when his shoulders lower slightly. He and I both know how my mom feels about him taking on interns all summer.

He glances up at the clock. "I suppose I could do that."

"Not could, Dad, *should*. You should do that."

Two hours later, John and I finish up all the packages, put away the extras, and check in with the evening staff who are in the middle of feeding. Although check-in sounds too formal. We say quick hellos and goodbyes.

"Ready for tomorrow?" I ask as we head to the parking lot.

John sighs. "I mean, other than showing up and wearing the

suit, there isn't a lot I need to be ready for. The girls got the tent all done today. His fiancée just told me to make sure my brother gets to the church mostly sober."

"Low bar." I laugh.

"He actually hasn't had a drink all month. I think he plans on uncorking that restriction tomorrow night."

I wince. "Oh, so it's going to be a sloppy wedding."

"What kind of groom wants to remember his wedding day?" John murmurs, smiling down at his phone like a moron.

"Nigel?"

He hmms in response while he taps a reply.

"He's not going to show up as a surprise tomorrow, is he?"

John's head snaps up, and a look of pure horror covers his face. "God, I hope not."

"I thought you really liked him. Why wouldn't you want him to?"

"That's way too much commitment, Nell. This thing is still new."

"Six months is still new?" My god, Teddy and I are in the embryonic stage if six months is considered new.

"Yes. We just had the 'Are we exclusive' talk."

"And are you?"

"Are we what?"

"Exclusive."

"Ish." He tips his hand back and forth.

"Ish?"

"Yeah, ish. We are exclusive-ish."

"How the hell can you be exclusive-ish? It's not an ish word. Either you are or you're not."

"It is what it is. Did you come clean to the Fletcher kid?"

I can feel the blush coming and quickly look down, trapping my lips between my teeth.

"Oh," John hoots. "I'm guessing it went well then?" All I can do is nod. "How well are we talking?"

"I don't know. We haven't talked about it beyond me wanting to take it slow."

"Well that's no surprise, you've always been a slow and steady type of girl."

Ish. I think. With Teddy, I want to savor every kiss, every look, every single smile. He feels like...it. But I refuse to say it out loud. This thing with Teddy is too new, too fragile to put that much pressure on.

"I like to weigh all the facts and possibilities. You know how I feel about wasting time."

"That I do. So, what are your first impressions on that front, then?"

"Right now it feels like the best use of time."

"And do you think he feels the same way?"

I remember his hands in my hair and the way he kissed me like he'd never get enough, and nod because I'm too busy biting my lip to keep myself from giggling hysterically.

"I look forward to meeting him one day," John says, pulling me in for a side hug before walking over to his car. "I'm leaving on Tuesday. Do you have any free time to hang out on Sunday evening or Monday?"

"I'm not sure yet, but I'll do my best to fit you in."

He lays his hand over his heart. "I am honored to fit into your busy social calendar."

"You should be," I say with the straightest face I can manage.

TEN

TEDDY

Nellie and Zoe are sitting together in the stands at my game. Unfortunately, my parents are nowhere to be seen. I knew my dad would opt to stay home, but I still felt a surge of disappointment when I didn't see them.

Over the years, their friends have drifted away, and my dad hadn't done much to stop it from happening. He insists that he isn't embarrassed, but it was either that or he's too worried that something else would happen to Mom. I flip-flop on how I feel about it. Zoe is adamant that he's just worried, and right now, I'm choosing that line of thinking. There is also a part of me that's happy my parents didn't come. I'm not sure I am ready to introduce Nellie to everyone. Zoe was enough for now, on several different levels.

Before the game starts, Nellie sneaks into the dugout while I am bent over, touching my toes. When I stand she's right in front of me, and I somehow manage to jump back while also grabbing a hold of her and hauling her with me. We land awkwardly on the bench, and after I'm done kissing her in front of my entire team, she beams shyly at them.

"Does that count as our lips breaking our fall?"

"Yours, maybe."

She kisses me quickly again and whispers, "Good luck, EG," before jogging back to the bleachers.

Jimmy's eyes narrow at me. "Does this mean she doesn't have a boyfriend, or that she's in an open relationship and you're fine with it?" He looks over to where she's sitting. "Honestly, I'd probably be fine with it myself."

"It means I'm the only one she's in—" We haven't really discussed anything. Going slowly probably meant that it was the start of a relationship but maybe not a full-blown one just yet. "A thing with."

"A thing, eh?" Jimmy's brows disappear underneath the brim of his cap. "Sounds serious."

"Shut up." I shake my head and stand to get ready to hit the field. I've never been overly competitive, but with Nellie here, I feel a need to win like never before. How I can throw a single pitch properly let alone several with one eye trained on her should be studied.

"I like watching you play," Nellie says, holding her can of pop up.

After the game, we picked up pizza and went to the beach. It's nothing special, but there's no one else here so it seems like a great place to spend a quiet evening together.

"I like you watching me play too." I tap my drink against hers before taking a sip. She'd gotten a bit of sun, and her cheeks and the tip of her nose are slightly pink. "Did you wear sunscreen today?"

"I put what tiny amount was left in the tube. I guess it wasn't enough."

"I wish you'd said something. I had some with me."

"You wishing I'd said something is starting to become a thing with us." Sitting this close I can see the tiny laugh lines that have begun to form at the corners of her eyes. The proof of someone who smiles and laughs often. The ache I feel to see those lines evolve is almost painful. I want to be one of the reasons they spread and deepen. I want to be able to count every smile she ever smiled because of me.

"What?" She's looking at me, head cocked, slightly crooked smile bright. I'm staring at her, probably with a sappy look on my face. She wants to take things slow, and I'm sitting here fast-forwarding to a time where she's telling me she looks old and I'm holding her from behind, staring at her in the mirror and telling her she's never looked more beautiful than today.

"You're really beautiful" is what comes out of my mouth, and it's totally worth it as her cheeks darken, and she looks everywhere but at me. "Hey," I say, taking her chin between my thumb and forefinger so she has to look at me. I was all ready to reiterate what I'd said, but the minute those dark blue eyes land on me, all I can think to do is kiss her. And so I do. It's slow and almost sweet but still starts to ignite something in me that is decidedly not slow so I ease back. "You really are," I say quietly before leaning back and taking her hand.

Next week we won't have time to see each other almost every day. It may help with the taking it slow part. Either that, or by the time I do see her I'll be ravenous for her affection and sloppy drunk after one hit of it. I can still feel her eyes on me so I point towards the lake with a slice of pizza. "The fish are jumping." When I allow my eyes to slide her way, she's looking at the water.

"They are indeed," she whispers, without so much as glancing at me.

"It's going to be weird next week not being up all night talking with you."

She sighs and leans back on her elbows. "I'm surprised we still have things to talk about."

"We've got twenty-plus years to talk about. I'm not surprised at all." I feel a bit guilty that I haven't talked about my mom at all. I don't think it's going to change a thing, but past experiences have made me a bit truth-shy when it comes to her. I don't know if I'm protecting my mom or myself.

I can see her fighting exhaustion when she smiles at me. "Are you looking forward to getting back to work?"

"Yeah. I like working outside, and it's a better deal than a gym membership. What about you?"

"I'm not so sure, to be honest. I'm looking forward to being back at the library. Working there helps keep systems in my head while I'm away from school. And I'm looking forward to the birds at the center, but I'm not so sure about the people."

"Not a people person?"

"It's not even that. I think my dad may have taken on a bit more than he should have this year. Last year, he had John as well as his two full-timers. Now he's got one less employee and four more interns. He's one of the best to learn from, but he's also dedicated in a way that makes me worry."

"Worry about what, exactly? Him? The interns? The birds?"

"Mostly worry about him, and the birds." She smiles sheepishly at me. "I don't care so much about the interns."

"Dads are resilient. He'll probably be okay in the end."

"Oh? Know a thing or two about resilient dads?"

This is the perfect opening. Seriously, I couldn't script it any better, and so I surprise myself when I don't take it. "Well, parents in general right? Just think of all the things they deal with that we never know about. Somehow they keep on going, working, parenting, and loving each other. Well, I guess not all parents—there are definitely shitty ones out there. But still, a lot are resilient. And resilient parents breed resilient kids."

She's looking at me as if she can see that I'm keeping something locked up, but all she does is lean further into my side. "You're probably right. I'll still worry about him, though."

"That's your right as his kid," I reassure her. I worry about my dad too. While everyone else is worried about my mom, I lose sleep worrying about him.

I watch as Nellie fights another yawn, and I look back at where our cars are parked. "Are you going to be okay to drive home?"

She nods. "I'll open the windows and blast some music. I'll be okay."

If the whole slow thing wasn't hanging over us, I'd suggest sleeping on the beach, although I know I'm already going to be sore tomorrow after sitting out here for hours.

I walk her to her car, and we recreate our post-hike kiss. "Text me when you get home, all right?" I tell her when we finally pull apart.

"You too." She gives me one more chaste kiss before we finally separate and head towards our respective homes.

Forty-five minutes after I get home, I am still staring at my phone, waiting for a text from Nellie. I am not sure if playing Candy Crush is helping me stay awake or lulling me to sleep.

LIBRARY GIRL

Home. Had to stop for gas and a friend from high school was working so I got home a little later than planned.

Glad you're home safe. How was the drive?

Uneventful. Not even a jaywalking deer.

It really is rude that they just think they can cross wherever they want.

Deer are notoriously unobservant creatures.

My front bumper knows that all too well.

Oh no!

First time driving solo too!

OH NOOOOO. I thought I hit a chipmunk once and was inconsolable for about 10 minutes. My mom finally got me to stop crying and pointed at the side mirror and the little fucker was just standing 50 feet behind the car, watching!

I am convinced for some species running across the road is a coming-of-age thing.

I suggested that to my dad once and he assured me it was not…I still think it is though.

Okay, I need to go put my phone down or I'm going to fall asleep with it.

Would that be the worst thing?

No. Goodnight, EG!

Night, LG!

ELEVEN

NELLIE

I stare down at my phone, my hand pausing mid-book scan. I'd woken up to a good morning text from Teddy, and then he'd sent a picture of a tree his team would be dismantling about an hour later. Other than that we haven't talked much today, which was to be expected with both of us returning to work. Still, despite the expectation, I find myself missing him more than I should.

Um… What kind of desire are we talking about here?

Get your head out of the gutter, LG. We're taking things slow, remember?

I wanna know what you'd love to do if given the chance to do it… something you'd be fine telling your parents about.

My current secret desires, the ones I keep under lock and key inside my mind, all involve Teddy, and because I had to go and state I wanted to take things slow, that is where they will remain for the foreseeable future. And I'm glad for that because I do want to take things slowly. He's just making it hard by being all nice and sweet, and his lips are all soft and pillowy and gloriously demanding.

"Cornelia, I've got a meeting tomorrow at one. Would you be able to cover the phones while I'm out?" my boss asks, walking up to the counter and not noticing that I've been scanning the same book for the last minute while I'm lost in thought.

"Yeah, sure, absolutely," I stammer, putting the book on top of the to-shelve pile. The library doesn't exactly have a busy phone line so I doubt she even needs to ask me. Sometimes I think she does this to give me a glimpse into the life of a small-town librarian. I love it here, but this isn't what I want for my future. I don't think it is, anyway.

When she heads back to her office, I pick my phone back out and reply.

> I would love to have a mobile library. One that travels to remote areas that don't have funding for a permanent library.

> That's really cool.

> What about yours?

I watch my phone for a few minutes, but no answer comes. When a reply still hasn't arrived by the end of the day, I send one more text before heading home.

> Is it that embarrassing?

By the time I pull into the driveway at home, there is a reply and I feel the nervous bubbles in my stomach ease.

I'm so sorry I got home and showered then laid down and passed out. Hauling logs and branches all day is exhausting.

Who could have guessed?

My secret desire is to travel around the world.

Where would you start?

Probably fly to New Zealand then make my way west.

So mine is to drive a van of books about three hours away from my home and yours takes a three-day journey.

Don't sell your desire short. You'll share ways for people to escape their realities. Far more accessible ways.

Is that why you want to travel, to escape your reality?

Dots appear and then vanish. I can almost see him typing something then erasing it, and I can't help wondering what he is trying to sort out. Assuming that he was hiding something seems like a good way to drive myself mad so I refuse to let my mind wander there.

Just a change of scenery for a while would be nice.

Change from what? When was the last time he had gone somewhere beyond my hometown or the city for a game? He'd commuted to university so hadn't lived in the dorms or an apartment.

Where's the farthest you've been?

When I was about 10 we drove out to British Columbia to visit my mom's family. That's the last time I went anywhere interesting.

So you're long overdue.

Sure am.

In one of our late-night talks, I'd told him about trips I'd gone on as a kid. Usually they revolved around Mom or Dad's work, but I don't remember them actively working on any of those trips. They always did feel like a proper getaway, even if I came home with more bird experiences than anything else. I can't imagine going so long without a real trip. But I guess if you don't do it all the time, it's not something you miss. Still, I want him to get the chance to explore the world, even if I have to stay here.

I'm going to turn in. Hopefully, in a few days, I'll have a routine and won't immediately want to go to bed when I get home.

The next morning I wake up to a text from Teddy with a timestamp of two a.m.

I didn't even ask how your day was, I'm a terrible person.

Did you wake up to ask me that?

His response is a guilty-looking emoji.

I hope you at least slept well. Wouldn't want you falling asleep on the job and being crushed by a tree.

Are you working at the library today?

I am. I start at 9.

By the time I leave for work, he hasn't responded, and again I try not to let that bother me. He's at work, work that requires his full attention and both hands. But when I pull up to the library, there is a large truck with a tree logo, and the sound of chainsaws fills the air. Even with the hardhat and his back to me, I can pick Teddy out of the crew as they cut and haul a dead tree to the chipper. I back myself through the doors so I can watch him for as long as possible before clocking in and getting to work. The library isn't busy at this time in the morning, and it's easy to hear Teddy's team working away. Around 10:30, the door opens and a few of the guys walk in. An older man asks me to point them to the washroom, and two of the three walk in the direction I gesture. The third guy stops in front of me, and when I look up I'm greeted by a face I have come to really appreciate.

"Surprise." He smiles at me, those canines pressing into his lower lip. Teeth that have done zero damage to me but still hold my attention.

I want to pretend to be cross that he hadn't told me, but my desire to do that is no match for the one that wants me to leap across the counter and plaster myself to him.

"Hi," I say shyly. "Are you all done?"

He shakes his head. "Nah, still a couple more trees to fell. We're just taking a break because our schedule allows it today."

I quickly look around. I'm the only one working until eleven so I slip around the counter, grab his hand, and drag him to a random aisle, hidden from anyone else who may be inside.

"Is this a small-town version of the stacks?" he whispers, his hands moving to my hips and pulling me into him.

"You seem taller," I observe, moving my hands to his neck.

He nods as he brings his lips to mine. "Boots," he says against me, that cinnamon breath brushing lightly across my skin.

If one day someone told me I'd be making out in my workplace with the hot tree guy, I would have laughed. But I'm not laughing now as we play "how hard can someone be pushed against these shelves before they topple over?" Turns out, pretty hard, because they're all bolted to the ground. It feels like flames are going to burst out of my body, and I wonder if Teddy can feel how hot my skin is as his lips trail down my throat.

"Goddamn, I've missed you," he groans just before his lips are back on mine.

I want to say I missed him too, but the desire to kiss him harder wins out as his hands graze the sensitive skin at the base of my shirt. Chills race through me, and I pull on his neck so his lips fuse with mine.

The sound of his coworkers leaving the washroom has us jumping apart so fast we may have broken the sound barrier. As I fix my shirt I watch him casually lean against the shelf across from me, looking down at his feet, eyes closed, and doing deep breathing exercises. Those pants he's got on may hide a lot now, but while we were plastered together everything was pretty obvious.

"Sorry about that," he says when we hear the main door shut. "That was the definition of not slow."

"I'm pretty sure I started it." I smirk back at him.

"That's true. You should be the one apologizing, I guess." I don't know if it's the one eyebrow he has quirked, his grin, or simply the inexplicable need to touch him but whatever it is has me erasing the distance between us. I thread my fingers through the loops in his pants, and look up at him with the most demure expression I can manage.

"Teddy..." I coo.

"Mm-hmm?"

"I'm very sorry."

He removes his hands from where they'd been holding him up on the shelf and runs them up both my arms until his fingers card through in my hair. Eyes locked on mine he lowers his face, and just when he's about to kiss me he moves to my ear and whispers. "I'm not." Then he drops his hands, straightens up, and walks away.

When he reaches the door, he looks back and smiles at me. "Thanks for making reading fun, LG."

After he's gone, I go back to the task he distracted me from and replay every second of today's encounter. My mind keeps reminding me that this is new, take it slow. But my body is telling me the opposite, and right now it may be winning.

TEDDY

One of my many secrets is that I love to cook. I'm pretty sure I got the love of it from my mom. She's currently sitting on a stool beside me as I prepare dinner. Sometimes I catch her looking wistfully at my hands as I chop or stir, and I can't help wondering how I'd feel if the ability to do something I loved was taken away.

I've made this dish so many times that I could do it in my sleep, but I still ask her questions as I go. "What do you think, rough chop or a fine dice for tonight?" I hold up the two options, and she smiles before nodding at the hand with the diced pieces.

Tonight she wants to stir, and I don't interfere. There are some days she stays far from the kitchen, and others she wants to do as much as possible. Before everything changed, she was the type to have the radio on, dancing and singing along as she prepared dinner. She insisted that cooking for her brood was her favorite way to unwind after school. It took a long time for her to come back to the kitchen after everything. Will took over cooking most meals until Dad felt like Zoe and I were old enough to handle the knives and gas stove. When Mom finally got back into the kitchen, it was Dad she bossed around the best she could. Her mobility has improved since then, but her verbal abilities never came back even after months of therapy.

When I've added the last ingredient to the pot and slide it into the oven, Mom looks at me over the top of her glasses. "What?" I know exactly what she wants to know. I swear losing certain abilities has only enhanced others, like mind reading. She is asking "Who is she?" with her eyes and a tip of her head. I don't know how she does it and I don't know how I know, but being able to communicate with her in any way at all is something I'll never take for granted.

"Her name is Nellie. We met on the train after a Jays game. It's new... but I really like her."

Her head tips further to the left, and her eyes narrow slightly.

I roll my eyes because I knew that wouldn't be enough information. "She just finished her second year at Ossington. She's really smart and funny." *She's beautiful and has this sexy demure thing going, yet takes charge like a champ. She nearly undid me against a bookshelf at the library yesterday, and I have a new appreciation for reading.* I don't say any of that, of course. Mom doesn't need to learn just how far gone I am for Nellie, not yet anyway. "Like I said, it's new but..." I trail off because Mom's just nodding and looking at me with the softest goddamn eyes. She reaches out for my arm, squeezes, and sighs.

As a kid, my parents talked about their love story constantly. My mom always said, "When you know, you know, and everyone around you will know too." I don't believe in love at first sight, but I do know that I've never felt this way about another person. It's this delicious anxiety that spreads through my body whenever I think of her, and it morphs into a raging inferno when I see her. Honestly, it feels a bit like the time I went skydiving. A mix of exhilaration and terror that I want to experience again and again.

Dad gets home just as *Wheel of Fortune* ends and *Jeopardy* is starting. We've watched these two shows together since I was a kid. My siblings and I would take turns doing the best impressions of the contestants yelling out the letters or sharing obscure facts to introduce themselves. Zoe was particularly good at yelling out "N" in a way that would have us all howling. She did it tonight, and Mom laughed just as hard as she always has. Mom may not be able to talk, but her laugh never left.

Dad bends down to kiss Mom on the head and squeezes my shoulder as he walks to the kitchen to get his dinner.

"So," Dad says, as he returns with his plate and sits beside Mom, "I was thinking that we'd come to your game tomorrow if that's okay with you?"

"Yeah, that would be great. I'd love to have you both there."

He nods, stirring his food. "We'll drive over separately, though, so we can leave if we're tired." He always uses "we" in place of "your mom."

"I totally get it. Do whatever you need to do."

"So, will your girl be there?"

I've been watching the TV through this conversation, but now I can't help but turn my head slowly towards him. He's chewing, but a smile spreads slowly across his lips. At this moment, all I see is Will when he's found out something that was a secret.

I swallow, and my eyes shift to my mom who is trying and failing to control her smirk. "Who told you?"

"Well, I ran into Keith yesterday on my way home from work, and he mentioned that you were a great addition to the team." He takes another bite of food and chews for what feels like a full minute. "He just wonders if you'll be able to make it through the week without making out with someone against a bookshelf."

So this is what it feels like when your heart stops. My mind is racing through the entire encounter with Nellie. We heard them come out of the bathroom and separated before they would have seen us. I mean, they could have seen me panting and figured it out I guess. Or, they had come out, seen us then went back, and made a louder exit as a warning.

"I... we've been... ugh, I was on a break." I must look like a deer caught in headlights being cross-examined, that is how I feel anyway. Dad, meanwhile, is clearly enjoying how uncomfortable I am, and I don't doubt for a minute that Mom feels the same way.

"Relax, kid." He laughs, reaching over to pat my knee. "You're twenty-two. This is the time to be doing that stuff. But I would like to know if she'll be at your game?"

Now I'm not sure I want her to be at my game. I don't think I could handle it if she doesn't want to deal with my family situation. Then again, wouldn't it be better to find that out now rather than later?

"Yeah, she should be there."

He looks at Mom, and they have one of their weird nonverbal conferences before he looks back and simply says, "Good. Now can you turn it up a bit? Alex seems to be talking quieter today."

I may as well be alone in the room because I've completely zoned out. Is it too early to meet the parents? It feels too early. But I should probably tell Nellie what's up and let her come to that conclusion on her own. If she wanted me to meet hers, I'd say yes only because it would mean more time with her.

I pull my phone out and begin texting her.

> Just a heads up, my parents are coming tomorrow

> I won't be offended if you decide not to come

> They're nice but it's early and so no pressure

> I'll be supportive of whatever you decide to do

LIBRARY GIRL

I'd love to meet your parents. Although, maybe you don't really want me to?

> No, I do, I definitely do. I'm just nervous

Don't be. Parents love me. I can bring a reference letter from my own if you'd like

Goddammit, did I just fall in love with her? Is this the moment I get to tell people it happened? It doesn't seem all that romantic. Also, I can't fall in love with her, not yet anyway.

> A letter won't be necessary, you seem trustworthy

I'm hauling a giant branch to the chipper and trying to control yet another yawn the next afternoon due to a lack of sleep brought on by the anxiety of how tonight is going to go. I want Nellie to like my parents and for them to like her. On one hand, if this is a disaster, at least we figured it out early before either of us was that invested. But on the other, if it is a disaster I may never sleep again. What I need to do above all else is tell Nellie about my mom. I hadn't planned on doing it yet, but if they are going to meet in a matter of hours, I really should let her know.

"Fletcher. Get your head out of the clouds, kid," my team lead calls to me, and I shake myself out of the spiral.

"Sorry, Keith," I mumble, which of course he can't hear due to the ear protectors and the sound of the chipper. I toss the branch into the feeder and watch as it's instantly turned into shavings. I hope tonight isn't going to do the same thing to my new relationship.

After work, I decide to call Nellie instead of texting her.

"Are you going to try and convince me not to come tonight?" she answers after the third ring.

"No, I was going to tell you that my mom, who will be at the game, is partially paralyzed and can't speak."

I could hear a pin drop on the other end as I'm greeted by silence. And then I hear a sigh. "Wait, are you serious?"

"Yeah, I'm serious," I say, and then prepare myself for the "I can't handle this" speech I've gotten used to. But just as she's been doing since the day I met her, she surprises me.

"Teddy, why didn't you tell me?"

"I didn't want you to decide I wasn't worth getting to know."

"Why would your mother have anything to do with me wanting to get to know you?"

"There's a history of... sudden disinterest, shall we say."

She's silent for a minute, and I feel the weight of it crushing the hope within me. "I'm going to be honest with you," she says slowly. "I want to meet your mom. But only if you are really okay with it. If it's too soon I understand, but I'm not going to run away. She's your mom, Teddy." She sounds exasperated, sad, and somewhat excited all at once.

"No, no, I do want you to meet her," I rush to say, feeling a bit lighter. "And my dad. I want you to meet him too."

"Good," she says, a smile in her voice. "Anything else I

should know before tonight? Does your family have a flying dog? Or perhaps a talking cat?"

I laugh, looking up at the cloudless sky, suddenly grateful for this woman. "No, unfortunately just a gravity-enabled dog, but both of those things would be pretty great."

"I'm not sure," she mutters skeptically. "A talking cat would probably have an insufferable amount of attitude. Imagine all the nonverbal judgment being vocalized."

"True, but a flying dog would be cool. Like Falkor."

"Agreed," she concedes. "Although, I think Falkor was a Luck Dragon, not a flying dog."

"Oh, well having a Luck Dragon would also be pretty cool."

We sit on the phone just listening to each other breathe for a minute. "I can't wait to meet your family, Teddy."

"I can't wait for you to meet my family, Nellie."

"See you tonight."

"See ya tonight."

Between every pitch, I find myself staring at where Nellie is sitting in the bleachers talking to my parents. I've heard my mom's laugh a few times, and knowing it was Nellie that caused it does things to different parts of my body. My heart is falling fast, my head is in awe, and I'm more turned on than I ever want to be when my family is involved. After I get the final batter to ground out, I walk slowly back to the dugout with my eyes glued to the woman who has flipped my world upside down. She looks over at me as she listens to something my dad is saying and smiles. I've never cleaned up my shit so fast.

"Great game, kiddo," Dad says as I walk up to where he's still sitting with Nellie and Mom. "I wasn't sure you had your head in the game, but you proved me wrong." He winks and tilts his head at Nellie along with a not-so-subtle thumbs-up.

"Thanks," I say to him, but my attention is on the woman sitting next to my mom. "Did you enjoy the game, Mom?"

"Omm," she hums while reaching over to squeeze Nellie's arm. Then she nudges Dad and gives him a look only he understands.

"Well, it's late so we're going to head out. You kids have fun," he says, helping Mom down. "Don't be a stranger, Nellie." He looks up as his hand covers Mom's on his arm. Mom's smile is bigger than I've seen it in a long time, and it's all for Nellie.

I join Nellie on the bleachers, and we watch as my parents slowly make their way across the field to their car.

"What happened?" Nellie asks, taking my hand and leaning into me.

"She had an cerebral aneurysm rupture when I was twelve. She was fine, and then she wasn't. We came home from school to find our aunt at the house, which was odd. Dad didn't come home for a couple of days, but that was only to shower and change. It took her a long time in various forms of therapy to get her motor functions back. Unfortunately, her speech never got better. She was a teacher..." I trail off and feel Nellie's arms wrap around my torso. I've told the story so many times, but this is the first time in years that I've struggled to finish it.

"She's really great," she whispers into my shoulder. "Your dad is too."

"Yeah, as far as parents go, I did okay." I look around to see that everyone has gone, and it's just the two of us left. "You wanna get out of here?"

THIRTEEN

When Teddy said his mom couldn't speak, I didn't know how to react. Obviously it wasn't a problem for me, but it hit me just how new we still were. I barely know anything about his family, and he barely knows anything about mine. It isn't that I need to be in the know this early on, but his mom's situation seems like a big deal.

In the end, though, I had nothing to worry about. I had a wonderful time meeting his parents, and I looked forward to seeing them again. What was more, I loved the way his parents looked at Teddy throughout the game and when he walked up to us after it. His mom, who had looked happy all evening, practically levitated when he made his way over, clearly the light of her life.

Teddy's friend manages a drive-in theater near the ballpark, and after a few texts, he gets us in for the second movie which is starting in half an hour. His car is a far better vehicle for a drive-in so I leave mine at the back of the theater lot and hop into his. After he finds a spot, he backs in and pops the trunk before getting out.

"Was all of this just in case?" I ask when I join him and see the blankets and pillows.

"Always be prepared, LG." He smiles down at me, gesturing for me to climb in. "You get comfortable, and I'm going to go change and grab snacks." And then as if he can't keep himself away another second, he draws me in for a kiss that has me sliding rather than climbing into the back on account of my knees turning to Jell-O.

I do a bit of reorganizing so that we have some support yet be able to get good and close. I am trying to figure out what position to wait for him in when he appears around the corner with his arms bursting with stuff.

"Did you leave anything for anyone else?" I laugh, leaning forward to take things from him before he drops them.

"Well, I didn't know what you liked, and Ed told the concession guy to give me whatever I wanted."

"You could have asked."

"Where's the fun in that?" he asks, climbing in next to me. "Besides, I may have been taking advantage of the situation." He holds up a couple of bags of candy. "If you don't like any of these things, they are now car snacks."

"Clever." I snag the bag of Swedish Berries out of his grasp. "I do happen to love these, though."

His gaze drops to my lips, a sly grin appearing on his lips. "Excellent."

"What's that look for?" I ask, popping a candy into my mouth.

His smile grows and he leans into me, his hand going to the back of my neck as he draws me closer. "I also happen to love Swedish Berries."

I only get out a small "oh" before his lips meet mine.

We spend most of the movie making out because both of us seem far more interested in each other's lips and bodies than tornadoes full of sharks. We only come up for air when we need to hydrate or freshen up our Swedish Berry breath. By the time the credits roll, I feel high on sugar and Teddy.

"It's late," I say, holding his wrist up so I can check his watch.

"It is," he replies, his hand pushing escaped pieces of hair behind my right ear.

"Don't you have to work in the morning?"

"Nope." He grins back at me. "I've got tomorrow and Sunday off. What time do you work?"

I shrug. I'm helping my dad with some pre-trip prep at the raptor center, but that's it. "Probably eleven."

"Hours and hours away," he says quietly, pulling me back to him.

"Sleep is very overrated."

An hour later, I manage to extract myself from his car and drive home, a stupid smile plastered on my face.

"Nellie?" I hear my name whispered from the living room when I walk into the house.

"Hey Mom," I say, walking in to find her curled up in the big armchair with the lamp on and a book open on her lap. "You didn't have to wait up for me."

She tips her head and smiles at me. "I know, but I always will." She stretches and closes her book, the page she was on folded over causing an involuntary shudder to run through me. "So when do we get to meet him?"

"Meet who?" I ask coyly.

Mom gives me that look she had mastered long before I came to be.

"Ooooh, Teddy. Well, maybe after your trip? He's got a busy schedule."

She walks over to me and puts her arm around my waist to pull me into her side. "Better yet, how about I stay home, and we can invite this Teddy for dinner? Your father doesn't need me."

I look down at her and smile sweetly. "I think that would be a terrible idea."

She laughs, squeezing me tighter. "Your sister was far easier to convince than you are."

"Maybe I've just learned what not to do from Sylvia. Besides, Caleb worked for Dad. We all knew him long before they fell into each other. Actually, I'm not entirely sure Dad didn't push her into him." My mom is looking at me skeptically. "No, really, you weren't there. I don't see how she tripped. He pushed her."

"'Pushed' seems awfully aggressive. Maybe he nudged her."

"Oh my god, he did!" I gasp.

She shrugs. "Remember, I wasn't there. I just can't see your dad pushing anyone, let alone his firstborn."

"We'll have to agree to disagree on this."

"I'm okay with that. Now go to bed, young lady. There's lots to do tomorrow before we leave." She lets go of me and heads for the stairs. "And don't think I've forgotten about meeting Teddy. Within the next month, you're going to invite the guy who keeps you out until the wee hours over for dinner."

"Deal," I say before she disappears from view.

In the kitchen, I pour myself a glass of water and pull my phone out to text Teddy, only to find one waiting for me.

ENVIRO GUY

I think Swedish Berries are forever ruined for me.

Oh no! Did you overdo it tonight?

Possibly...

Just thinking about them turns me on now.

I cough as water enters my windpipe and stare down at his words. I begin to answer, then stop only to repeat those steps.

I made things weird, didn't I? Is it too late to unsend? Can you pretend you never read that?

Depends, is it the berries that do it or the thought of me?

I can see him typing and then stopping, clearly struggling with finding the right words.

It's always you.

It's always you. Never have three words caused all the oxygen to leave my body before now.

Too forward?

No, just the right amount. Night, EG xx

Night, LG

Teddy and I follow the same kind of schedule for the next month. We both get even busier with work but always find a way to see one another no fewer than four times a week, which never feels like enough.

"Six weeks," he says, after kissing me hello outside the raptor center one evening.

I quickly do some mental calculations. "You're right, although it feels like longer." I can tell he isn't sure if I mean that in a good or bad way. "In a good way," I add, kissing him for a bit longer this time.

We're still taking things slowly. I'd slept with my ex by six weeks, multiple times. But there is just something about Teddy that makes me want to savor the build-up to that moment. I don't want to rush a thing. At least my heart and mind are on the same page. It turns out that my body is very impatient.

"You must be Teddy." My mom's voice has me jumping back and stepping in front of him defensively. I have no idea why this is my reaction, she's harmless. "Or at least I hope you are."

My mom ignores my stance, passing right by me and pulling Teddy in for a hug. He's about a foot taller than her and smiles brightly at me over her head. At least one of us is chill.

"What are you doing here, Mom?" I stammer.

"Your father left his reading glasses on his desk." She rolls her eyes.

I narrow mine. "Dad has like thirteen pairs of reading glasses. And at least two in his car." I know this because every time he loses a pair he buys another at the drugstore and inevitably finds his old pair within fifteen minutes of making the purchase.

As if on cue, I hear my dad yell. "I found them, ducky," he calls from beside the car where he's standing, waving a pair of glasses above his head.

"Oh, well, would you look at that?" Mom says innocently. "Although, now that we're all together, how would you like to go get some dinner with us? That way we can get to know Teddy here."

I immediately try to think of an excuse why we can't do that while Teddy says, "That would be great."

She clasps her hands and beams. "Wonderful. Why don't you two finish up whatever it is you were doing, and we'll head to Norm's. Do you like gastropub food, Teddy?" Mom asks, looking concerned.

"I love all food, Mrs. Woodcroft."

"Oh no, please call me Jean," she insists.

Teddy nods. "We'll see you in a bit, Jean."

I watch as my mom practically skips back to the car. Both my parents wave as they drive away, and I release the groan I've been holding in since I heard her voice.

"I'm so sorry about that," I say, taking Teddy's hand and leading him into the center. "My dad said he was leaving early today, and I guess I was a bit too enthusiastic about it. He's usually not that perceptive."

"Don't be sorry. I've wanted to meet your parents."

"Why?" I laugh, looking back at him.

He pulls me back to him and wraps his arms around me. "Why wouldn't I want to meet your parents? They made you."

I stare up at him, waiting for a punchline that doesn't come. "Can I see your ID?"

"Why?"

"Because I don't believe you're only twenty-two. What twenty-two-year-old says things like that?"

He shrugs, dropping his arms and taking my hand again. "What can I say, I'm an old soul. Now I want to go meet Mr. Fitzgibbons, the man I'm in competition with." Teddy begins pulling me in the wrong direction, and I stand my ground, halting his progress.

When he looks back at me I point towards the opposite side of the room. "The feathered love of my life is that way."

At nine weeks, Teddy's parents have shown up at five more games, and I swear he plays better than ever when they're there. His smiles were as much for me as they were for his parents, particularly his mom.

During the few hours I'd spent with Teddy's mom and dad,

I'd seen bits of Teddy in each of them. He has his mom's eyes and wavy dark hair while his laugh and height are all his dad's. At the third game, his mom took my hand and held it for most of the game, squeezing when she needed to cheer so I'd cheer a bit harder for both of us. That night, she'd touched my cheek when they said goodbye, and Teddy blushed from his nose to his ears. When I asked what it meant later, he had just kissed me followed by a murmured thank-you. I didn't understand what he was thanking me for, but I didn't want to stop kissing him to ask.

I'm still riding the high of his post-game kisses the next morning while helping my dad prepare for another quick work trip when I start to feel a bit off. My mom asks quietly if I'm pregnant. Unless you can be impregnated by aggressive over-the-clothes action, there is no possible way that I could be. Still, she insists that she is more than happy to stay home with me, the perfect excuse for not going on another bird-related trip. I know she'll have a good time, though. She's never been good with the buildup of things, so I push her out the door, insisting I will be fine.

By nine a.m. Saturday morning, I'm curled up next to the toilet after texting my boss to let her know I won't be making it in today. I feel bad as it's pouring, which means the library will likely be busy with parents trying to occupy their kids. Just thinking of the energy it takes to deal with children all day has me retching.

Around noon, I get myself down to the couch with the designated puke bowl from my childhood, a sleeve of saltines, and a bottle of some electrolyte drink my mom keeps on hand for heavy workout days.

ENVIRO GUY

Game is canceled tonight, want to do an early dinner?

I look at Teddy's message and immediately feel my stomach flip. Something it always does when I see a text from him, but this was definitely more to do with the thought of dinner than the guy I was falling for.

Can't. I'm sick.

Oh no! Want me to come over?

No! I'm probably contagious. I'm just going to slowly die on the couch while watching a British period drama.

An hour later, there is still no reply from Teddy. Thirty minutes after that, there's a knock at the door. I lay there glaring through the house, willing the person to go away. There's another knock before I hear it open. If I had any energy at all I would be running to the kitchen and grabbing a knife, but instead, I lay there, accepting that I was about to be killed, robbed, or both. And then Teddy walks around the corner.

"What are you doing here?" I screech, horrified that he is seeing me decked out in sick girl couture.

"You're sick." He shrugs, walking towards me holding a large canvas bag.

"I know, that's why I told you not to come over," I mumble.

"Why? Because you didn't want me to see you sick? You still look hot, for the record."

I roll my eyes and sit up a bit. "No, doofus, because I don't want to get you sick!"

He shrugs again. "I have the immune system of a bat."

I stare at him. "I don't know what that means. Do bats have good immune systems?"

"One of the best," he says, plopping down next to me. "I brought you sustenance." He puts the bag down and begins pulling things out. A heating pad, Gravol, ginger ale, tissues, crackers, a loaf of bread, the book he'd bought with me, a container of some kind of liquid, and a box of tea bags.

"You didn't even know what was wrong with me. What if I just had a headache?"

"You said you were contagious."

"Right, I did say that." I give him a small smile. "What's that?" I point at the container with the mystery liquid.

"Soup."

"Did you make it?"

"Not this one. This is one of Zoe's creations." He picks it up and tips it back and forth. "Don't tell her I told you, but she is the better soup maker between the two of us."

"Do you cook a lot?" I ask, sitting up more before thinking better of it.

"A couple times a week. After Mom's aneurysm, we all picked up the things she did the most. Dad and Will did most of the cooking until Zoe and I could be fully trusted alone in the kitchen. Although to be honest, we are rarely alone. Mom loved... loves cooking so she's often in there with us, overseeing things."

"I hate what you've all been through, especially your mom, but it's pretty great how you all stepped in."

"That's what family does. You face an issue head-on, you don't run from it."

"Is this you facing an issue head-on?" I gesture at the pile of stuff on the coffee table.

"It is."

It still feels like my insides were thrown into a blender and then poured back into my body, but the way he looks at me, even when I'm several shades too green, does make things a bit better.

"So." He gestures at the things he's unpacked. "Can I get you anything right now?"

I survey the items again and feel the bile rise the minute my eyes land on the soup. "Maybe just the Gravol for now. I don't think I could keep anything else down." He nods and pops a couple out of the package, handing them to me.

"These will probably knock you out, but at least you won't be throwing up."

"One of those things is definitely better," I murmur after I swallow the pills and snuggle back into my pillow.

"This that British drama you were talking about?" Teddy asks, sitting back and nodding towards the TV.

"Yes, but we can watch something else."

He throws his hands up, "I would never dream of inviting myself over and then making you watch something else. Just give me the Coles Notes of what's going on so I'm not totally lost."

"Okay, so it basically all takes place at this estate in the English countryside, and there are usually two main storylines. One with the owners and one with the staff. Very upstairs-downstairs stuff. The family is the parents, their three daughters, and the dad's mother. But his heir died, and so they had to find someone else in the line."

"Wait, the heir died? But he has three other kids."

"Apparently in the early 1900s, women couldn't be the heir."

"Typical." Teddy rolls his eyes. "Sorry, continue."

"They end up finding this guy who is a lawyer, and so he and his mom show up and it's all snobby upper-class vs self-righteous middle-class people being dramatic. This is the first season. I think you'll catch on pretty quickly."

"Oh, you've already seen it?" I hold up three fingers. "You've seen it three times?" he asks, eyes wide.

"It's my comfort show. I watch when I'm sick, which isn't often, or I'm homesick or just want something familiar."

"Huh, I don't think I have a show like that. I don't think I have anything like that, actually."

"Well, I will happily share this one," I assure him before restarting the episode.

"You don't need to restart it," Teddy says as if I've offered to donate a kidney.

"I was only fifteen minutes in. Trust me, EG, rewatching any part of this show is not a hardship for me."

Teddy manages to get right into it, and halfway through our second episode he's formed opinions about every character.

"I do not like the direction this relationship is going with the valet and that maid." "I feel so bad for the blonde sister; she's basically an outcast in every way. Do you think they cast her because she looks nothing like the others?" "Grandma is hands down the best character on this show. She dies in the next episode, doesn't she? Wait, don't tell me." "I would not mind cooking in that kitchen. Imagine having that much counter space."

I've never watched with someone else, and I am enjoying the commentary, especially on things that play out over several seasons. I'm asleep by the third episode and wake to the sound of heavy rain. Teddy is sitting at the end of the couch, ankle crossed over his knee, with a book in hand. I don't say anything for a couple of minutes, soaking up the view of a hot guy reading.

"How are you feeling?" he asks without looking away from his page.

"Marginally better than I did earlier."

"Better enough to try some soup?"

I think for a moment, and when the idea of eating soup doesn't make me gag, I nod. "Would you mind putting it in a mug? They're in the narrow cabinet next to the fridge."

He comes back with two mugs, spoons sticking out of both. "You could have used a bowl for yourself," I say when he hands a mug to me.

"Careful, it's hot. I happen to prefer soup in a mug. Well, broth-based soups anyway. There is something about cream soup in a mug that just doesn't work for me."

"No, I get that. Something about the viscosity of it." We both make a face and laugh. "Thank you for coming. I just really hope you don't end up in the same situation."

"Me too, but of all the people who could get me sick, I'd be least upset if it was you." He would say the most romantic thing I've ever heard when I have a fever and may actually be hallucinating.

FOURTEEN

TEDDY

As the words leave my mouth, I think maybe I've come on too strong. Watching Nellie's face twist this way and that makes me start to panic. "I mean, ultimately I'd really prefer not to get sick." I laugh, trying to break the tension.

She finally smiles at me and raises her mug to blow across the top. "Wanna keep watching?"

"Absolutely. I need to know what that cranky lady's maid is up to." She probably thinks I'm just placating her, but after three and a half episodes, I am absolutely hooked.

Nellie finishes most of her soup, and I convince her to try a piece of toast. She encourages me to make myself something more substantial so I make a couple of peanut butter and jam sandwiches. When we are done eating, I clean up quickly and get her to put her pillow onto my lap. She manages to keep everything down and within half an hour of her head hitting the pillow and my hand combing through her hair, she's sound asleep again. I am grateful for the slower pace of the show since I spend half the episode watching the flutter of her eyelids as she dreams, her mouth occasionally turning up in the corners.

She wakes briefly and goes to brush her teeth. When she returns, she is the one who reorganizes our positions on the couch so I'm on my back and she's wrapped around me, head buried in my chest. I am convinced that when we get up, I'll have a Nellie-shaped sweat spot. Between how hot she is and my body temperature, I feel a bit like I'm melting. But if melting from our combined heat is how I'm going to go, I'm fine with it.

The next day I wake to a clear sky and Nellie wrapped around me like a sloth. I'm going to be sore from sleeping on the couch, but when Nellie wakes and announces she's feeling better, I decide the minor aches are worth it. She makes me eggs and toast and just toast for herself, and we have breakfast on the deck next to the pool.

"You don't have to run off, do you?" she asks, brushing the crumbs off her fingers.

"Nope. All yours for the day, LG."

"Feel like going for a swim in a bit?"

I'm still desperately trying to take things slowly, and having her pressed against me all night has chipped away at my resolve. "I didn't bring a suit. I didn't expect you to be feeling up for a dip."

"I'm sure I can find something for you," she says, standing and grabbing our plates. "I'm going to change and see what I can round up."

"Sounds good," I lean back in the deck chair and watch her walk into the house. Right before she passes through the patio door, I nearly suggest that we say to hell with suits and just skinny-dip. But I know that will absolutely lead to other things, and she hasn't even tried to go there yet so I keep my mouth shut.

She comes out a little while later wearing an oversized T-shirt that ends mid-thigh, leaving her long legs on display. I don't notice at first that she's carrying a pair of swim trunks.

"These still have the tag on them." She rolls her eyes. "My dad doesn't use the pool much, but my mom still buys him a new pair of trunks every summer."

After changing, giving myself a much-needed pep talk, and brushing my teeth, I rejoin Nellie on the patio. Her eyes sweep over me as I walk towards her, and I see her lips turn up at the corners ever so slightly. She likes what she sees apparently. Next, it's my turn to appreciate the view as she slips the T-shirt off. She's in a one-piece, but it's the kind I've only ever seen on vintage pinup posters. If someone had asked me if Nellie had a pinup model body before I would have said no. But goddamn if she doesn't look incredible.

"I like the polka dots," I say lamely, pointing at her suit.

"Oh yeah? Like anything else?" She spins slowly giving me the best 360 view I've ever seen.

I take a step towards her and when her eyes lock on mine, I move even closer. "There is one thing," I say, laying my hands on her waist.

"And what's that?"

"I just think it's a bit too dry." And with that, I wrap both my arms around her and launch us into the pool.

When she pops out of the water, she's laughing, and I'm momentarily frozen in place watching her wipe the water from her face as she treads in place. When she sees me, she smiles sweetly and starts swimming my way. I back up until I'm against the side of the pool but she keeps coming. Her hands land on my shoulders and she wraps her legs around my waist, my hands immediately go to hers.

"How about now? Wet enough?"

"Careful, LG, that sounds like a euphemism."

She moves her hands from my shoulders to cup my face. "Answer the question, Enviro Guy."

I slide my hands up and down her sides, my eyes still on hers. "It's sufficiently wet," I answer.

"Good." She releases my face and waist and pushes off the wall, rocketing away from me. After a couple of deep breaths, I follow her across the pool.

We spend the next half an hour lazily swimming, never touching for more than a couple of seconds at a time.

"If we hadn't met, what would you be doing this summer?" I ask as we float on our backs.

"Working, mostly. Basically, all of my high school friends moved away for school and spend the summer wherever they went or they travel," she says, looking over at me.

"Glad I could break up your summer between jobs."

"What about you?" Her hand brushes mine briefly and I feel it to my toes.

"Probably drinking more, partying, more hungover mornings, and arguments with my brother."

I hear a thoughtful little hum come from beside me. "So having me around is good for your liver and relationship with your brother."

Having you around, I think, *is better for every part of my life.* "It would seem that way." I smile over at her.

Eventually, Nellie swims to the edge and hoists herself up. But she doesn't stand and walk away like I expect her to. She turns and sits with her legs dangling in the water, watching me with a flirty little smile. As I swim closer, the smile grows, and when I set my feet down and stand so her knees are framing my sides, she's got a full-blown grin.

She brushes the hair off my forehead, and I watch her eyes sweep across my face as if she's mapping every inch. "Hey," she finally says.

"Hey." I smile back just as I make a decision. Planting my hands on either side of her hips, I raise myself out of the pool so our faces are level. "I'm going to kiss you now, LG," I say.

"Yes, please."

It's a wonder how I manage to keep myself upright as our lips meet. This woman unbalances me in the best way. Her fingers slide through my hair, her nails scraping deliciously across my scalp. I want to stay like this forever, but my arms betray me, unlocking so I fall away from Nellie and back into the water. Seconds later, she slips back in and closes the space between us. She wraps her entire body around me before her smiling lips meet mine again. I keep my hands at her waist, wanting to slide them lower but knowing that will only lead to frustration later on.

Slow down, slow down, slow down, I chant to myself. Every molecule in my body wants to blow right through taking things slow. It feels almost unnatural, which is why I slow our pace and eventually pull away.

She doesn't vocalize her question, but I hear it anyway. Why?

I lean forward and peck the tip of her nose. "If we keep that up, going slow is not going to happen."

"Maybe going slow is overrated," she says, as if in a trance. She licks her lips, her eyes on where they had just been.

"It's what you wanted, Nell. It's what I agreed to, happily. And I'm not going to let this"—I gesture between us—"happen for the first time in a pool."

She wraps her legs tighter around my hips, causing me to suck in a breath. "We can get out of the pool, you know." Her smile is a bit wicked as she says it like she's thinking of all the things we can do once we hit the deck.

I stare at her for a moment, trying to read her expression. It doesn't take me long before I find what I'm looking for: a touch of doubt sitting at the corner of her lips. I've seen it before, I'm realizing. When she told me she had a boyfriend, and when she winked at me in the bookstore. My Library Girl may like the idea of blowing through the yellow light, but she's still going to treat it like a red.

I reach up and trace those telling lips with my thumb, stopping right where her doubt lives. "I don't want to rush a single thing with you, Nellie," I say when her eyes meet mine. "I've never wanted to savor anything more." I watch her lips turn up and the doubt disappears.

"You're very romantic, EG. What twenty-two-year-old guy is this romantic?"

I shrug. "I told you, I'm an old soul."

"I suppose one of us needs to be the mature one." Then without warning, she's pressing down on my shoulders, dunking me, and swimming off towards the side.

I can hear her laughter underwater and don't give a second thought before I push off the bottom and rocket after her.

We spend the next fifteen minutes acting like children, dunking and splashing before Nellie admits to being exhausted. On the deck, I reach for her towel first and wrap her in it, pulling her towards me as I do. She looks up at me with those big blue eyes before reaching up for a kiss that leaves my legs feeling a bit like my arms. There are promises of things to come in each kiss, and I cannot wait to find out what they are. An involuntary shiver runs through me as the breeze picks up, and she breaks away, reaching for the other towel, which she throws around my shoulders.

"Come on, let's go change and warm up." I keep the fact that with her so close I don't feel the need to warm up to myself, but I nod and follow her lead anyway.

When she comes back downstairs, I can't help but laugh

when I see that she's wearing the T-shirt version of my sweatshirt.

"Great minds," she says, stepping into the living room.

"I believe they only let those into the school." I walk over and wrap my arms around her.

"Mmm," she murmurs into the fabric of my sweatshirt. "I have heard that. So." She looks up at me. "What do you want to do now?"

Absolutely everything, I think. If she suggested going for a colonoscopy I think I could get on board. "Do you want to maybe..." I stare down at her and grin. I see her eyes heat thinking I'm about to suggest something else. "Read on the patio with me?"

Her face lights up and she pulls back, her hands landing on my hips. "That may be the hottest thing anyone has ever said to me."

"Really?" I ask.

She nods and pulls me down for a kiss. "Really." I feel her smile against my lips right before she pulls out of my arms. "I'm just going to go grab my book. I'll meet you outside."

FIFTEEN

I've read the same line twelve times. We're sharing a lounge chair, my back to Teddy while his arm is around my waist and his thumb traces patterns across the surface of my T-shirt.

"You're cold," he says, as goosebumps begin to rise on my exposed arms.

"I'm fine," I assure him. It's not the chill in the air; it's the way he's touching me. It's his body pressed to mine and the memory of how he felt against me in the pool. No, the unseasonably cool weather isn't to blame for a single thing I'm currently feeling.

He clearly doesn't believe me though, because he sets his book down on my lap, removes his arm, and tips me forward a little. He pulls the collar of my shirt to the side, and his lips drop to my shoulder, kissing the spattering of freckles I have there. They travel up my neck, and then they're gone, and he's pulling his sweatshirt down over my body.

"Now you're going to get cold," I say, leaning back against his chest.

"Nah, you're hot enough for the both of us." He nips at the

skin just below my ear, causing my goosebumps to have goosebumps.

"Keep doing that, and I'm going to need your pants too," I tease, tilting my head just a little more, inviting him to finish what he started.

"I don't think I could concentrate if you were wearing all my clothes."

"It also doesn't seem that fair," I murmur, as his lips continue their journey down the side of my neck.

"To me or you?"

"You."

"Oh, LG." He sits back and looks down at me, "Don't worry about me. Seeing you in my clothes does things to me that I'd rather not think about right now."

His eyes have turned stormy, and I can't help myself from spinning around and straddling him.

"What kind of things?" I ask as innocently as possible, while I push my reading glasses into my hair.

Teddy's gaze tracks every movement and a little smirk appears on his face. "Things that are not slow." I lean in to kiss his jaw and then begin trailing my lips down his neck like he had done to me. "Things—" He swallows, and I feel his Adam's apple move under my lips. "Things that I've done with you in my dreams."

"Tell me," I whisper, sliding my teeth down his earlobe. The noise he makes sends a thrill through me, so I do it again.

He's gripping my hips so hard that I won't be surprised to find his handprints there tomorrow. "Fuck, Nellie," he grits out before flipping us over so he's hovering over me. "I'm." He kisses my neck. "Not." His lips move to the other side. "Going." They meet mine. "To." Harder now. "Rush." He sits back and looks down at me, his hands pulling the sweatshirt down where it has ridden up my torso. "This." He finally breathes out.

I'm relieved and disappointed all at once. I meant what I said about taking it slow, but I also want to just blow through the waiting period. But I get the impression he feels the same way, like he's not stopping this just because of me.

I sit up and cup his face in my hands. "I'm sorry," I say, searching his eyes. The storm clouds have moved on and they've returned to their pale blue. "I don't want to rush things either, I just..." I don't know what to say. I don't want him to get tired of waiting.

"Hey," he says quietly, taking my hands in his. "I'm not going anywhere, LG. You get that right?"

I nod and squeeze his hands. "Promise me one thing?" I ask, looking up at him through my eyelashes.

"Sure."

"When we're done taking it slow, you'll show me what we did in your dreams."

A laugh bursts out of him. "Sure, LG. I'll give you a play-by-play."

I behave myself for the rest of the day although I don't know how. I deserve some kind of reward for my efforts. Around two, we extricate ourselves from the patio furniture to go in search of food.

"We've got a couple of cucumbers, a bag of baby carrots, a..." I pull a tub of hummus out to see if it passes the sniff test. "Seemingly okay tub of caramelized onion hummus and a block of cheddar so old it'll turn to dust if you so much as breathe near it."

"That's the only kind of cheddar I eat." Teddy grins and takes a few of the ingredients from me. "Any eggs?"

I pull the carton from the fridge and open it to reveal six.

"Okay, put two of those in a pot and cover it with water."

Not too long after, we are curled up together on the couch

with a board of odds and ends from the kitchen displayed beautifully.

"I'm not loving this guy's holier-than-thou attitude," Teddy proclaims, pointing a carrot at the screen.

"If I was alone I'd be fast-forwarding through every single one of his scenes."

"Are they important?" he asks with one eyebrow quirked.

"Sadly for your first viewing, yes. He's basically the main servant."

"Damn." He slumps back against the couch, his head rolling in my direction. "What?"

I'm staring at him with an amused smirk. "Nothing. I just kind of love that you feel the same way."

"Are there Mr. Bates fans out there?"

"Many. In fact, I'd say most people are. Actually, I didn't feel this way during my first viewing, but I've grown to despise him." I pull my feet under me and turn more to face him. My head resting on the back of the couch, mirroring his. "Maybe you're a better judge of people than I am."

He reaches and tucks a piece of stray hair behind my ear. "I'm not sure about that. I do know that I was right about you, though."

Christ almighty, is he doing this to me purposely? Does he know what hearing him say things like that does to my head and heart? It takes every bit of self-control to stay exactly where I am and just smile back at him. The stopping and starting today has been a lot, and I don't want to stop again so I will not start. It's times like this I wish he'd say normal twenty-two-year-old-guy shit. Drop a few more "bros" and "dudes" and a few less Mr. Darcy lines.

"And what convinced you to try and be right about me?" I ask and mentally punch myself because I know whatever he says next is going to melt every piece of me.

"Your glasses," he says without hesitation.

"My glasses?" Okay, so no melting.

"You had them pushed into your hair." He's looking at the top of my head like he can see them there now. "I don't know why. I just thought, damn, I like that."

"Huh" is the only response I can muster.

"Not what you were expecting? Or hoping for maybe?" He grins back.

"No, I just didn't have that on my bingo card."

"What did you expect me to say? That I thought you were hot? That I wondered what these lips"—he runs his thumb along my bottom lip, and I fight the urge to open my mouth and let it in—"would feel like under mine?"

I nod slowly.

"Oh, I definitely thought you were hot and I absolutely wanted to feel these lips." His thumb continues to trace. "But it was the glasses that made me think 'her.'" Okay, commence melting. "It's the same voice that makes me look at Mr. Bates and think 'asshole.'" The spell breaks when we both start to laugh. It feels like all the tension that had been building releases at once, and I feel a sense of relief as we slip back into each other's easy presence.

Around eleven, Teddy reluctantly pulls himself from my embrace. He has to be at work for seven and still has to drive home. I tell him he should have brought more clothes, and he reminds me that he hadn't even planned to stay over one night, let alone two. I'd prefer he never go at this point. Tying him up and forcing him to remain seems a bit extreme though, and I suppose, very illegal.

At the door, I manage to stretch our goodbye out so by the time I hear the car door close it's eleven thirty. I fall asleep to the sounds of a hushed argument featuring Mr. Bates and his nemesis and my lips still tingling from Teddy's kisses.

In the morning there's a single text from Teddy.

ENVIRO GUY

xxxxx

I can't help running my fingers over my lips, remembering our goodbye last night. It's one of those moments I'm glad I'm alone for because I don't need my family asking why I'm floating around the house like Sleeping Beauty after the dance in the woods with the prince. I want to reply with language that would be inappropriate for this early in a relationship. This is very much the honeymoon stage, and I have to rein myself in a bit.

Xxxxxxx

Thank you again for taking care of me. It was the best sick experience I've ever had.

I spend the next several hours waiting for a reply that never comes.

SIXTEEN

TEDDY

The team is giving me shit for staying up late watching some British soap opera when my boss pulls up behind the truck. I glare back at them as they continue to recount just how many times I yawned before we break for lunch. Dale certainly doesn't need to know how tired I am as I'm sure he'd have something to say about me feeding tree parts into the wood chipper. I need the shifts because I need the paycheck.

As Dale comes into view, the teasing stops abruptly.

He points to me and gestures for me to step onto the sidewalk. "What's wrong?" I ask when I reach him and he can hear me without yelling above the chainsaw above us.

"It's your mom. You've gotta come with me."

"What about her?" He looks at the ground instead of me and I know but I still need to hear it. "Dale, what about my mom?"

He looks up again and over at the team lead before his eyes finally meet mine. "She's gone."

The chainsaw is suddenly too loud. My coworkers yelling at one another filling up every millisecond of silence when it stops. Then a buzzing. Not the saw or an insect, just a static buzzing that I can feel in my eyes and throughout my body.

"Teddy?" I barely register my name being called until I feel Dale's hand land on my arm.

I give my head a shake, and the sounds around me die down as I focus my attention on my boss again.

He said she was gone. A tiny voice in my head asks where she's gone. She can't drive, she doesn't go on walks by herself. She can't just be gone without help. "My dad?"

"He's at the hospital. Your brother called and asked me to come get you."

"And take me to the hospital?"

"To the house."

Right, she's gone. Why would I need to go to the hospital?

"Right." I'm suddenly unsure of what to do next. "So I'll just..." I look around and realize that other than my bag, there is nothing for me to grab. So I just gesture to his truck and then follow. The expressions of my coworkers seem frozen in a state of pity as we drive by. Hands raise in unenthusiastic waves which I return. It all kind of seems automatic, like my body is doing what it should be doing, without me having to think about it.

The drive home is quiet. Dad's car is gone, but Will's is here. The only time I ever see Will's car here is when he's on Mom duty.

"Don't worry about work, okay?" I hear Dale say.

I nod and slip out of the truck without so much as a thanks for the lift as my legs carry me towards the front door. The door opens as I'm reaching for the handle, and Will is there, already pulling me in for a hug. This is weird, we don't hug. My brother is *not* a hugger; he'd sooner punch me in the stomach as a form of greeting than hug me. My arms wrap loosely around him as he holds me like a vice. Zoe is on the couch just staring off into the distance, and I want to push Will off so I can go see what's wrong. *She's gone, you idiot*, I remind myself.

Mom is gone.

When Will pulls away, I get the first look at his face. His eyes are red-rimmed, and he looks like he's aged ten years since I saw him on the weekend.

"What happened?"

"She was fine, we were having breakfast at that diner on Seventh. You know the one with…"

"With the extra-thick-cut chips," I finish for him.

"Yeah. She was laughing and then…" His eyes widen as if he's watching it for the first time. "She just stopped laughing, said 'ow,' and fell forward. But she was alive. She was alive when the ambulance came. She was just unconscious so I didn't… I didn't…" Tears fall as he mouths words that I can't hear.

"Why isn't anyone with Dad?"

"Brenda's there. She's going to drive him home. He's not exactly in a state to drive."

I can't help but laugh at how obvious that statement is. "No shit," I mumble, pushing past my brother to go kneel in front of Zoe. If anyone saw us, they'd think she was looking at me but she's not. She's looking through me like I'm not even there.

"Zoe?" I take her hands in mine and wait until I see her eyes focus on me. It's then that she seems to realize I'm home.

"Oh my god." She throws herself at me, buries her face in my neck, and crumbles.

I don't know what to do other than rub her back and tell her it's going to be fine. I don't know that, though. I have no idea what comes next. I don't think I'm fully understanding any of this. Rationally, I know what Mom's gone means. I understand why Will hugged me and why Zoe is a sobbing mess. Irrationally, I'm telling myself this is all just a misunderstanding.

Mom just passed out from the heat or she had a mild stroke. She's gone for the time being, but she'll be back tomorrow.

We stay like that on the floor until my legs have gone numb and Zoe's sobs die down to whimpers. Will has moved to the front window and watches the driveway with his arms crossed, Morris watching along with him.

I eventually get Zoe back in the chair and go to the kitchen to put the kettle on. I remember when Mom had her first aneurysm. Brenda came over to take care of us while Dad was in the hospital with her.

We'd arrived home from school to find our aunt in the living room watching her "stories," and she'd told us she was staying for a few days while the doctors tried to figure out what was wrong with Mom. Brenda made us tea and told us it would help soothe our worry. So that's what I do, I make tea. I don't even know if I've had tea since that day. I don't think anyone has, as is evidenced by how far back in the cupboard I find the tin of tea bags.

When it's ready, I take mugs out to the living room and set them on coasters in front of Will and Zoe, and then I go back and get one for myself. An hour later, the tea remains untouched and the only sound is that of the clock in the front hall. An ominous ticking, counting down the minutes and hours since Mom left. I still don't think I've grasped what that means.

Three hours after I arrived home the door opens, and Brenda walks in, followed by the shell of my father. Will and I stand to hug our aunt, but Zoe has gone back to staring at dancing dust particles. After I hug Brenda, I look at my dad, and it's in that moment, as his hazel eyes meet mine, that things click. Mom's gone. She's dead. She's not coming home... ever... again.

Sitting beside my sister, I join in staring at nothing, only hearing bits of what my father, aunt, and brother are discussing. Paperwork at the hospital, arrangements at the funeral home, pre-selected plan, something about British Columbia, service type. Things I recall hearing about after all my grandparents had passed away. Normal things that need to be taken care of following the death of a person. But this isn't just a person, it's Mom.

My mom wasn't even sick.

She was fine.

She ate a toasted tomato sandwich this morning.

Two nights ago, she was laughing at Zoe's ridiculous stories and bugging me about not bringing Nellie over for dinner. I'd invited Nellie just to get her off my back. Then it hits me: she's never going to bug me about anything again. No more sly little looks that let me know she knows everything. No more evenings of her bossing me around in the kitchen. No more driving her to appointments or seeing her cuddling next to Dad on the couch. Just, no more.

I'm suddenly way too hot, still in my work stuff, bits of sawdust still clinging to me.

"I'm going to change," I say quietly, not sure if anyone hears me, truthfully not caring if they do. Upstairs I pull off my soiled clothes. The sound of something hard hits the ground, and I look down to see my phone. *Nellie*, I think. *I should call Nellie.* I keep thinking I should call her while I change into a tank and shorts. I need to let her know that we can't do dinner because my mom's dead.

My. Mom. Is. Dead.

I leave my phone on the floor and grab my running shoes, which I slip on at the top of the stairs. Mom hates—no, wait, *hated*. Fuck, it's all past tense now. Mom hated us wearing our shoes in the house, but she's gone so she won't know about me doing it now.

The first tear falls then. My rebellious action of wearing shoes in the house is what finally breaks me, and as I run down the stairs and out the front door, the tears begin to come faster. I only ever run when I need to clear my mind as if I can run away from the anxiety or sadness that's living in my brain. But by the time I'm about three kilometers away from home, I realize there is no outrunning this. I can't outrun anything so I bend and unleash all my rage, confusion, and emerging sorrow into a scream. I'm sure people come out of their homes because I've done it in the middle of a subdivision, but all I can hear is a roaring within my head. Once I've pulled myself back together, I'm off again, continuing to run away from home.

Eventually, I make my way into a wooded area that runs next to a golf course. Technically, I'm not allowed to be here, it's part of the private club, but fuck them, my mom's dead.

It's quiet in the dense trees and I feel like I can take a proper breath for the first time since Dale showed up at the work site. I walk until I reach a shallow creek and drop down next to the water, drawing my knees into my chest.

My brother's words float back to me. *"She was laughing."*

Mom's laugh was distinct and very loud. I have no problem hearing it. But for how long will it be easy to hear? I have tried to remember what my dad's father sounded like but can't. People talk about missing the physical presence of someone, but it's the forgetting her laugh that has me rolling onto my hands and knees and throwing up my breakfast and lunch.

I hate Will at that moment. I hate that he got to hear her last laugh. I hate that his memory of it will be so fresh in his mind while I sit here not knowing when I heard it last. I don't know if she was laughing at me or something I said. Or maybe Zoe and I were making fun of someone on a game show. I hadn't seen her the last two nights because I was with Nellie. I missed her last days because I was too preoccupied with Nellie.

My most recent memories are all of her, and I do my best to push them aside, but Mom's off in the distance.

She's been gone for a few hours, and she's already fading from my memory.

When I finally get home, Dad is in the kitchen, sitting alone. A full mug sitting in front of him.

"Dad?" I whisper as I walk over and sit across the table from him.

"Zoe..." I watch as he swallows, trying to finish his sentence. "Your sister is upstairs going through your mom's clothes. It would be nice if you helped her pick out something for your mom to wear."

I nearly ask where she'd be wearing the clothes. But of course, there was only one place they'd be worn, never to be removed again. I nod and stand before walking around the table to awkwardly hug him. He pats my arm and then goes back to staring at the mug full of tea.

I find my sister down the hall sitting on my parents' bed, clothes strewn around her. She's holding a black dress, the one Mom had worn to her father's funeral. Zoe looks up at me with red eyes, taking in my shirt and shorts. No doubt smelling the sweat on me.

"Have a good run?" she asks bitterly.

"As a matter of fact, it was shit," I say, dropping onto the bed beside her.

"Good."

I reach for the dress in her hands and toss it behind us. "She can't wear black, Zo."

She sniffs and leans into me. "I know that."

"What about that pink one she wore to their anniversary party last summer?" Everyone had complimented Mom when she'd shown up in it.

"It doesn't have any sleeves," Zoe says quietly.

"What does that matter?"

"It matters, Teddy... It..." I can hear her start to break, so I put my arm around her and hold her tightly against me as I stare into the closet. "I don't want her to get cold," she finally whispers. And that thought, the thought of Mom never feeling again is what cracks me wide open.

The next three days fly by in a blur of planning, arguments, and so many tears that we all seem to have accepted that puffy eyes and red raw cheeks are just part of life now. The current altitude isn't helping with my permanent headache.

We're on a plane to British Columbia because that's where Mom wanted her ashes spread. Half in the mountains and half on the coast just like her parents and grandparents. I haven't been to BC since I was ten when we came to visit Mom's parents, who had moved back shortly after Mom and Dad had gotten married. I remember loving it there and begging to go back. If I knew what would take me back, I never would have wanted to return.

"Here," Will says, holding out a travel-sized bottle of pills. "These'll help."

I take the bottle, dump a couple of pills in my hand, and throw them back dry. He says something else, but I've already turned my attention back to the clouds passing by out the window.

I've never wished to believe in something greater than

myself until now. The comfort of the belief in Heaven or something more spectacular being out there brings must be nice. Dad said Mom's wishes were to be reunited with her family, as if it would help me understand why we were making this trip. It just pissed me off more. We're her family. If she thought throwing her burned existence into the air was going to reunite her with her long-dead ancestors, why wouldn't she want to stay close to *us*?

Why the fuck doesn't she want to stay with the man she's loved since they were kids?

Why wouldn't she want to stay with Will, Zoe, and me?

What was the point of us sacrificing our childhoods to care for her if the minute she could leave she could without thinking of us?

I dream of Nellie. Of Swedish Berries and floating beside her in the pool. Her laugh echoes in my mind, bouncing off the grief and confusion that have taken up residence. I keep trying to tell her something but can't seem to get it out. I'm too distracted by her smile, and I don't want to do anything that makes it go away, so I just watch her and float.

"Teddy Graham." Zoe's jostling me and whispering my name over and over again.

"Ugh, fuck's sakes, Zoe, what?" I mumble, swinging my arms out to block her from pushing me again. Nellie's smile fades completely when I open my eyes.

"We landed like fifteen minutes ago, asshole," she hisses back, causing my eyes to snap open all the way. When I look around, I see it's just the two of us left at the back of the plane. "Everyone else already got off, let's go. Unless you want to fly back to Toronto."

I consider it for a split second but then remember that Mom's not there either. I drag myself out of the seat and pull my overfull backpack from the overhead bin. I don't even know what I packed; I opened drawers and pulled stuff out in a fog of grief. Mom was very specific about not wanting anyone in suits or stiff black anything.

"It looks like you're staying for more than three days," Zoe says as she pushes me down the aisle.

"God, why are you so pushy today?" I glare back at her and manage to dodge more physical encouragement.

"I just want to get off this damn plane," she says, pushing me once more for good measure.

The two flight attendants standing near the exit smile sadly at us as we pass, and I feel my stomach drop. They had to do a lot of gentle coaxing to get Dad to stow the ashes away during take-off. He'd insisted on holding the little gray box for the entire flight. "She's scared of flying." he'd told the attendant quietly. I don't think he was embarrassed to say it. I think he genuinely believed he'd embarrass Mom. Hard to embarrass a dead person, though. Every time I had a thought like that, I felt a new bubble of fury float to the surface.

"What the hell did you give me?" I ask Will angrily as we wait at the car rental booth.

"Something to help you sleep. It worked, didn't it?"

"Will, what was it?"

"Ambien or something like it."

I stop dead in my tracks. "What the hell, Will? I took two."

"Right, so definitely not Ambien." He shrugs. "Relax, they're leftover pills a friend had after flying back from Europe. She got them in Latvia—no, wait." He looks skyward as he thinks. "Maybe it was Lithuania. Definitely not Luxembourg, I'd remember the x in there. It was some L country in Europe. Anyway, she told me they'd help me sleep."

"And you didn't think to find out what it was?"

"Teddy, if there is anyone who needs to just throw a couple of pills back and not ask questions, it's you." He pats me on the back and follows our father and Zoe as they head towards where our car is.

An hour later I'm standing in between my siblings listening to my uncle tell a story about Mom falling out of a moving car after their father took a corner too sharply. Apparently my uncle didn't say anything right away because he was in shock. It's the first time I feel inclined to laugh in days, the visual too funny to ignore. Within minutes we're all trying to catch our breath and wiping tears of laughter from our eyes. It's what my dad says next that has every ounce of joy leaving my body.

"When the doctor gave her five more years..."

I miss what he says next because I keep repeating *five more years* to myself.

"We knew it was coming..."

Knew what was coming? What the fuck is he talking about?

I look at the rest of my family as they nod along, not one of them looks surprised by what Dad just said.

"I'm sorry," I interrupt. "What are you talking about? What did we know was coming?"

"The aneurysm they couldn't get to after her first aneurysm ruptured," my aunt says like she's reminding me of a fact I have just forgotten.

"He didn't know," Zoe says quietly, avoiding looking at me. "Mom didn't want us to tell him. I only knew because I overheard Dad telling Will, and then he swore us to secrecy."

For the first time in my life, I get the saying "seeing red." It looks like the world around me has a red filter on it. They knew. They all knew. Everyone except me was in on this monumental secret.

The same thing happens. All the noises above me grow louder. Birds, insects, voices rise like a tidal wave before crashing into silence. They all knew.

I whirl around to face them. "So, what, you've all been preparing for this for what? Ten fucking years?" I'm angry and embarrassed and completely confused as to why my family, why my mother, didn't want me of all people not to know. Is this why they always seemed more paranoid than me? My memories race through every cold, cough, and fever.

"She didn't want you or Zoe to know," Dad says, almost pleadingly.

He reaches for me but I step back, the last thing I want is to be touched right now. "But you ended up telling her." I jab a finger in Zoe's direction. "Why didn't you just tell me too?" I look over at my twin trying not to let the feeling of betrayal show too much on my face. Judging by her expression, I fail.

"You were always so hopeful that she'd end up getting better in the beginning. And then you were the only one who didn't act like there was a deadline."

I think of how much time over the last couple of months I could have been spending with Mom, but I was off with Nellie or playing baseball or working. Zoe and Will never switched around their schedules to avoid time with her while I'd been doing it since school ended. They didn't do it because they knew time was running out, and instead of letting me know, they let me carry on, wasting the most precious time in the world.

There's that question people ask: if you knew you were going to die soon, would you want to know, or would you rather be surprised? I can't answer that for myself, but I sure as hell can for the person I love—loved—most in the world. Hell yes, I'd want to know. I should have known.

Run, a voice in the back of my mind I don't recognize whispers.

"Give me the key," I say emotionlessly to my dad. He looks from my hand back to my face like he doesn't know what to do. "I need to be alone."

He nods and fishes the key out of his pocket. I look at the box he's holding in his other hand one more time, then turn and walk back down the trail.

At the car, I pull my phone out of the front pocket of my backpack. There are several unread texts from Nellie, and I open them now.

I focus on the last one she sent this morning.

LIBRARY GIRL

I thought you were one of the good guys.

I always did too, but grief mixed with anger does things to a person. Right now I hate her name on my phone. I hate that I spent so many of my mom's final hours with her, and I despise my family for making me resent every fucking smile she flashed my way.

Guess not.

I turn off the phone, shove it back into my backpack, lock the door, slide the key into the wheel well, turn, and walk towards the road. I have no idea where I'm going, but I can't stay here and I certainly won't be going home.

SEVENTEEN

NELLIE

I stare at my phone for what feels like an eternity. I don't understand what's going on. His brother must be messing with us. Teddy would never go three days without a word and then answer me like this. The guy who showed up uninvited at my house to take care of me while I was sick wouldn't do this.

Unless... An intrusive thought slithers in. *Unless you were too clingy.* Maybe he woke up the next morning and decided it was all too much too fast. Or it was all too much and not enough because we weren't having sex. But he was the one who was abiding by my "let's go slow" request better than I was. He was the one who stopped anything from getting too hot and heavy.

I tell my coworker I'll be right back and head outside. I need air. Maybe by the time I get out there, he'll have texted me an apology. He'll let me know that Will stole his phone. He'll apologize for ghosting me for the last three days, and then he'll tell me he's planned a picnic or a movie night.

But when I get outside, there is no new message. No apology or clarification. Just those two words jumping off my screen. *Guess not.*

For the next week I mope around work and home, obsessively checking my phone, talking myself in and out of reaching out to his sister or dropping by his place before my mom asks what's wrong. When I tell her, she doesn't seem to want to believe me. "That boy had it bad," she insists. "There's no way he'd just disappear."

I thought maybe he had it as bad as I did, but the proof is in the text. It's in the lack of any new texts. It's in the absolute absence of my social life or my desire to get out of bed. The proof is in what I can only describe as a broken heart.

Four Years Later

Marley is home from an extended assignment regaling us with tales of lust in the most recent conflict zone she was sent to.

"He was hung like a jack rabbit," Marley whispers, demonstrating with her fingers.

Izzy asks the question I'm thinking. "How do you know how hung or not hung a jack rabbit is?"

"I have absolutely no idea." Marley laughs. "But he sure moved like one." She gives us a look, and we both crack up. "The way he kissed should have given him away, but I'd been shot at like six times that day and needed something to take the edge off."

"And did it?" I ask.

"It did not," she confirms solemnly. "He seemed to have a

good time though, so I'll consider that my good deed for the month."

"How was that date last night, Nell?" Izzy asks, switching her attention to me.

A nice guy, Kenneth Smith, had taken me out to a movie and a nice dinner and proceeded to bore me to tears. But he did kiss well, so I'd said yes to another date. "There's potential there."

"Is that what you want there to be?" Izzy prods.

"Maybe she just wants to get her rocks off and not chase potential, Iz," Marley scoffs.

"No." Izzy points at her. "*You* only care about 'getting your rocks off.' Nellie here is a 'meant to be' type."

I used to be, I think.

Seven Years Later

"You look stunning babe," Mark says, pulling me close and kissing my neck.

"You don't look half bad yourself." I pull back and give him an approving once-over. "Definitely the only groomsman I want to go home with."

"He's totally going to propose after his brother's wedding." Izzy had said when I walked out of the dressing room in the dress I was currently wearing. "He may do it during the ceremony. I would."

Being married to Mark wouldn't be so bad. My parents seem to like him. He is nice-ish, and I feel good with him. It isn't an all-consuming feeling, not like I kept expecting to feel, but it's more than nothing. I'm sure the big 'I would die for this man' feelings are just around the corner.

. . .

Seven Years and Three Months Later

"What do you mean you said no?" Izzy squawks from where she sits beside me on the couch.

"He asked me to marry him and I said no," I explain again. "I didn't even want to move in with him. Does that scream 'this is the one' to you?"

"Meant-to-be person, remember?" Marley whispers. She's currently in some half-destroyed hotel in god knows where and doesn't seem at all bothered by the large booms coming from somewhere in the distance.

"But you two seemed so good together. Shit, I owe Tom a..." She stops abruptly, her cheeks pinking slightly. "I lost a bet."

"Blowjob, Izzy. It's okay, you can say it. This is a safe space." Marley laughs as another boom sounds from somewhere closer.

Mark had asked in a restaurant, and I'd sat there staring at the large diamond ring he held out to me. And I felt absolutely nothing.

"At least you don't have to move or anything," Marley says with a shrug. "Small mercies."

"Has it ever felt right with any of the men you've dated? Maybe the timing was wrong?"

One guy, I think, and the timing was terrible apparently. "No," I say slowly.

"Liar," Marley huffs and then covers her mouth while I glare at her.

The interaction doesn't go unnoticed by Izzy's mother-of-two gaze. "What? What does that mean?" She turns to me. "What don't I know?"

"It was a summer fling."

"With whom?"

"Just a guy. It doesn't matter. He took off, and I haven't seen him since." That's all I ever told Marley. Teddy has always been "just a guy" to those who didn't know me back then.

Izzy sits back and crosses her arms. "So is this fling the reason you said no?"

"It was a fling when I was too young to get it. Things were great until he peaced out. I'd say that is a clear indication that he wasn't the one."

"If you expect it, it'll never happen," Marley says.

"So you're open to the unexpected, are you?" Izzy asks.

"I thrive on the unexpected, Iz. It really gets me going." She winks at us, and we laugh.

My two best friends could not be more different in how they approach relationships. Izzy was married by the end of her first year of university and still managed to finish and go on to get her master's and PhD. Marley has no interest in spending more than one night with the same guy. Then there's me, refusing to acknowledge that when it comes to my heart, no one has ever measured up to Teddy. It's exceptionally annoying since he was only around for two months. There is no logical reason he should still have my heart under lock and key.

Twelve Years Later, December

I could barely sleep last night. The thought of getting Marley back to Bennett was too exciting. I felt like I was about to give someone the best gift, like a puppy or new car. But instead of either of those things, I was taking my anti-relationship best friend to the man who'd rescued her in the middle of the woods when she'd sprained her ankle. I would have put money on this happening eventually; when Izzy and I picked Marley up in October, her body came willingly but mentally she seemed elsewhere. It only took nearly dying in Syria for her to realize what, or rather who, she wanted.

I watch Marley fidget next to me. Her fingers tapping nervously on her thighs as she peeks over her shoulder at Pip, her Syrian rescue pup. The fact she brought a dog home with her was all Izzy and I needed to confirm how she had really felt about leaving Bennett's.

Three cars sit in Bennett's driveway, and I see Marley tense. He'd always been alone so I can practically see the scenarios that are playing out in her mind: *there's another woman here; he's moved on.*

"You good?" I ask as I put the car into park.

"Yeah, it's just real now. Just... give me a minute."

We sit there for a few moments, and I watch her hype herself up out of the corner of my eye.

"Okay," she breathes out, slowly wrapping her scarf around her neck and slipping her gloves on. "Wish me luck."

"You don't need it, but for your sake, I'll say it. Good luck, Marley." She offers a tight smile in response and peeks once more back at Pip before sliding out of the car to follow the single set of footprints that lead to the barn.

A little while later I see her exit the barn and head towards the forest. Bennett must be out with the dogs on a pack walk. It seems fitting that's what he was doing when he found her and now she's off to find him.

"What do you think, Pips McGee?" I say, looking back to the tan and black puppy sitting with his little nose pressed to the window. "Should we go into the nice warm barn to wait for the two lovebirds?"

I'm greeted just inside the door by a woman with wild red hair, or rather Pip is greeted by her; I'm just an afterthought. I get it, though; Pip is adorable.

"Well, aren't you the sweetest creature on the planet," the woman coos at the squirmy pup.

"This is Pip. He's—ugh, the woman who was just in here, Marley, he's her dog," I stammer as I'm divested of Pip.

"Hi Pip! I'm Cass," she enthusiastically introduces herself, dropping to the ground to play with him. "If you're waiting for Marley, I don't think you'll be needed." She smiles up at me. "Bennett has been counting down to today, even if he won't admit it."

"Yeah, I had a feeling that would be the case. I tried to tell her, but I think she's still struggling with the fact that someone may care about her the same way she cares about them."

A door closes nearby, and as I turn toward the sound I hear a sharp intake of breath. Pale blue eyes greet me, and I feel all the air sucked from my body.

"Nellie?"

Holy shit.

Teddy.

He's different then he was the last time I saw him. His wavy dark hair is longer, and his beard is thicker than any of the scruff I'd ever seen in our early twenties. Twenty-two-year-old Teddy had been long and lean, but thirty-four-year-old Teddy fills out a shirt the way the old version never could.

It's those damn eyes, though. The pale blue flash of recognition as my name leaves his lips, the way he looks like he's seeing a ghost, and then how that look quickly turns to nervous joy. I briefly glance down to see that Cass has disappeared with Pip before looking back up at him.

"Teddy?" I barely get it out, as if saying it will cause him to disappear again.

He nods absently, and I feel the shock and attraction start to give way to the pain I'd felt for so long after he'd sent that last message.

A slow smile starts to form on his face, his hand going to rub the back of his neck. "Hey, Nellie."

How fucking dare he flash that crooked grin at me? How dare my eyes go straight to those teeth that fascinated me so long ago? How dare he be here at all?

It takes me a few tries before the words actually leave my mouth. "What are you doing here?"

"I work here," he says, as if it's the most obvious thing in the world.

"How— Of all the places you could work— How the hell are you here right now?" I'm barely keeping it together. Part of me wants to sink into the floor while another part wants to run back to my car, go home and forget any of this happened.

"Can we talk?" he asks, taking a tiny step toward me.

"*Now* you want to talk?" I spit, stepping back to keep the distance between us in place.

"I think I owe you an explanation."

"You owed me one twelve years ago." I look toward the door, planning my escape.

"I know." He looks down at his boots. "I let a lot of people down back then, you more than anyone else."

I should tell him to scream the explanation into the ground for all I care; I don't want what he thinks he owes me now. But for a split second, despite the added muscle and hair, I catch a glimpse of the Teddy who stole my heart with his goodness.

If you leave, you'll just keep wondering, I tell myself. *Get the reason and put this all behind you.*

"Fine," I say like a petulant child.

"We can talk in the office." He motions with his head toward a set of stairs and leads the way.

The office is less a workspace and more of a storage room with a laptop.

"You can have a seat if you want." he offers, moving a box off the desk chair.

"No thank you," I reply, crossing my arms and letting my

eyes wander around the room, looking everywhere but at him. "Well?" I order impatiently when he doesn't start explaining immediately. "I'm here. Explain."

"My mom died."

My eyes stop wandering and snap to him. Of all the things I thought he'd say, that hadn't ever crossed my mind.

"What?" My feet automatically take a step closer.

"That's the reason I disappeared. She died, then I found out something that hurt me, and I took off."

"Wait, back up," I stammer, trying to put what he just said together. "When did she die?"

"The morning after I left your place. I was at work and my boss showed up and, well, she was dead. That's why he showed up. He took me home, and then the rest is kind of a blur." He's so calm that I have to remind myself that he's been sitting with this for twelve years. To me it just happened.

"Why didn't you tell me? Teddy, I could have been there for you." It's weird to suddenly feel the need to apologize to the person who's apologizing to me.

"I know. I know you would have been there in a heartbeat, but I wasn't in a good place, Nellie. It wasn't until a couple of months later that I was able to think again. And by then, I convinced myself that I'd messed up too badly."

"Your mom died. Who would be in a good place?" I'm not sure anyone has ever thawed so quickly. All I want to do is cross the small distance between us and hug him, the way I would have if I'd known all those years ago.

"I still should have told you, let you in." He sounds so broken that before I even know what I'm doing, my arms are around him. He doesn't move, his arms limply at his sides, and I'm pretty sure he hasn't taken a breath since he told me.

"Oh, for the love of god, would you hug me back, please?" I

mutter into his flannel. When his arms fold around me, I can feel layers of what was left of the ice melt away.

This, a little voice hums.

We stand there holding each other for enough time that our breathing seems to sync. It's suddenly like no time has passed. As if it was just yesterday we kissed goodbye and then we texted until we fell asleep. I let myself live in the fantasy for a few more minutes before I pull away. He lets me go, but when I look into his eyes, I can see him at war with himself. Heat, pain, and sorrow battling for his attention.

"I'm sorry," I say, looking down at my hands because I can't handle looking into those eyes any longer.

"You have no reason to be sorry." He shakes his head, looking pained.

"Hey, Marley's friend?" I hear Cass yell from somewhere below us.

"Marley's friend," Teddy says quietly, shaking his head like he can't believe it. I get it. I can't believe it either.

"I should..." I point toward the door.

"Yeah." He nods and lets me lead the way back down to the main floor where Cass is waiting with Pip in her arms, her gaze shifting between me to Teddy, a little smirk on her lips.

"Just wondering if this guy can have some play time in the snow?"

"Oh, yeah, I'm sure he'd love that," I assure her. "His outdoor time got cut short this morning."

I can feel Teddy behind me as we head outside, Pip bounding around with excitement as if he knows what awaits him beyond the door.

When Bennett and Marley get back, I am still distracted by the fact Teddy is here and that there's a part of me that wants to keep him here. I can't stop looking over at him, each time catching his gaze already on me. Each glance adds another match to the spark of interest. It's as if we've slipped back into our early twenties, when all that mattered was when we got to touch one another again.

After Marley confirms that she is in fact not returning with me, Teddy offers to walk me to my car. We're quiet on the walk out, the snow beneath his feet the only evidence that I'm not alone. The air crackles around us when we stop in front of my door. I have every intention of thanking him for telling me the truth, and for walking me out, but when I look up at him nothing comes out. We just stand there staring. Then movement, so fast I don't know which one of us leans in first. All I know is that as our lips collide the only thing on my mind is *this, him, us.*

It's not until I've been sitting in my driveway at home for a while that I realize I'm crying. After I get into the house, I walk straight to my bedroom, flop down on the bed, and let the tears flow freely. I cry for Teddy's mom and for him losing her so young. I cry because I feel guilty for hating him for so long. I cry because of what he took from me without realizing it. I cry because the day my best friend put her heart back together, mine feels like it's being split into pieces all over again.

NOW

EIGHTEEN

NELLIE

MAY

For the past five months, Marley has sent me nearly daily updates on how the puppies they had rescued just before Christmas are doing. When she's away for work, she tasks Bennett with updating me. I know he's only doing it half the time because his messages are just quick updates with medi-ocre images. I know it's Cass doing it the other times because those images all have Teddy in them, and I can guarantee he isn't aware of most of the pictures she's taking. I hate how my body heats ever so slightly when he's a bit more in focus. I cannot stand how my eyes only briefly land on the dogs before finding him and staying put for way too long.

The picture I'm currently looking at is of Teddy holding out a large stick in the center of several jumping dogs. He's wearing a light blue Henley, dark jeans, and a baseball cap. If someone asked me how many dogs were in the picture or what color they were, I'd be at a loss. But I could tell them that Teddy's lips are pulled to the right ever so slightly and he hasn't shaved in a few days. I could tell them that the top two buttons of his shirt are undone and that there is a stain on his jeans, just above his right knee. I won't tell anyone, though; no one else needs to know how or what I feel. Especially since I can't quite figure it out for myself, and there's no point in trying to unravel over a decade of feelings now.

I get ready for bed and curl up with the latest in Maira Sahni's The Forest of Despair series. What started as a trilogy quickly bloomed into a never-ending saga that has grown with me. Unfortunately, the main character, Amira, has faced a similar fate when it comes to her love life. Well, maybe "unfortunately" isn't the right word. It's kind of nice having someone to sympathize with when someone you loved just fucks off, even if they are fictional.

After trying and failing to read more than two pages, I slap the book down on my bedside table and throw myself into the ridiculous amount of pillows I keep on my bed. My mind wanders back to our reunion, not in the car but in the office. He had told me that he had learned something that set him off, but we never got to it. I try to convince myself that I don't care, but I know that's a lie. My mind drags me back to all the encounters we've had since that first one.

At Christmas, the memory of him in the car was still present on my body. Every place his fingers had grazed, every caress of his lips, every exhale that touched my skin still burned. When he walked into Bennett's kitchen, brushing snow out of his hair, the pull was strong. I'd been reminded of what I had been missing only days before, and I'd quit that feeling cold turkey. I allowed my gaze to linger longer than I should have. His pale blue eyes had met mine across the room, and we'd been locked like that while people introduced themselves to each other. I tracked every movement he made as he removed his jacket and boots. Tried not to focus on the way his sweater stretched across his shoulders or how I knew what those locks of hair felt like slipping through my fingers.

For the rest of the night, I tried to stay away. Tried not to look at him and then let my eyes linger. Forced myself to leave the room when he'd walk into it. Ignored his hopeful smiles or suggestions of puppy snuggles, which was a whole other kind of torture. Nothing about being near him and yet not being with him felt natural, and still I'd forced myself to keep the shields in place. *Stay strong*, I'd repeated to myself.

Then, on St. Patrick's Day, I could tell he had wanted to talk, I felt those blue eyes on me more often than not, but I avoided him the entire time. Or rather I avoided talking to him. I know he caught me looking almost as much as I caught him.

Tomorrow will be the first time I've seen him since March. Bennett is throwing a party for Marley's birthday and her return home from another trip abroad, and Izzy, her husband Tom, and I are driving up to help prepare while they're driving back from the airport. I don't know what's going on with me. Teddy showed up and made me remember that feeling of euphoria just by the presence of the other person. I don't know if I haven't felt it again because I'm too afraid to let my heart go all in again, or if it just was Teddy.

As I lay in bed with visions of Teddy dancing in my head, I can't help wondering if staying strong is akin to being cruel to myself. Protecting myself seems logical but I'm not sure how right it feels. What's more, I'm not sure I can keep it up. I don't know if I can ever fully forgive Teddy and I certainly don't know if I can trust him again. The wounds he left were deep, and trusting my heart with anyone has become nearly impossible. But trusting myself around Teddy may be the most difficult task yet.

NINETEEN

TEDDY

"Are you excited to see Nellie?" Cass asks, coming into the food room with a bag of alfalfa chunks for Lloyd, our rapidly growing calf. The grassy odor immediately replaces the smell of dog food that lingers in the air.

"Are *you* excited to see Nellie?" I respond, without looking up from the new feeding requirements the vet left after her visit.

"I'm not the one who made out with her the first time she was here and then somehow watched her obsessively while also ignoring her at Christmas and then again at the St. Patrick's Day party," she says, sitting on top of the chest freezer.

I could deny it, but apparently Karl announced the make-out session to everyone after he and Nancy walked by Nellie's car. "Blips."

"She's the one, isn't she?"

"The one what?" I finally look up and regret it immediately.

"Who was perfect, but you fucked up." She grins down at me the same way she does every time she knows she's right about something. I'd told her and Bennett about Nellie in a roundabout way, well before I ever saw her again. Of course Cass would remember the conversation.

"And if she was?" I go back to studying the sheet.

"Well, for starters, you can fix it."

"It's not that simple."

"Sure it is. You just have to try. It's the starting-to-try part that isn't simple. Get over yourself and try."

"And if I already tried?"

"When, four months ago?" she scoffs. "Teddy, you made out with her, let her leave, then twice since then you've spent hours in the same room and didn't talk once. That's hardly trying. Why do all the men in my life need me to spell it out? You're worse than Foster."

Foster is Cass's brother. I don't know much about the guy, but she rolls her eyes a lot when she brings him up. I'm not sure I want to be in the same class with him. "How do you know we didn't talk once? Were you watching us the whole time? And what was I supposed to do? Tie her down and tell her all my deep dark secrets? She told me she wasn't doing this again."

"We all talk about you two. There's even a group chat. But two apparent strangers who make out randomly in the middle of the day—sort of in public, I might add—probably have some things to discuss."

"What? No. That was, I don't know, leftover sexual frustration."

Cass looks at me with wide eyes. "Sure. I get it—you're hot, she's hot, you're just drawn to one another. Hell, I'd make out with both of you if I was into that sort of thing."

I just blink up at her trying to follow her line of thinking. "I'm sorry, like a threesome?"

"God no. If I was into making out, I could imagine either of you would do, due to your level of attractiveness."

More blinking by me, slower this time.

"I'm not into physical relationships, but you two seem to be, so I say just, like, bang it out and see what happens."

"Did you miss the part where I said she wasn't interested? Also, I'm not sure this is an appropriate conversation for the workplace," I stammer, trying to refocus on my work.

"Oh, it's not. That's why it's fun." She jumps down and heads out of the room. "Teddy?"

"Yeah?" I look up to where she's leaning around the door.

"If she's the one, there's only one thing to do. Start small, but *start*. If progress takes ten years, it takes ten years, but at least you're progressing." She shrugs like she hasn't just given me a pretty stellar piece of advice, and walks out of view, whistling.

I never did tell Nellie what made me run away. I was so surprised she let me get out what I did, I didn't want to push my luck.

When Nellie walked in, I knew who she was immediately, and it took everything I had not to drag her to me. Those dark blue eyes didn't miss a thing, widening ever so slightly when they landed on me. I hadn't expected her to hug me when I was telling her about my mom, and I certainly didn't expect to be pushed into her car and have her climb on top of me when I'd walked her outside. I knew it was a bad idea, but I shushed that little voice the minute it started to protest. Nellie was grinding into me, moaning into my mouth. My Nellie, the girl who had captivated me by merely existing, was back. It wasn't until she slid off me and said that would never happen again that I realized I wasn't lost in some dream. The Nellie in my dreams never stopped; I just always woke up.

I'm lost in thought, running through possible scenarios for tomorrow when Bennett's head pops into the room. "I'm about to head out. You need anything before I leave?"

He knows by now that Cass and I have everything in hand, but I'm convinced he still has a hard time admitting that. "Nah, we're good," I say, looking back down at the list in front of me. I can still feel his eyes on me though and raise my head to see a look of concern on his face. "What's up?"

"You going to be okay tomorrow?"

"I assume so, are you?"

"Marley is going to be home. I'll be more than okay." The smile that spreads across his face could power a small city.

"So we'll both be good." I smile back, hoping that will be the end of the conversation.

"It's just that at Christmas you and Nellie seemed a bit"—I can see his brain working on how to say awkward as fuck in a more diplomatic way—"less warm than we had all expected seeing how things had gone the first time. Then in March…" he trails off.

In March, Bennett and Marley had hosted a St. Patrick's Day party. It turns out that Bennett loves a gathering, and his neighbors, Nancy and Karl, have both implied that having Marley around has just made his desire to host that much stronger. Nellie had arrived with Izzy and Tom, and I'd been so distracted by the tight green sweater she was wearing that I'd fallen up the porch steps.

She'd stifled a smile, and I remember thinking that I'd fall up every single flight of stairs if it got her to look at me with anything other than disinterest. She spun away from me before I'd even reached the door, her dark auburn hair flying out dramatically as she moved further into the house.

Cass had found a fiddle somewhere, and after a few pints, I gave into playing it. I hadn't played the violin in years, not since before Mom died, and yet between the booze and company, my fingers seemed to know what to do. Nellie's eyes had been glued to me as I played. I'd never played for her before, only told her that I had, and this felt like I was letting her in a bit more. Revealing more of myself. Into the second playing of the only song I remembered, I'd fumbled when she'd stood abruptly and left the room. Marley was the only one who had noticed, and when I'd looked over at her, she'd tipped her head as if to ask, "What the hell was that?"

Marley and Bennett tell each other everything, and so it's no surprise he's bringing March up. It's on days like this that I miss the solitude of working in the middle of the forest, alone. Or mostly alone. My thoughts haven't given me much peace over the last decade. I set my clipboard down and turn to fully face Bennett. "Nellie and I have a history. A history that I tainted. If you want to know how, you'll have to ask her. If she tells you, that's fine, but you're not going to hear it from me."

He watches me for a few seconds before nodding. "Okay. I'll see you tomorrow evening."

I don't feel my shoulders relax until I hear the door shut, but my thumb's got my ring spinning at hyper speed. I know they all want to know the story; they're all a bunch of tea grannies when they get wind of drama. Usually, it's about someone in the farming or rescue community, though. I hate that I'm at the center of it now.

I'd been holding my breath since Bennett told us what the plan was for tomorrow night. I'd seen Nellie twice since the car, and both times were sweet torture. She was there, but she was untouchable. If her gaze landed on me, it was with a question she never vocalized. I'd do anything she'd ask of me, even leave; if that's what Nellie wanted, that's what I'd do. But she never said a thing, and so both times we danced awkwardly around one another, trying to not give anything away while clearly being very obvious that there was something else going on.

As it stands, neither of us is going anywhere, so I have to

either accept this uncomfortable existence, or I have to take another step towards fixing what I'd broken in the first place. Tomorrow seems like a good opportunity to start, even if it is the tiniest step forward. As Cass had so eloquently put it, progress is progress.

"It's a girl," Zoe squeals, and I have to pull the phone away from my ear. I'm sure the dogs below me just perked up. "We didn't even make it to the car before checking the envelope."

"That's amazing, Zo. Congratulations! What did Dad say?" I ask, leaning back against my headboard and trying not to yawn. Zoe had told me that if they were having a girl, they'd name her after Mom.

"He cried. At first I thought he was upset but then he smiled."

"That's awesome. I'm glad he reacted well." In the years since we lost Mom, Dad has been hot and cold about some things. One minute he'd want to reminisce about her, and then the next he'd shut us down if she came up. We've all encouraged him to get back out there so he wouldn't be alone, but he maintains that she was it for him and he doesn't want to make anyone feel like they'd never live up to her. It's a feeling I relate to more than I'd like to admit.

I soak up every second I speak to my family. It took me so long to reestablish any kind of relationship with them, but once I got my head on straight I started by calling Zoe, then Will, and finally our father. Repairing our relationships hasn't been the easiest thing, but I'm glad we have gotten as far as we have.

When I hang up, I wonder how things are going to work with Nellie. I'm the only one at fault in our relationship, or whatever you'd call us now. She owes me absolutely nothing, while I owe her years of apologies. I had dreamt of seeing her again but never knew how she'd react if she saw me. Would she even care? Had we meant anything to her, like we had meant to me? That first day back in December sure made it seem like I had meant something, but since then... Well, she's made it clear that nothing more was going to happen, and she's made that easy by keeping her distance every chance she got.

I don't know what is worse anymore, having her back but not being with her or not seeing her at all.

TWENTY

NELLIE

"It's not that I want them to die," I say, peeking through the window that faces my backyard. "I just don't want them to be there anymore. A retirement home, or just a different house that's not next to me, or... spontaneous combustion."

"To be fair," Izzy says, coming up beside me, "spontaneous combustion would most definitely result in death."

I shrug as I catch sight of Mrs. Dipietro squinting into my backyard from her deck. "Okay, maybe death is the best option. There's no coming back from it," I huff, sitting back down on my stool at the island and immediately feeling guilty.

"Why do you let them control when you can and can't be in your own yard?" Izzy asks, still staring out the window.

"Because I'm afraid that one day one of them is going to say something so unforgivable, I'm going to end up saying something that will shock them so thoroughly they'll drop dead."

"Problem solved!" Izzy claps.

"I don't want to kill them, Iz," I gasp. "When they die, I want it to be of natural causes, preferably peacefully in their sleep. And not until it's their time."

"Well, excuse me for taking this conversation to a dark place."

"Okay," Tom says, sighing heavily as he walks into the kitchen. "The faucet is no longer dripping every three seconds. It was a pretty simple fix. You probably could have done it yourself."

"She's aware, honey. But she also knows that she didn't want to do it, and if it happens again, she won't want to do it then either."

I point over at Izzy. "That's exactly it. Besides, I had to finish the salad."

"Is it the one with grapes and asiago?" Tom asks, walking over to the counter where a saran-wrapped bowl sits.

"It is," I reply slyly.

"Okay, we're even."

"Also, when I get a dog, you get to come play with it whenever you want. Unless I'm entertaining, then you have to wait."

"You're not getting a dog," Izzy says, as she starts packing up stuff to go to Bennett and Marley's. "You don't have time."

"Well, that's because I pick up extra work, due to the fact I don't have a life. If I had a dog, it would give me some more"—I pretend to think—"damn, what's that thing called when you work but also do stuff you want to do for fun? There are scales and shit..."

"Work-life balance?" Tom tosses out.

I snap my fingers and nod. "Yes, work-life balance. I think a dog would help with that."

Izzy's eyes narrow at her husband. "Don't for one second think that's an excuse for us to get a dog. You balance plenty with work."

"Babe, golf is work."

"Oh?" Izzy looks taken aback. "Is that why you practically

skip out the door for tee time while you grumble the whole way out the door when you're going to the hospital?"

"Balance." He grins at her.

"It's going to be a long fucking drive." She grabs the bag of party decorations and heads for the door. "May as well get it started now."

Despite Izzy's mood as we walked out the front door, she laughs with Tom and me for most of the drive. She's always been the most buttoned-up out of the three of us. Marley is the adventurer with the mouth of a sailor. Izzy is the adult, married with kids, and I'm the nerdy serial dater, unable to find the right guy. On paper we don't work, but in practice there are no two other people I'd rather call my best friends.

"Are you and Teddy going to be weird again?" Izzy asks from the front seat as we pull onto the gravel road to Bennett's.

"We aren't weird."

"You're weird," Tom and Izzy say in unison.

"There's this strange energy with you two," Izzy says, turning to look at me, her eyes narrowing as she studies me. "I've never seen two strangers act like scorned lovers who wanted to be loving lovers before."

I sit up straighter and run my suddenly sweaty palms down my thighs. I haven't told anyone a thing. Izzy doesn't even know about how Teddy and I got hot and heavy in my car when I brought Marley back last winter. Yet she's looking at me as if she's been told about it.

Shrugging, I look her straight in the eye with as much confidence as I can muster. "I don't know what to tell you, Iz. How should we act? Like old friends? Like current lovers?"

"You could talk?" Tom suggests from the driver's seat, his eyes finding mine briefly in the rearview mirror.

"That is a good and normal start," Izzy agrees. "Act less like he's oil and you're vinegar."

"I can act as mustard for you if you want," Tom says.

My traitorous imagination immediately flashes an oiled-up Teddy, which is appealing until Tom appears wearing a French's yellow mustard costume and an inappropriate grin. "That sounds like a euphemism for threesome." I cringe.

"She's right, it sounds like a line they'd use in a porn about an orgy in a restaurant," Izzy adds, turning back to face the front. "You know they'd use lots of oil too."

"As a doctor, I'd have to advise against using mustard," Tom says thoughtfully. "Especially Dijon."

I sit back and listen to them as they continue discussing what edible things could be used in place of mustard as an emulsifier in a porn setting. Their voices fade the minute Bennett's place comes into view, and I see a tall dark-haired figure walking towards the house, five dogs zigzagging around his legs.

If how I felt was visual, it would be TV static. Black and white dots vibrating below the surface of my skin, warming and cooling me at the same time.

Teddy stops just before he reaches the porch and turns to watch Tom park, then waves when we are all out of the car. I realize my hand is in the air, returning it before I know what I'm doing. A smile, albeit a small one, appears on Teddy's face, and when I look away, I find myself greeted by Izzy mouthing, "Good start." Doing my best to keep my face neutral, I start gathering stuff to bring inside, only then to discover that Izzy has dragged Tom behind the car to have what appears to be an intense private conversation. I glance back toward the house where Teddy is standing, hands in his jean pockets, head tilted ever so slightly to the left, eyes on me. His hair is shorter, as is his beard, and I can't help but wonder if he's tidied up his rugged appearance for me.

As much as I wish, or partly wish, that I could avoid him

forever, he lives in the apartment in the barn now, and from the way Marley talks, Teddy and Bennett are the best of friends. I need to just suck it up and be an adult. Sure, Teddy and I had tried the friend thing once, and it bloomed like a rose bush on speed to something more, but I'd been there, done that, and could probably stay the course now. Then he has to go and pick up a dog who I now realize is one of the Christmas puppies, and I'm suddenly filled with an incredible sense of want.

I straighten as much as possible, plaster a cordial expression on my face, and walk toward Teddy with as much confidence as I can muster. The feeling only lasts for a few seconds however as my toe catches the edge of the flagstone path, and my confidence plummets only slightly faster than me and the porcelain bowl that has slipped out of my hands. I do manage to think *Nightmare, this is a nightmare* just before my body makes contact with the ground.

I look up just in time to see Teddy step on what I think is an escaped grape and watch helplessly as his arms windmill in a desperate attempt to grab air to stay upright. He fails, of course, on account of air being, well, air.

"Oh no," I hear Tom say as he approaches. "The salad."

Izzy, on the other hand, is holding onto the hood of the car as she laughs hysterically. "I'm going to piss my pants," she manages to get out. I know she means it too; I've witnessed a few very close calls with her.

"Are you okay?" Teddy asks in the middle of jumping up like he didn't just perform the most perfect comedic fall I've ever seen. He holds out his hand, but I'm more concerned about the dogs making their way over to investigate.

"I'm fine, but can you keep them away from the food?" Pointing at the dogs. Teddy looks back towards the dogs as they reach us. "There are grapes," I shriek, scrambling to cover what little poison bombs I can reach.

"I'm on it." Tom jumps into action, grabbing a couple of the smaller dogs and jogging towards the fenced-in field.

"Be right back." Teddy gives a sharp whistle and the others immediately follow him.

"That was one way to make an entrance," Izzy says from above me.

"Do you think anyone noticed?" I laugh, shifting onto my butt.

"Nah, I think it was subtle enough to fly under the radar," she says as another fit of giggles racks her body.

"He hasn't looked at Tom or me since we arrived, by the way. That clumsy man only has eyes for your clumsy ass. So when he offers you his hand again, you better suck it up and take it," she hisses as the guys get back sans dogs.

While Tom bends to help Izzy with the rest of the mess, Teddy once again holds out his hand, and this time I take it, although I do so reluctantly. His hands, once soft, are now rough with permanent calluses. Something I'd briefly noted as they glided across my skin a few months ago. Shivers spread through my body at the memory, and the minute I'm standing, I drop his hand.

An involuntary hiss leaves me as I take the first step. Teddy looks down at my jean-clad knee. "Sure you're okay?"

"It's just bruised." I shrug as we make our way to the house. I bruise like a rotten peach if there's a stiff breeze. I'm sure my knee is going to look like an eyeshadow palette exploded on it within the hour.

"I guess now we're even," he says when he opens the door and gestures for me to go first.

"How?" I ask, slipping my shoes off in the entry and heading straight to the sink to wash my hands.

"That day in the woods when I slipped and fell." He holds

a towel out for me to dry my hands. "That remains the most mortifying moment of my life, but less so today."

That day in the woods, out for an innocent hike that led to a first kiss that still lives in my head rent-free. Who has their first kiss in front of a waterfall, serenaded by birds and witnessed by no one else? Come the fuck on.

"Did you hit your head and forget the part where you also fell today?"

He shrugs and offers me a grin that shouldn't make my knees as wobbly as they suddenly feel. "I can claim I was falling to make you feel better." He used to make me feel better just by being there. Everything used to feel pretty great when Teddy was there. I miss him being there.

I was going to wait and figure out how to bring up the vibes we are giving off, but the words leave my mouth before I even think. "I want to be friends," I blurt out.

"What?" Teddy asks, towel held out between us as I stand there staring at it, not at him.

"Or I want to pretend to be friends, or friendly at least."

I take the towel, look up at him, and watch as he registers what I'm saying. "Okay," He draws out the word, his right hand returning to his pocket while his left begins to fidget with the ring on his forefinger. It is an action that will always make me think of the train. "Why, exactly? I mean, why exactly do we have to pretend? Why can't we just be friends?"

"Because I'm not ready for that yet." *We need to go slow*, I think to myself. Where have I heard that before?

"And we are pretending to be friends for their benefit?" He points to the door.

"Comments have been made about our not-so-subtle avoidance of one another. And I don't want to tell them why because I don't want them to hate you the way I did for so long."

"Do you still hate me?" He has stopped spinning the ring and has both hands in his pockets now.

I look up into those pale blue eyes, the same ones that captivated me so long ago. The only difference being the fine lines that have appeared at the corners. "No," I admit quietly. "Hate is an exhausting emotion. I don't know how I feel about you now, but I don't hate you, Teddy." Right now I feel a bit like I did all those years ago. I want to kiss him, but I also want to push him away and never see him again. I don't feel equipped to deal with these emotions. Him leaving wasn't like any other breakup. I didn't know it was coming, there was no warning, and until a few of months ago, there was no reason. Twelve years is a long time to sit with heartache coated in questions.

"I'm sure she'll make the salad again this summer, babe," Izzy drawls as they come through the door. "Oh, sorry if we're interrupting, I've just really gotta use the toilet."

I drag my eyes from Teddy's and watch as Izzy hustles to the hall bathroom and then looks back at Tom, who stands sheepishly in the entry staring at us while holding what remains of my bowl and salad.

"I'm not sure what to do with this," he says, nodding down at his hands.

"Here." Teddy pulls a garbage bag out of a cupboard and holds it open for Tom. "I'll go through it later and separate the food from the bowl."

"How green of you." Tom grins, tipping everything into the bag.

"Have to balance with the number of balloons Cass is inflating in the barn. Speaking of balloons, I thought the kids were coming."

"Izzy's grandmother is over from Korea, so her parents thought it would be nice for them to spend some more time with her. Apparently they will be doing a lot of cooking."

"That'll be nice for them," I say, bending to wipe up the drops of water that fell from my fingers while I stood awkwardly in front of Teddy. "Izzy has some great stories of cooking with her. Come to think of it, she's got some good ones of cooking with her Polish grandmother too."

"The woman can fold any kind of dumpling like a pro," Tom tells us. "Anyway, I was thinking as we were cleaning this up, it's a good thing you weren't carrying the cake, eh?" His eyes widen comically at the thought.

"I'm not sure Izzy would have been laughing so hard about that," I agree.

TWENTY-ONE

TEDDY

Operation Appear Friendly is going well so far. Nellie and I are currently winning what has quickly become a competitive game of Code Names. We already took down Marley and Bennett, and we're one round away from taking Izzy and Tom down. If Karl and Nancy stayed up later than nine p.m., we would have probably beaten them too.

"When do you leave again?" Marley asks, taking a bite of birthday cake.

"In two weeks." Nellie sighs, as she resets the cards in front of us. "It feels like I have a million more things to do, but at least most of the books are gathered."

"Where—" I start to ask but it comes out weakly, so I clear my throat and try again. "Where are you going?" I manage to sound less like a thirteen-year-old mid-voice change.

"It's a new mobile library program the university is launching," Nellie says, looking right at me and holding my gaze. "I'm going to be hauling a converted mini Airstream up to this remote town..." She stops to think. "I actually think it's a hamlet, definitely not big enough to be a town. Anyway, they don't have easy access to library services. I'll be working with one of the locals to set up something that can kind of serve as a hub for the whole area. It's a pilot project." It's the first time she seems genuinely interested in talking to me. Her face lights up in a way I haven't seen for over a decade, and it feels like warm sunshine hitting my face. I'm positive I'm wearing my goofy smile because she's doing the thing she dreamed of doing.

"Where will you be going?" Bennett asks.

"Somewhere between Timmins and Moosonee. It's called Marmot Point."

"Alone?" I blurt out before I can stop myself.

"Alone," she confirms.

"Huh." Bennett looks at Marley, and something unspoken passes between them before they look between Nellie and me, smiling.

Nellie's eyes narrow with suspicion. "What?"

"Nothing. Hurry up and take those two out so we can go out and make smores." Marley smiles sweetly at Izzy and Tom. Marley is nice and everything, but sweet is not a word I'd use to describe her even if I've heard Bennett murmur "sweetheart" to her on occasion. How he's come to that conclusion is for them to know in private.

"You haven't even finished your cake," Izzy points out.

"I'm sorry, are you judging me? On my birthday?"

"I'm not judging you for wanting s'mores, I'm just pointing out that you haven't yet finished your first dessert."

"You're basically a nighttime hobbit." Nellie laughs. "She's had one dessert, yes, but what about second dessert?"

Marley chews thoughtfully before nodding. "Dessert hobbit. I like it."

Izzy looks between her friends, clearly confused before turning to her husband. "Did you understand any of that?"

"You didn't?" She shakes her head, quickly glancing at the

rest of us. "Maybe you should have come to see *Lord of the Rings* with me back in high school."

"You know I don't like movies with goblins, Thomas."

"Orcs," Marley says, setting her empty plate down. "The gobliny creatures are called orcs."

Izzy's eyes are comically wide. "I don't like movies with those either."

"I know, babe. I still love you." Tom pats her knee.

It only takes fifteen minutes for us to win the next game and for Marley to declare that it's time to head out to the fire pit. We pack up fast, and while everyone grabs a sweatshirt or blanket, I head out to get the fire started. I'm poking a couple of logs around when Nellie sits across from me, the firelight illuminating her and more specifically the sweatshirt she's wearing. It's the university sweatshirt I left at her house on our last day. The one I slid over her body in a way that felt like I was claiming her. For a solid minute, I'm convinced I'm about to fall headfirst into the fire pit, swallow my tongue, or stomp over to her, pull her into my arms, and drag her back to my apartment. I do none of those things, of course, opting instead to look back into the flames like I never noticed in the first place. For the rest of the night, I'm quiet, but I assume everything I'm feeling is loud and clear whenever my gaze lands on her.

In the morning while everyone is sleepily sipping coffee and devouring Nancy's maple walnut scones and, in Nellie's case, a chocolate chip cookie, Bennett reveals what the look meant the night before.

"Ya know, I've been meaning to connect with the one

rescue just north of Timmins. They're a smaller operation but vital. Maybe we could do a joint trip? Help each other out."

"I doubt Marley wants to go on that kind of road trip when she just got back home," Nellie says sympathetically.

Marley laughs, and then her eyes land on me. "Not me—Teddy. He's been so good with outreach." That sweet smile is back again, and it nearly gives me a toothache.

"Teddy?" Nellie practically chokes out.

"He can go with you and help with the book stuff and do some work with the Spencer Lake Rescue."

"Oh, I don't know," Nellie says slowly. "I mean, it's a lot of driving and then just sitting around hoping people come to check out the books."

A lot of time alone with Nellie is more of a selling feature than I think she realizes. A month to try and repair what I broke. Cass had said I needed to just start, and this seems like a very solid way to do that.

Straightening, I turn to Nellie. "I'll go." Her dark blue eyes widen in surprise.

"Yeah, you will." Cass smiles over at me and winks.

Nellie's gaze bounces off everyone else at the table before it lands back on me. "You don't have to. I am absolutely fine with going alone."

"What if you sprain your ankle in the middle of nowhere? Do you think a handsome man is just going to appear to rescue you?" Marley asks innocently. "It's not exactly realistic, Nell."

Izzy snorts from the end of the table, and we all turn to look at her in time to see the coffee she had just taken a sip of dribble out of her nose. "Oh my god, it burns!" she squeals, fanning her face while Tom scrambles for napkins.

Nellie stares at Izzy for a minute before looking over at Bennett. "But you have so much going on here. Surely you can't spare him."

"I have two students coming to work for the summer so between them, Cass, Marley, and me, I think we'll be alright. Remember, I used to do this all by myself."

Before she can come up with another excuse, I resort to begging. "Please let me come, Nellie." And because I don't want to make her uncomfortable, I add, "Bennett has been talking about connecting with Spencer Lake for a while, and it's harder to do electronically. Showing up in person builds goodwill. And maybe we can bring a few dogs back if they need some relief." I see the moment she decides. It has nothing to do with me, but the thought of the dogs that does it. It should hurt, but it doesn't.

"I'd also suggest bringing one along with you," Bennett adds.

I know exactly what dog we should bring along with us. "Kevin is the most social and calmest of the puppies. He'd be a good one to take."

"You'd be doing us a huge favor, Nellie," Marley says enthusiastically. "Plus, after traveling nonstop for years, I'm sure Teddy is ready for a bit of a trip, even if it's just a few hours north."

"I am actually," I agree.

"I mean, I guess the solo travel thing sounds better than it would probably be," she concedes.

"Awesome." Marley punctuates her glee with a loud clap. "You should probably exchange numbers now so you can plan things without one of us." She gestures between herself and Bennett.

We both take our phones out and pass them to each other. When I select add new contact, I immediately type in Enviro Guy only to be asked if I want to update an existing contact. I look up at Nellie quickly, but she's busy inputting her details. I don't know if I should update the contact or add it under my name. I opt to create a new contact, counting this as starting fresh with her.

I know everyone sitting at this table thinks they just got away with something diabolical because they are all giving one another mental fist bumps.

After breakfast, everyone spreads out around the house or yard. Tom and Izzy announce they're going for a hike, something that seems to surprise both Nellie and Marley. "Like, in nature?" Marley asks, her eyes sliding to Nellie.

"Well, we aren't going to do laps around the house," Izzy scoffs. "We get so little time alone so we're going to use it."

"Okay, sure, this seems totally normal," Nellie says slowly. "Make sure you bring your phones in case you get lost."

"In our pockets." Tom smiles back at us before guiding his wife out of the house.

"And remember poison ivy has three leaves, so if you're gonna do stuff, don't do stuff near leaves of three," Marley hollers as the door shuts.

"One of them is going to come back itchy," Nellie says.

Marley and Bennett suddenly have to go look at something in the Hores' cow barn that can't wait until later, and within five minutes of cleaning up breakfast, Nellie and I are standing in the kitchen alone.

"Do you want to go out and play with the dogs for a bit?" I ask, not knowing what the hell else to do.

"Sure," she says, already getting her shoes on.

After a while, I find myself sitting on the bench in the pasture next to her while the dogs do their dog stuff. "Is it really okay if I come along, or were you just saying that for their benefit? Because you can say no, Nellie." I'd have a hard time saying no to all those faces, and I'm not a people-pleaser like Nellie is. At least I get the impression she's still one. Like she'd let everyone else on the train before she got on herself.

She doesn't answer right away, just stares out at where Pip and Daisy are chasing after a surprisingly speedy Yogurt. "On one hand, it would be nice to move forward. Neither of us is likely going to be out of this bubble anytime soon. We may as well make an effort. I did tell you I wanted to try the friend thing. And nothing forces two people to mend fences like a road trip."

"Stuck in a car together, forced to entertain one another. I've also heard the same said for putting together Ikea furniture," I add.

"Three years ago, the head librarian at the university decided that a fun team-building exercise would be to put together the new whiteboards for the meeting rooms."

The thought of that being something to bring people together makes me laugh.

"That was also my reaction. I grew up with two parents who never fought. I didn't even think they were capable of it. Then they bought me a bed from Ikea—you know, one of the ones with the drawers?" I nod. "Yeah, well, my dad slept in the guest room for a week after they finished."

"My brother finds stuff like that relaxing," I say, almost to myself.

"I'm sure both of my parents would have if they'd attempted it as a solo project, but for some reason, they thought it would be a good relationship activity. In the end, I was the only one who had a few good nights of sleep in a row." She laughs, absently taking the stick Norman Barkwell offers her and tossing it. "Anyway, all of that is to say that I can't see it ending with us worse off than we are now."

"That's the confidence I was looking for." I smile over at her and notice as her eyes dip to my mouth and catch there for a few seconds. "We worked as friends once."

She blinks a few times. "And that will be all we can work as going forward. If you can agree to that, then I don't see a problem with any of this."

So this is what a heart-sinking feels like, hope withering and dying in the center of my chest. I swallow the disappointment down. "They may never let us team up for a game night again."

"Probably not." She smirks at me.

"You can tell them, you know. What I did. I'm fine with being the bad guy because it's the truth."

Nellie looks down at her hands for a minute before answering. When she looks back up at me, it's with the saddest eyes I've seen in a long time. "The thing is, Teddy, I'm not so sure anymore that you were or are a bad guy. But every time I see you, it's like the wind gets knocked out of me again, and for the first little while, I feel nothing but the betrayal, anger, and sadness that I felt the day you said, 'Guess not.'" Those two words take me back to that mountain parking lot in BC. The place where I hit send and blew up my life. "Before the end of this trip, the earlier the better, I want to know what made you go from the guy who showed up for me when I was sick, but wouldn't even give me the chance to do the same when he faced the worst day of his life. I want to know why you couldn't face this"—she gestures between us—"head on."

"Deal," I say as she stands and walks away from me.

It feels like we've just reached the end of a chapter, and I'm eager to turn the page and start a fresh one. Chapter Four, Teddy's Redemption Begins.

TWENTY-TWO

"I don't think I even have room for all these books, Dad," I call from the living room where my parents have stacked boxes of ornithology books. Some my father wrote, but most are just gifts he's received over his thirty-year career.

"You never know, chickadee, people may surprise you." Mom walks in with yet another box. "Also, you'd be doing me a favor."

I try again to use logic. "I have limited space. You've seen the trailer."

"I thought you were taking Bennett's pickup. Surely there is ample space in the... the..." She gestures wildly for the word.

"The bed?" I suggest.

"Yes. I know his employee is taking stuff for that shelter or whatever, but I'm sure you'll still have plenty of room."

After my parents expressed concern for the twelfth time that I was going to be driving into the wilds of the province to deliver books, alone, I told them that Bennett had asked if one of his employees could join me to do some outreach. I didn't tell them who the employee was. As far as they know, I haven't heard from Teddy in over a decade.

"What about some of *your* books?" I ask my mom.

"I think one of these boxes has some copies of the early releases." She starts rummaging through the boxes on the coffee table. "This one has some the publisher sent for other authors. Oh, and about six of mine."

I peek in and see a few covers of scantily clad women and bare-chested men. "Those will be a nice break for the non-bird enthusiasts."

Every single book in that box was written by my mother. She either has no idea or is in deep denial that I know she writes the steamier stuff under a pen name. When I was sixteen, I decided to take one off her shelf only to realize the hero was word for word the high school boyfriend she had recently told me about. I don't think I've ever shut a book so fast. I'm fine with my mother writing steamy books; I just don't feel the need to be in her imagination when it comes to that stuff. It's just literally too close to home. The me pretending she doesn't write it and her thinking I don't know about it arrangement works well for our relationship.

My phone lights up beside me, and I have a moment of panic when I see it's just Izzy.

IZZY

I've got the kids books all read

ready*

Although they also have all been read, which is why they are going with you

I'll swing by on my way home from my parents

How are you feeling about everything?

> Fine

> Have you talked to him?

> Just a few texts for confirmation purposes

> Hot!

> I needed three cold showers after the one exchange

> I bet you did

"Lunch is ready, my loves," Dad calls from the kitchen.

It's not until I'm walking towards the deck that I notice how clean the house is. "Did you two do a full decluttering while getting the books together?" I watch my parents have a silent conversation and start to get nervous. "Is someone dying?" I ask, half joking but half terrified of the answer.

"Oh lord no." Mom laughs. "But we do have some news."

"Are you selling?" They have talked about selling the house and moving somewhere a bit smaller for a while, but this feels sudden.

"Not exactly," Dad says, looking at Mom as if looking for permission to continue. When she nods he does. "We're moving to the Philippines for a couple of years."

This was the last thing I expected him to announce. "I'm sorry, what?"

"Well, after retiring last December, I've been, well, bored. Caleb casually mentioned that if we were interested in a change of scenery, he may be able to help with the boredom." He's not looking at me while he goes on to tell me about the work Caleb and his team have been doing for various endangered birds. My father wouldn't need much more convincing than that. "Also, this way your mother can do a proper book tour in Australia and New Zealand. Her latest comes out down there in two months." He reaches over and squeezes Mom's hand, and I silently watch the interaction.

I've had my parents nearby my entire life. This is a chance for my sister to have some more of their time. Although she's the one who moved away, not me.

"Are you going to say something, chickadee?" Dad asks.

"Sorry, I'm just in shock. When are you leaving?"

They do the silent conversation again, and I feel my anxiety begin to spike. "Well, in two weeks."

"Two... As in fourteen days from now?"

"Twelve days, actually." Dad winces.

"Twelve days!" I shriek, unable to contain the sudden burst of emotion. "I'm leaving in three. I'm going to be away when you leave. I won't get to say goodbye to you." I suddenly feel like a child on the verge of a tantrum.

"We'll come up to you the morning you leave."

"I'm going up to Marley's the night before I leave." I pout.

"Then we'll come up and see you off the night before. Regardless, Cornelia, we will have a proper goodbye even if at the time we are both still in the country."

"And," my dad adds excitedly, "you can come have a nice Christmas in paradise with your whole family."

The idea of spending Christmas with palm trees and an ocean breeze may sound appealing to some people, but I am not one of them. However, if it means being with my family over the holidays then I can probably suck it up.

"And who knows," Mom adds. "Maybe by then you'll have someone in your life and you'd rather spend every minute alone with him."

Cue my traitorous brain showing me a highlight reel of every smile Teddy has ever flashed me. I may have told him friendship was all I was willing to try, but if you took a peek into my brain you'd call me a big fat liar. It's like a teenage bedroom plastered with posters of my crush in there. Stupid long-buried feelings.

I do my best to pretend I'm on board with the move and my initial reaction was just a blip. On the one hand, I am happy for them. I know my mom loves the heat and being close to the ocean, and my dad will be in heaven studying new birds. I catch myself rubbing my thumb over the malkoha tattoo on my arm every so often as they talk and try to remember how much fun we had over there.

I don't cry about the news like I keep expecting to. I wait for the tears as I pull out of the driveway, and then again as I leave the town limits. When I tell Izzy, I'm surprisingly calm and unemotional about the whole thing. When I get home, I continue to wait for the tears that never come.

TEDDY

Look at this!

Teddy has attached a picture of Kevin wearing a blue-and-white vest, and I melt on the spot.

Cute

I thought it may be good to have a life jacket in case we want to take him swimming at some point

I'm not sure how much time we'll have for swimming

I put my phone face down and go through my suitcase for the tenth time since I packed. I'm sure I'll go through it another twenty before I actually leave. After I close it, I head to the kitchen to figure out how much I can get out of the rest of the food in the fridge before I leave. Halfway through making a salad of random ingredients, I see Mrs. Dipietro pointing into my yard from her deck.

"That's it," I seethe and stomp back to my bedroom to get my phone. I don't know what exactly I'm going to do with my phone—record her to prove she is, I don't know, to prove she's a nosy and obsessed with my yard? "And who do you need to prove this to, Nellie?" I ask aloud, standing in the bedroom holding my phone.

I see there is another text from Teddy.

> Oh come on, you're going to deny this face swim time?

Attached is perhaps the cutest picture of Kevin that I have seen yet.

> This isn't fair

> Sure it is

> It's manipulation. You're manipulating me with cute dog faces

> Technically just the one face

Another picture comes through, and this time it's the bottom half of Teddy's face while Kevin is perched in his arms.

Now I'm standing in my room staring at my phone trying to remember why I even came in here in the first place. I look back at my suitcase and then at my dresser. I know there is a swimsuit at the back of the one top drawer, but I also know that I haven't worn it in two years, and if—and that's a big if—I decide to wear one around Teddy, it's not going to be a forgotten swimsuit from the depths of my undergarment drawer.

Ten minutes later, the salad and my nosy neighbor are forgotten, my phone is set to silent, and I'm halfway to the mall. If I'm doing this, I'm doing it with a new suit. *It's normal to want to look hot in front of an ex-turned-maybe-friend*, I tell myself while I shuffle through the rack of suits, all annoyingly regular priced because it's the start of the season. I find a vintage-cut suit that I know will highlight the hourglass shape I've grown to love, and even better it's blue and white so it kind of matches Kevin's vest. I don't know why that feels relevant.

Thirty minutes after the last picture from Teddy, I'm back home sitting on the couch and eating my soggy kitchen sink salad, and the swimsuit is packed along with sunscreen and a giant floppy hat. There is rarely a checkout sale that I can say no to, hence the additional things.

You're going into any lake first to check for leeches

As you wish

Do you have everything ready?

I think so

Well if you forget anything I'm sure we can find it before we actually reach the middle of nowhere

Which is why I'm not stressed about it

Good

Do you have everything ready?

Would you believe everything is already in the truck?

Even Kevin?

*Picture of Teddy's hip and a sleeping Kevin next to him on the couch.

He's getting all his sleep in now

Well, he does have to keep me awake during the long stretches

I'm more than willing to help with that too

I stare at the message trying to figure out if it's innocent or not.

I'm a really good shoulder flicker

Innocent it is.

TWENTY-THREE

TEDDY

I reread my last message to Nellie no fewer than ten times. *I'm a really good shoulder flicker.* What the fuck does that even mean? I sent the message about helping her stay awake during the long stretches, then I immediately went somewhere dirty in my mind, and I panicked. Now I'm pretty sure I've come off as a weirdo.

NELLIE

So I'm in good hands

I wish she was in my hands. I wish I had handled everything better twelve years ago. But that's easy to think now, when hindsight is indeed twenty-twenty. I know for a fact that if I could go back to my past self and say to my face, *Walking away is going to be the biggest mistake of your life,* I'd still do it. I'd still send those last two words to Nellie and walk away. Sometimes we need to get lost to find ourselves, and I had to get real lost.

And paws!

The cutest lil paws!

I can practically see her typing that. Her nose scrunches up as she makes an adorable 'aw' face, thinking of Kevin's little paws.

The conversation has been steady so I decide to test my luck.

What are you up to?

Eating salad and watching Downton

I look up from my phone at the show muted on the TV. So much of my time with Nellie has crept back in over the years. When I started to feel more leveled out, I picked a book up again, a well-loved copy of *The Forest of Despair* I found at a hostel in Australia. While staying with a friend in Hungary, I stumbled across *Downton Abbey* on TV, and I started watching it again. Things that were only in my life in the first place because of her. And now a couple days away from our trip north, we are sitting in our own homes, watching the same thing and texting each other. This is totally something friends would do.

You?

Just being lazy with Kev until I've got to feed the dogs

The life!

At ten to six, I head downstairs to start the task of delivering the food to the dogs' designated areas. While they eat, I get all the cleanup stuff ready. Everyone gets excited when they find out where I work, but they don't think about the stuff that doesn't involve cuddling or playing with dogs. For instance, thirty-two dogs create a lot of waste. This isn't a case of running out quickly with a poop bag. Picking up dog shit is half of what I do on an average day. But no one wants to hear about that part of the job. "I had a shitty day" means something different in this line of work.

Marley comes out when I'm almost done to take over the last little bit of pick up. I'm grateful because it gives my back a break. It doesn't take long though before I sense she has an ulterior motive to being so helpful.

"So how are you feeling about the trip?" she asks, dumping a shovel full of shit into the bucket.

"Great. I'm looking forward to seeing Nellie's operation and, of course, seeing the shelter up there."

"Good thing Bennett had the extension built this spring, eh?"

I look up at the barn and rub my neck nervously. "He may need to start thinking about another one at this rate." It's a beautiful setup, and I can't think of anywhere better to be a dog. Hell, I can barely think of anywhere better to be as a human. When Bennett offered the apartment to me, I didn't hesitate to say yes. I have my own space but get to socialize when I want, and he refuses to charge me rent. Sometimes I wake up in the morning and have to pinch myself. I never expected to land so steadily on my feet when I moved back to the country.

"He has promised to be better with the adoption side of things this year. Although I have yet to see that come into practice." Marley rolls her eyes as she puts the lid on the bucket and carries it back towards the barn.

"I can do that," I insist, jogging after her.

She throws an exhausted look over her shoulder, and I back off immediately.

Marley has an independent streak a mile long, and since

her injury, she is almost militant in her need to prove she's capable of doing things on her own. Nancy said it was because Bennett coddled her a bit too much when she had gotten hurt. Which I can imagine since Bennett is the biggest empath I've ever met.

"Have you had dinner yet?" Marley asks after she's put everything away.

"I'm about to."

"What are you having?"

I have no idea. I was going to spend the next half an hour rummaging through my kitchen with the intention of making something hot only to decide on a couple of sandwiches.

"Come over. Bennett's got enough on the barbecue to feed the entire town."

She doesn't even wait for me to confirm, just walks back towards the house. Being fed wasn't part of this arrangement, yet I find myself eating with Marley, Bennett, and occasionally Cass no fewer than three times a week. I usually say yes, but some days I just don't have it in me to be in the presence of two people who only have eyes for one another. I'm happy for them, but they remind me of my parents, and even after all these years, it's hard. I can't help but grieve for their future when one has to let go while at the same time, I'm envious of them for having to face that one day.

After assuring Marley I'll be over soon, I head up to my apartment to change into something a bit less single-guy-who-lives-in-a-barn. Once I've done that, I pull out the machine I have used regularly since I've been back home. I hate the squeeze of the cuff as the sensors read my blood pressure. Still normal after three readings.

Three years ago, shortly after giving birth, Zoe had been getting severe headaches at the back of her head while sick with a vicious cough. It was dismissed as neck muscle strain until they took her blood pressure. She was immediately sent for an MRI, and sure enough, there at the back of her brain was a small unruptured aneurysm. Something we had all silently feared could happen to one of us. A fear that had only grown in intensity since Mom. So far, the doctors have advised that no surgical intervention is needed, but Zoe has pleaded with me and Will to pay attention to our health. "You can get this cuff," she'd said, sending us a picture of the portable blood pressure meter she had. "And maybe get in for a scan. Dr. Tascioni will requisition one, I'm positive."

I take a picture of the average and then head down for dinner. I could tell myself it's because I want to spend the evening with company, but I know if I stay home, I'm probably going to text Nellie again, and I'm trying damn hard not to come across as desperate.

"You do realize that Nellie is going to want to keep Kevin, right? This is going to be a trial run that they'll both ace." Marley's reaction is about what I expected after I told them I was serious about taking Kevin along for the ride.

I'm well aware. I may not have spent much time engaging with Nellie since December but that doesn't mean I haven't been paying attention. Despite the Christmas puppies all looking alike, aside from Eggnog, she has always gravitated toward Kevin. Choosing him wasn't a coincidence.

"Well, Bennett does keep talking about finding homes for the pups." I lean back in my chair, and both Marley and I turn to Bennett with knowing looks.

"What?" he asks innocently. "It's not my fault the applicants are subpar."

"All of them?" Marley says.

"Every. Single. One," Bennett enunciates before standing to clear the plates.

Marley looks over at me with narrowed eyes, and I give my

head a subtle shake. There have been countless adoption applications, and most of them were suitable. They just didn't meet some impossible standard that Bennett has set. I'm sure the standard is that they aren't clones of him and this place.

I stand and start gathering the serving dishes, but Marley bats me away. "You two stay out here. This is the one thing I get to do without an argument."

"We can help bring stuff in, Mar," Bennett says, lifting the plates out of her reach.

"Fine, but you put them down and get out of my kitchen." She huffs.

"*Your* kitchen?" Bennett asks.

"When it is time for dishes, it's my kitchen. When it's time to cook, it's yours and when—" Bennett sets the plates down and covers her mouth with his hand so fast half the cutlery slides across the table. I watch as a blush creeps up his neck to his face, and when I look over at Marley her eyes are crinkled, giving away the giant smile she's got underneath his hand.

"We'll drop things off and leave," he assures her but keeps his hand where it is for a second longer. When he drops it, he does so slowly as if he's expecting whatever he was trying to keep in, to try and come out again.

Marley smiles up at him and then leads the way inside.

As promised, we set what we're carrying down and then head right back outside.

"So, how are you really feeling about the trip?" Bennett asks, sitting back down across from me.

I could lie to him, but I am tired of keeping it in. "Honestly? A bit terrified. I feel like I have another chance at a relationship with Nellie, and I'm worried I'll fuck it up again."

"We're talking about a romantic relationship?"

"I'd take friendship at this point, which is all she wants." Saying it out loud physically hurts.

Bennett studies me, from across the table. "Is that all you want?" he asks.

I have said time and time again that if people wanted to know our story, they would have to ask Nellie, but I feel compelled to keep talking.

"We tried to be friends once. We were good at it too, but the attraction proved to just be too much for her." Bennett laughs along with me as I buy time to think of what to tell him next. How much can I reveal without letting him see it all? "I don't know if it was like this for her, but all I could think about when we weren't together was when we'd be together again. The first time I saw her, all I knew was that I wanted it to not be the last."

"Love at first sight." Bennett nods sagely.

"No, I don't think it was love at first sight. It was intrigue and attraction. There was this want I felt just to meet her and then that turned into a need to know her. And in turn for her to know me. And at the time I thought I might be someone she'd maybe want to get to know."

"For the record," Bennett says thoughtfully, "it wasn't love at first sight for me either. I didn't even realize I loved Marley until she was gone, and even then, I battled with it. On one hand, I wanted to fully give in, but on the other, what if she never came back? I allowed hope to slip out here and there but until she was standing in front of me—" He looks out towards the forest as if lost in a memory. "It was as if seeing her just cracked every bit of fear I had right off my body. She jokes that I was too easy on her, but I knew that if she was back it wasn't to test the waters, it was to dive in. And there was no fucking way I wasn't diving right in with her."

"I think you have a different view of it than the rest of us did." I smirk at him. "You seemed fully in before she came back, whether you realized it or not."

"And you clearly want Nellie to get to know this version of you—a version, by the way, that reveals itself a little more every time she's around. When you started, you were this man of mystery, nice enough but guarded. Then you get some Nellie time, even if it's from afar, and the curtain gets pulled back a tiny bit more. We all see it."

"No shit," I say, rolling my eyes. "Not a single one of you has been subtle about it, either."

"Life is short." Bennett shrugs. "Screw subtlety."

Life is indeed short, I think.

"Listen, I don't know what went down between the two of you, but if repairing the relationship is really what you want to do, I'm sure you'll succeed. Just don't lose hope."

I nod back because the little bit of hope I have seems to be lodged in my throat.

TWENTY-FOUR

NELLIE

I wave to my parents until they turn off my street, and still I don't cry. I should have cried at least six times by now, but my tear ducts remain drier than an academic journal.

I'd insisted they leave before me. For some reason, I wanted them to see me in their rearview mirror rather than me seeing them. It's a reminder that they're the ones leaving me behind. I'm just doing a few weeks north of here. They're the ones moving away.

One more walk around the little Airstream to double-check that nothing is going to open or fall off on my drive to meet with Teddy. Teddy. I would be lying if I said I wasn't excited about spending time with him. Even if I'm also dreading it. The human heart is an interesting thing, capable of holding great hope and the capacity for immense heartbreak at the same time. After I confirm no doors are going to swing open and dump books on the highway, I slip behind the wheel, reverse out of my driveway, and head toward a new adventure.

Twenty minutes later, Marley calls. She was going to call earlier but must have gotten busy.

"Hey," she says out of breath.

"Hey yourself. Are you out for a run?"

"No, Jason stopped by." Jason is the Hores' bull and the most prolific escape artist since Houdini.

"I assume he's back home."

"For the time being anyway." I can hear her eyes roll from here. "But enough about runaway bovines, how are you? How was the goodbye?"

"Far more painless than I had expected."

"Still haven't cried?"

"Nope. Apparently you've had more of an influence on me than I realized."

"Come talk to Bennett, he'll have you bawling in minutes." She laughs. Marley wasn't a crier, but apparently on her first full day with Bennett, she set some kind of personal record for tears.

"If this goes on much longer, I may take you up on that."

"Deal. He'll love it." Her voice has taken on a tinny quality.

"Where are you?"

"The bathtub," she says as if it's the most normal thing in the world.

"Why?"

"I'm spying."

"On who?"

"Teddy."

"Um... okay. Why?"

"Nell, the guy is a nervous wreck. He has checked the contents of the truck at least eight times today. Did you threaten him or something?"

"Does that seem like something I'd do?" I scoff.

"True. Did Izzy?"

"Not that I know of. Maybe this is always how he travels. You check things a bunch. It's not unheard of."

"Well, that's because if I forget tampons or something, there isn't a Shoppers just down the street."

"Marley, stop spying on Teddy. He probably knows you are," I scold.

A pfff sound comes through my speakers, most likely accompanied by an eye roll I can't see. "Seems unlikely. I'm very good at being invisible."

"Marley, Teddy asked me to come tell you to stop watching him," I hear Bennett say from somewhere nearby, and I laugh at the visual of Marley being told off while hiding in an empty bathtub.

"I'm just watching to make sure he doesn't drop from exhaustion. Has he even hydrated during all his trips to and from the truck?"

I hear Bennett chuckle softly then what sounds like a kiss. It's still weird to think of Marley in a relationship, let alone one where she's open about absolutely everything. Sometimes too open.

Bennett says something that I can't make out, and by Marley's reaction, I'm glad to not be in the know.

"You two are gross," I grumble.

"You're just jealous. You could be gross with someone too if you let yourself be. Think you're willing to try allowing that?"

"Marley, there are nearly twelve years of history I'm going to have to wade through to even reach a place where friendship is possible."

"Are—" she says at the same time as I say "But—"

"Go ahead."

I take a deep breath and work up to what I've been telling myself since we decided to do this thing. "But I am actually looking forward to trying because when I think back to the before times—"

"BM!" Marley exclaims.

"Bowel movement?"

"No." Marley snorts. "Before Marley."

"Oh." I laugh too. "Yes, in the times before you, before everything went from blissful young something-or-other to shit, I was happier than I'd ever been."

"And then poof?"

"Then poof."

We stay silent for a few minutes. Marley, I assume stretched out in an empty bathtub, and me, staring at the near-empty highway in front of me.

"Once upon a time, I was the one who poofed," she says quietly.

"Yes, I remember. It wasn't that long ago, you know."

"Feels like years now." I can practically hear her smiling. "In a good way. But sometimes I wonder what would have happened if I'd come back and Bennett hadn't been receptive."

"Marley, you had a good reason for leaving. You two also weren't actually in a relationship."

"So you *were* in a relationship with Teddy?" Marley's voice manages to sit up and take notice.

Shit, I knew I'd have to reveal all this one day, but I thought I'd maybe do it in person.

"For a couple of months when I was twenty."

"Wait..." She squeals. "Is he the summer fling? How did I not put this together? You just said twelve years of history. Oh my god okay, hold on. No, wait, I'm shutting up, go on."

"I don't know what else to say. We just worked, and things were so good, Marley. Obviously too good. He was the quintessential good guy, and I remember thinking, wow, they do exist. Remember, I had just finished my second year at school, and most of the guys I encountered were hoping to sleep with more girls than the guy down the hall. Anyway..." I take a deep breath. "One day he just disappeared. The day after he had taken care of me while I was sick, might I add. He brought me soup and watched *Downton* with me."

That's the part that always gets me the hardest. We'd just spent all those hours together, and yet it was so easy for him to just cut me out.

"He watched that boring show with you? That's love. Did he tell you where he went?"

"No. He did tell me—" The telltale sound of a dropped call fills the car. "Dammit." I try to call back, but I seem to have entered a dead zone. I'm thankful it's Marley I was on the phone with, though, and not Izzy or my mother who would immediately think something horrible had happened and would already be googling a disaster in the general area.

Teddy is walking towards the truck when I pull into the driveway, and I have to wonder what trip number he's on. I'm almost shocked not to see a path worn into the grass.

"Hey," I say as casually as possible when I get out and walk toward him.

"Hey." He smiles easily at me, although his thumb is spinning the ring on his forefinger like he's trying to power the sun.

"Come to walk me to the house so I don't crash again?" I joke, pulling out my backpack from the backseat.

"Actually I was just double-checking that everything was in the truck."

"Double-checking?"

"Double times ten. No clue what that would be called."

"Paranoid, probably." I give his arm a playful, friendly little push as I pass him. "Come on, let's give Marley something else to do besides watch you walk back and forth."

I watch as his head tips back and he releases a deep sigh. "I knew she was watching me."

He's probably watched more than he realizes, I think to myself. "Teddy, everything is in the truck, and if it's not, it wasn't meant to be. Let's go." I turn and lead the way to the house where Marley comes bursting out the porch door.

"I knew you hadn't been eaten by some giant lizard."

"There was a close call with a porcupine, but it thought twice."

"If only they crossed at their designated signs," Teddy says from behind me.

I can feel my cheeks heat and try to ignore the look Marley gives me. "That would be convenient," she says, looking over my shoulder to address him. "Drop your bag in the bedroom, and then we're going to go for a pack walk. All of us." She looks between us seriously before heading out to the barn.

"She's so bossy now," I mumble.

"Now?" Teddy asks.

"Yeah, as in she didn't used to be." I don't mean for it to come out so passive-aggressively. I don't even know where that came from.

"Okay then. Well, I'll be." I look back to see him point back outside. "Unless you don't want me to come on the walk."

"No, of course, you should come." I plaster on the most sincere smile I can muster and hope it comes across the way I intend it to.

His face relaxes but only slightly. "See you out there."

It only takes me a couple minutes to drop my bag off, but I take a few more to make sure I look decent. I haven't changed too much in the last twelve years, but I wonder if Teddy sees the fine lines that have started to appear around my own eyes, or the lines across my forehead that seem to deepen with every school year. Does he think I should be dyeing my hair to hide the premature grays that have sprouted? Did he like the little bit of extra padding under his hands that time in my car? By the way he'd responded to me, I can't imagine any of it was a deal-breaker.

"Friends," I say to my reflection. Friends don't care about that shit. I certainly don't care about how he has filled out. Or how his once-soft hands have turned rough.

"Okay, keep going," Marley says, tugging on my arm to slow me down while the guys put even more distance between us.

"I'm trying to, but you're holding me back."

"Nellie, what did he tell you?"

"His mom died," I say quietly, turning more toward her and hoping my voice doesn't carry.

"That's why he left?"

"She died, and I think he just was caught up in that and then he said he found out something and... I don't know what that was, but he said he'd tell me while we're gone."

"Huh," she says, stopping mid-stride. "So a metaphorical meteor hit his world, and his strategy was to run away."

"I guess, but that sounds kind of heartless when you put it that way. His mom died, and he adored her. You should have seen them together, Marley, the way she looked at him. He was her world, but I don't think I realized just how much of his world she was." I look ahead where Teddy is becoming smaller with each stride, and I'm struck with the sudden need to hold him.

"You're crying." Marley's voice pulls my attention away from Teddy as I raise my hand to wipe away the tears that have begun to fall. "Did I just help someone else have a breakthrough?" Marley looks elated. "Is this how it feels to therapize someone? No wonder Izzy is so into it."

"I'm not sure that's what you did." I laugh, wiping the remaining moisture from my face.

"Well, maybe I didn't use the same methods, but the outcome is the same." She shrugs. "Just let me have this, Nell. It's so nice to be the one who isn't a mess for a change."

"I'm so glad I could help you out."

Marley shocks me by pulling me in for a hug. "You did help me out, though. You're one of the reasons I didn't keep going down that path I was on. You're one of the reasons I am here with him. Consider my being pushy about sorting shit out with Teddy me paying you back."

"What if I don't want to be paid back?" I sputter into her shoulder.

She pulls back and studies me. "Is that what you want? Because if you don't want to try with Teddy, I'll make up some excuse why he can't go with you, and we'll forget any of this ever happened. Hell, I'll come visit you all the time instead of you coming here. Because as much as I love you, I don't think Bennett is willing to give up his new best friend. And it's nice to see him have a friend that doesn't live... wait, never mind. It's nice to see him have a friend his age." Her face softens, and I brace for what's coming next. "Teddy, on the other hand... Bennett claims that when he first came he was broody and a bit of a loner. Now he eats with us multiple times a week and is actively involved with the social media stuff and outreach. And I get it, Bennett is amazing, but I don't think Teddy's about-face has anything to do with him."

I look from her to Teddy, who is jumping around with most of the dogs while Bennett plays tug-of-war with Yogurt. Lloyd is standing off to the side, eating leaves off a bush. I don't want to not come here anymore. This place is like Disney World for animal lovers.

"I've had months to come to terms with Teddy being back. I'm not mad at him anymore. I'm just scared that we won't work as friends."

"Why do you think you won't work as friends?"

I watch them for a few minutes more. I'm in a constant battle with my feelings when I see Teddy. The urge to touch him is always there. The need to be closer is at war with the barricade I've put up around my heart. I go back and forth between thinking of how amazing it is that of all the places he could be, it's here, and cursing the universe for doing this to me.

Finally, I pull my attention away from him and focus back on Marley.

"Avocados," I murmur.

TWENTY-FIVE

TEDDY

We've been on the road for about forty-five minutes and have said a total of fifty-two words. Most of them are directed at a very excited Kevin who is currently balanced on my thighs with his nose pressed against the window. I've got one hand on his chest while my other fidgets with the only thing that has stayed with me since I was diagnosed with anxiety at eighteen. The smooth silver of the ring glides over the surface of the stable metal below as it goes round and round. Before I had the ring, the skin on my thumbs was constantly raw and I was self-conscious about it. It was Zoe who found the ring online, and I've worn it since the day it arrived.

My anxiety doesn't tend to manifest in other ways. Sometimes I don't even realize I'm feeling anxious until I notice I'm spinning the ring continuously for a while. Jobs that depend on using my hands help too. Despite my very hands-on job at Morgan Estate Rescue, I've noticed that I've been spinning the damn ring a lot more since that day with Nellie in the car. I've also noticed that I've craved this anxious feeling like never before. Nellie-induced anxiety makes me feel more alive than just about anything else.

"So," she says suddenly, drawing my attention to her profile, "I already have to pee so I'm going to be stopping at the first rest stop I see. I guess we'll have to take turns staying in the car with Kevin."

That was not what I was expecting her to say but at least it's something. "I don't have to go, but I'll take him out to see if he does."

"Okay, well if you change your mind between now and"—she squints at the sign we pass—"twenty kilometers from here, just let me know before we leave. I want to get to the first stop before dark."

I see her jaw set again and figure she's done talking, but I don't want to be. "Where exactly is the first stop?" I got used to not planning while I traveled, so for some reason I decided to take the same kind of approach with this journey. Seeing how it's a small town out in the middle of nowhere, I figured scheduling down to the minute wasn't necessary. It turns out I was right. The shelter is actually run out of a couple's house, and the wife, Betty, told me not to worry because she'd "be around."

"Cyprus Creek, about three hours north of Algonquin. I think we could actually push it further, but I'd rather be off the road when the animals start to think about crossing en masse."

"That's fair." I nod.

"And there's a campsite there with showers and a bathroom so it seemed ideal," she adds.

I'm sleeping in the truck with Kevin while she uses the bed in the Airstream. I do have a tent packed as well if I decide that the truck is too much of a tight squeeze.

"Do..." I start to say, but when her eyes land on me briefly I lose my train of thought. "Um, sorry, forgot what I was going to ask," I say, shaking my head and looking back out the window.

"Do I want you to tell me what made you disappear for over a decade?"

"I didn't disappear, I was just gone."

"You *disappeared*, Teddy."

"I'm sorry," I say in a strained whisper.

"Stop saying that," she grits out. "I don't need any more sorry's. I got enough of them after you left. 'I'm so sorry he's gone, Nellie,' 'I'm sorry he broke your heart, Nellie,' 'I'm sorry I left, Nellie.' I have a cabinet of sorry's, and it's near bursting."

I genuinely don't know what to say to that because "I'm sorry" is the only thing that comes to mind. So I say nothing.

"I want you to tell me why, and I don't want another apology. I know you feel bad. I just want to know why."

"Not yet," I say.

"Why?" she snaps.

Because I don't know if you'll drive into a tree or break down when you hear it, I think.

"Listen, I don't know how you're going to react, and in all honesty, I'd rather not find out when you're behind the wheel."

She looks over again, and I see her face soften slightly. "Well, now I'm even more nervous."

"You have nothing to be nervous about."

"Teddy." She exhales my name like she is giving up. "I thought the worst of you for so long, and then I come to find out that your mom died. Now you won't tell me why you fully disappeared because you're worried about how I'll take it? I'm sorry, but I won't just be shrugging it off."

"I don't know what to tell you, other than to repeat that you have nothing to be nervous about."

Her only response is another deep exhale, and we sink back into silence.

Twenty-five minutes later, we pull into a rest stop, and she jumps out without saying a word. I watch her walk towards the building and don't get out with Kevin until she has slipped through the door.

Kevin pees the second his feet touch the grass, and I am suddenly relieved that she stopped when she did because we seemed to have been on the doorstep of a disaster only a few hours away from home.

Nellie returns carrying two coffees and silently hands one to me. "I needed one so figured you might too."

"Um, thank you," I stammer. "I think I'm going to try and —" *Try and what? Where are you going with this, you moron?*

"Go for it," Nellie says, saving me from myself and taking Kevin's leash.

I pop the coffee in the truck and jog inside. I really don't have to go, so I wander around the food court and into the little convenience store. They have a wall of candy, and I am immediately drawn to bags of Swedish Berries. She brought back coffee for me, so we can clearly treat each other to things, and unless she has completely changed, she probably still likes them. I grab a couple of bags and check out.

"You remembered?" she says in awe when I drop the bags on the center console. Of course I remember. I remember everything about her, about me when I was with her.

"Saw them, and it jogged a memory." She's probably thinking that I remembered the drive-in, but it was the intense fear I felt after I told her that it was always her I was thinking about.

I lost track of how often something jogged a memory of Nellie while I was gone. I left and thought I'd set her free from having to deal with my angry grieving heart. But it just so happened I'd left my heart with her.

TWENTY-SIX

NELLIE

I don't know what it is about the smell of Swedish Berries, but I can feel myself relax a bit as soon as the bag is open. It relaxes me to the point where I think I can actually start a conversation with Teddy that is not based on Kevin, bathroom breaks, or destinations.

"Is it safe to ask where exactly you went?" I hate that I'm so curious about where he was instead of coming back to me.

"All over really," he begins tentatively.

"I really am interested, unless you think it's going to impact my driving?" I look over at him quickly.

"No, I can't imagine it will cause an issue." He smiles back. "I started in New Zealand. My boss here, from my summer job, got me in touch with a guy who he'd met when he was doing forestry work in BC. He's high up in the New Zealand Ministry of Forestry."

"Fancy."

"His job may be, but I spent all of my time mostly doing what I'd done here, except I had to learn real quick how to get up in the trees myself."

"Still afraid of heights?" I look over just in time to see a look of surprise, like he's shocked I remembered.

"Would you believe me if I said no?"

"I might. Repeated exposure is a known way to get over a fear of something. It's how I got over my issues with blood."

I see him turn to me out of the corner of my eye. "How much blood were you seeing?"

"Story for another time. Is that where you've been this whole time? Seeing New Zealand without me?" Once upon a time, we had talked about nerding out in Hobbiton together.

"No, I was only there for three years."

"Only three years," I repeat as if three years is nothing.

"Yeah. Then I went to the Philippines." I can't help it as my grip tightens on the steering wheel "Is your sister still there?"

"Mm-hmm," I grind out. My jaw locking as he continues.

"I wasn't there long. I spent most of my time in El Nido. No forestry work there, but I did get my PADI certification. Scuba," he adds quickly.

"I have mine," I say, my voice clipped with unintentional annoyance. My father had insisted on getting certified on one of our family trips. "We do it together or not at all," he'd proclaimed, and since Sylvia was desperate, we all did it.

"Of course. Anyway, after three months, I stopped to volunteer with an elephant sanctuary in Thailand, and then I went to the Czech Republic. The forestry community is pretty tight-knit, and I was able to land places through friends of friends. I bounced around Europe for a few years doing forestry stuff and getting involved with some dog rescues before settling for a bit in Newfoundland." I tense again. He had been back in the country for years. "I was living in the middle of nowhere, basically a glorified ranger station. But it's where I finally real-ized I needed to go home."

"What about the rest of your family?"

"I kept them in the loop occasionally in the beginning. Basically every time I landed in a new place. The embassies always knew where I was, but... well, I had my reasons, even if now they seem petty." Reasons I'll hopefully know soon, and reasons that hopefully won't make me drive away and leave him in the middle of nowhere. Although out of the two of us in this car, I'm not the one most likely to do that. "Things are better now. We see each other occasionally and obviously text. I regret not being there for my dad now, but back then..." he trails off.

"Hindsight," I say mostly to myself.

"Hindsight has been a tough lesson," he replies, and I can see those pale eyes slide my way.

We slip back into silence, and I decide that it's time for some music. It's just a mix, but I put some Shinedown on the playlist, and I can't help wondering if they're still his favorite band. Six songs in, "I'll Follow You" comes on and I feel those eyes on me again. When I glance over his attention is on Kevin, who remains dedicated to watching the formations of the Canadian Shield shift as we pass by.

After another three hours of driving, I'm directed to turn off the highway onto a long gravel road. I wince, hearing the stones bounce off the Airstream and the truck, and suddenly imagine the cost of fixing a million tiny dents on Bennett's new vehicle.

"Kevin!" Teddy shrieks as Kevin pops straight off his lap into the air.

"That was a shockingly good Catherine O'Hara," I say.

"What?" he asks, looking over after Kevin is firmly secured in his arms.

"In *Home Alone* when the mom realizes they left their kid behind."

"Oh yeah, on the plane."

"Yeah, it was a good impression, even if it wasn't intentional."

Cue another long stretch of silence. In the BM times, the only time Teddy and I weren't talking is if one of us had fallen asleep. Even if we were making out, there were words. This silence feels uncomfortably foreign and somehow like something we need to go through to repair things. The little glimpses I get of the potential are addictive, and I long for more.

There is a hut about ten minutes down the road and I pull over, assuming it's the place I need to check in for the night. The signage isn't exactly helpful, but sure enough, there is a greasy guy inside wearing a T-shirt with the name of the campground.

"Hey," I say, walking over to the desk that looks like it was rescued from the side of the highway after it fell off a very tall truck.

I instantly regret wearing a tank top as his eyes trail down my body as I approach. The shiver of ick that passes through me must be visible because the guy's eyes snap to my face. He stands quickly, straightening his shirt. Now that is the way to greet a paying customer.

"Welcome to Sleepy Pines campground. Do you have a reservation?" I'm about to answer when it dawns on me that he's looking over my shoulder.

"You'll have to ask her, I'm just a hitchhiker," Teddy's voice comes from close behind me.

I turn back to him ready to tell him off, but he's not even looking at me; his eyes are lasered in on Jim Bob behind the desk. And if I am being honest, it's kind of hot.

"I do have a reservation. Should be under Three Rivers University." I look down at the old dusty computer and wonder if the thing can even be connected to the internet.

Greaseball McGee doesn't even look it up, just hands over a pair of keys. His eyes, which are now wary, remain on Teddy. "Lot fifteen," he squeaks out. "Three roads down on the right."

I snatch the keys from his hand, lean into his sightline to Teddy, and smile sweetly. "Thank you so much for your help." I turn on my heel and walk out of the hut.

Once we're back in the truck, I look down at my top and sigh.

"I probably should have popped on a different top," I say, pulling back onto the road.

"Why? Because you've got some cleavage on display? Nellie, you aren't responsible for how someone reacts to you. He's a grown-ass man, it's on him for making you feel uncomfortable."

"I wasn't uncomfortable," I insist.

"You stiffened like a corpse going into rigor the minute you stepped in there."

"The whole setup caught me off guard, I wasn't uncomfortable."

"Sure, Nellie, whatever you say. Regardless, you wear whatever you want, and no one gets to make you feel bad about it."

I slam on the brakes, bringing the truck to a halt and pitching us forward in our seats. "Should I feel bad about wearing a tank top?"

Teddy looks over at me, shock on his face. "No, never, that's not..." He shakes his head, his mouth moving with unvocalized words. When he seems to have his composure back, he levels me with a look that has me rooted to the spot. "I don't know why I said you shouldn't feel bad, that's not what I meant. I meant what I said about it being on him that you seemed uncomfortable. He sucks, you're great, I'm sor—" He stops himself from apologizing and deflates. "I don't know how to talk to you anymore."

Letting go of the wheel, I sit back and just look at him. Now this is uncomfortable. I'd rather be mentally undressed by every skeezebag out there than be stuck in this moment with Teddy. It's just a giant spotlight on what used to be and what is now.

I sigh. "I know."

"It was so easy in the beginning."

"There's more emotional real estate in between us than there was then. Our reunion was confusing, we checked every box you could check, and then we closed ourselves off. And now we're spending hours in a car together to appease friends. We can't force ourselves to go back in time."

I watch as he worries his lip, his thumb running over the silver of his ring before finally looking back at me. "But do you want to go forward with me in your life?" he asks, each word deliberate.

Yes, I think to myself, *but also no*. "I don't know yet. I don't know the Teddy of today yet. And frankly, you don't know me. I don't know if I've changed all that much in general, but when it comes to you..." I let out a long, exhausted sigh and glance over at him. "Your choice has had an effect on how I conduct myself in relationships." I put the truck back into drive. "Let's just get to the site and go from there."

For the remainder of the short drive to the campsite, I remind myself that when it's all out, it will stop feeling like we're going in circles.

Teddy helps me get everything hooked up. I'd had a lesson and watched countless YouTube videos, but I had visions of doing something wrong. I was grateful for his help but even more grateful that he didn't do everything like he was teaching me.

While he takes Kevin for a walk, I start making dinner. There was no kitchen in the trailer since all but the bathroom had been converted into shelving space for books, but I'd stowed away a bag of charcoal and various utensils for making meals. I refused to spend the next month living on restaurant food, not that I expected to be in the vicinity of many restaurants. We certainly wouldn't be stumbling across a Starbucks anytime soon.

"There's a lake about ten minutes down that trail," Teddy says, coming around the airstream carrying a very tired-looking Kevin.

"Ah buddy," I coo, standing from the pot of simmering broth, "are your little legs no match for Teddy's?"

"He did okay, considering." Teddy chuckles, handing him over to me and going to stir the pot. "Want me to toss the noodles in?"

I look down and realize that if we wait much longer I'll have boiled the liquid so far down that there won't be enough left to cook the noodles. "Yeah, probably a good idea." I set Kevin down and can't hold back a laugh when he immediately flops onto the ground. "Should I feed him?"

"I'll do it after we finish. If he eats too early, he'll have me up at the crack of dawn for breakfast."

"Don't you usually wake up at the crack of dawn?"

He nods. "I was hoping to learn how to sleep in again on this trip. And that won't happen if this guy thinks it's his job to wake the world at four a.m."

"Four a.m.? Is that the crack of dawn?"

"No, but he doesn't know that. I thought you were a morning person?"

"I am, but I'm not a dawn person," I clarify, sitting in one of the chairs I'd unpacked. "And even then I like to stay in bed for a solid twenty minutes after I wake up before I get up and begin my day."

"Can't do that when you've got twenty-plus dogs barking below you." Teddy grins at me, and I have the sudden desire to see him first thing in the morning. I'd seen it once, and it had been pretty glorious. But that was twenty-two-year-old Teddy. Thirty-four-year-old Teddy is a whole other level of delicious.

TEDDY

Nellie calls it a night early, and I can't decide if it's an avoidance technique or if she's tired from the drive. I choose to believe she's just tired.

I'm not ready to test out the back seat yet so I grab my book and read until my eyes are straining with only the dying fire-light. By the time I force myself to get some sleep, the sound of mosquitos and the odd branch snapping are the only sounds around. I had hoped to hear a loon, hoped that maybe we'd gotten lucky with the nearby lake, but no calls come.

Tossing and turning on a back bench seat of a pickup truck is one of the least ideal ways to spend the night. I'd rather accept the disdain in Nellie's eyes for the rest of the trip than sleep in here again. When dawn breaks through the trees, I officially give up and swing my body into a sitting position, rousing Kevin from where he's curled into a tight sausage ring.

He stretches and gives a little grunt, and I reach down to scratch behind his ears as a consolation. "Sorry, bud. I think I jinxed us by opening my mouth last night."

The morning is already warmer than I expected, and I

decide to change into swim trunks and a sweatshirt, snap on Kevin's lifejacket, and head to the little lake we found yesterday. Nothing like a whole lake to yourself to start the day.

Except someone else seems to have had the same idea. There is a towel folded on a log and a pair of flip-flops next to it. I scan the water but don't see anyone so take a few more steps towards the shore.

Nellie's head breaks through the surface seconds later, and I can't hold back my smile. She doesn't notice me right away and glides across the smooth surface on her back, eyes closed, fully at peace. Of course, that's when Kevin decides to lose his mind and goes bounding to the water, his hoarse little bark echoing across the lake.

"Well, now the forest is awake too, Kev, thanks."

Nellie's head is turned in our direction, and her hand lifts to offer a dripping wave. I nod back and stay where I am, remembering. Our last day together we'd been swimming. Nellie in that polka dot one-piece, looking straight out of a pinup poster minus the red lips. The memory stirs something deep within me, and I let myself slip back there for a few minutes. Back when things were perfect.

"Are you coming in?" Her voice breaks through my thoughts, and I look up in time to see her swimming towards me. She stands where the water is waist-deep, and I feel the breath leave my body. The suit has the same lines as the one from the past, but it's solid blue with white borders, and past Nellie has nothing on present Nellie with the way she fills it out. She's got her hair up, but the pieces that have come loose, stick to her skin. I want to brush them away from her face so a single freckle isn't hidden. Her tattoos are a stark contrast to the prim suit, and my fingers itch to trace each one. There are so many new ones to discover.

I am ogling her, I know I am, so I force myself to look at her face. Despite the warmth of the morning, her lips are trembling enough that I can see it from where I stand. "I, I... um, I don't want to barge into your space."

She looks around holding her arms out. "Teddy, I think this is more than enough space for two people and a dog."

"I thought I had to go in first to check for leeches?" I suddenly remember.

Nellie shrugs, and I momentarily find my attention drawn to her shoulder. The water droplets speckled there around the cluster of five freckles I once claimed with my lips. Then she lifts her foot out of the water, and I see she's in water shoes.

"You do realize they don't just go after feet, right?"

"I know, but I figure this lowers the odds of meeting one." She lowers herself back into the water and begins to retreat. "It's nice. You should come in." Smiling, she disappears back under the water.

She's not going to have to suggest twice. I slip off my sandals and sweatshirt and step into the water holding Kevin.

It's fucking freezing. I don't know how she's out there swimming like it's lukewarm. I can't turn back now though, so I take a few more steps, feeling the goosebumps rise across my body. Lowering Kevin so his feet touch, I hear Nellie's laugh ring out across the lake. Kevin's legs immediately start moving in a swimming motion, but he's pulled them above the water.

"That alone would be worth finding a leech." She swims closer to us. "Want me to take him so you can get it over with?"

"Get what over with?" I ask without looking up, which takes all my effort.

"The plunge," she says dramatically. "Once you get in past your, um..." The pause has me glancing up, thinking she's noticed the tattoo on my chest. But instead, my eyes are on her just in time to see her tongue swipe across her lips, those dark blue eyes glued to my abs. "Middle section."

"My eyes are up here, Nellie." I point at my face and watch as a blush spreads up her chest to her cheeks. I want to track it with my tongue, kiss every millimeter of where the pink touches her.

She laughs. "You get those from climbing trees?"

"Among other ways," I grin back.

She only blinks back at me and then reaches out. "I'll take Kevin, you dive in." Kevin swims through the air adorably, and when Nellie's hands connect with mine I have the urge to throw the dog off to the side and pull her to me. He'd be fine; he's got the lifejacket. Thankfully, Nellie's got a firm grip of the dog before I've finished the thought.

The cool of the water enveloping me puts a quick stop to my thoughts of what I'd do once I got Nellie against me. But she was right, because of course she was; it is better once I'm submerged. The water is murky, but I can just make out Nellie's legs from where I am. Instead of swimming back to her though, I take off in the opposite direction just to stretch my body out. The movements feel good, and within a few minutes, I'm feeling a bit more balanced than I had when I woke up.

"He's a natural," Nellie gushes when I return. Kevin is swimming after her as she propels herself backward.

This is the most unreserved I've seen her since those few minutes of total abandon in the car. Her smile is wide, and she's laughing as the dog chases her slowly through the water. Looking around, taking in the view, I breathe deeply, and allow myself to be present. Trees, water, blue sky, a dog, and best of all, Nellie.

"Tell me," Nellie says, handing me a mug of coffee with one hand while the other holds out a tray of maple cream cookies. "Tell me before we leave here."

I take the coffee and wave away the cookies. "Are you sure?"

"Consider this me taking the plunge, ripping off the Band-Aid. You and I were never good at taking it slowly, anyway. Why start now with the truth?" She says it with such conviction I launch straight into the truth I promised her.

"Some of this is going to be a repeat of what I told you years ago, but I feel like I need to say it to keep things straight."

"However you need to tell me is fine, as long as it's the truth."

"It is." I take a deep breath to collect myself. I haven't been this vulnerable in front of anyone in a while, and it feels like it carries more weight being like this in front of Nellie. "My mom had a cerebral aneurysm rupture when I was twelve." She nods; that part she knows. "Well, when they took her into surgery that first time, they found another one, another aneurysm. They couldn't get to it without possibly doing further damage, and because they didn't know how much damage had been done from the first one, they didn't want to risk it. So they waited until Mom was conscious enough to see how she was cognitively, and the surgeons gave her and my dad the options. Operate and possibly prevent a future rupture, but with the risk of her getting worse. Or leave it and basically hope it didn't rupture. They gave her five years. Will said she'd been acting a bit different the morning she died. She clearly had a headache, but she wouldn't admit it."

Nellie is sitting across from me, but I can tell she is fighting with herself to stay put. If she touches me right now I'm not sure I'll be able to finish. I'll break.

"Everyone knew," I say quietly.

"Knew what?" Nellie asks, leaning forward.

"Everyone knew that there was another aneurysm that could rupture. They all walked on pins and needles, and I never realized why."

"Wait, how come you didn't know?" Her face scrunches in confusion, as if what I'm speaking in another language.

"They didn't want to tell me. Zoe found out by accident, and Mom wanted at least one of her kids not to treat her like a porcelain doll."

"When did you find out?"

"On the side of the mountain we were spreading her ashes on."

She shakes her head. "A mountain?"

"In BC. She was from out there and wanted her ashes to be in the winds or some shit with her parents."

I watch as she swallows and stares at me for a breath. "So." She swallows again, blinking rapidly as if to keep from crying. "So, you found out this huge secret far from home, grieving and vulnerable."

"That's the gist of it, yep."

"Teddy, I'm—" I watch a single tear slip down her cheek and can't stand it.

"Don't say sorry," I say, cutting her off. "Let's remove that word from our vocabulary, at least when it comes to one another."

"Okay." She nods, although her eyes are a beacon of sorry.

We sit with the truth for a few minutes before Nellie breaks the silence. "So your mom died suddenly, and everyone but you knew it was coming?"

I nod, anger giving way to the grief that still lives deep within me. "Imagine finding out after it was too late that you should have been soaking up every single moment you had with the person you loved most."

When I look up from my hands I see the realization in her face. "But you were with me all the time." I nod again. "So you were mad at me too," she states matter-of-factly.

"I thought I was, in the beginning, but no, Nellie, I was never actually mad at you. I was mad at my family for robbing me of the choice. I would have still wanted to be around you all the time. But I probably would have been more open to you being around my family more too, if that was something you would have been open to."

"Of course I would have been open to that, Teddy. I so desperately wanted to be part of your life and vice versa."

She rises as if to come to me, and I raise a hand, hoping to stop her, then watch in relief as she sits back down. "I'm not telling you any of this for pity or so that you'll want some kind of relationship with me. I'm telling you this because I owed it to you after what I did. It took me months to get my head somewhat on straight, and I could have reached out then, but I wasn't ready and I was afraid of your reaction. Anger is one thing. Pity is too much. I got it enough because of Mom's death."

Nellie may not be saying it, but she is oozing *I'm sorry* with every blink, every move of her lips. *I'm sorry* is sitting in wait like a predator.

"We should get going. I'm sure you want to get to the middle of nowhere well before the crowds show up."

She smiles at me, the pity fading from her eyes. "Probably should have hired security for crowd control," she says thoughtfully.

"Nah, I can deal with the crowds." I flex my arms. "Only guns I need." The roll of her eyes sends the last of the sadness rolling along with them, and when she looks at me again it's just with the clear deep pools of blue I fell into years ago.

Packing everything up takes very little effort, and we are

back on the road in no time. At the end of the campground's road, I feel pressure on my arm and look down to see Nellie's hand.

"I missed you, Teddy," she says, giving my arm a friendly squeeze and then turning her attention back to the road ahead.

I missed her too, so fucking much.

TWENTY-EIGHT

The drive to the middle of nowhere isn't as uncomfortable as the trip had been yesterday, but we're still not overly chatty. Telling me probably made Teddy relive some of what he had been through twelve years previously. And I've spent the majority of the three-hour drive processing what he said.

When I told him I had missed him, it was the truth, and it felt as close to sorry as I could get. The truth doesn't stop me from wishing he had reached out at some point in those first couple of weeks, but I also understand more now why he hadn't. Still, I can't help wondering where we would be today if he had talked to me. Would we have even met if he'd known the truth? Selfishly, I hope so, because despite the immense amount of hurt I felt, having Teddy even for a little while would have been better than not having him at all.

"What's on your mind?" Teddy's voice cuts through my thoughts.

"Hmm?" I glance over.

"You look like you're ready to storm a building."

"I'm just thinking."

"That's obvious. What are you thinking about?"

"Nothing," I say with a wave of my hand.

"So, about what I told you, then."

"Can you blame me?"

"No, not at all. I'm still thinking about it over a decade later. You're allowed to dwell for as long as you want." *I just hope you don't take too long* goes unsaid, but I know he's thinking it.

"I think I'm going through the stages of grief, or I'm beginning to anyway."

"Skip right to anger?'

"No. My first thought was it can't be that simple." I keep my eyes on the road because I don't think I can look at him right now. "So, denial. Denial that you had a legitimate reason and that the reason wouldn't destroy me the way I had expected."

"What had you expected?" he asks quietly.

"That what we had had all been in my head and you just got tired of it. That I was too clingy. That at twenty-two, you weren't ready to feel..." I can feel the tears burning behind my eyes and stop. I see him move out of the corner of my eye, but I lean away and he drops his hand on the console briefly before returning it to rest on a sleeping Kevin.

"Nellie," he starts but I shake my head and he stops.

"Fuck," I mutter, bringing my hand to wipe my leaky left eye. "I don't want to talk right now okay, at least not about this. I'm still processing."

"Okay. Do you want to talk about anything?"

"What are your plans for the shelter up here?"

"Honestly, Bennett said 'Tour the facility.'"

"Is there something special about it?"

"Not that I know of. I was instructed to help out if they

needed to transport dogs south. Marley also wants me to check out their adoption process."

"Does she think it will help you go through with one?" I laugh.

"I think that's her hope. She just wants Bennett to learn how to let go a bit more, I think. He gets attached easily."

"Exhibit A: Marley."

Teddy starts laughing, and the sound makes me smile. "He tried to tell me that he hadn't dwelled on her coming back."

"I was there the day she left. I've never seen someone look at another person that way before." The look on Teddy's face when he realized it was me came close, but it had faded almost as fast. Bennett's never budged. Not until we were driving away, and heartbreak crackled across his face. "Honestly, I nearly pushed Marley out of the car."

"I met him mid-pining," Teddy says, looking out the window. "He kept this list, Things to Tell Marley, but Cass and I would find notes around the barn. Like he randomly thought of something and grabbed the nearest thing to write it down. 'At therapy today all we did was talk about you." Stuff like that."

"Marley told us he had a long list of moments to tell her about. Sometimes I check in with her just to make sure he hasn't vanished."

Teddy looks over at me like I've lost it. "Oh, he's not going anywhere without her," he assures me.

"No, but he may vanish because he's not actually real."

"He's not perfect, Nell...ie." Teddy tacks the end on my name almost as if it's an afterthought. "Nell" felt right, but it was also a reminder of where things still stand between us.

"I know that. No one is perfect."

"Sophie's boyfriend seems to think he's pretty damn close."

"You got that from the one time you met him?" I roll my

eyes. Men are so threatened by one another. Sophie Hore, the daughter of Bennett's neighbors, introduced us all to her boyfriend at Christmas. He's a few years older than her and quite established, but there's nothing wrong with that.

"No, I get that from the three times I've met Gregory-not-Greg, and because of the things Karl and Cass have said about him. Although Cass tends to bring her brother Foster into every conversation about Sophie and Greg." I laugh at the way he says "Greg" in such a mocking tone, as if he knows the guy will sense the short form, and Teddy is reveling in it.

"He's nice, though, right?" I don't know Sophie that well, but she is one of those people you'd thowdown for in a heartbeat without a history with.

"Foster? I have no idea, I've never met the guy. If he's anything like Cass, he's probably great. All I know is that he's a ginger too and he lives abroad, but that's about it."

"No, not Foster, Gregory," I clarify, forcing a terrible British accent.

"He's just an academic."

I force my lips to stay shut. I work in a university library and consider myself to be a bit of an academic, not to mention my father is an actual academic.

"Not that that's a bad thing," Teddy finally continues. I don't know if he realized what he said was somewhat offensive or if he just didn't know how to carry on with his thoughts. "He's the kind of guy who will stand up on a plane when someone calls for a doctor. Bro, you know damn well what kind of doctor they need, chill."

"Okay, I guess he did give off those vibes," I agree. "How is Zoe?" I realize we are doing an excellent job talking about other people in our lives rather than addressing the elephant in the room, but we're talking and that seems to be more important.

"She's"—there's a brief pause—"good. She's married with a

kid and another one on the way." We can circle back to that pause later.

"And your brother?"

"Married too. Three kids, a white picket fence, and a golden retriever."

"You sound surprised telling me that."

"That's because I am still surprised." Teddy guffaws. "I think we both expected to be in the other's shoes."

"You with the idyllic nuclear family and him the nomad?"

"Well...Maybe just the nomad part."

It feels like we have circled back to where we start discussing his mom and why he left, so when I see our destination is only five minutes away, I feel a wave of relief wash over me.

"Marmot Point," Teddy reads the name on the map. "There's probably some dark reason behind the name."

"Probably sounded better than Groundhog Point," I say as I slowly enter the hamlet.

I was told to park at the gas station, which has one very old pump. The building itself appears to serve as the post office, liquor store, and... "Does that say taxidermist?" Teddy asks, squinting at the sign squeezed between the two others. I see him pull Kevin into himself a bit tighter and can't help the smile that spreads on my face.

"It's not exactly what you expect to see, but I guess you make do."

"Well, no, for sure." Teddy nods. "Every town needs a gas station, liquor store, and good taxidermist. Those are the essentials."

"Absolutely," I agree, slipping out of the truck and immediately stretching.

Through the window, I watch Teddy do the same, and I allow my eyes to lock onto the slip of his abdomen that's revealed when his shirt lifts a few inches above the waistband of his pants. Teddy had been all lean muscle when he was twenty-two, but there is nothing lean about the man in front of me. It's not that he's bulging or bulky; it's more that he now has the body of someone who worked to get it rather than just existing with it. I can feel my cheeks heat when I remember how he caught me staring at the lake. I never thought of myself as a hairy-chest lover, but on Teddy, I have the urge to grab on and never let go.

"Earth to Nellie," I hear my name, and my vision starts to clear.

Teddy is leaning into the truck looking at me like I've lost my mind. "You good? It was like you were in a trance."

I slap on a smile and shake my head. "Too much driving, I think. I'm good."

"That who we're meeting?" He points towards an older woman who seems to have materialized out of nowhere. She's got an old Toronto Maple Leafs hat pulled low, a long-sleeved shirt, cargo pants, and some pretty heavy-duty-looking boots on. Behind her there are seven children, walking in single file, wearing nearly the same thing.

"I have no idea." I shrug, unable to look away from the troop as they march towards us.

"It's like the Von Trapp kids, but a northern Ontario edition," Teddy murmurs from beside me. I have no idea when he moved, but I am far too enamored with the sight in front of me to care.

"Cornelia?" the woman says as she nears.

"Cornelia?" Teddy chuckles.

I elbow him before stepping forward and holding out my hand. "Margaret?"

"Only my husband called me Margaret, and that old

bastard took that name to the grave with him six years ago. It's Midge."

"Midge," I say, shaking her much rougher hand. "Please call me Nellie. Only my parents and people who have access to my government ID call me Cornelia."

"Nellie." Midge smiles warmly at me before turning her attention to Teddy. "And who's the wiener?"

I look up at Teddy, horrified, only to realize he's holding Kevin. "This is Kevin," Teddy says easily.

"And you handle the wiener?" Midge asks, completely straight-faced.

"I am the wiener handler, yes," he replies, equally straight-faced.

"Midge." She holds her hand out, and Teddy shifts Kevin so he can take it.

"Teddy."

"Well," Midge says, relaxing her stance and glancing back at the kids, who have remained in single file. "I guess we should get down to business. These are the majority of the kids in town." She gestures behind her, and I admit, I'm a bit disappointed when each kid doesn't step forward and introduce themself in song.

"Just seven?"

"Seven of the twelve permanent minors in town. There are a few more who come up at different times during the year. These happen to be my grandchildren. My sons and their wives work for the mill so the kids spend most of their time with me. I'm grandma as well as their teacher. Taught for thirty-five years down in Windsor before we moved up here to be closer to the kids and grandkids."

"Wow, that's dedication," I say, amazed by someone's willingness to move from a city to a place with a gas station-liquor store-taxidermist combo.

"That's love." Midge smiles up at us, her eyes dancing between Teddy and me. "Grumpy Al's got the plans all set up in the office." She starts to walk towards the tiny building, and it takes a second before my feet begin to follow her.

"Should—ah, the kids, Midge?"

"Hmm?" She turns mid-stride and waves us off. "They'll find something to do. Devon," she yells, and I watch a blond boy peek around a taller boy. "No roadkill today. If you see something, leave it for the crows."

"What if—"

"Not even if it's a saber-tooth tiger young man," she calls back as she continues her walk. "Boy's got an unhealthy love of turning dead things into decor," she mutters, shaking her head. "Not saying there's no future in it, but there's no future in any more glass-eyed raccoons in my living room, that's for certain."

Teddy slows his stride to match it with hers. "To be fair," Teddy says, "if he found a saber-tooth tiger, I'd suggest that be an exception to the rule."

"I bet you would," Midge replies, her gaze assessing as it goes from the top of his head to his shoes before she pushes into the building. "Al, you in here?"

"Goddamn, Magpie, you don't gotta shout. I'm not deaf yet. You keep that up, though, and it won't be long." A very tall, very gangly man rises from behind the small counter that houses an old cash register, chocolate bars, gum, a stack of pamphlets, bug and bear spray, and a sign that says LIVE BAIT. "Ah." His brown eyes crinkle with a smile when he sees us. "You must be the book people."

"Librarians, Al," Midge says, leaning against the counter and rolling her eyes. "This is Nellie, the wiener is Kevin, and the one holding the wiener is Teddy."

"George," Al introduces himself.

I look at Teddy who just shrugs. "Oh, so not Al?" I clarify, reaching out to take his hand.

Al or George laughs softly and looks down at Midge with an expression I can't quite read. "Only Magpie calls me Al."

"Okay, George it is."

"Now I know you had a plan for where they could set up, but I was thinking maybe I should look at it before they do," Midge says, very business-like.

"Magpie, just because five Marmots agreed you should be their representative in regional disputes does not make you the city planner. I've got them setting up shop at the north side of the lot, far enough from the road to keep the kids safe from traffic and a good distance from the woods to keep them safe from ornery mooses."

"It's moose, Al, for the three thousandth time. The plural for moose is moose."

"And for the three thousandth time, I've been saying mooses for seventy-two years, and I ain't changing now."

"So the setup area?" Teddy interrupts the argument about the moose, and both George and Midge look in our direction.

"I'll take you over there now, and you can get situated." George comes around the counter, ducking under the fishing nets hung across a beam.

"Other than my brood, you should be expecting some locals to visit within the next couple of hours. I told everyone they had to be here and gone before five," Midge prattles on as we all follow George out of the store.

"Oh, they don't have to be so precise," I insist.

"Nellie, if you give these Marmotans an inch, they will take it and stretch it into a mile. Best set a hard time and be done with it."

"She's not wrong there," George calls over his shoulder.

"Besides, that will give you two plenty of time to get set up in the bunkie before dinner."

"Bunkie? Oh, Teddy has a tent, and there's a bed..."

"I told the lady from the library...Amaranth?"

Amaranth? "Amelia?" I ask. My boss has a very slight accent, but I can't imagine her name would have sounded that far off.

"Ah, yes, reception isn't what we're known for up here." Midge laughs off the misunderstanding. "Amelia is much less of a mouthful. Anyhow, I told her you'd have proper accommodations for the time you were here with us."

"That really isn't—" I try and continue only to be cut off again.

"The bathroom isn't the most ideal, but other than a few bugs and the odd porcupine mucking about, it's private and has a real flushing toilet."

I look up at Teddy who mouths, "A flushing toilet," as his eyebrows bounce up and down.

George stops in front of a patch of gravel, outlined in orange paint about fifty meters behind the gas station that is about an equal distance from the road and the forest. "This is it, the literary playground," he says dramatically.

"It's ah, well, perfect. Thank you, George," I say, taking in the area I'll be parking the Airstream on. There's enough room to have a couple of portable shelves outside as well as a few folding chairs for those who'd like to read and return within the same day. The gravel isn't ideal for the outdoor rug, but the rug will still add to the atmosphere. "I'll just go bring the trailer around, then we can start getting set up."

Teddy follows me back to the truck and the minute the doors are closed he lets out a laugh.

"What's so funny?"

"This entire thing is going to be a blast. I feel like we fell through the looking glass. I'm only slightly disappointed that Midge isn't a rabbit and George isn't a moose himself."

TWENTY-NINE

TEDDY

Only about twenty very enthusiastic people visit the library on our first afternoon, and most of them spend the majority of their time playing with Kevin. Apparently, a dog of his size is unusual around these parts. "Good-sized meal for a decent-sized bird," George had said, squinting up at the sky.

Nellie is in her element. She has helped several of Midge's grandkids find books highlighting their favorite hobbies, including a taxidermy for dummies book for Devon. He insisted he wasn't a dummy, but once he opened the book, we'd lost him for the remainder of the day.

"How long can we have a book for?" one of Midge's grandkids asks me.

"Oh, um," I stammer, looking around for Nellie who had just been rearranging some books on the one carousel. "Just let me—" I hold up a finger and head towards the Airstream.

Nellie is bent at the waist, rooting through a crate of books, and it stops me in my tracks. It hasn't been lost on me how the dark denim of her jeans hugs every curve from her waist down, but in this position it freezes me, even my breathing seems to have halted. I shamelessly watch as she shifts her weight and pops a hip before peeking back at me.

"Can I help you, Teddy?"

What I want to say is, "Yes, but you'll have to remove my pants because I can't seem to move at the minute. Then maybe we can just bang it out, and maybe, just maybe, this unbearable need I feel every time I look at you will ease a bit." The skin on my palms almost begins to itch with the need to feel that ass in my hands again, like in her car and all those years ago in the pool. A sensory memory that has never faded.

I finally manage to swallow and clear my throat, "Uh, one of the kids was asking about borrowing time for the books."

Nellie straightens and slowly turns towards me. "Seven days, although unlike a regular library, we don't have cards to track or fines for being late. I asked about maybe doing a temporary card system, but that would have been too expensive. And this was already a gamble with the cost of the Airstream and me being gone for so long. Anyway, you asked a simple question, and that was a diatribe. Seven days is the official time." She looks nervous suddenly. She used to look like that when she'd get lost in a thought. Telling me about a bird or some fact she'd read about. I'm not turned on so much now but I seem to be lost in my astonishment.

She's so similar to how she was before. The way she holds eye contact with me and the slight tilt of her head. I'm still stuck in place when her face crinkles in concern. "Are you okay?"

"Yeah, no, totally fine, maybe just a bit tired."

She nods in understanding. "You'll definitely sleep better in the bunkie." She turns back to the crate and grabs a few books before moving towards me, or the door.

"Oh no, you can have the bunkie, I'm fine in the truck."

She stops in front of me, her eyes nearly at the same height as mine as I remain a couple of steps down. "Teddy, I could practically hear the truck rocking last night while you tossed and turned. And unless you had a surprise guest, I'm guessing it wasn't because you were sleeping well."

"Okay, so the truck isn't the most comfortable thing in the world, but I can't imagine that two-inch mattress is much better," I say, pointing up at the just visible flip-down bed.

Nellie's eyes follow my hand. "No, but my whole body fits on it so I can stretch out."

"I'm also not leaving you out here alone while I go to wherever the hell this bunkie is."

"I don't need your protection, Teddy." Nellie's expression has turned stormy. I know she's about to give me a lecture on how just because she's a woman that doesn't mean she needs some man to watch out for her.

"I know you don't need protection, Nellie," I cut in. "You're very capable. I just know that no mattress is going to help me sleep better if you're not nearby. Maybe it's me that needs protection, ever think of that?"

Nellie gives me a very long, slow, deliberate once-over before stepping even closer. I can smell the lake on her mingling with her soap. Her breath tickles my ear as she says, "It's me you'd need protection from, Teddy."

I'm left wondering what the hell that means as she pushes past me and back outside. I don't know how she made it sound like a threat and a proposition. And I don't know how the hell I'm even more turned on now with the thought of it being both. Prying my feet from where they have been stuck to the steps, I close myself in the tiny bathroom just to collect myself.

When my mind and body have calmed down enough for me to leave the trailer, I find Nellie chatting animatedly to a guy only slightly taller than her. Part of my brain tells me to stomp over there, punch the guy, and carry her away. Clearly the less evolved part of my brain. The other part wants me to let things go because Nellie can do whatever she wants, which includes talking to and flirting with whomever she likes.

"Dad!" I hear Devon call out, and I look up to see the guy squat down as Devon approaches with a book. The guy looks up at Nellie and smiles, and I watch as she lowers herself to join in on the show and tell. *She doesn't want kids*, I remind myself. But she had admitted that to me at twenty; my brother changed his mind at thirty. People change their minds.

"He's a flirt, just like his dad," Midge says, making me jump halfway out of my skin.

"Sorry?"

"My son." She nods towards the guy. "Only one of my boys who's single, but that's his own doing."

"Because he's a flirt?" I force myself to look down at her.

"That, and he let his wife leave. Didn't fight for her."

"Maybe she didn't want to be fought for," I suggest, looking back at Nellie who is laughing at something Devon is animatedly describing.

Midge is quiet for a minute, and when I look back she's studying me. "Hmm." She narrows her eyes. "You're not together."

"Nope."

"But you want to be together."

"Nope." I shake my head.

"Liar." She smirks up at me. "But then again, you are a man, so it's a habit."

"I'm not lying."

She studies me some more before shaking her head. "Then you're a dumbass."

"Wow." I can't help but laugh. "I don't know what's worse."

"If you're lying about wanting to be together, there's a reason. If you really think you don't want to be together, then,

Mr. Wiener Handler, that's all you're ever going to be, a wiener handler. You can take that however you'd like to."

She walks away from me to join the remaining grandchildren gathered on the rug, fawning over Kevin.

Instead of trying to figure out how I've just been insulted, I begin to take some pictures of the setup, careful not to get any faces in the images. Kevin's nose poking under a thigh and then over a shoulder, through a fan of hair. Nellie crouched down, laughing with a kid and his flirtatious father. A moose wandering across the road towards us. Holy shit.

"Um, Midge," I whisper as loudly as possible. "A moose is heading our way."

Midge stands quickly and looks towards the road. I watch in awe as she squares her shoulders and marches towards the giant creature. "Now, Morticia, we've talked about this. You stay on that side of the road until the people are gone, missy." Midge is still heading towards the moose, and she's got her finger out wagging away. She appears to be lecturing the lumbering animal. "I know you're starved for attention, but you'll simply have to wait." She stops at the edge of the road and plants her hands on her hips. The moose, to her credit, has stopped halfway and seems to be weighing her options. She's massive, and honestly it seems likely that if she wanted, any option at all is open for the taking. But after a few seconds of deliberation, she seems to decide with a great sigh to turn around and head back into the woods she came from.

Midge watches her disappear into the bush until no sign of her remains before turning and heading back towards us. "That's our cue to head home, troop," she hollers. "Let's help Nellie and Teddy get things cleaned up, and we can lead them back to the homestead."

"Staying in the bunkie, eh?" I hear Midge's son say.

"Well, Teddy is. I'll be back here." She points at the trailer, and I watch in horror as a slow smile creeps along the guy's lips. People look at me and think I'm the kind of guy who has gotten into my share of brawls, but the truth is I've never actually thrown a punch that wasn't at Will. I'm the kind of guy who would walk towards a prospective fight and have to repeat, "Your thumb stays on the outside of your fist" the entire time.

"If you want any company, just say the word." I overhear him say, and I cannot contain the disgust I feel that he just said that to her in front of his kid.

"Oh, don't worry, I will." Nellie smiles at him as she walks away, her hips swaying more than usual. The guy with no boundaries watches her walk away, his eyes glued to her ass, his tongue clenched between his teeth.

When I turn my attention to Nellie, it's obvious by her expression that the tone and way she's walking away is not conveying how she feels. Her jaw is clenched tight and her brow is furrowed as if she's holding herself back from letting the guy know how she really feels.

Twelve years ago, Nellie lied to me about having a boyfriend to avoid being hit on. Today, she could have easily used me as an excuse and didn't, despite being visibly uncomfortable. If she thinks for one second that I'm sleeping farther from her than I have to be, she's in for a rude awakening.

THIRTY

NELLIE

Tanner—thirty-six, father of two, estranged from his wife, blond hair, hazel-eyed—McIntyre immediately plants himself beside me at the picnic table in Midge's yard. His plate is piled high with two burgers and a sausage on a bun, potato and maca- roni salad, and three kinds of pickled vegetables. He's already chewing when his ass hits the bench.

"You're gonna love staying here," he sputters around a mouthful of something brown.

"Is it the company that will win me over?" I ask, biting into a carrot stick.

He takes a swig from his beer, swallows, and gives me a big smile. "Oh, it's definitely the company." He continues to watch me while we eat, as if I've given off some vibe that having my every move watched is a turn-on. For the record, it is not. At least not when it's Tanner's eyes on me.

As subtly as I can manage, I look around the yard trying to pinpoint where Teddy is. It takes me no time to spot him, even through the deer fencing. He's slowly walking through the garden with Florence, Midge's oldest granddaughter. I see her gesturing to different plants and Teddy's appropriately enthusiastic response. I don't need to know his background to know he's in his element out there. He looks like he was meant to be out there with the growing things.

"My wild girl," Midge says fondly, sitting down across from us. "She took to the garden like a duck to water. It's nice of him to indulge her."

"Oh, I guarantee it's not a hardship for him. Teddy is a nature guy."

I watch Midge study the pair for a while longer before she nods. "I see it."

"He doesn't look like a hippie," Tanner scoffs.

"He's not," I say, a tad defensively. "He just has a deep respect for the environment. Teddy has a degree in Environmental Science and spent years traveling the world working as an arborist."

"You together?" Tanner asks, his eyes narrowing.

I answer "No" at the same time Midge says "Yes."

I see a warning in Midge's eyes and settle on, "It's complicated."

He holds his beer out to me, and I tap it with my can of root beer. "Been there. So, uh, before, you weren't flirting back?"

I mean, I kind of was but not really in a I-hope-this-goes-somewhere kind of way, which I realize now seems cruel. "No?" it comes out like a question, and I hope he drops it.

"Cool, cool, good to know." The whole cocky guy aura Tanner has been glowing with fades, and he looks almost relieved.

"Hey Dad?" Devon says, sitting down beside Tanner.

"What's up, bud?"

"Catelyn said Mom's getting us at the end of the summer, is that true?"

Tanner looks over at Midge. "Mom?"

Midge shrugs. "News to me, kid."

"Can you go find your sister and you two can meet me inside in a few minutes?"

Devon nods, and Tanner begins cleaning up his half-eaten dinner, his appetite seemingly snuffed out by talk of his wife. "If I don't see you before you folks head out, thanks for doing this library thing. The town needed some excitement." He smiles sadly at me before making his way into the house.

"He's not a terrible guy," Midge says, her eyes on her son. "He's just unsure of himself, and because of that, he can be a bit too forward, a bit too much for some. I think he took my criticisms about him not fighting for his wife as advice to jump into every possible new relationship with gusto."

"Overcorrection." I nod and look back toward the garden to see Teddy walking up the slope towards us. "I know what that's like."

"That garden is spectacular," Teddy gushes, sitting down where Tanner had just been, although he leaves more space between us than Tanner had.

Midge's eyes seem to register the distance, but her attention is quickly pulled to her left as Florence sits down. "It wasn't until this one," she says, wrapping her arm around her granddaughter's body and pulling her in. "I have no idea where she got her green thumb from, but we sure are glad she's willing to share it with us."

"I'm afraid of what's going to happen to the garden when I go away to school," Florence frets from behind a curtain of hair. She's certainly not as comfortable outside of the garden.

"What are you going to school for?" I ask, leaning into Teddy's heat.

"Plant science, and then I want to come back up here and use that to create more sustainable growing habits for a more northern climate."

I'm impressed. I don't know what I had expected, but it wasn't a group of kids so driven. Although, with Midge leading the way, it's not all that surprising. "That's really interesting," I say and hope she knows I'm being serious.

"That's only the second nerdiest major at this table." Teddy bumps my arm.

"By a long shot," I agree.

Midge bats us away when we try to help clean, and Teddy and I are left alone at the table in the fading light.

"I thought Bennett's was peaceful, but this place...It's on a whole other level." Teddy sighs, tipping his head back and breathing deeply.

I watch as his chest inflates and deflates and fight the urge to lay my head on it. "I'm sure the dogs have something to do with it." I look under the table to where Kevin is sprawled on his side and sound asleep. "That being said, seven kids is a lot."

"I don't know how Midge does it."

"Love, probably. That, and she spent so many years in classrooms, seven probably seems like nothing."

"Except at the end of the day they don't go home to their parents, they stay." Teddy stretches and then we sit in silence. An owl hoots from somewhere off in the trees and a tree groans, and still we sit, absorbing the silence as if we are drawing strength from it.

"My mom was a teacher," he says suddenly. "Her career was cut short, obviously, but she lived and breathed teaching. For a while, I thought about becoming one, but I just didn't like kids the way she did."

"You'd never guess it by the way you've been today. I bet she'd be proud to see how you are with them."

"I didn't say I hated kids, Nellie." He smiles over at me, and the silence somehow becomes even quieter. "I just don't love them the way she did." Those pale blues watch me for a few seconds. "You still on the no-kid track?"

I'd told him I didn't want kids that summer. We had been hanging out after one of his baseball games, and one of his teammates was trying to comfort his son who was having a meltdown about being given the wrong ball, even though it looked identical to all the others. It just came out of my mouth. "Ugh, I could never do that."

"Do what?" he'd asked.

"The kid thing."

I'd expected him to tell me I'd change my mind or that he desperately wanted them, but he'd just said, "Then we're on the same page." And we just left it there, a big-ticket conversation over in the blink of an eye.

"Staunchly," I say. "Same for you?"

"Same for me." He nods.

Midge breaks us out of the apparent trance we've both fallen into by inviting us to follow her to the bunkie.

"Both beds have fresh linens," she says, flinging the door open and leading us into a cramped single room with a single bed on each side. "Now I'd ask if there is going to be any hanky-panky, you move some blankets to the floor, since I'm not sure the beds could withstand what I'd imagine is vigorous lovemaking." She then winks at me and leaves.

We stand there, watching as she grows smaller in the distance, and then I hear Teddy start to laugh.

"I wonder if she's related to Cass. They have to share DNA," he says in wonderment.

"Because they're so blunt?"

He looks at me, and I can tell there is something specific he wants to say, but instead he just nods. "Please stay with me tonight."

I open my mouth to argue, but he continues, "I desperately

need to sleep, and I'm not going to if you're five kilometers away on the side of a road in the middle of nowhere. This is no different than sitting in the truck together. It's not like we're sleeping together-together."

He looks wary and exhausted, and so I agree. After both of us have completed our nighttime routines, the lights are off and we're in our respective beds.

"Are you sleeping?" I hear Teddy ask softly from across the room after a while.

"No," I reply.

"Why not?"

"I can hear you breathing." It's not the truth. I can't sleep because he's there, so close yet so far. A whole gulf of emotions shared and intimate histories spread out between us in the form of an old wood plank floor.

"I'm sorry, I'll try and breathe quieter," he says.

"It's not your breathing," I murmur, but no response comes, just the sound of a mattress shifting.

"Nellie. Nellie." Teddy's voice and the gentle push on my shoulder bring me into consciousness on our fourth morning in the bunkie.

"What?" I yawn.

"I found a lake."

"And you had to wake me up to tell me?" I'm so confused.

"The loons are out."

Loons. I sit up, and I feel him step back quickly, our foreheads brushing. I'm out of bed and slipping my shoes on so fast that I forget that the mornings are much cooler up here than they are at home. I'm halfway down the front steps when the cool air hits my arms. I turn to go back inside and run straight into Teddy. His arms wrap around me and keep me from falling backward.

"Arms up," he commands, and I follow without a second thought. Heavy fabric slips down my arms and over my head, and while my bare legs are still covered in goosebumps, at least my upper body is protected from the chill.

"Thanks," I get out before I'm striding the rest of the way to the ground and across the yard. Stopping abruptly, I turn to see Teddy on the other side of the bunkie.

"You could go that way, but you probably won't get to the lake before noon." I don't know why I assumed I knew where the hell I was going. Turning on my heel, I jog to catch up with Teddy and Kevin, who is eagerly prancing at his feet.

The minute I hear the loons, the frantic feeling I felt upon waking dissipates. How did he remember my love for loon song?

THIRTY-ONE

TEDDY

Watching Nellie listening to the loons is going to go down as one of the best moments of my life. Forget bungee jumping in New Zealand or volunteering with elephants in Thailand—this morning as the fog rises from the lake with Nellie beside me tops the list. For so long, this felt like the most unreachable goal, finding her again and convincing her to let me back in.

While she watches the lake, her eyes wet with emotion, I get the coffee ready. When I'd snuck out to the truck to grab the supplies, Midge caught me and had me come into the house for a thermos full of her freshly brewed stuff.

"I like it strong, but I have a feeling you'll both need it like this today," she'd said while sealing the thermos up and shooing me out the door.

"You made coffee?" Nellie asks, wide-eyed but reaching out eagerly.

"Midge made coffee. But I did contribute something," I say, reaching back into my pack and pulling out the box of maple creams.

"Oh yes." I can't help laughing at how her innocence transforms into greedy need.

"When did you become a cookies-for-breakfast person?" I ask, slipping one out for myself and watching as she dunks hers into the hot liquid for a few seconds before transferring it to her mouth. Her eyes close as the flavors hit her tongue and she looks completely blissed out. I suddenly want to make her face do that, no cookies or coffee involved, just Nellie and me.

She chews, swallows, and then shrugs. "My first job out of university, I had a coworker that made these incredible chocolate chip cookies. She'd bake them when she got up so they could cool while she got ready. I swear you could taste the dedication. I liked having one with my coffee in the afternoon, but did you know that caffeine can negatively impact your sleep?"

"Get out of town," I joke.

"Well, it's true. So I started having a cookie with my morning coffee, and then it just became a habit. I prefer a cookie with coffee, and since I don't drink coffee past noon, morning cookies it is."

"And when did you choose to have coffee with maple cookies?"

"That's a pure nostalgia thing." She smiles dreamily out at the lake. "My great-aunt and uncle had a cottage, and we'd go there in the summers. My aunt always bought those cookies. Since I was coming north, I figured I'd grab a pack. Kind of wishing I'd grabbed a few now." She watches me bite into the dry cookie, and her eyes narrow. "At least eat it properly, EG."

Dropping my hand, I stare back. "What?" she asks, her hand quickly brushing invisible crumbs from her mouth.

"You called me EG." *Do it again*, I want to beg. Teddy on her lips is music; EG is a fucking siren song.

"I did," she says slowly, as if she's just realizing it herself. "Feels right." She looks at me for another few seconds and then turns back to gaze out at the water, the loons greeting her attention with their calls to the morning.

"George was telling me there's a woman on the outskirts of town that's got a"—I raise my fingers in quotes—"'menagerie of manky mongrels,' and he was going to see if she wanted a visitor."

"That could be fun. Or hostile. May want to ask Marley for some advice." Nellie's eyes are still on the view in front of us, but she's smiling as she takes another sip of coffee. "What the hell would be considered the outskirts of this place? It kind of all feels like the outskirts." She's not wrong.

"He then told me the name, and it's the rescue Bennett wants me to go check out. So that's convenient."

Three mornings later, I'm hauling a shelf of books down the steps of the airstream while Nellie gets things organized for the day. Kevin has finally caught his tail and is currently rolling around with it in his mouth.

"Why does it feel like him doing that is the most productive any of us is going to be today?" Nellie asks, hands on hips, looking down at Kevin. The minute he sees her looking at him he drops his tail and bounds over. "Hey buddy," she coos, bending to pick him up. "Are you ready for more socializing?" Laughter bubbles out of her as Kevin goes in enthusiastically for all the licks. "Okay, okay, that's enough of that for today." Nellie lowers him back to the ground and uses the arm of her shirt to wipe her face.

"Mornin'," George calls from halfway across the lot. "Teddy, I got Betty on the phone, and she said she's already spoken to you. Also asked if you had any heartworm tablets?"

"Yeah, I've got a decent supply. Any clue how many she needs?"

George shrugs, looking lost. "Didn't ask, and she didn't say," he shouts as an ATV pulls up to the gas station. George waves to the person who gets off the machine. When they take off the helmet, I'm shocked to see someone far younger than I had expected. "That's Neulla. She'll be watching the place while we go."

"Oh, you're coming? And you want to go now?" I ask, looking over at Nellie.

"Just waiting for"—George turns to the trail from Midge's, and I see someone coming towards us—"Florence. Betty has quite the greenhouse, and that one never misses an opportunity to visit."

"Are you going to be okay?" I ask Nellie.

She rolls her eyes dramatically. "Well, I don't know, Teddy. It's an absolute madhouse here. At least I'll have Kevin to supervise."

"You joke, but a little power is going to go straight to his head. He's already a mini-Yogurt."

"A GoGurt?"

"Isn't that a travel yogurt?"

"Well, he is traveling," she counters.

"Touché." I laugh, gaze locked with Nellie's.

A throat clears, and she looks away.

"Well if you two are done whatever this is, we better head out. I told Midge I'd have Flo back by the end of the school day."

"Have fun, kids." Nellie tosses me the keys to the truck.

"She'll be fine," George says as we are pulling onto the road. I drop my gaze from the rearview mirror onto the road ahead. "You two could probably use some time apart anyway."

"The tension is three c's thick," Florence agrees from the back seat.

"I don't have a clue what that means," George grumbles. "But it sounds accurate. Turn left at the next road and then drive until it ends."

"Ominous."

"Just keep your eyes open for moose and their young."

"Hey, you said moose, plural."

"I know proper English." George grins over at me. "Getting Midge hot and bothered about grammar is what counts as entertainment around these parts."

"Gross," I hear Florence say quietly from behind me.

It turns out that the outskirts means a thirty-five-minute drive in any direction. George points at a crude hand-painted sign that reads Spencer Lake Rescue nailed to a tree at the end of a long gravel driveway and I turn in. Betty's property is, as expected, large. There is a barn with runs and kennels, and every single one has an occupant. Most look to be huskies or lab mixes. Working dogs. Florence is off to the large glass greenhouse behind the house the minute I put the truck in park.

"That'll be the last we see of her for a few hours," George says as we watch her rush away from us.

"Welcome!" A middle-aged woman with gray-streaked brown hair greets us from her porch, coffee mug in hand. She's wearing a flowing tunic and tights along with a pair of Birkenstocks.

"Thanks for putting clothes on for the occasion, Betty," George chuckles.

"I know how our lifestyle makes you uncomfortable." She waves away his comment. "You must be Teddy." She pushes my outstretched hand aside and pulls me in for a hug. "None of that stiff handshake shit here, city boy. We Marmotans hug."

"That Marmotan hugs," George corrects.

"Nice to meet you," I manage to get out as the woman crushes me to her.

"Coffee?" she asks, holding up her mug.

"I'm fine, thanks," I say, looking up at the two-story home with its weathered white siding and black trim.

"I'll take one if you don't mind. Is Joshua inside?" George asks, already halfway to the door.

"He should be in the living room. He insisted on doing everything himself this morning so he may be in quite a state."

"I am forewarned so I shall be forearmed," George orates before disappearing through the creaky door.

"My husband had a stroke in January." My face must convey my concern because she continues quickly, "He's here, that's what matters, but he did lose some mobility on his right side. A woman comes from the hospital in Timmins once a week for physio, but other than that, I'm his nurse, physiotherapist, and wife."

"I'm sorry to hear that. This must be a lot of work for you then." I gesture around the yard.

"Do what you love, and you'll never work a day in your life." She beams at me. "Although having Flo come by now and again is helpful. She's a wonder in the greenhouse."

Betty leads me through the whole operation. It's not nearly as open as Bennett's, but with the amount of wildlife around it makes sense. Half the dogs would end up forming a pack and running wild if she did things Bennett's way.

As I had expected, many of the dogs had outlived their perceived usefulness to their previous owners. Dogs young enough to still have a decent life but a burden to their owners because they weren't able to do the work they had been bred to do. Before Betty, many would have just been euthanized.

"Joshua drove a truck for the mill up here, and one day he brought this dog home. We hadn't had one in years, and it was just so nice to have one in the house again. Pretty soon he was bringing one home at least once a month." Betty sighs. "People got wind that Joshua's wife couldn't say no, so they would find him and leave dogs left, right, and center. Now, keep in mind these are working dogs so they don't have the same need to be loved. At least they don't appear to when they arrive, but they learn pretty fast how nice it is."

"That's my favorite part of the rescue process."

"What is?"

"When they give in," I say quietly. "When you watch that light appear in their eyes when they see you. The moment you become their world."

She smiles. "Follow me." Betty leads me to the back of the barn where a large black dog is pacing along the fence of its kennel. "That's Rumi. He wasn't a working dog. This guy was illegally bred and trained to hate." Rumi stops pacing and lowers his head, his lip curling defensively, one yellow and one pale blue eye glued to mine.

"Wolf?" I ask, unable to look away.

"Half."

"What's the other half?" I'd guess he was a full wolf by the look of him.

"Not sure. Husky is my best guess with that eye color. I've thought about doing the DNA thing but." She shrugs. "Maybe one day when I can get close to him without tranquing him."

"Why's he back here alone?"

"The other dogs act differently if he's around. More skittish, occasionally more aggressive. I'm at a bit of a loss with him, if I'm being honest. None of this feels fair. Not to him, the other dogs, or me quite frankly."

"What about a wolf sanctuary?" I suggest hopefully.

"There is one in Québec that's considering it. But he's been rejected by two in Ontario and one in Alberta, so I'm trying to manage my expectations."

"I'll let Bennett know. Maybe he can put in a call."

"He has pull with the conservation people?" Betty asks skeptically. "Does he have friends in the government?"

"No, not that I know of," I say. "But he does have a lot of money." Bennett isn't flashy with his money, but I doubt he'd think twice in a case like this to let it do some talking for him.

"Well, I won't say no. Now, let's go chat about how you and your Mr. Moneybags can help out these dogs."

As we approach the house, I see George sitting beside a man who, at first glance, looks a little tired but the closer I get I can see the telltale signs of facial paralysis. The way his eye droops just so, as if weighed down at the corner and his mouth is pulled back in a half grimace. Despite his condition, however, it's clear the man, I assume is Joshua, is smiling at me, or more specifically, his wife.

Betty walks over to her husband immediately and drops a kiss on his head before introducing me. "My love, this is Teddy. He's going to help us find Rumi a home."

"Well, it's about time," Joshua says slowly, each word taking more effort than it likely would have before his stroke. I want to tell Betty to bottle each of those words and cherish the sound of them.

I laugh and reach out to shake his hand. I know my mom hated when people avoided doing normal societal shit with her because people assumed she couldn't. She could and she did. Joshua's mouth tips up on one side, and the smile shines through in his eyes. "I've heard we have you to thank for half the dogs down there." I gesture behind myself.

"All she had to say was no." He looks over to his wife, and I watch Betty shrug.

"I wouldn't be surprised if Betty put a call out for people to bring their dogs to Joshua. She once brought home a bear cub, calling it a puppy." George laughs.

"The look on my mother's face." Betty cackles. "I did learn my lesson, though. I didn't bring home any more animals that could end me with a swipe of their paw."

"Just every other one," Joshua teases, joining in the laughter.

"Someone's gotta," she defends.

"No one's gotta. Sometimes you've just gotta let nature be nature," George says sternly. "You've got a bleedin' heart, that's your problem."

"Not a problem," Joshua murmurs, reaching over and taking Betty's hand. I feel the emotion rising quickly and have to look away, blinking hot, unwanted tears from my eyes.

"Okay, that's enough. Teddy and I have some business to attend to. You two behave." She stands and guides me into the house.

There's a wheelchair set to the side just in the entryway, and the hallway is clear of all obstacles. The patches of darker wood on the floor revealing where furniture may have once sat. A house amended to better serve its occupants. A house that feels far more like a home than any I've been in since Mom.

THIRTY-TWO

There is something different about Teddy when he gets back. I can't quite figure out if he wants to be left alone or needs a hug.

"How'd it go?" I ask from the Airstream doorway.

"Good," he says but doesn't elaborate.

"Well, that's good." I hate how uncomfortable I feel at this moment. This morning at the lake, I swear I could feel things click back into place. It was as if we'd been stretching for days and had finally warmed up.

"Yeah." He smiles at me but it doesn't reach his eyes. "I'm going to head back to the bunkie to make a call. I have better service in there."

"Do you want to take the truck? I can walk back when I'm done."

"Nah, I need to stretch my legs a bit. Let this guy do the same." He points to Kevin who is sprawled out under a chair.

"Okay, well, I'll see you for dinner."

Teddy nods, gives me one more half smile, then heads down to the trail to Midge's. His shoulders are slightly hunched, and I could swear by the movement of his head he's muttering to himself. Or maybe he's talking to the dog.

"Hey George," I call out when I see the man heading toward the air pump on the side of the station with a hammer in hand.

He stops and turns towards me. "Yeah?"

"Did anything happen while you were gone?"

George thinks for a minute then shakes his head. "Nope, although that boy was a tad quieter on the way back than he was on the way there."

"But nothing happened?"

"Not that I can think of. Mind you, I was with Joshua most of the time while he was in the house with Betty."

"Joshua?"

"Betty's husband. Had a stroke a couple of months ago so I get up there when I can. People in that situation can feel pretty isolated, and I figure we're isolated enough as it is way out here."

"That's nice of you," I murmur, my gaze going to the place I'd last seen Teddy, his mood becoming a bit clearer. "Well, I'll let you get back to...you're not going to hit someone with a hammer are you?"

"Just the compressor. It acts up now and again. One good smack with this, and it'll spring back to life for another four months."

"Well, good luck with that." I back away before turning just in time to see a car pull in next to the truck. A family of five jumps out, and the kids immediately run to where the books are.

"Jasper, Dustin, and Tabitha, what did we say in the car?" a man I presume is their father shouts.

When none of them answer, the woman who got out of the passenger side raises her voice. "Kidlets, answer your father, or you are getting back into this car and we will drive the three hours back home." She sounds stern, yet the term kidlets makes her seem less so.

I watch in astonishment as the kids halt, turn, and all say, "Be careful with the books."

Their mother nods, and they resume their hustle towards the library.

"That was impressive," I say when I reach them.

"I'm the oldest of six, so three kids is nothing." The woman laughs. "I'm Donna, and this is my husband Frank."

"Nellie." I give a lame wave.

"When we heard that the university picked Marmot Point for their pilot project, I got so excited."

"She did," Frank confirms.

"That's so good to hear."

"I was worried you'd be farther west. Three hours is about as far as I want to be traveling to get to a library," Donna says.

"I heard you say three hours, but I assumed you were exaggerating." I may have driven for sixteen hours to get here, but I can't imagine traveling three just to go to a library.

"No exaggeration. I applied for the pilot program but lost out to Marmot here."

"Oh." I'm suddenly uncomfortable. "I'm so sorry. I had no say in where this was happening. I just volunteered to bring the books."

"Are you a librarian?"

"I am, although here I'm just a book fairy with an advanced degree."

"Well, whatever you are"—Donna rests her hand on my shoulder—"you have made my whole summer."

Something warm blooms in my chest. This is the feeling I have been missing while working at the university.

"I'm so glad." I smile back.

"I better get over there, or they'll toss the place." She rolls her eyes, straightens her shoulders, and marches off towards her very well-behaved children.

With the family of five, a handful of Midge's grandchildren coming by again, and a few middle-aged couples stopping by, the library has been considerably busier today than yesterday. By the time I get everything shut away and back to Midge's, everyone has already started eating. Except there's no sign of Teddy. When I don't find him in the bunkie, I push down the urge to go in search of him and opt instead to join the others for dinner.

"Cold plates tonight," Midge says when I reach the patio door.

I have no idea what that means so I just nod like I understand. The kitchen island has a spread I'd describe as dorm charcuterie. Or maybe, in this case, kids' charcuterie. There are lots of vegetables but also recognizable lunch meat rolled up alongside cubes of cheese and pickles. Leftover macaroni and potato salad complete the spread.

"Has Teddy eaten?" I ask before popping a pickled onion in my mouth.

"I haven't seen him," Midge says with her head inside the fridge.

"At all?" I put my plate down and walk over to the window above the sink as if he'll be right outside.

"No, honey, not since he got coffee this morning. Why?"

"He said he was going to walk back and make a call in the bunkie, but he's not here."

"I'm sure he's fine. It's easy to get lost in these woods, but easy enough to find your way back." She tugs my arm gently and hands me back my plate. "Sometimes we've gotta let people lose themselves for a bit."

I spend the rest of dinner and my evening with Midge and

the kids looking over my shoulder, always expecting to see Teddy approaching with a guilty wave. By the time I crawl into bed, the feelings I'd experienced twelve years earlier are bubbling to the surface. I don't want to believe he'd disappear again, but I know he's capable of it. Not just that, he's good at it. Long after all the noise of the world dies away and the night soundtrack has reached its climax, the bunkie door opens with a slight squeak. I know it's Teddy just from the sound of his footsteps, but I don't turn to him or give any indication that I'm awake. I'm too angry. Angry at him for disappearing, even for a short time, and angrier at myself for caring.

"Sit," I hear him whisper to Kevin followed by the sound of Kevin's tiny teeth crunching something. Then the unmistakable sounds of clothes coming off and a body sliding between the sheets.

I want to roll over and demand to know where he was so badly, but I hold myself in place, desperately trying to keep my breathing even.

I don't sleep at all, and at the first sign of morning, I slip out of bed. In the bathroom, which doubles as a change room and is not nearly as scary as I had been warned, I put on my bathing suit and cover back up in my sweatpants and sweatshirt. Then I grab Kevin's lifejacket and a towel from the truck before grabbing the very sleepy pup from the foot of Teddy's bed. I'm exhausted, but the minute I hear the loons I can feel the anger I've been holding onto start to evaporate.

This lake is warmer than the last one, and it doesn't take me long to acclimate. Floating on my back while Kevin paddles like mad beside me, I close my eyes and try to just be.

"Hey buddy." Teddy's rich voice breaks the silence. My eyes fly open just in time to see Kevin's front legs trying to cling to Teddy's bare shoulder. "How long have you been out here?" It takes me a minute to realize he's asking me and not the dog.

"Ugh, I don't know. I may have fallen asleep."

"Real safe, Nellie," he scolds.

"Says the guy who disappeared yesterday. I see you haven't lost your touch. Really dealing with things head-on still, I see. Thanks for not waiting over a decade to come back," I spit, shocking myself with how unfiltered I let myself be.

I'm angry again, on the verge of a tantrum. I slip beneath the water and swim as fast as I can to the shore. Not looking back, I grab my towel, wrap it around myself, and head towards the trail.

"I didn't disappear," I hear him shout. "Nellie, I didn't disappear. I'm here." I can hear him swimming, but I keep walking. "Nellie, where are you going?" He's behind me now, his feet pounding on the packed earth.

Where am I going? I whirl around just as he reaches me and nearly smack into his chest. His hands grab my arms to keep me from falling backward. Water drips from his hands down my arms, causing me to shiver, so I step out of his hold.

His hands drop to his side. "Don't run away from me, Nell. Stay and talk, let me explain."

"I'm not running, Teddy. I'm walking away from you. Don't you recognize the gesture? Or did I not do it right?" I seethe. "I'm walking away from you before you can do it to me again. Because I have stupidly let you seep back into here." I rest my hand over my heart. "Because the thought of you being here and gone again is too fucking much. And I cannot even begin to tell you how much that pisses me off. Also, I was enjoying my morning and then you had to show up, so thanks for that."

"So tell me," he pleads as I take another step away.

I spin back. "What?"

He takes a step towards me. "Tell me what pisses you off. Lay it on me. Every single thing you wanted to say to me but didn't get a chance because I fucked off. Tell me what a coward

I was. Tell me I don't deserve a second chance at any kind of relationship with you. Unleash every single feeling you've hidden away because you didn't want to make a single situation awkward for anyone else." He takes another step, and he's so close I can feel the heat radiating off him. It would be so easy to lean in and soak it up. "Break my heart as thoroughly as I broke yours and don't leave a single piece of it mendable."

My gaze is fused to the tattoo that I refuse to acknowledge. "You really want to know?" I ask and finally look up to see him nod. "I convinced myself that this"—I gesture between us, cursing when my hand brushes his skin—"was supposed to happen. It was all fate or some shit, and now it feels like a giant reminder that I'm maybe too trusting, too forgiving. Too Nellie from twelve years ago. I could be married right now, did you know that? I could be Nellie Holmes, but I'm not because despite being comfortable in my relationship, he didn't do a thing for me in here." I smack my chest. "You broke me, Teddy. You took my heart and cut it off from feeling more for anyone else, and I didn't even realize it until you came back. You're fucking selfish."

I'm watching him the entire time I speak, and I see his heart break as clear as day. The way his forehead crinkles and the lines at the side of his mouth deepen. I watch him swallow as his shoulders begin to curl in ever so slightly. I watch the fight fade from his whole body, and it's in that moment I have the shocking realization that I don't want it to. I want to be fought for. Specifically by Teddy.

"Then you come back. Completely out of the blue, poof, there you are, and you had this brilliant, horrible, heartbreaking excuse for leaving. And I hate you so fucking much for that. Because it's the only reason you could have given me that made any kind of sense for the guy I fell for. You left, and for years I was convinced that I had done something to push you away.

Imagine how that would feel, Teddy. If I had done this to you, and then you find out you had absolutely no role in it. You were just a goddamn casualty."

I stop to catch my breath because if I keep going I'm going to have to grab onto something to keep upright and the closest something happens to be Teddy. His eyes are burning into me, unasked questions fading in and out of focus. I can't look at him anymore so I turn my gaze toward the trees that seem to stretch into oblivion.

"And the worst part," I say, calmer now, "the worst part of this entire thing is underneath all this pain is a woman who is so happy you're here. And I don't understand it."

We stand there silently together, my breathing jagged and his calm.

When my breathing returns to normal, and the silence is overwhelming, I finally look back up at him. "Is something wrong with your phone?" He shakes his head again. "You could have sent a text last night. Called. Yelled."

"I could have, and I should have. I'm s...not going anywhere, Nellie. I was still here." He spreads his arms indicating he was still in the vicinity. "I had planned to talk to you about it when I got back, I just got back later than I thought I would. It wasn't intentional." *Not like before*, I think.

He tips his head towards the shore, a stupid hopeful little smile appearing on his face. "I brought coffee."

There is no harm in listening to this, at least I'll get an explanation right away. "Did you—"

"Bring the maple cookies? Yes," he confirms.

"Fine." I grunt and lead the way back to the rocks where I now see a thermos and a little baggy of cookies.

When half my coffee is gone, I ask the question I should have asked yesterday before he had a chance to walk by me. "So what happened?"

Teddy, to his credit, doesn't look away from me. He sets his coffee down and looks me straight in the eye. "Betty's husband —"

"Had a stroke," I finish for him and watch as his eyes widen. "I asked George about your trip, and he mentioned it."

He clears his throat and blinks rapidly a few times and I fight against the need to reach for him. "It wasn't even the stroke or the fact he had similar paralysis as my mom. It was this moment between him and Betty. It was like I was back at the kitchen table with my parents. Despite the fact their reality was far from ideal, they just made it work, for them. They made the life they wanted fit. And..." I watch him swallow and finally look away from me.

"We don't—"

"No," he cuts me off. "No, I want to, I need to. I wasn't running away yesterday, Nellie. I was trying to pull myself back into the present. When I was gone, I spent half of my time grieving my mom and what I had as a son and brother, and the other half grieving us, you."

I understand the grieving us part, I did it myself and it was hard. I have no idea what I would have done if I'd lost my mom and then discovered what felt like a monumental betrayal.

He takes another deep breath, and I watch a tear escape and track down his cheek. "I know by now I should be over this. I know I should have moved on from this sadness that taints every single relationship I have. I will never be able to make up for what I did to you. There is no erasing the hurt my actions and inaction caused. I should have called you that first day. I should have written you a thousand letters. The shame that consumed me after the grief eased kept me from following through on a single thing when it came to you. You had twelve years stolen because of me. I know I shouldn't look at you and hope you still see the good guy somewhere inside me. But I do."

"I do, even if it's hard to admit it." It comes almost as a question, as if I can't quite believe I'm saying it myself. I may still hold some anger about being left, but I've been denying the fact that the guy I fell for is still very much who this man in front of me is. "I see the good guy. I also see a guy who's struggling to come to terms with the life he left behind. I see a son who desperately misses his mom and his family." I see the reality of how time doesn't necessarily heal as fast as we hoped it would. It most certainly doesn't erase moments we wish we could redo.

I move a little closer, but I still don't touch him. "I see the boy I was falling for so long ago in the eyes of a man. I see you Teddy, the you from before and from today, and all the versions in between. I see it when you smile, even if you don't smile as much as before. I hear it in your laugh and when you talk to the dog like he's going to answer you. I see you, Teddy." The last words are a whisper, and before I know it I'm rising on my knees and wrapping my arms around his shoulders.

Teddy's arms encircle my waist, pulling me into him. Head on my chest, trying to control his own emotions. When I went to bed last night the last thing I would have imagined was this scenario. If anything I could have imagined an angry fuck at most, but this feels far more appropriate for friends.

"They're hugging, Grandma," a little voice yells from somewhere in the forest.

"Hugging?" Midge replies at the same volume.

"Yeah, but Teddy is shorter than Nellie."

"Martin Vanderkraats, you march that butt back here right now and forget what you have seen." Midge's voice sounds panicked, and I feel Teddy shaking with laughter against me.

Looking down, I watch his gaze meet mine, tears of sadness turning to tears of laughter. "I bet she's going to have to move a certain health lesson up now," I say before crumbling into him in a fit of giggles. "Feel better?" I ask, pulling back and out of his grasp.

"Much. You?"

"Yes." I slide back to where I had been sitting before the need to hug him overwhelmed my ability to think straight.

I pick my mug back up and watch as he does the same, although neither of us drinks. His eyes are still on me, and I can't help my gaze dropping to his lips. Heat pools in my core as I remember what they felt like. What harm would kissing him do? We're adults; we can kiss and move on like, well, adults. We did that back in December and then carried on. But now we can have conversations, and it doesn't have to mean anything.

"We should get back before Kevin shivers to death," Teddy suggests, and the spell I was under breaks.

"Oh god." I throw back what's left of my coffee and reach for my bag. "If he dies, Bennett will never let me adopt a dog," I groan, watching as Teddy stands and tucks Kevin into his zip-up hoodie.

"Relax," he says, reaching down to pick up the thermos and mugs, "He's a wiener. He shivers when a warm breeze touches him."

If anyone saw us on the walk back, we'd look like two friends walking back from a swim at the local watering hole. They'd never guess that I was two seconds away from giving into every primal urge I've ever had.

THIRTY-THREE

TEDDY

Every morning starts with a trip to the lake and a visit with the loons before Nellie heads to the library and I drive out to Betty's. Some days we talk, and others we just swim quietly. I don't know if we've slipped back to the summer we spent together or if I just wish we had, but it feels a bit more like that than the frosty distance we've had since.

Getting out of the lake on day twenty-three of our residence at Midge's, Nellie slices her foot open on a rock. I'd finally convinced her to lose the water shoes, and within an hour there's a puddle of blood pooling on the rock where we sit and have our coffee every morning.

"Shit," Nellie curses, reaching for her towel and immediately pressing it to the wound. I watch in horror as the blood seeps through the towel. Nellie, on the other hand, calmly folds the material again and presses it back against the cut.

"Nellie, Jesus, you're bleeding like a hemophiliac." I grab my towel and kneel beside her at the ready, tiny pebbles pressing into my skin. Then I remember what she'd said about getting over her fear of blood. "Wait, are you?"

"Am I what?" she asks without looking up at me.

"A hemophiliac?" That would explain being afraid of blood and getting over it right? Constant exposure tends to ease fears.

"No, it's—well, it's a disease, but it's not hemophilia." When she looks up at me, she quickly continues, "It's like hemophilia light. It won't kill me. I just have a hard time clotting, but I will, eventually."

I barely hear what she says next because she's in my arms and I'm off back through the woods towards Midge's. She's still talking and I can hear Kevin yapping, but the blood pounding in my ears muffles everything.

Midge is sitting in a Muskoka chair sipping her coffee when I burst out of the forest.

"She's bleeding. She won't stop," I manage to get out.

"Bring her inside," Midge says far too calmly, standing to lead us through the door.

I'm panicking, I know I am, but much like the bleeding, I can't stop. I set Nellie down on the old patchwork sofa and kneel next to her foot, unwrapping the soiled towel and calling out for a first aid kit. At least I think I do, I think I may be hyperventilating. Midge is next to me in seconds and gently shoves me to the side so she's closer to Nellie's foot and I'm closer to her head.

I can feel hands on my face, but I feel a bit like I'm floating. Movement around me, cold on my neck, my name far away, slowly moving closer.

"Teddy, Teddy, it's okay, I'm fine." It feels like my heart is trying to escape through my neck. The hands slip from my face as I scramble backward. I don't know how I get on my feet or back outside, but I suddenly find myself bent with my hands on my knees, staring at the coffee and maple cookies I'd had before swimming as silver stars dance through the air.

Run, a tiny voice whispers, and I feel the urge to give in.

But I stay put. Running wasn't the answer last time I did it, and it most certainly isn't the way to handle this.

A hand lands on my back. "The bleeding has slowed down," George says from beside me. "I think she may need medical attention, though. The cut is deep, and who knows what got in there from the lake."

"I'll get the truck—"

"No," George states firmly. "You will not be getting behind the wheel in this state, young man. You're not even wearing shoes. I'll bring mine around. You can come with us as long as you pull yourself together. Nellie is fine, but if you aren't, that's not going to help her."

"Right." I take a deep breath and finally look over at the old man. "Wait, when did you get here?"

He laughs, his hands slipping into his pockets as he tips back on his heels. "I've been here the whole time, kid. Was sitting beside Magpie when you came running out of the woods like there was a grizzly on your heels."

"I, I didn't notice you," I stammer.

"No shit!" He laughs harder. "You looked like you had the love of your life's life in your hands."

I did, I think.

"The blood, it, it wouldn't stop. I didn't know what else to do."

"Well, you did the right thing, albeit maybe a tad more dramatically than it needed to be done. Maybe bring the panic down a bit." George pats my arm before gently leading me back towards the house. "Now, deep breath. You good?" he asks, sliding the patio door open when I nod.

Nellie's eyes meet mine over the rim of the orange juice she's drinking, the minute I'm through the door I feel myself deflate. She's fine, but she looks worried, probably about me. I hate that she's the one who's hurt and she's sitting there concerned about my lame ass.

"You okay?" she asks, her head tilting a little to the left.

I breathe out heavily and nod. "I'm fine. I don't know what that was."

"That was a bloody panic attack," George inserts unhelpfully.

Midge sighs, handing me a glass of juice. "I don't know if that was a clever turn of phrase or inappropriate. Drink that, then we'll get this one to the clinic."

Taking a sip, I stand there awkwardly, not sure how to conduct myself now that I've calmed down. I feel like the biggest fool. Then I remember that we're not exactly close to any hospitals. "Where is the clinic?"

"Dr. Arnaud lives about forty minutes away. He has a small practice, but he'll be able to treat the cut quickly and either glue or stitch it up."

"Flo and I will manage the library," Midge says. "Al will drive you. No arguments." She holds her hand up, stopping the words about to come out of my mouth immediately.

George's truck is significantly older than Bennett's, but it has a back bench seat. Nellie sits behind George with her legs across the seat, her injured foot resting on my thigh so it's slightly elevated. She and George discuss how things have been going with the library and another run-in with Morticia a couple of afternoons ago, and I sit there silently, replaying how I handled the morning.

Nellie and I have grown closer over the last two weeks, and this morning had felt like we were about to push through a barrier. She'd reached for my hand as we floated beside each other, Kevin paddling around our heads biting at the water bugs as they zipped across the surface.

"Remember that day in the pool?" she'd asked, eyes glued to the sky.

"The day you nearly undid my resolve."

"I did not." She laughs.

"Nellie, by that day my resolve was being held together by a frayed piece of twine." I looked over at her to see if she would look back at me. Her attention remained on the sky, but her small smile gave away that she knew exactly what I was talking about. I continued to look at her. At how her tattoos became a little distorted by the water. She has so many new ones, and I'm desperate to explore them. "How many tattoos do you have now?"

"A few," she said coyly.

"A few more than that day in the pool."

She turned to look at me, her dark blue eyes traveling down my face to where my chest sat just above the water. "You have at least one more than you had that day."

My hand automatically covered the small artwork that sits over my heart. "I was wondering if you were ever going to say anything."

"I wasn't sure I wanted to acknowledge what it may mean," she said quietly.

I tightened my grip and pulled her closer, letting my lower half sink and encouraging her to do the same until we were facing each other, treading water.

"What do you think it means, Nellie?"

Nellie's hand reached out, and I shivered as her fingers danced across the blue jay in flight across my chest. "I think it means you really like blue jays," she whispered. Then she'd put both her hands on my shoulders and dunked me before racing off towards the shore.

"What do you think?"

I blink away visions of this morning and see Nellie looking

at me, one eyebrow raised. Forest passes by out the window behind her, and I take a split second to reorientate myself with where I am.

"Sorry?"

She tilts her head, eyebrows knitting in concern. "I was wondering how many dogs you think Bennett will take?"

"Oh, we only have room for two comfortably. Cass said they already have applications filled out for them, and Marley and Betty have approved a couple of candidates. So as long as their meet-and-greets go well, they'll have homes within hours of us getting back."

"Does Bennett know?"

I can picture Bennett trying to make his case to keep the dogs there for longer and then inevitably forever. "I'm pretty sure Marley put her foot down. He has no reason to keep them. It's a good trial run, using tried-and-true methods from Betty." We pass a maintenance truck on the side of the road with a wood chipper attached, and my attention is momentarily captured.

"Do you miss it?"

"Hmm?" I turn back to Nellie.

"The tree stuff?"

My shoulders rise and fall before I can even vocalize an opinion. "Sometimes I miss the rush of it. I think my body misses it most of all." Nellie's eyes slowly sweep down my side, and I feel my body heat.

"You still do some stuff at Bennett's though, right?"

Nodding, I force myself to keep looking at her, despite the heat of her stare. "Here and there. I can't complain, though. The job is pretty great."

"What was your favorite part of working in the trees?"

The quiet, I think, although it's not exactly a quiet profession. "There is this moment, right when you get up high. The noise of the ground is muted, and for a time all you hear is the tree. Gentle creaks or leaves rustling. I remember the moment I went from being afraid to craving it. There was this mountain ash in New Zealand we had been doing some work on for a couple of days. It was early in the day, and I hadn't slept well the night before so I had been dreading work."

"Climbing trees on little sleep seems ill-advised." Nellie laughs softly.

"Yes, although I was kind of in a trance-like state so I wasn't thinking about my underlying fear of heights. I get up to the top to start pruning and—" I pause because how do I describe the moment things started to change? "This is going to sound woo-woo or something, but I felt my mom with me."

Nellie doesn't say anything, just offers a small smile.

"It was an incredibly weird sensation for someone who doesn't believe in anything." I laugh nervously, my thumb immediately making contact with my ring, drawing Nellie's attention. "I just let myself feel it, no questions or judgments. I've never even told anyone before."

"I'm honored to be the first you've told," Nellie says, followed immediately by George clearing his throat. "George is honored too."

"What you experienced there, Teddy, is the sensation of your soul healing after great grief," George affirms quietly, his eyes meeting mine briefly in the rearview mirror.

Nellie leans forward and gently takes my hand. "That's a beautiful thought," she says, squeezing my fingers in hers.

The rest of the drive is quiet. Nellie's hand wrapped around my own, resting on her knee. My attention remains on the passing scenery, but I can feel hers on me.

THIRTY-FOUR

NELLIE

Teddy crashed the minute we got back into the truck after Dr. Arnaud glued my foot back together. I'd assured him over and over while sitting on the exam table that I wasn't going to cut myself and drop dead. I'd received my diagnosis of type three Von Willebrand Disease at twenty-three, after having my wisdom teeth out. Apparently, excessive dental bleeding is a tell, and my body picked that surgery to do all the telling. Suddenly, heavy periods and bruising easier than a rotten peach made sense. The hematologist who discussed treatment with me told me since I had never had surgery or even a filling before it wasn't surprising that I hadn't been tested. It's rare, but on the scale of rare diseases, it's more of a nuisance than anything else.

I'd had an IUD inserted to help manage my period, took iron supplements, and had my blood tested every six months or so. Other than that, I just tried not to cut myself, mainly to avoid reactions like Teddy's.

Even in his sleep, he still looks worried. I can't help wondering if he's thinking about his mom. I'd done some research on cerebral aneurysms after meeting her. I'd gone down the rabbit hole of clots, strokes, and aneurysms. I'd always been of the mind that an aneurysm and a stroke were roughly the same thing. An aneurysm could cause a stroke, but a stroke didn't lead to an aneurysm. I still don't know the path of Teddy's mom's life. What I had learned, though, was that there were loads of blood-related things that could forever alter someone's life.

Teddy stirs when we pull into the lot at the gas station and immediately apologizes for sleeping the entire way back.

"Don't be, you needed it." From what I'd heard from a friend, panic attacks could zap your energy pretty thoroughly. "Feel better?"

"I should be asking you that," he says, his brow furrowed so deeply that it would be hard for an onlooker to know if he was mad or worried.

"I will live to cut myself and bleed excessively again. But I will also survive that, and the time after that too. And you will just have to learn to live with that."

Teddy's gaze holds mine, and I realize what I've said makes it sound like he's going to be there for all the future cuts and bruises. And I feel no reservations about that.

We have a week and a half left at Midge's, then we'll pack up, secure the Airstream so it's semi-permanent, meet Betty to grab the dogs, and begin our trip home. I've taken a few steps back from the library, overseeing more than anything, and I'm not worried about leaving it in Midge and Florence's hands.

"You know," Teddy says from the other side of the empty vegetable bed we're weeding two nights later, "we both fulfilled our secret desires."

"And just as I thought, yours was way more ambitious."

"I ran away. You stayed and helped pioneer a program that brings books to people who want them but don't always have access."

"Do you regret leaving?" I ask, unable to look at him.

"Every day," Teddy says. When I look up, he's staring at me. "What I did was unfair to you. I made you question your worth, and that was never something I wanted. I was so consumed by my anger, I wasn't thinking of anyone else."

"We don't have to talk about this again, Teddy. I know you're sorry. I've forgiven you." I sit on the edge of the waist-height garden with a sigh, running my hands over my shirt to get some of the dirt off.

Teddy does the same before making his way around the bed, stopping when he is in front of me.

I watch as he sinks to his knees, taking my hands in his and resting them on my knees. "Ask me," he implores.

"Ask you what?" I whisper.

"About the blue jay." His eyes settle on my throat as I fight with what I think I know and what I may believe. "Ask me, LG," he practically begs.

My breath catches when I hear the nickname. "What's with the blue jay, EG?"

He takes my hand and places it over where the blue jay is etched into his skin, just below the fabric of his shirt. "You have lived here since the moment I saw you on that train." I don't know what I had expected him to say, but it wasn't that. A tattoo doesn't erase the feeling of abandonment I felt for years. "I'm not telling you that so you forget everything. I'm telling you that so you know a day didn't go by after I left that I didn't think of you. When a few of my coworkers decided to go get tattoos one weekend, I didn't even hesitate on what I wanted." Twelve years later, and he's still reading my mind.

I pull my hands back from him and sit up straight. I can tell he's starting to second-guess his decision to say something, so I reach for the side of my shirt and pull it up slowly, revealing a simple outline of a tree, the only non-avian tattoo I have. Most of my other tattoos have been on display when we've been swimming but this one has remained hidden, my secret until now.

His eyes widen as he takes it in, flitting to mine before going back to the tree. He reaches out and traces the outline with his dirt-stained fingers, and goosebumps scatter across the surface of my skin. I want more than just that finger on me, desperately.

"Nellie?" He looks up at me with wonder in his eyes, and all I can do is shrug in response.

"It was a spontaneous decision after the heron on my back was done. I saw a sketch on the artist's wall and asked how long it would take." She'd been shocked that I was interested in something that wasn't a bird but had pointed out that trees and birds went hand in hand, or branch in talon. I think deep down I always knew who it was for but was too afraid to admit it.

A tear sits at the outer edge of Teddy's eye and I reach out to wipe it away, but before I can, he grabs my hand and presses it to the side of his face, kissing my palm and holding it against his skin. It's then that I realize how tired I am. Tired of fighting every good feeling I have. Tired of looking for signs that he's going to run again. Tired of craving him and not letting myself have what I've wanted for so long. I'm also incredibly tired of talking about it all.

"Teddy," I say, spreading my knees just enough that he understands what I want. He shuffles forward, eyes on mine the whole time. "I don't want to talk anymore." Taking his face between my hands, I guide his lips to mine.

The minute I kiss him it's like a dam bursting, like that day in the car but this time I'm not doubting a thing. It's all yeses and questions like *why have we been wasting so much time not doing this?* I can't hold back the moan when he sucks my tongue into his mouth or stop my legs from wrapping around him, pulling him tight against me. It's only when my back hits the dirt, I'm reminded where we are.

"Wait, wait." I push against Teddy's chest until he pulls back. His face is flushed, and he's breathing like he's just run a marathon, pupils blown wide so the light blue of his eyes are just thin rings. "We can't do this here." He blinks rapidly, and I watch those silvery blue rings expand.

He looks towards the house and then back at me. "No one is home," he reminds me "They're all at that barbecue."

He's right. We told Midge we'd head over after we finished in the garden. Everyone had been working out here, and we thought maybe we could finish it up tonight as a surprise so Florence and her cousins could get started on the late summer planting first thing tomorrow.

Making out in the garden leaves us exposed to not just the elements but to anyone who may come home early.

"We'll hear if anyone comes back early, right?" I ask as my heart rate speeds up at the thought of being discovered.

Teddy's eyes dip to my lips, and he nods. "There's no way she'd let anyone walk back when it's getting dark." His hands have already begun to creep back up my thighs. "We can be fast," he says as his fingers curl around the waistband of my shorts. "If you want," he quickly amends.

I shake my head. "I don't want to be fast."

He taps my hips, and I raise them so he can pull my shorts down. I should feel weird about sitting on the wood border of a garden bed in just my underwear, but there's something about it that thrills me. The fact there's no hiding my arousal from him thrills me even more.

Teddy tosses my shorts to the side and focuses on what he's unwrapped. Biting his lower lip, he groans, taking me in. "The way I have dreamt of tasting every part of you, LG." He hasn't moved yet; he's just looking, his hands applying enough pressure to keep my legs from closing even a millimeter. I want to beg him to act out everything he's ever dreamed of, but I stay silent, just watching him drink me in.

"May I?" he asks, eyes glued to where he desires to move to. When I don't answer right away, he looks up. A strangled "Please" slips through his lips. I'm so captivated by the way his eyes are drinking me in that when I open my mouth to respond nothing comes out, but I must nod because he moves.

His hands slide back up my legs, a trail of tiny shocks left in their wake. Once he's reached my hips, he tugs my ass to the very edge of the bed. I lower my elbows and lean back just enough so I'm relaxed and so that I can watch as his head disappears between my legs.

Teddy doesn't remove another scrap of clothing, just moves my underwear to the side, the graze of his fingers alone sending waves of pleasure through me. The touch of his tongue breaks every mold I've ever put myself in.

"Fucking finally," he says against me. At least that's what I think he says. I know it's what I'm thinking.

I don't know how I'll ever be able to smell dirt again without immediately being turned on. My back lands fully in the soil as Teddy pulls me forcefully against his mouth, moaning into me as his tongue does delicious things. The brush of his beard adds a whole other sensation I've never experienced before. I keep expecting his fingers to join in, but they remain at my hips, holding me down until a wave of white-hot pleasure crashes into me, forcing my back to arch and my hips to strain against his hold. Teddy's mouth stays locked onto me until the last tremor eases and I'm left breathing heavily in the dirt.

"That was worth every second of waiting," Teddy says, the brush of his beard against my thigh causing another bolt of pleasure to course through me, before rising on his knees to look down at my spent form. "I hope you enjoyed yourself, Library Girl, because I'm not sure I can survive without doing that again soon."

THIRTY-FIVE

TEDDY

I don't think I've ever been this hard. Feeling Nellie lose control on my tongue is the hottest thing I've ever experienced and the thought of experiencing even more makes my brain turn to mush. All I want to do is rip off those very wet panties and bury myself deep in her. But I manage to keep some composure as I suck on the hollow at the base of her gorgeous throat.

"Teddy," she says in a breath.

"Yes," I reply against her skin, unwilling to remove my lips from her. Desperate to never be parted again.

I feel her hand on my hip and then my knees buckle when she grips me through my shorts. "Fuck," I breathe out, my hips moving into her hand unconsciously.

"Get on the ground," she commands, pushing me back.

Who am I to argue with the woman of my dreams? I lay back between two of the garden beds and lazily watch Nellie slide off the side of one, onto her knees. I'm not going to last long. I'm shocked I didn't go off the minute I felt her arch against my mouth.

She swings her leg over me and rests her perfect ass on my thighs while she unbuttons and then unzips my shorts. The wait is torture.

"Lift," she commands, and I do as she says immediately. "Good boy."

Fuck yes.

She slides my shorts off, and I get harder at the sight of her eyes widening in glee when I'm free.

Dropping my shorts to the side, I watch motionless as she moves up my body until her lips meet mine in a kiss that will be forever imprinted on my soul. She takes my bottom lip between her teeth, and my hips involuntarily leave the ground. The combination of the sting of her teeth and the glide of her core against my length stops my breathing. The little "mmm" she hums out has me ready to grab her hips and keep her right where she is.

But she has other ideas.

"I've been dreaming of tasting you too," she whispers against my ear, nipping my lobe and disappearing back down my body.

She wastes no time wrapping her lips around me. My head slams back into the ground and I do my best not to fuck her mouth, letting her set the pace.

I've got my jaw clenched so hard I'm a bit worried I'm going to break an entire row of molars, but as she grazes her teeth against me, I accept my fate of a future with expensive dental bills. My hands find her hair, and I hold on for dear life. She moans when I pull a little, the vibration doing magical things to my body.

"Nellie," I grind out, trying to warn her about the imminent situation. I tug a bit harder which only earns me another long moan as she doubles down on her efforts. "I'm—" I pant just as my body stiffens. I watch in awe as she stays put until the last spasm and then slides her mouth off me, capping off the fantasy by licking her lips and smiling demurely. "Fucking hell, Nellie," I say, trying to catch my breath.

"I hope you enjoyed yourself, Enviro Guy, because I'll be wanting to do that again later too."

A surprised laugh escapes me as my body sinks into the earth, utterly spent. "Just say the word, LG."

As much as I'd like to carry her back to the bunkie and continue checking things off our collective wishlist, we decide that we better at least make an appearance at the barbecue. If we do that, we can spend more time alone tomorrow without someone making comments about not showing up, so we clean up quickly and head to the truck.

Nellie doesn't argue when I get behind the wheel and she doesn't flinch when my hand lands on her thigh. She even spreads her legs a bit when my fingers begin to wander. Now that they're soil-free, I am desperate to sink them into her, which is exactly what ends up happening two minutes after I slam the truck into park before we even reach the road.

"You're going to ride my fingers until you come undone, pretty girl. Then you're going to spend the entire time at the barbecue wet, knowing it's because of me."

"Yes," she gasps as she writhes in my lap, my other hand in her hair, pulling it back to expose her throat.

"Fuck, you're beautiful, LG," I growl against her skin, holding myself off from tipping over the edge. And she is. She's always so in control, but this version of her is chaos and desperation and it's hot as fuck.

"I, I, I—" she chants until I force her lips to meet mine. This time she unravels on my fingers with my tongue in her mouth.

"Holy shit, Teddy." She leans back against the steering wheel, and I slowly pull my fingers from her, bringing them to my lips. She looks at me with hooded eyes and a wicked little smile. Her tongue traces her lower lip as she watches my every move.

"I'd share, but I'm greedy," I say before sliding my middle finger into my mouth without breaking eye contact.

"Friends, that's all we're ever going to be," Nellie had said before we left. But friends don't go down on one another in a garden or get each other off in a car. Friends are not what we were ever destined to be. The taste of her on my tongue proves that.

"We were wondering if you two were going to make it," Midge shouts when we finally get out of the truck. The air smells like grilled chicken, and my stomach rumbles immediately.

Nellie looks from my stomach up and smiles. "I guess I didn't satisfy your hunger," she pouts.

I bend down as we walk, getting my mouth as close to her ear as possible. "I've been starving myself for twelve years, LG. It'll take a lifetime of feeding before I'm satisfied." I can't help the smug grin that appears on my face when she turns red.

"Nellie!" Devon calls from where he's sitting at a folding table holding Kevin. "I found a raccoon today, and George says he'll teach me how to stuff it."

"Don't say that in front of the dog, dummy," Devon's little sister Catelyn hisses.

"He doesn't know what I'm saying," Devon shoots back. "Besides," he says, looking down at Kevin fondly, "I'd stuff Kevin if he died. Then he'd always be with me."

"Okay, I think that's enough talk about stuffing things." Midge laughs, scooping Kevin out of Devon's lap and snapping the long line onto his collar before setting him down. "Run free, lil wiener," she whispers loud enough to wake the dead.

"We were able to get the garden ready for planting so the

kids can do that tomorrow," I say while piling chicken and various salads onto my plate.

"Turns out Teddy and I are quite a team." Nellie smiles across the table from me as she goes to add baked beans to her plate before seeming to think better of it. "Stop looking at me like that," she whispers to me.

"Like what?" I ask as innocently as possible but letting her know I know exactly what she means as my gaze runs the length of her body, pausing briefly where I know she's wet.

"Like you've planted anything in my garden."

I hold my hand up in surrender. "But I haven't planted anything...yet." I let the T pop and watch again as she blushes.

We manage to make it through dinner with no further incidents, and when the local band starts playing, people make their way to the dirt patch dance floor. Tanner is back and asks Nellie to dance immediately, and I watch him lead her to the center of everyone like a predator watches its next meal.

"There's no rule that says you have to wait until the song finishes before you cut in," Midge says conspiratorially from beside me.

"If Nellie didn't want to dance with him, she would have said no." I shrug as though I'm fine with her choice. I am, but I also don't like how Tanner's hand sits low on her back, far too close to where my hands made their claim today.

"Well, if you aren't going to step in and get your girl back from that prick, then you may as well ask me to dance," Midge says hotly.

"Prick? He's your son. You can't call your son a prick."

"Exactly, *my* son. So I can call him anything I like, and he *is* a prick. Just like his father was in the end." I roll my eyes and lead her out to join everyone else. "That's not entirely fair," Midge concedes, looking over at where Tanner and Nellie are laughing. "He's not nearly as bad as his dad." She pauses, eyes still on her son. "But he is still a prick."

"Noted," I say as I spin us closer to the only person I want to be dancing with.

Nellie sees us move and stares at me. When she knows I'm not going to look away, I watch her mouth, "I'm so wet," and good lord, I have no idea how I manage to stay on my feet as I stumble to the side and take poor Midge with me.

"Whoa there," Tanner says, reaching for his mom. "You okay?" he asks her.

"Just fine, but I think I'd rather dance with you now, kid." She pulls her son away and leaves Nellie and me alone.

"She's good," Nellie says, walking up to me and wrapping her arms around my neck.

"She really is." I smile down at her and pull her close, letting my hands dip a little further than Tanner's had been. Possessive but PG since we're surrounded by kids. "How much longer do we have to stay?" I ask as we make a second turn of the space.

"I figured one of us could start yawning a lot. You know how it is when you have to share a small space with someone. Best to get ready for bed at the same time." She winks at me.

"Ah yes, always key to a good night's sleep." I relish the way she blushes again and dips her head shyly. She wasn't so shy a couple hours ago when she was ordering me to get on my back and removing my clothes. Or when she eagerly climbed into my lap in the truck. But here she is, almost bashful at the mere suggestion of things to come.

The sound of Nellie's ringtone cuts me off, and I watch as she reaches into her back pocket and brings out her phone, "Mom" flashing across the screen. A pang of jealousy stabs at me as she holds up her finger with a smile and accepts the call.

"Hey Mom," I hear as she walks towards the edge of the

forest, one hand up against her other ear to block the noise around us.

I watch her expressions change as she speaks and then listens. Minutes of a conversation that likely won't be remembered but will always exist. Nellie hasn't fully admitted to me how upset she is that her parents have moved so far away, but I hear it when she tells me about an update.

I turn back to the other guests to give her some privacy and catch sight of Midge dancing with George. His hands are definitely below friend level, and the way Midge is smiling up at him has me thinking that there may be more to their morning coffees than meets the eye.

"Devon told me that they've been a thing for three years now." Nellie's voice makes me jump as she comes up next to me holding Kevin.

"Three years?" I ask, looking back at the apparent couple.

"But they like to pretend they aren't a couple. He doesn't get it, but it's clearly a kink."

"Speaking of kinks, you got a thing for dogs watching?"

She looks down at the impressionable pup in her arms and back up at me, horror-stricken. "I didn't even think about it. We're going to traumatize him."

"Just go see if Devon wants to have him for a sleepover. Kids love puppies."

"That'll give it away," she hisses back.

"How?"

"Devon will say, 'Hey Grandma, can Kevin sleep over?' and then she'll be thinking, 'Oh, because Teddy and Nellie are doing it.'"

"Doing it?" I laugh.

"Fucking" she mouths, and I'd be lying if I said that the word leaving her lips has me ready to say to hell with what anyone else thinks. But we're technically here as part of her job, and I don't want her to feel like she's being unprofessional, despite all the things we've done already.

"We'll just have to be discreet." I take Kevin from her and start walking towards the truck. "Time to get this little guy to bed," I call out to Midge and George as they sway slowly back and forth. "Have a good rest of your night." I wave quickly before getting in the truck. Nellie climbs in seconds later looking nervous.

"They all know," she says, slamming her head against the headrest.

"Even the kids?" I joke.

"Well no, probably not the kids, but the adults do and they'll talk and then I'll be the naughty librarian."

"You're not making that sound like a bad thing, LG. Besides, from my experience, you have a bit of naughty in you and you are a librarian, so you might as well own it." I start the truck up and do my best not to peel out in a spray of gravel, even though I want everyone to know that I'm about to get laid by the naughty librarian.

THIRTY-SIX

NELLIE

Florence is sitting outside when we pull in. She had brought a couple of the younger kids back early. Kevin practically jumps from my arms when he sees her, and I hear Teddy's soft laugh as he bounds over to her.

"Maybe Kevin will make this easier on all of us by choosing to have a sleepover."

"He's a very perceptive dog," I say quietly, watching as Florence puts her phone down and bends to pick the dog up.

"He's yours for the night if you want him," Teddy calls to her.

"Really?" Florence calls back, the lights hanging around the fire pit illuminating the huge smile on her face.

"If you want," he assures her.

"Awesome, thanks." She waves, and Teddy tugs me towards the bunkie.

The second the door closes, I'm on him. "The last three hours have been torture," I breathe out as his lips connect with the space between my neck and shoulder.

"Three hours is nothing, Nellie. My balls have been blue since you kicked me out of your car seven months ago."

"I'm sor—" I start to say before remembering our rule as I begin working my hands under his shirt so I can slide it off. "I promise never to do that again."

"Never say never." He turns me around and I stick my hands out just in time before I crash into the wall. "We're going to see just how sturdy this little bunkie is," he says as he grinds himself against my ass. "Your ass in these shorts, LG, criminal." His hand slips down the front, and he groans as his fingers dip into my underwear. "I love that this is because of me." His other hand grasps my hair and pulls my head back right so his mouth can devour mine.

Right before it feels like I'll run out of air, I turn and push him towards the bed. He lands heavily when the backs of his knees make contact with the mattress, and I pounce. I'd told him that maybe it was me that he needed to be protected from without really thinking. Now as my teeth graze his jaw and I begin moving my hips, I think it was because part of me knew if we got to this point, I'd be fucking feral.

"You keep moving like that"—Teddy closes his eyes, fighting for control as his hands land on my waist—"and this is going to be over real fast." His words aren't matching his actions as he holds me firmly against him.

I slow my hips just enough that his eyes open in time to see me pull my shirt up and over my head. I watch his lips part and his tongue sneak out to wet them. Next goes my bra, and that's the moment Teddy reclaims the upper hand.

Flipping us faster than I ever thought possible, he kisses me almost viciously before he starts an agonizingly slow path down my body. I hate that he acquired any of these skills without me, but I also feel the need to send out thank-you letters because I'm the one who is now benefiting from his extracurriculars.

He wastes no time removing the rest of my clothing and then stands and looks down at me, fully taking in every inch of skin on display. Teddy-less Nellie never liked to be looked at naked. I've always been a lights-off lady, but Teddy's eyes can have all the time they want. And he takes his time looking as he slowly undoes his shorts. I am captivated by the way he watches me. It's how I've seen artsy people study paintings or how music people savor the perfect harmony. I watch as his gaze gets to my thighs and then the look of panic suddenly crosses his face.

His head snaps up, and I feel the mood shift instantly. "I didn't bring condoms," he says, almost to himself. "Did you?"

I push up on my elbows and feel my heart sink, "No, I wasn't exactly expecting to end up here."

"Me either."

"I don't know why, but that makes me happy," I say. "Not the no protection part, the no expectation part." I look around the small room as if a box of Trojans will spontaneously appear on the nightstand and then decide to suggest something I've never even contemplated before. "I haven't had sex since I was last tested and it came back negative for everything." I twirl my hand in the air. "And I have an IUD because it helps with the whole bleeding too much thing, so that's roughly ninety-nine..." I trail off, because he knows the stats.

Teddy looks at me skeptically. "Same, except for the IUD. I don't have one of those. Are you sure, though? I don't want to pressure you. I, we can wait. We've waited this long."

"So you keep saying," I say, sitting up and wrapping my arms around his waist, resting my chin at his hip and peering up. "I don't want to wait another week, day, or fucking hour. I trust you. I trust that you wouldn't have let me put my mouth on you earlier today if there was even an ounce of doubt."

Teddy still looks hesitant, so I decide to try one more tactic to prove I'm okay with it, and if it doesn't work I'll give up and accept a night of aggressive spooning. Sliding back on the bed, maintaining eye contact the entire time I lay back and slowly slide my hand down my body. I watch his chest begin to rise and fall faster as he watches my fingers begin to work.

I hear his shorts hit the floor at the same time his hands grab my ankles and he pulls me to the end of the bed, wrapping my legs around his hips.

His fingers circle my wrist and he pulls my hand away from my body. "That's my job now, pretty girl," he growls out.

"Then you better do it." I rock my hips against him and we moan in unison.

He lets my hand fall so he can grip my waist, holding half my body off the bed. "Tell me," he demands, his eyes almost black in the low light.

"Make me regret kicking you out of my car," I challenge. I already regret it, but now he can show me what I've been missing all these months.

That's all I needed to say as he slides all the way home. My back involuntarily arches to the point only my head is left on the bed as his movements push me back even as his grip keeps me firmly in place.

The bed is protesting with every movement, and I try to ignore the sense of dread I feel at the thought of it breaking. Midge had warned us after all.

Teddy seems to sense what I'm feeling because he bends at the knees and pulls my body to him. Moving to the wall he leans me back into it, using it as leverage. My eyes close as my head tips back against the wood paneling, and I feel his hand leave my waist before it settles at my throat.

My eyes fly open to see his lasered in on mine. I'll never know why, but I nod the tiniest bit and lean into his touch. A breathy "yes" leaves my lips, and his fingers tighten ever so slightly. He's not even messing with my air supply, but knowing the power he wields in this position does something to every pleasure center in my body.

"You regret it yet, LG?" he asks, squeezing a little more so he can pull my body back against his.

"Almost," I manage to get out as his mouth claims mine again.

The kiss goes from primal to sensual quickly, and I feel Teddy's grip loosen and my body begin to lower. When my feet hit the ground, he spins me around and places my hands back on the wall in front of me while his feet spread mine farther apart. His lips connect with my shoulder while his hands press down on my back, encouraging me to arch. Not like I need any encouragement though.

"Fuck, LG, remember when I said I'd dreamed of all the things I could do to you?"

I look over my shoulder and watch him scan my body. "I believe you told me you'd let me know one day."

"This is one of those things." He smirks before sliding back into me without warning, causing a long slow moan to escape me. "And that's the sound I heard every." He snaps his hips. "Single." Snap. "Time." Snap.

I hope to god Florence is long gone. The bunkie isn't right next to the house, but I'm pretty sure every syllable out of my mouth is carrying through the trees. Usually, I'd be concerned, but present Nellie doesn't care who or what hears her. That's future Nellie's problem.

Future Nellie, now present Nellie, is pissed. As I open the door to the crisp morning air, I am greeted by a suggestive whistle originating from one of the two people sitting in the Muskoka chairs. I practically skulk behind the bunkie towards the bathroom and take my time with my morning routine. Teddy had already headed inside to get coffee for us, and I can't help but wonder what kind of greeting he received. Knowing how men can be, I imagine he'd strutted over like a fucking peacock.

My reflection gives little away. It doesn't show the slight soreness in my back or the rawness of my skin from his beard. I also half expected to look like a sex bomb, but I just look like me after very little sleep. No overnight, sex-induced transformation has occurred. I'm still just Nellie.

I pull out my phone to shoot a text to the girls.

It finally happened!

IZZY

You DNF'd a book?

MARLEY

You slept with Teddy!

IZZY

Oh, I like that better. Did you?

I peek back up at my reflection and smile at the fact I get to say yes to that.

Let's just say very little sleep was slept!

MARLEY

FUCK YES!

IZZY

Well, that sounds very promising.

MARLEY

Bennett just high-fived me!

MARLEY!

MARLEY

He doesn't know why... yet...

I raised my hand and he automatically did it.
He spends a lot of time around dogs.

IZZY

Importrant question

*Importrant

IMPORTANT FUCK

MARLEY

HAHAHAHAHA

IZZY

Will you be getting very little sleep again?

MARLEY

Have you seen him?

IZZY

One cannot assume.

Assume away!

MARLEY

Another high five!

IZZY

Is he even questioning these high-fives?

MARLEY

It was from Cass this time. She called this
btw.

Called what?

MARLEY

You and Teddy not lasting the whole trip
without ...

Three little dots appear then disappear, and then it

happens again.

Marley, without what?

MARLEY

Sorry, I couldn't remember the exact word.
Without coupling.

IZZY

Ew, I do not like that termite

MARLEY

Does anyone like termites?

IZZY

*Term

This new phone hats me.

I can't hold in the laugh as I picture Izzy cursing silently at her phone. She's such a perfectionist that I know this will be driving her mad.

MARLEY

Maybe you're just dumb like the rest of us!

IZZY

*Hates

And never.

There's a soft knock at the door just before it swings open revealing a shirtless Teddy. Probably because I've got his shirt on. He leans against the frame and takes me in from head to toe, a slow smile curling up the edges of his lips. I expect him to say something, but he remains silent as he watches me put my phone down and remove the toothbrush from my mouth.

"Do you need something, Teddy?"

He shakes his head, that damn smile shifting as his jaw

slides left then right. "Just wanted to let you know that coffee is ready."

"I'll be there in a minute." He nods and turns to leave but catches himself on the door, spinning back around. "Oh, and Midge was wondering how the bed held up." My mouth drops open, and he turns and walks back down the steps, laughing.

Goddammit it, past Nellie.

THIRTY-SEVEN

TEDDY

ZOE

MRI came back clean!

I stare at the message and feel my shoulders relax.

That's great! Thanks for letting me know.

Have you been having any headaches up there?

Not really.

What the hell does not really mean? You have but not many?

A couple but nothing too intense. Nothing to worry about.

Maybe make an appointment with Dr. Tascioni just to be safe.

Zo, I'm fine. Stop stressing. You know it's not good for you!

I hate that she worries about us like this. One of the things the doctor was pretty clear about was not letting stress get to her. She seems unbothered by her diagnosis though and is constantly worried about me and Will. We've had scans done, and we both have no signs of anything wrong. The machine is in a duffle in the truck, and I'm trying to decide whether or not to go do a reading so I can show her when Nellie saunters back into the bunkie.

She's wearing one of my T-shirts, and I have to bite my lip to keep the moan from escaping. It hits mid-thigh, and I can't stop myself from running my hands under it to trace the edges of the bathing suit she must have just put on.

Nellie's not looking at me like she's about to beg for more, though. "Everything okay?" Her forehead creases with concern.

"Yeah." I smile up at her. "Why?"

"I don't know, you looked worried when I came in." She looks down to where my phone sits in time to see another notification from Zoe pop up, this time a call. "I'll be at the lake. Take your time." She bends and kisses me in a way that leaves me wanting more when it ends too quickly.

"Zoe?" I answer, watching Nellie quickly grab her bag and Kevin's vest. She gives me a quick wave before disappearing out the door.

I realize that Zoe has been talking but I didn't hear anything. "Sorry Zo, lost you, what did you say?" I lie.

"I said, you being flippant about things stresses me out."

"I'm not being flippant. I know what to watch out for, and I'm being honest when I say the headaches I've had haven't been anything to worry about. I'd sooner be worried about a brain tumor than an aneurysm at this point."

"That's not fucking funny," Zoe hisses.

I sigh and lay back on the bed, knowing there is no way I

can win. "If I go take my blood pressure now and send you a picture, will that ease your mind?" I stand and head for the door, grabbing the keys from the cabinet.

"That would be preferable to you claiming you're fine, yes. Cold hard evidence is always appreciated."

"You sound like a lawyer."

"Well at least that degree isn't completely going to waste."

When I open the door, the yard is empty so I don't feel like I have to sneak to the truck. It's not that I don't want people to know; I just don't want them to worry, which they tend to do. Exhibit A: me with Nellie's cut.

"Okay, the cuff is cuffed, and I'm about to start it. Tell me something good."

Zoe tells me that Jordan's pregnancy is going well, better than hers had been with my nephew Keenan. Will and his family were over last night for dinner, and she assures me she pestered him too. At least she's consistent.

The first cycle ends, and I report the numbers to her as the cuff starts to restrict again. Three rounds, and the average is normal which finally convinces her that I'm not about to drop dead. We say our goodbyes, and I slide off the tailgate to start putting things away.

"Everything okay?"

I must jump three feet in the air as George walks up to the truck.

"Christ, George," I gasp, leaning on the tailgate, trying to get my breathing to even out. I bet my blood pressure wouldn't be so normal now.

George leans on the truck, his eyes glued to the bag I was in the middle of zipping. "What's wrong with ya?"

I love how people over a certain age don't care about societal norms. They'll ask you whatever they want, whenever they want. and small-town people are even better at it.

"Nothing. I'm fine."

"Fine people don't generally check their blood pressure in secret."

"They do if they're making sure they stay fine," I say with as much confidence as I can.

"Why wouldn't you stay fine?"

"These are pretty personal questions, George."

He shrugs and looks back towards the bunkie. "If you're protecting that girl from something, I'd recommend just being honest with her."

"I have been honest...I am being honest. This"—I zip the bag the rest of the way—"is nothing. It's something to keep my sister off my back."

"It may be nothin' to you, son, but I guarantee it would be somethin' to her if you don't tell her. At least check things in the bunkie rather than sneaking out to the back of the truck like some addict." He pats the truck a couple of times and backs away. "I'll see you in a few hours for our trip out to Betty's."

I'm fine; I know I'm fine. But I also know how I handled Nellie's bleeding, and I doubt I would have reacted that way if I'd known about her condition. At least I hope I would have kept it together a bit better. The words *I'm going to lose her, I'm going to lose her* kept running through my head. I'd lost her once because I couldn't handle something. Telling her had to be at the top of my list. Being honest with her even if it seems insignificant proves that I care about her and I care about her caring about me. I refuse to hear her say that she wishes I'd said something earlier.

"Come on, Kev!" I hear Nellie holler as I'm nearly at the lake.

She's patting the water and waiting for Kevin to start towards her then she dips below and pops up on the other side, repeating the process. He pursues her just as enthusiastically each time. *I get it, buddy,* I think to myself as I hang back in the shadows and watch for a few more minutes, wondering if I could freeze time. What if we just stayed here in this middle-of-nowhere bubble? Nellie runs the library, I work for Betty—ideal in every single way.

I'd once called the little town of El Nido in the Philippines heaven on earth, but it doesn't hold a candle to this place, not when Nellie's with me. Hell, the back seat of a beat-up old Ford pickup is Heaven when she's there. Forget remote beaches, banana pancakes, fresh fish every night, and forgotten coral reefs. Nellie is all I need.

I announce my presence by diving in and swimming straight for her. She yelps as I grab her around her middle and pull her to me. It doesn't take long for her arms and legs to wrap around me. There is absolutely nothing sexual about this, just two people in a remote lake hugging. Heaven.

Eventually, I let go and allow my body to stretch out with a few short laps to the shore and back to where Nellie and Kevin continue to play their little hide-and-seek game. After that I join in, only to discover that I'm not Kevin's favorite. It's a slight hit to the ego, but if I'm being completely honest, I get it. I'd pick her too.

"You seem to be a bit more like yourself now," Nelly observes as we sit across from each other on the rocks. Her water-shoe-clad feet resting alongside my bare ones.

"I'm with you, in nature, and Zoe isn't bugging me about my health," I say after a long sip of coffee.

Nellie sits up straighter, leaning toward me, concern etched across her beautiful face. "Your health?"

Setting my coffee down, I mirror her body position. "Let me preface this by saying that I am fine, and I have the tests to prove it." Her eyes widen, but she says nothing. "Zoe has an aneurysm, unruptured." I tap the back left side of my head, showing where it is. "They found it three years ago after she gave birth, but it's small and so they opted to monitor rather than do surgery. But she insisted that Will and I get blood pressure monitors and check periodically as well as keep track of headaches."

"I can understand that. Between your mom and now her, I'd be doing the same thing," Nellie says. "And so far you're good?"

"I am happy to report that my blood pressure is award-worthy, I have an MRI scan proving my brain is clear, and the only headaches I tend to get are from eye strain from reading in low light."

"You know they have these nifty things called lamps right? They can help with things like low light." Then she holds up a finger and reaches into her bag. "Also, these are great." She pulls out a long U-shaped thing and clicks a button. "Well, you can't really tell in daylight, but you wear it around your neck and there are lights here and here." I watch as she demonstrates how this very simple reading light works, and my imagination goes to work.

Nellie, next to me in bed, reading well into the night, far too enthralled by whatever adventure she's on to sleep. Nellie, reading to me in bed, doing all the voices like she does when she reads to kids. Nellie, wearing only that thing, moving above me. The lights pointed down, illuminating just part of her body, acting out one of our favorite scenes in The Forest of Despair series.

Cold water hits me, and I'm shocked out of my daydreaming. "Were you imagining me in just this reading light, EG?" she asks innocently.

"No!" I protest. "I was imagining you reading... in nothing but the light."

She smiles back shyly. "Maybe if you're a good boy today, I'll read to you tonight in nothing but this light."

"Don't tease, LG," I warn.

"I'm not teasing," she assures me. "You." She shifts so she's on her hands and knees. "Me." I freeze as she crawls slowly towards me. "No clothes." I remain motionless even when she's between my legs, hands resting on either side of my hips. "And a book." Her lips are a millimeter from mine. "Heaven," she breathes out, and I strike, grasping her head and claiming every part that I can reach.

"Teddy," Betty calls the minute I'm out of the truck. "I've got a proposition for you."

"Have fun, kid." George winks as he heads to the house. He's been talking about coffee all morning, and I'm trying to figure out if he's interested in coming to keep Joshua company or for the Nespresso.

Betty and I take a walk out to the dogs. Over the last couple of weeks, I've been helping her plan out an outdoor space where the dogs can socialize safely. When we round the corner of the barn, I see she's been busy. Bright orange spray paint has been used to outline where future fencing will go, deep into the ground so dogs can't easily dig their way out and nothing can easily dig its way in.

"This is going to make a huge difference," I say, hands on my hips as I take it in, already imagining the space full of dogs.

"I spoke to Bennett last night. About this and about something else." I look over at her and see she looks excited and nervous.

"What else?"

"You."

"Me?"

She nods and turns back towards the house. "It'll be winter before we know it, and Joshua's nurse told us two days ago that she's done traveling after October tenth."

"That means you'll have a lot more work."

"It does. The thing is, Teddy, I'm not sure I want to do it." She looks over at the dogs and back at me. "I love it, but Joshua needs to be my priority right now, and our daughter suggested we move to Timmins for a few months so we can be closer to the hospital."

I'm starting to put the pieces together. "Is that what you talked to Bennett about?"

"I was curious about the possibility of him loaning you out for the winter. If you want to, of course. I just wanted to make sure it was something he'd be on board with before I asked you. Don't wanna step on any toes."

"I'm guessing he said he'd be fine with it?"

"If you were, he would be," she says calmly.

I look over at the dogs. I could be useful here. "When would you need to know by?"

"In a couple of weeks. If you can't, I'll have to figure out something else. Possibly send the dogs to other rescues."

There aren't enough rescues willing to take this many dogs. Some would end up in high-kill shelters, and we both know it. "I need to talk to Nellie." I finally say.

"He said you'd say that."

THIRTY-EIGHT

NELLIE

I read a book once about a vampire that turned the woman he was in love with into one, with her consent of course. They became obsessed with one another to the point it was dangerous to be around anyone else. She could sense he was on his way home from fifty miles away and started getting all hot and bothered, then she'd be ripping the door off the hinges the second he pulled into the driveway. He'd be equally agitated and they'd collide with such a force that would have killed them if they were human. In short, they were addicted to one another, and that's how I feel right now. When Teddy is gone, I become agitated. I have a hard time focusing on the kids who have questions or adults looking for a recommendation. All I want is for Teddy to pull in so I can jump him.

It took me a while to realize that our December reunion was essentially us colliding after too long apart. And then three nights ago in the garden, another collision after far too many months of teasing. It feels like I was only fighting the inevitable, and you know what they say about inevitabilities: it's only a matter of time. I felt this way years ago, but it feels more intense now. This doesn't feel like a honeymoon stage anymore, it feels like a triumph after reaching the summit.

"Al's wife loved this book," Midge says, holding up one of my mom's more popular releases.

"Oh yeah?" I shake off my Teddy withdrawal and walk over to the display she's standing by.

"*The Ghost of North Bakers Lane.* She read it so many times the pages were practically falling out."

"I'll let my mom know," I say nonchalantly.

Midge stares down at me as if I've just said something insane. "Why would you tell your mom?" she asks slowly.

"Because she wrote it."

"Your mother is Jean Woodcroft?"

"She is indeed."

"Oh, Natasha would have loved to meet you. She would have loved to meet you anyway since you brought more books. But her favorite author's daughter. Oooeee."

I wonder how close Midge was to George's wife. "When did she pass?" I ask.

"Oh, let's see. Stewart died six years ago, which means Natasha died eight years ago thereabouts."

I gasp. "That's not why you call George Grumpy Al is it? Because he was grieving?"

Midge looks taken aback. "What kind of heartless bitch do you take me for? I started calling him Grumpy Al the first time I met him, which was twelve years ago."

Twelve years. She met George the same year I met Teddy. Wild.

"But why?" George is the farthest thing from grumpy.

"I walked into this little station to pay for gas, and when I walked in, he got all grumbly because I'd interrupted his penny counting. I smacked down a twenty and turned right back around but not before calling 'Night, Grumpy Al,' over my shoulder."

"When did you find out his real name?"

"Natasha dragged him over the next afternoon to welcome us to the neighborhood. When he saw me, he got all aggravated, and after explaining who I was, Natasha told me we were going to be best friends. Al said, and I quote, 'Over my dead body.' Turns out he's never been good at threats because not only is he still here, he encouraged the friendship."

I'm momentarily distracted when a truck pulls in. Disappointment must show on my face when it's not Teddy because Midge pats my arm. "It's nice to see that you two have repaired whatever had been broken."

"Hmm?" I glance down at her.

"You and Teddy. There was clearly some barrier between you two when you arrived, but it seems it's been removed?"

There is absolutely no point in trying to lie to this woman; she's a bloodhound. Whether it's getting to the bottom of someone's love life or detecting which grandkid tracked muddy footprints through the kitchen, she will find it out.

"I think so," I say slowly. "Early days yet."

"What are you worried about?" She takes me by the elbow and guides me to one of the chairs, sitting me down before sitting next to me. "Pretend they aren't here." She gestures to the three kids sprawled on the rug, one sitting on a big bean bag chair one of the residents had dropped off.

"We have pretty different lives. Well, not exactly different, we just don't live near one another."

"Distance is a terrible excuse. Why else?"

"No, it's not so much the distance. It's just that... well, he loves his job and I lo... like mine and it's not like we can just relocate to do it."

"In three years, is that job going to welcome you home from

a long day? Is it going to hold you when you've had a bad day? Cook for you? Make your toes curl with its kisses?"

"No," I say quietly.

"A job is just a job. It doesn't give a shit about you."

"Grandma!" one of her grandkids gasps. "Language."

"Kelly, we have discussed this. I am tall enough to say whatever words I want without getting in trouble. When you are this tall, you may do the same."

Kelly scoffs and goes back to her book. "Her mother is a bit of a prude," Midge whispers to me. "Lovely woman, works admin at the mill, but..." She gives me a look that shows she has little patience for her. "Now." She pats my knee heartily. "Back to this make-believe conundrum. I know it's hard to find a job you lo... like and you went to school for and all that. I loved my job, sometimes more than the one I had at home, if I'm being honest. But at the end of the day, it was Stewart that made me happy, not the classroom."

"I thought you hated your husband." Midge hasn't had a kind thing to say about the man since we arrived.

"He wasn't well in his last couple of years, and he changed. Sometimes it's easier to remember that person... easier to remember the pain he caused me—never physically," she quickly reassures me when she sees my eyes widen. "Emotionally. He was unstable, and life was hell, quite frankly. Out here in the middle of nowhere, I'd just lost my best friend, and the man I'd spent forty years head over heels in love with seemed to hate me. But when he took his final breath at the hospital holding my hand, he looked at me and I saw him there, the Stewart I'd married. The man who had never raised his voice to me or called me a terrible name. And I realized that I had grieved that man already."

"That's a pretty big realization," I say, reaching out and squeezing her hand.

"And I lied about it." She laughs. "Al was the one who made me see it. Still in the throes of his grief, two years after Natasha left us. He said he'd watched me go through the same stuff, heard me say the same things he was thinking even though Stewart was still here physically."

"I'm sorry Midge."

"Nellie, don't be sorry. I got years of happiness with a man I was mad about. How lucky am I? Some people never get that. Now." She slaps her thigh. "I came today because I have something to discuss with you."

Teddy still isn't back when it's time to close up the library, so I pick up a copy of *The Forest of Despair*, curl up in the beanbag chair, flip to my favorite part, and start reading, Kevin dreaming by my side, chasing after a chipmunk perhaps.

Dusk is settling when George's truck pulls in, and I slip my glasses onto my head and unabashedly watch Teddy unfold himself from the passenger seat. He and George exchange goodbyes, and he starts to make his way over. Kevin greets him halfway, and I feel my insides turn to mush when he picks the little dog up for a snuggle.

"Hey you," he says, dropping to his knees beside me. "I should have known you'd be reading your favorite book."

"How was your day?" I ask after I kiss him quickly. Something that feels new and somehow like the most natural thing in the world.

He eyes the top of my head, and a soft smile forms. "Ah, it was interesting," he says slowly, reaching up and gently untangling the glasses from my hair and holding them out for me.

"Mine too," I muse, slipping them into my bag, alongside my book.

"How was yours interesting?" he asks, leaning in for a quick kiss.

I shake my head and pull him back when he starts to retreat. "I want to hear about your day first," I murmur against his lips.

He hums in response before sitting back, his hands resting on my knees. "Well, it started with this hot make-out session at the lake." Teddy's eyes rake down my body, and I feel my skin heat. "Then I think I was offered a job, or a temporary job anyway." He seems confused by what he's telling me.

"What kind of job?"

"Betty asked if I'd be interested in taking over the shelter for a bit. Joshua could use more treatments and more regular visits with his physiotherapist to help him get back on his feet. Their daughter suggested that they move in with her in Timmins so they could be closer to the hospital. Especially for the winter."

"And what did you say?" I ask nervously.

His gaze holds mine and I feel like he's going to wreck me again. "I said I'd think about it. I wanted to talk to you first."

"Why? You don't need my permission."

"No," he says. "But that doesn't mean I don't want your opinion or your input in any way I can get it." He takes the book out of my hand and sets it aside, then takes both my hands in his. "What are you thinking, LG?"

He looks nervous despite how steady his hands are. His eyes are giving him away. "What was your first instinct? Was it to say yes?"

He shakes his head slowly. "My first thought was of you. Just *'Nellie.'*" My breath catches at the way he says my name like a prayer.

"I can't factor into your decisions, Teddy. You need to do what is going to be best for you. Not me, or Bennett, you."

Rising on his knees so he's above me, he gently takes my face in his hands. "You're what's best for me, Nellie." When I close my eyes, he pleads with me to look at him, and I do. His nervous expression has given way to determination and something softer that I can't quite name. "Does the idea of us scare you?"

"No," I whisper. "It should, but it feels far more right than knowing you're out there and not with me."

"Since December, I've felt..." He pauses, thinking of the right word. "Settled. Like you showed up, and that was that. I was home, even if you weren't with me. You existing nearby made me feel like I was home. I hadn't felt like that in so long, Nell. I've questioned so many choices since I left. But when it comes to you, I've never questioned how I feel." He sounds like Marley. Someone is saying this about me, and I'm nearly speechless.

"And how do you feel?" I ask quietly.

"Like I could conquer anything as long as you're by my side. Like I've won some grand prize I didn't even know I was entered for. Like this was inevitable. You...you've had my heart since the train. It just feels like I've been reunited with it after a very long absence. It has a reason to beat again. It's—" I stop his words with a kiss. I don't need him to carry on coming up with ways to tell me how he feels without saying the words everyone focuses on. I don't even need them, just the fact he wants my input tells me where I stand.

I draw back slowly. "I think you should say yes."

THIRTY-NINE

TEDDY

I can feel the panic begin at the base of my spine. *I think you should say yes.* I told myself it was too fast, things may have heated up quickly physically between us, but that doesn't mean she's ready for more. I've done this to myself, again.

"Midge brought me some interesting information today," Nellie says, although it sounds like I'm underwater and she's speaking to me from above. "Teddy?"

She grabs my hand to stop me from fidgeting, my thumb no longer able to spin my ring. "Sorry?"

"I said, Midge brought some interesting information to me today. About a library application she submitted to the regional council. Marmot Point has received funding for a proper library. It would serve not just Marmot Point, but the surrounding communities with a mobile unit. I don't know all the details yet, but Three Rivers University is one of the partners." I don't know why she's telling me this. Maybe she thinks I'll be happy to know that if I stay, I'll have easier access to books. "She suggested I stick around to help them."

"Wait." I give my head a shake. "We were both offered opportunities up here on the same day?"

Nellie tilts her head, grinning at me. "I think these Marmotans have been trying to play matchmaker since the day we got here. But what do you think? Should I take the role? At least to help them get started?"

"You're asking if you should take a job that's about half an hour from where I'll be living? Is that a question you don't already know the answer to?" I ask.

"I hate assumptions," she replies. "I'm still trying to work through some feelings, and I don't know if this is all just"—she looks off into the distance, the lines on her forehead deepening slightly as she searches for the right word—"a phase," she finally says.

"A phase? This?" I gesture between the two of us, and she nods. "Did anything I just say sound like something someone says in a phase." I grab her hand and place it on my chest. "This beats for you. Nellie. Nellie. Nellie." She laughs, her fingers curling in my shirt.

"Not Library Girl?"

"Too many syllables. I think it would be considered a very irregular heartbeat." She laughs harder, the force of it causing me to join in. "We officially have a week left here. If you decide it's not what you want, we go home and never come back. If it is what you want, we go home and get things settled so we can come back together."

"Together," she mouths, the sound barely reaching my ears.

"So what exactly would you be doing?" I ask Nellie, who is sitting across from me on the floor of the bunkie.

She draws patterns in the smear of hummus on her plate with a carrot. "Honestly, Midge just gave me a very basic overview. But it sounded like a nice change from what I'm currently doing. Don't get me wrong, I enjoy working in an academic environment, but I've done it my entire working life. Being here has reminded me of my summer job at the library. Getting to work with kids and adults who want to read. People who yearn for a good book." She drops the carrot and looks up at me. "I don't think it's something I want to do forever. I don't see myself up here for years on end. But being part of something from the ground up would be pretty cool."

"What about your parents? What do you think they'd say about you changing jobs?"

Nellie winces. "I don't know. They've always been the type of people to encourage dreams. But they will also question walking away from a pretty stable, well-paying job. I'll have to have my arguments well-constructed before I talk to them. I'm an adult and can do whatever the hell I want, but..."

"You don't want to disappoint them," I suggest.

"Exactly."

"You haven't talked much about them moving away. You doing okay with that?"

I watch as she looks back at her plate and begins to worry her bottom lip. She's blinking rapidly and I am about to slide over to her when she looks up at me. "I was upset when they told me. It felt like they were abandoning me. I kept expecting to cry or lash out in some way. Spoiled, remember?" She laughs, pointing at herself. "But I just kept reminding myself that they're just a plane ride or phone call away." She looks at me, and I see it in her expression. They're still here, physically still here.

When Nellie wants to call Marley after dinner, I take our plates back to the house. Midge is snuggled next to George on the well-worn couch reading from the same book. It's ridiculously cute.

"I heard you had a job offer today," she says the second she sees me.

"Well, a temporary job offer," I amend, sliding the plates into the dishwasher. "It's just until Joshua is better. Mind if I?" I say, pointing at the armchair next to them.

"Please do." Midge smiles up at me. "What's your story?" she asks as George closes the book and pulls her in closer.

Only two people outside of my family know everything, and now that I've told Nellie, I don't feel the same anxiety about telling anyone else. Everything pours out of me in one long stream of consciousness, and when I'm done, Midge and George are looking at me with eyes full of tears.

"She's the reason for every breath you take," George says softly.

"Such a romantic," Midge scoffs, although her expression softens further making her tone carry less weight.

"I would doubt that, but it sure felt like I took my first real breath in years back in December."

"How did you end up here together?"

"That would be Bennett and Marley's scheming. They claimed to not like the idea of Nellie coming all this way alone, and then Bennett mentioned Betty and Joshua's rescue."

"So everyone around you sees it?"

"What?"

"That you're in love with each other," Midge says plainly. "Head over heels, only have eyes for the other, dumbstruck, truly, madly, deeply."

"Take it from two olds—" George begins.

"Olds?" Midge sputters, looking highly offended. "Speak for yourself, sir."

"That's what the kids call us when they think we can't hear them, on the account of being old."

"What kids?"

"Your blood relations, Magpie. All the wee Midges running around this place."

"They would never."

"They do," George and I say at the same time.

Midge leans forward and glares out the window to see her grandkids are up to various activities in the yard. "Those rude little buggers."

George shrugs. "I've earned the stamp of old. I don't take it as an insult, and I don't think they mean it as one." His words don't seem to do anything as Midge remains in her current position, wearing the look of someone planning revenge. "Embrace the feeling, Teddy," he says to me, ignoring what Midge is doing. "You more than just about anyone know how fleeting time can be. This thing between you and Nellie is years in the making. It has been challenged, and at the end of the day, it has triumphed."

I lean back and look out the window just in time to see Nellie jump back from the snake Devon is carrying. He grins and then he's chasing her with it, the other kids joining in. I can't help laughing at a memory that starts to play. We had just finished a picnic and were walking back to the car when a garter snake slithered across the path. Nellie said a very loud "Nope," threw the basket she was carrying to the side, and took off at a run. I'd stood still, watching her disappear as the damn thing made its way to the forest floor, totally unbothered.

"This was her dream," I say, watching as Nellie runs toward the truck.

"What? To be chased with a snake?" George asks, confused.

What a weird dream that would be. "No, to have a mobile library."

"I believe it," Midge says, finally done with her death stare. "She's got a wanderer's spirit. I have a hard time imagining her now stuck in one place."

I look over at Midge. "How long have you known about the library being approved?"

She looks at me with a guilty little smile. "It was approved before you arrived. Nellie's boss had suggested that she might put Nellie's name forward for the position."

"But there isn't a position available yet."

"The trailer will stay put as a temporary library until things are set. It's going to be a long winter, but spring comes eventually, and with it a new adventure. The trailer then will be able to be used as a mobile library."

"Those kids are psychotic," Nellie gasps as she bursts through the patio door and collapses dramatically at my feet.

FORTY

NELLIE

After Teddy does a sweep of the yard to ensure there are no children with snakes ready to jump out at me, we head to the lake.

Teddy sits behind me with his arms wrapped around my body while Kevin gnaws on a stick that's far too large for him.

It's the first time we've been like this with one another since our reunion. It feels like before, when the reality of just being together was enough.

Sighing, I lean back into his embrace. "This is nice."

"It is," Teddy says quietly, tightening his hold ever so slightly and dropping a kiss to the top of my head.

There's a splash from somewhere at the end of the lake, and we both lean forward trying to see what made it. Kevin, who most definitely has better eyesight, starts barking aggressively. Or as aggressively as an eight-month-old puppy can manage.

"Our protector." I laugh, reaching over to grab the dog. "See anything?" I look over my shoulder to see Teddy still focused on the distance.

"It's either a moose or a bear," he says. "Definitely not a giant snake."

I jab him with my elbow. "Not funny."

"It's a little funny," he murmurs into my neck, no longer concerned with what made the noise. "It wasn't even alive."

"Being chased with a dead snake doesn't make it better," I insist. "That kid is so weird. Not a bad thing. I mean, weird kids make awesome adults. But he's unnervingly obsessed with dead things."

"We need those people, though," Teddy replies thoughtfully. "Everything dies eventually. It's good to have people who care about that part of it. And look at it this way: he's not *creating* the dead things."

"That's true. I guess if he was obsessed with that part of it, we'd have a reason to be worried."

"There ya go." His lips glide over the exposed skin of my neck, and I feel myself relax against him more. "So, I was thinking."

"Dangerous."

I feel his breath replace his lips, humoring me with the smallest laugh. "When we get home..." I tense at the word "home." No more bunkie sleepovers or early morning swims. I've managed to forget that this isn't my real life.

"Hey," Teddy says softly, scooting around so we're facing each other. He distracts Kevin with a stick and then picks up my hands. "Don't freak out."

"I'm not," I squeak, giving away the fact that yes I am indeed starting to freak out. "Okay, maybe I am a little bit."

"Why?"

"Because home is real life. This place is"—I look around and take a deep breath—"a fantasy."

"Your fantasy involves twin beds in a one-room hut?" Teddy's eyebrows arch comically high.

"No, but this place feels like a vacation."

He looks down at our hands. "So am I just some guy you had a vacation fling with?"

I'm shaking my head before I even know what I'm going to say. "You've never been a fling, Teddy," I say so quietly, at first I don't think he hears me.

"When we get home," he starts again, "we are going to try this thing for real. You and me. No meddling townsfolk or meandering moose. Just Nellie and Teddy going for dinner or a movie. Just us finding each other again."

"We can't go back, Teddy."

"I know," he says with a sad smile. "But going back was never part of my plan. Once upon a time, I fell for this library science student named Nellie. She had wild auburn hair that she always got her glasses stuck in. She loved books and birds and drove me wild. One day a shadow darkened my world, and not even Nellie's light could lead me out of the darkness. Then many years later, back in the world of light, I fell for a librarian named Nellie. She has wild auburn hair that she always gets her glasses stuck in. She loves books and birds and driving me fucking wild."

My face is probably as red as a tomato. "You should be a writer," I tease.

"I really should be. I didn't follow my true calling of writing very basic and repetitive fairy tales about the woman I'm in love with."

"It's too soon," I whisper.

"It's too damn late," he says with conviction. "At twenty-two, I was too dumb to recognize what it was. I thought it was infatuation or basic feelings. Nellie, it turns out I have felt those things for other people." I hate those people. "But I've never felt what I feel for you. It came back to life in December, this constant reminder of who you were."

"And who am I?" I ask, my voice somehow not giving away the nervous excitement bubbling away in my brain.

I watch those pale blue eyes search mine and I know exactly what he's about to say. "Mine," Teddy whispers back. It's not a possessive mine or an expression of ownership. Probably because I feel the same about him. Like he has been mine since the start.

We both reach for the other's faces at the same time, and a nervous laugh bubbles out of me as he wipes a tear from my cheek because I was about to do the same to him.

"On a scale of one to ten, how corny was that?" he asks.

I pretend to think about it, hemming and hawing until he gives me an exasperated look. "About a nine. But I like corny so feel free to be as corny as you want when it comes to telling me how you feel."

"So you're up for trying?"

"Very much so." I manage to say before his lips crash into mine. I've never kissed someone I've decided is mine, and it turns out that it's a pretty spectacular experience. Five stars, would recommend.

Teddy pulls me into his lap, and it doesn't take long for his back to hit the rock beneath us. I chase his mouth with my own and give over to every instinct in me. His hands grip my hips and pull me so hard against him that he breaks the kiss, gasping for air, his pupils blown wide as I establish a rhythm.

It's getting dark, and I know we are very alone out here, so I do something I have wanted to do since the day we were caught hugging. I reach between us and undo his shorts. Teddy catches on quickly and does the same with mine. Seconds later and after some slightly creative maneuvering, I'm sinking torturously slowly down onto him. When I'm fully seated, I hold still and watch him try to stay in control. Bending down I kiss him slowly, our moans trapped between us. When I give my hips the smallest swivel, Teddy's head drops back, his mouth open in a silent moan.

When his gaze meets mine again, I smile down. "Mine," I say and watch as his eyes darken ever so slightly.

His grip goes from feather light to bruising and I love it. I want his fingerprints seared into my skin. I want to feel them for days so that when I get home I can remember this wasn't all a fever dream. My head tips back, and his left hand reaches under my shirt to pull me free from my bra. I'm almost too sensitive as he tweaks and pinches. He shifts beneath me, and his hand goes to the back of my neck.

"Look at me." His warm breath hits my throat and the added sensation makes me shudder.

He's sitting up now, his arm like a vice around my hips while his other hand maintains a light grip on my neck. "Hey there, pretty girl," he purrs when our eyes meet. "This feels like a dream."

"A good one?" I ask, the tension building to an impossible height.

"The best," he exhales against my lips right before he kisses me.

"So close," I murmur against his lips.

I'm only vaguely aware of his hand moving down my body, but when his thumb connects with me, I feel every part of me come alive. Every tiny hair stands on end, every single cell is engaged as pleasure detonates within me.

"So beautiful," he rasps, burying his face into my chest and letting out a strangled cry.

"Betty and Joshua have a lake not far from their place," Teddy says as we head back to the bunkie, batting mosquitos the whole way.

I look down at where our hands are connected and lean into him. "You should have mentioned that earlier. I would have said yes immediately."

"That felt like cheating. I wanted you to want to stay for me, not the lake."

"Can't I have both?" I look up at him, and I'm greeted by that serene smile I haven't seen in years.

"You can have everything you want," he whispers, leaning down to kiss me.

Kevin is trotting in front of us, his little tail wagging away. "Do you think we've traumatized him?" I bite my lip with worry.

"He chewed on that stick the whole time. I don't think he knew anything was going on," Teddy reassures me.

I head to the bathroom when we get back to get ready for bed. Halfway through brushing my teeth, my phone lights up with a text from Teddy.

TEDDY

DON'T LEAVE THE BATHROOM

I smile down, thinking he's about to come in and ravish me in here too. The counter is the perfect height for bending me over, or sitting me on and—

Morticia is in a standoff with a bear right outside the bathroom.

The fire that had started to reignite turns to ice. I look at the door that now seems a bit too flimsy, and try to figure out what to do if a bear or a moose decide to use the bathroom as an escape route.

"How did she die?"

"Oh, she was run over by a moose in a bathroom of all places."

"Shame."

At least my death, while tragic, will be kind of funny. I decide to huddle on the floor of the shower. The walls in here seem a bit more reinforced.

George is getting his gun.

No, don't kill them!

I don't think he's planning on shooting at them, just near them, to scare them off.

Okay, good.

You okay?

I'm sitting on the shower floor hoping nothing comes through the wall.

Also, I kind of want to watch.

Don't you dare open the door, LG.

Distract me.

Please.

When we get home, we are going straight to my very sturdy bed.

To sleep?

To tire ourselves out!

What happens after we do that?

I slide my left hand down my body and into my shorts. I'm

still sensitive from earlier, but I can't help touching myself as I eagerly await his reply.

> I get to pull you into my arms and sleep with you there all night. Then I'm going to crawl under the covers and wake you up with my mouth.

The fire has reignited as my breathing quickens. My phone rings.

I answer with a breath.

"Are you distracting yourself with your hand, pretty girl?"

I barely manage a breathy "Yes" as my fingers go to work.

"Good. Imagine your fingers are my tongue."

"Teddy," I whine, just as a loud bang comes from outside and I drop my phone and scream.

"Nellie? Nell?" I hear Teddy's voice through the phone and then from outside.

The door flies open, and he slides over to me, pulling my shaking body to him.

"I'm so sorry. Fuck, I didn't expect it to be that loud. You're okay."

"I know. I don't know why I'm shaking," I croak, leaning harder into him. "Kinda pissed I didn't get to finish though."

"Hurry up in here, and I'll help with that back in the bunkie. I don't want to end up trapped in here for the night." His eyes catch on the counter, and I watch him realize the same thing I had earlier. "Although..." He looks at me as a wicked little grin appears.

"It was a far better thought when there wasn't a threat of a bear bursting through the wall," I say, shaking my head.

"Fair."

Teddy helps not once but twice back in the bunkie, and I fall asleep no longer hearing the gunshot.

TEDDY

"We'll be back soon," Nellie says as she hugs Midge. "I cannot wait."

"You'll let us know if you change your mind, though, right?" Midge asks.

"I absolutely would, but that won't happen."

"And you," Midge says, pulling me down for a hug, "take care of our girl here."

"I will." I hug her back as tightly as she's hugging me. "We'll see you soon." I release her and wave to the gathered townspeople.

Betty brought two dogs over at dawn, and they're howling away in the truck. Kevin is looking at me like I've betrayed him. "Gonna be a long drive with those two," George says, patting me on the back.

"They'll settle down, I'm sure of it." Nellie waves off his concerns, and I don't have the heart to tell her that it's probably going to be like this for the next sixteen hours.

Sixteen hours driving right through, at that.

We pull out of the gas station-liquor store-taxidermist

parking lot with a lot more fanfare than we pulled in with. Both Nellie and I wave out our windows as we pull back onto the main road and head for home.

Three hours later, Nellie is looking over at me like she may murder me. "Why are they still going?" She looks back at the two huskies still chattering away.

"They're huskies." I shrug, reaching over with my right hand to take hers. "They talk."

"Do they ever shut up?" she asks, looking worried.

"I'm sure they will when they run out of things to say."

After another three hours, Nellie looks like she's near tears.

"Do you want me to just open the door and let them out because I will? For you, I will."

She laughs and then scolds me. "Don't make me laugh. I've gotta pee so bad."

"Why didn't you say something?"

"We're making good time, and I didn't want to ruin it."

"Are you going to piss your pants?"

"Possibly," she says guiltily.

"Is that better than stopping briefly?"

She shakes her head and pouts. "I don't want to ruin Bennett's truck."

"There's a gas station in a few klicks, so we'll stop there. I'm sure the dogs have to go too."

"Maybe that's why they're so chatty," she says hopefully.

When we arrive at the station, Nellie runs inside, and then I see her scurry out and around the building to where the bathroom is. In the meantime, I manage to get each dog out one at a time for a pee break. Both huskies are quiet after I get them back in the truck, and I think maybe Nellie was right.

Ten minutes pass, and Nellie still hasn't come back. Another five minutes, and still no sign of her. I text her only to hear her phone ping from inside the center console. Now I'm worried so I pull the truck up to the bathroom and jump out.

"Nellie, are you okay in there?" I call through the door.

Her reply is muffled, but at least she's able to reply.

"I didn't hear you." I try to turn the knob but it's locked. "I'm going to see if they have another key, just a minute."

I head into the station, and the guy hands a key over way too easily. What if I was some creep wanting to break into the bathroom?

"I'm coming in," I shout as I turn the key and slowly push the door open. I keep my eyes closed though just in case there's a situation she doesn't want me to see.

"There's no toilet paper," she whimpers, and I open my eyes to see her holding an empty roll.

"Oh...I'll just go." I point to the door and leave again.

Shockingly the guy gives me a harder time about the roll of toilet paper than the key. His priorities are alarmingly skewed.

"How long were you going to wait?" I ask when Nellie gets back in the truck.

She shrugs. "However long it took to air dry down there?"

"Take your phone next time."

"Ew, no. I mean it's iffy in a normal bathroom, but a gas station bathroom? The grossest."

"That bathroom had nothing on some of the ones I've seen," I say as I pull back onto the road.

"Oh? Do tell," she goads.

"I'd really rather not. But let me just say that a lot of people aren't great with aim when it comes to squatting over a hole."

Nellie shudders. "Okay, say no more."

The silence between us on the way home isn't like it was on the way up. For one thing, Nellie's hand is in mine. When I look over, she's got her head turned towards me, smiling serenely. I wonder how many smiles I've missed over the years. Knowing Nellie, millions.

"Question," she says after an hour of quiet.

"Yeah?" I ask, looking over at her briefly.

"You know the song 'Dead or Alive' by Jon Bon Jovi?"

I chuckle. "Do you mean 'Wanted Dead or Alive' by Bon Jovi?"

"Sure. Did you know the lyrics are about a 'steel horse' and not a 'stale horse'?"

"Why would it be a stale horse and not a steel horse?"

"I don't know, I always thought it was a song about riding a tired horse. Like it's so tired it's stale."

"It's about their time on the road. Pretty sure the steel horse is a tour bus."

She makes a tiny "hmm" sound, and I look over to see her staring ahead, her face twisted in concentration. "I've lived my entire life singing the wrong lyrics. I wonder how many people noticed but never said anything."

I squeeze her hand. "I'm sure no one noticed, and if they did, they didn't say anything because it's really cute."

She huffs and her head thuds against the headrest. "I wonder what other lyrics I've been singing wrong."

"Probably loads," I assure her. "I'm sure we all sing the wrong lyrics all the time." I lift her hand to kiss it and watch her face relax. "Whatever happened to that jaywalker in your hometown?"

"Edith?" she asks.

"Right, I had forgotten her name."

"She was still jaywalking last time I checked."

"Go Edith," I cheer half-heartedly.

"She was uncontested in the last vote."

"Jaywalking falling out of favor with the townsfolk?"

"Terrible benefits," Nellie says.

"Typical."

A large bird swoops low in front of us, and Nellie leans forward, her eyes following it as it lifts into the sky again.

"Anything interesting?"

I feel her eyes on me and look over. "Depends on what you mean by interesting."

"Rare."

She sits back, threading her fingers through mine again. "Just a red-tailed hawk, exceptionally common. But endlessly interesting."

"You're such a nerd," I tease.

"You love it," she says, resting our hands on her thigh.

She's not wrong. I keep my eyes on the road ahead but allow a goofy grin to spread across my face. "Whatever happened to that guy who worked with your dad? The one who was in the UK."

"John?"

"Yeah."

"I haven't talked to him in a while. God, it's been what..." She sighs, her fingers tapping on her right thigh. "Seven months, I think. He was on a video call with my dad when I was over the one day. Calling from the middle of the Amazon, if you can believe it. But he was good, happy, still very into birds, and still very much not my boyfriend."

"Well, that's a fucking relief." I grin over at her, earning a flirty little smile that has me considering pulling the truck over for a little mid-drive intermission.

Nellie has been asleep for two hours. She'd taken over driving for about five and then we'd stopped for food, and by her third yawn, I insisted she let me drive again. Kevin is curled up beside her, her hand is still in mine, and the huskies haven't made a sound since our last stop. Alone with my thoughts, I allow myself to replay the last month.

There had been signs that Nellie wasn't going to stick to her claim of nothing more happening. I'd catch her watching me, and she'd turn away as soon as I looked, but as time went on, her gaze would linger. I have no idea if she realized it or not, but it was a welcome change.

The first time she'd clasped her arms around me at the lake I'd been terrified of doing something that would push her away. I don't doubt things would have gone further if I'd kissed her then, but something in me screamed that it didn't feel right. When she kissed me in the garden, though, that was a rebirth. A fresh start that I'd been desperately wanting, and she gave it to me and then some.

Tonight we plan on crashing in my bed. While I'd obviously love to do all the things with her, I'm most looking forward to just holding her all night long. Tomorrow we're heading to her place so she can start preparing to rent it out. She let me know a couple of days ago that she was going to take the position in Marmot Point. Her boss had informed her that it was a role still within the university program due to the partnership with the region, so she'd still be able to return to her old job later if that's what she wanted. She hasn't said so, but something tells me it isn't.

"Where are we?" Nellie yawns, her hand leaving mine as she stretches and rubs her neck.

I reach over and take over neck duties, earning a long groan that takes a little too much brain power to ignore. "About two hours from Bennett's."

She looks back at the sleeping huskies and smiles. "They are beautiful dogs when they're quiet."

"You do realize Betty's place has mostly huskies, right? Sure you still want to do this?" I glance over at her, thinking I'd see panic. But no, she's turned her head towards me and looks completely content.

"I think it'll be fine if I'm not stuck in a confined space with them singing away."

"That does make it more tolerable, yes. You being there with me will make everything more tolerable." I glance over again, and she somehow looks even more content. Like the idea of being together chases all the worries away. A month ago this seemed like a dream that would never come true.

"Teddy?" My name is almost a whisper.

"Nellie?"

"I'm glad you got to explore the world. Even if it wasn't with me, I'm happy for you." Both of her hands are grasping mine. "But going forward, please take me with you."

"You were always with me, Nellie, but next time I'll make sure you're right beside me."

"I really would appreciate that." She raises my hand to kiss my palm. "We're really bad at—"

Nellie's words are cut off by screeching tires and horns, and I'm momentarily blinded by headlights before the world goes black.

FORTY-TWO

NELLIE

It feels like my body was used as a crash test dummy. I'm so tired and everything hurts.

I remember the huskies howling and Kevin's little whimpers, and then Teddy springing into action to get out of the truck, which had flipped and ended up on the driver's side.

"Are you okay?" That was the first thing he'd said, and despite a minor headache and neck pain, I'd assured him I was fine.

We'd kicked the windshield out and crawled onto the road, the dogs following. One was limping, but otherwise they seemed fine. Kevin's whimpers appeared to be from fear rather than injury. A transport truck lay on its side a few meters away, and two other cars were in various states of disarray.

"I'm going to go see if anyone needs help," Teddy said as he turned and jogged towards the car that was still right side up, but before he got there I watched him slow down for a second only to shake his head and continue. By the time I had tied each dog to something so they didn't escape, Teddy had helped two people get out of their vehicles. I ran to help the one woman who was limping sit before following Teddy to the car that was on its roof.

"Two people," he shouted over to me. He bent down and told the driver to cover their face before smashing the window.

"My wife," the man sputtered. "She's not moving. I'm not leaving her like this."

"Sir, we can't help her if you're in the car," I said calmly, kneeling beside the car, stones or maybe shards of glass cutting into my knees. "If we can get you out, then we can check on your wife."

Sirens in the distance had me breathing a sigh of relief as Teddy continued to try and convince the man to let us help him.

"Nellie, can you..." Teddy started to say but stopped. I watched as he shook his head and tried to ask me something again.

Then, as if in slow motion, he fell to his knees and keeled over. My screams split the night.

Now, two hours later, my hands won't fucking stop shaking. It shouldn't be taking me so long to get into Teddy's wallet. His license is already sitting on the table in front of me, but his health card is wedged behind some paper. Everything falls to the floor when I get it free, and I feel more tears gather.

"I've got it, hun," a nurse whispers. She sets the wallet and most of its contents on the table in front of me, and I stare at them for a while. Two credit cards, and a very old stamp card from Subway.

Bending down, I unsuccessfully manage to grab the rip piece of paper which slides farther under the table and I have to drop to my knees to reach it. It's not a piece of paper, though; it's a picture. It's from one of the very few games I was at with his parents. In it, I've got his mom's hand raised in mine as we cheer from the stands. The rip runs down his mom's left side, his father removed from the memory. I kneel there on the hospital floor staring down at a picture I never knew existed. A picture that, judging by the creases, has been folded and unfolded countless times. A picture he no doubt carried around the world with him. His mom and I from another time, cheering for the guy who made up so much of our worlds.

"You sure you don't need anything?" Marley asks, sitting next to me.

I shake my head, refusing to look away from Teddy. He looks so small in the hospital bed. He'd woken up momentarily when he was brought back to his room after having a plethora of tests done, but he'd only blinked at me a couple of times before his eyes closed again. He's going to be okay, though. I keep repeating that over and over to myself because the thought of him not being okay is not something I am willing to entertain.

"How's your head?"

"Better," I mutter.

"Whiplash is a bitch. Make sure you report any changes okay?" Marley says, squeezing my arm.

"I finally got Teddy's dad on the phone," Bennett announces quietly as he returns to the room. "He's going to call his brother and sister, and they may head up."

"Good," I reply.

Watching Teddy fall was the single most terrifying moment of my life. I could handle being left. I could not handle him leaving like that, though. Not after how far we'd come. Not after reuniting after years of being apart just to have him taken away from me because of some idiot falling asleep at the wheel.

I thought he was dead. I thought every dream we'd started to dream together was dead too. And I kept telling him I couldn't do this without him, not now, not after letting him back in, the entire way to the hospital.

He was diagnosed with blunt liver trauma from when the airbag deployed, and he'd had some internal bleeding, which explained why he'd passed out. Adrenaline can only keep a person going for so long. The doctor had said a lot of words about what they'd done already and then what would be happening going forward, but I don't remember anything other than the five at the end: "He's going to be alright." I refuse to let myself believe the doctor had said anything other than that, despite knowing deep down a doctor would never say anything with such certainty.

Now I replay the events of last night over and over again. I think I'd just told him to take me with him next time. I start to cry again as images of him falling replace everything else. He had been so close to leaving me. I feel Marley's arms come around me, and I let go.

"He almost left me again," I sob into her shoulder.

"I know, Nell, but he didn't. He stayed," she murmurs into my hair. "He's never going anywhere without you again, okay? He's staying." She rubs my back and lets me cry until my sobs turn to soft hiccups and I catch my breath.

At some point, Bennett convinces someone to bring in a cot, and after Marley assures me they'll wake me up if Teddy wakes before me, I fall asleep.

"Is that... Nellie?" I hear a voice ask somewhere in the distance.

"It looks like her," another voice pipes up.

Then a voice that I've been longing to hear confirms groggily. "Yes."

I sit up fast, too fast, and I tip back onto my side. "Slow down, Nell," Marley says, sitting next to me.

"He's awake," I mumble quietly, using my arm to push myself back up as slowly as I can manage. "Why didn't you wake me up?"

"I told her not to." Teddy's voice is gravelly from sleep. "Hey, LG," he says softly when I finally look over.

He's sitting up, wide awake and alive. His dark hair shoots off in different directions and his blue eyes are sleepy, but it's the best view I've ever seen. I know there are more people in the room than there had been when I fell asleep, but I don't see them. I just see Teddy as I grab his face and kiss him.

"I'm so sorry," he says as tears fall down his face.

"For what?"

"You could have died. I nearly lost you." He's searching my eyes as though he'll find confirmation there.

I shake my head and grip his face a bit tighter. "No, I'm fine. But I nearly lost you. You're not allowed to scare me like that again, do you fucking understand me? You had just promised to take me with you next time and then you..." I can feel the panic start to set in again, and I force myself to take a few deep breaths. "You nearly left me again." It comes out as a whisper.

Teddy lifts his IV-less hand and rests his palm on my cheek, his thumb wiping tears away. "I didn't mean to, LG," he whispers. "I'm so sorry."

I can't help but laugh at that fucking word. "We are not good at not using that word."

He laughs then grabs his abdomen, his hand falling from my face as he winces in pain.

"Shit, EG, don't laugh," I scold.

"Then don't make me," he grunts.

I bend to lay my forehead against his and his hand covers mine on the bed.

"Ahem." Someone behind me clears their throat, and I straighten to see two men and a woman standing by the end of Teddy's bed.

"So," Zoe says, pointing between the two of us with an eyebrow quirked and a shit-eating grin on her face, "when did this start up again?"

"You're sure his head is good?" Teddy's father asks the doctor for the third time since they arrived yesterday evening.

"Teddy's scans all came back showing no signs of trauma to his brain or spine. He's lucky it was just the liver and some superficial cuts." The doctor turns back to Teddy. "We'll keep you here under observation for about five days and continue to monitor the bleeding. Right now, we don't think you'll need surgery, but that could change. Bed rest is essential."

"I'll make sure he listens," I tell the doctor but keep my eyes on Teddy. I never want to look away from him again. Even though we have been told again and again that everything looks good, watching him collapse is branded in my memory.

After two days of sitting vigil by his bed, Marley persuades me to take a shower and change in her and Bennett's hotel room.

"Feel better?" Marley asks when I finally leave the bathroom. She's lounging on the bed watching some terrible daytime TV show, eating an apple.

"The heat felt good," I admit. "Thanks for bringing that shampoo."

"No problem," she says around an oversized bite. "Think you'd be up for food that doesn't taste like disinfectant?"

I haven't had much of an appetite since the accident, but when you've got so many pairs of eyes watching you, you just eat whatever they bring. I couldn't tell you if what I was eating tasted like disinfectant, tuna, or a crème brûlée.

"Sure."

"Bennett mentioned ordering something into the hospital, but that seems cruel to Teddy, so I suggested we just grab something at a restaurant nearby."

"I don't want to be gone for too long," I say, looking at the time.

Marley gets up and comes to me, tossing her core into the trash as she passes it. "Hey, we'll just grab burgers quickly, and then you can go back, okay? He was sleeping when we left, and chances are he's still sleeping." She takes both my shoulders in her hands and looks me in the eye. "Deep breaths in, one, two, three. Out one, two, three." We stand across from one another breathing in and out slowly, and I have to admit it is beginning to help. "Better?"

I nod. "Thank you."

She wraps her arm around my shoulder and guides me out of the room to the elevator. "You'd do the same for me. Hell, you practically did. It just looked a bit different."

"When are you two going back?" I ask while we slowly descend.

"Trying to get rid of us?"

"No, I just know Bennett is probably anxious to get home. He's probably in dog withdrawal."

Marley studies me for a minute before answering. "He's loosened the reins a bit since you've been gone. Cass has stepped up in Teddy's absence, and the students he took on were quick learners. We even had a weekend away, if you can believe it."

I'm genuinely shocked. "Really?"

"Yeah, we went to a cottage Sophie's fancy professor boyfriend owns or part owns... At any rate, he has—" she starts to say as the doors open.

"Nellie!" I stare at Marley, eyes wide. "Chickadee." I can feel the hot tears rise and then I'm being pulled from the elevator and my parents are wrapping me in a joint hug.

FORTY-THREE

TEDDY

I'm very over being poked and prodded. My entire abdomen hurts, but I feel fine otherwise. At least I think I feel fine. I'm not allowed to do much other than lie here. What I know for certain is that I'm fucking starving and thirsty. I look up at the bags dripping nutrients and painkillers into my body and feel the sudden desire to rip them open and drink.

While I was being wheeled for another scan this morning, we had to wait for an elevator while breakfast was being delivered. I caught a whiff of a banana and nearly rolled out of bed to get to it. Hell, the idea of eating hospital food right now has me salivating.

The sound of shoes squeaking on the floor draws my attention away from the IV bags, and I see Nellie walk through the door. She looks a bit more refreshed, and she's changed her clothes. I don't care how she looks; all that matters to me is that she's here.

"Hey," she greets me with a kiss, and I catch a whiff of her shampoo.

"How was your shower?" I ask, reaching for her hand.

"Do you really want to know?" She looks so guilty, and I feel bad that she feels like she can't even enjoy a shower right now.

"Please let me live vicariously through you. Tell me everything," I plead.

Nellie proceeds to describe every part of her bathing experience, from removing her clothes to lathering her body. I regret asking as I start imagining being in there with her and my body starts to wake up.

"Okay," I cut her off. "Tell me about the dogs now." I watch her glance down at my body and smirk.

She sits lightly on the bed. "The huskies are doing well, according to the firefighter who took them home, and Kevin has managed to pee all over a paramedic's new hardwood floors. From the sound of it, Bennett may have to find two replacement dogs for the people who'd been approved for the huskies' adoptions."

"And Kevin?"

"We are not at risk of someone else insisting on adopting Kevin. Marley and Bennett are planning to pick him up before they head home."

"They're leaving?" I ask. I had assumed they'd stick around until I was discharged. Nellie and I don't have a way home otherwise.

"They are, but only because we have another way back." I raise my eyebrows in question. "My parents are here," she says slowly, gauging my reaction.

"In the country?" I ask.

"In the hospital," she clarifies.

I don't know if I should be grateful or terrified. I don't think I'd be thrilled to see the man who broke my daughter's heart.

Nellie must notice the fear I'm feeling. She rests a hand on my shoulder, squeezing gently. "They're just happy we're okay. I told them everything. Dad cried." She smiles reassuringly down at me. "My parents don't hold grudges, Teddy. They forgive you because I forgive you. You're not the only one who is an excellent judge of character."

I tug her shirt gently, urging her to kiss me. "I love you," I murmur between kisses and relish the feel of her smile as it meets my lips again and again.

"Knock, knock," a woman's voice calls from the door. "Sorry to interrupt."

Nellie breaks away slowly, and I miss her lips instantly. "Mom, Dad," she says, turning to greet her parents who make their way very slowly into the room. "You remember Teddy, right?"

They flank the bed and smile down at me. "We are so glad you're alright," Mrs. Woodcroft says, reaching to squeeze my hand.

"I'm sorry you had to come home," I say, my eyes bouncing between Nellie's parents.

"Don't be," her dad says. "Our girl needed us." He gazes across to where Nellie is sitting, eyes full of love and pride. It's how I look at her, although there's always heat in the mix too.

"Are you sure you're comfortable?" Nellie fusses over me from the passenger door. "It's not too late to book a patient transfer so you can fully recline."

I reach for her hand before she can check the seat belt for the fifth time. "Nellie, I'm good. I'm full of painkillers and feel like I'm floating on a cloud. If something feels off, I promise to let you know."

When the doctor said I was ready to be discharged, Nellie had asked him several times throughout the conversation if it was indeed the right decision. Her forehead is still pinched with worry as she climbs into the seat directly behind mine. My head is practically in her lap, but this way she can keep a very close eye on me. Her hands start to gently massage my head before her father has even put the car into drive and between that and the drugs, my eyes grow heavier. *I'll be fine*, I think just before I'm out.

"As long as you need us to," Nellie's mother is saying when I wake up.

Nellie's upside-down face fills my vision when I open my eyes, and I decide it's the best way to wake up. Maybe not the upside-down part, but certainly her face.

"Hey you," she whispers, kissing my forehead. "Have a good sleep?"

I swallow and give her a lazy smile. I almost close my eyes again but realize we aren't moving, nor is the car making a sound. "What's going on?"

"We're home."

"Home?"

"Well, we're at my house, your house until you're more mobile," she explains.

I smile up at her. "You're home," I murmur.

"Yes, my home."

I shake my head. "No, you're, apostrophe R. E. home."

The need to explain again that we're at her house gives way to soft eyes that fill with tears and lips that tremble ever so slightly.

"Home," she says quietly, brushing her hand across my forehead.

NELLIE

"I'd like to propose a toast," Zoe says, standing from the table with her glass held high. "To finding the love of your life not once but twice, and to believing second chances are sometimes very worth it."

"Hear, hear!" my dad cheers, raising his glass a little too enthusiastically as lemonade sloshes over the side onto his plate of salad.

"Thank you, Zo," Teddy says lovingly, squeezing my thigh under the table.

It's been a long two months. Teddy has been very good at following doctor's orders and letting me do as much as I can for him. My parents and his family have stepped in from time to time so I could go back to work a couple of days a week once my body was feeling better. Tonight's dinner marks the end of my parents' stay and our final week of being here for the foreseeable future.

"Um, Nellie," Zoe whispers from across the table. "Why does your neighbor keep glaring over at us? Are we being too loud?"

I look back in time to see Mrs. Dipietro's lip curl when she catches sight of Kevin zooming around the yard, right before she turns back to her precious tomatoes.

"I believe she's just upset that dogs exist." I shrug. "Don't let that miserable woman ruin your night. Be as loud as you want. You too," I call to Kevin who is now squirming around on his back, legs swimming through the air.

"What time does your flight leave tomorrow?" Teddy's dad asks my parents.

"Two-thirty in the afternoon, thankfully. We couldn't believe there was a flight at a reasonable time."

"Straight through, or do you have a layover somewhere?"

"A quick stop in Vancouver, and then straight to Manila. But we then fly from Manila to the island we're living on. That's the part of the trip I'm dreading." Mom shudders. "Feels like a plane made out of popsicle sticks."

"The woman who doesn't love to fly married a man obsessed with birds." My dad laughs.

"My wife hated to fly too," Teddy's dad says sadly. "Yet she wanted to be thrown into the wind."

I look over at Teddy, knowing he hadn't been there for that part, but he's chatting with his brother and didn't seem to hear.

While we're cleaning up, Zoe pulls me into the hall, and I watch as she pulls a small pouch from her purse. "I, or we, have something for Teddy, but I'm not sure how he'll respond," she whispers.

"What is it?"

She tugs the strings on the bag and shakes out a black rope bracelet with a silver ring.

"It's lovely, but I'm confused why you think he'd have a problem with it. I don't think he's against wearing a bracelet." Maybe there's some history there I don't know about, but I can easily see it on his wrist.

"We kept some of Mom's ashes," Zoe falters, her voice breaking and I automatically pull her into me. "He had been..." She pulls back and looks down at the bracelet, her thumb tracing the circle. "Well, let's just say he wasn't thrilled about Mom's post-mortem plans. I think he had felt betrayed by her for leaving and then wanting to be spread so far away from us. So we held some back, some of Mom. I had no idea what to even do with them until I saw a video online of putting some ashes into jewelry. This way, she'll always be close. It sounds nutty when I say it out loud, but he wasn't handling it well even before he found out about..."

"The second aneurysm," I finish.

Zoe gives me a grateful smile. "Yeah. I'll never forgive myself for not telling him."

"He understands, Zoe. Obviously it hurt him, but he understands why you did it, why you respected your mom's wishes. I think he'll be incredibly touched by this gift."

"Would you mind..."

"I'll go get him and Will and your dad, then leave you to it?"

She tilts her head and mouths a quiet thank you.

Teddy is standing at the kitchen counter, sorting plates when I walk up behind him, wrap my arms around his chest, and rest my head against his back. "I'm so glad they all came, but I cannot wait until I get you all to myself," he says quietly.

I answer with a soft "mmm" because since we've been home there has always been someone else here, and until his doctor gave him a solid progress report, I had refused to do anything more than kiss him. I'm as desperate as he is to be alone.

"Your sister wants to talk to you in the living room."

"Oh?"

"I'll finish this. You go talk." I step beside him and bump

him with my hip. He drops a kiss on my head before turning to leave the room.

I step outside and let Will and his dad know Zoe wants to see them, and then I sit with Will and Zoe's wives, Stephanie and Jordan, and my parents on the deck so they have the house to themselves.

"What's going on?" my mom asks, nosy as ever.

"Family meeting," I say.

Will and Zoe's wives look at one another before looking over at me, both with tears in their eyes.

"Seriously, what is happening?" Mom pleads, leaning to look through the deck door.

"I'm sure she'll tell us later, ducky," Dad says, patting Mom on the arm.

"I love that you call her ducky," Stephanie coos. "Will calls me baby, and I kind of hate it."

"Does he call anyone else baby?" Jordan asks.

Stephanie looks appalled by the question. "No."

"Then embrace it. Sure, it may be a common endearment, but only one person is calling you that, and it happens to be the one you swore to love, honor, and cherish until the end."

"What does Zoe call you when we aren't around? I've only heard her say Jor."

Jordan blushes and shakes her head. "That's only for us," she says as she absently rubs her very pregnant belly.

"Nellie?" Stephanie turns to me. "What does Teddy call you?"

"Other than 'The One,'" Jordan adds with air quotes.

"He doesn't call me 'The One,' I can tell you that." I laugh.

"Maybe he doesn't say it to you, but that's how he has always referred to you. We never heard him say your name. We only found out what it was from Zoe."

My parents both look like they're about to melt into a puddle as they watch me blush.

Nellie, Nell, LG, and once in a while when he's making me feel good, pretty girl. But I don't feel like sharing with anyone right now. If he uses them in front of others then they can know, but they won't sound right on my lips. However, if he uses pretty girl, we may have to have a very serious conversation and also never see any of them again.

Thankfully the Fletcher clan joins us before they ask me again. It's clear to everyone that tears have been shed, and I watch my mom scrutinize every single person before her eyes land on me. I can tell she's desperate to ask what happened.

Teddy sits beside me, and his hand immediately goes to my thigh. I look down to see the bracelet affixed to his wrist. When I look up, my eyes meet that serene smile I love most.

I do not doubt that this is who is supposed to be next to me until I cease to exist. Teddy told me George had called our relationship years in the making, like it was inevitable. And you know what they say about inevitabilities.

EPILOGUE

Teddy

Despite the mid-October chill in the air, I still insist that sitting on the deck is the best way to enjoy my late morning break. We've been living at Betty and Joshua's for three weeks, and it finally feels like we've settled into a routine. The fence was installed our first week here, and since then, I've been working to gradually acclimate the dogs to their new reality. Lots of social time without barriers. So far, so good. Kevin and our senior rescue, Stanley, live in the house with us due to several factors, the main one being their physical limitations. We're afraid Kevin would seem like prey, and Stanley just doesn't have the mobility to keep up with the others.

Nellie has attended a couple of planning meetings and works at the mobile library a couple of times a week, but otherwise she's here with me, learning the ropes of what it takes to keep a place like this going. I've never seen someone look so happy to pick up dog shit. Yesterday, I caught her singing the wrong lyrics to Bon Jovi's "Living On A Prayer." I'll tell her that the word "naked" does not appear in the song another time. But she was singing and dancing away, and all I could do was watch her fully enjoy her time once again picking up dog shit.

"Holy shit!" Nellie squeals from the house. The door bursts open, and a second later, her phone is in my face. "Did you know?" It takes a second for my eyes to adjust, but I'm looking at a picture of a sapphire ring on a finger. It takes another few seconds to realize that I know the blurry people in the background.

Nellie looks elated, like she could float away at any second, so I reach out and take her hand to pull her into my lap. "Did he tell you he was planning this?" she grills me.

"Bennett never had to tell anyone he was planning it," I say, holding back my laugh. "I'm shocked he didn't do it the day she came back."

"But did you know when he was going to do it?"

I shake my head slowly as she goes back to looking at the picture. "Do you think I would have kept it from you if I'd known, LG?" My tone is deadly serious.

She finally looks at me, setting her phone down. "I kind of wish he'd done it while we were still there." She pouts. "But I guess he wanted to do it on the first anniversary of when they met."

"It's hard to believe that it's only been a year." My head thunks against the chair's back.

"When you know, you know. Time doesn't matter." She shrugs, taking my face gently in her hands and moving so her knees are hugging my thighs.

I pull her harder against me and watch her expression heat. "Do you know?" I ask as my hands slide under her sweater.

"I know," she says, shivering under my touch.

As the hem of her sweater moves up with my hands, I reveal the new tattoo, a loon, its wings splayed above the water, the head stretching up along her sternum. I bend to kiss it, and she sighs out a fact. "Loons can stay underwater for up to five minutes." A smile curls my lips as I slowly make my way up her body.

"How long?"

"Five minutes," she pants. I love how fast she loses herself in these moments.

"Have you known?" I ask, pulling my hands from under her sweater and raising one to her jaw. I slide my thumb over her lips and down to her chin so I can tip her head, forcing her to look at me. "How long have you known, LG?"

"The day we met," she says quietly. Her lower lip slips between her teeth, and I watch as she recalls that day. "It was the panic I felt when you were getting off the train. I'd lied to you and was afraid you wouldn't actually text me."

"There was no way in hell that I wasn't texting you, Nellie," I assure her. "But even if I hadn't, I'm not so sure we wouldn't have met again at some point."

My phone lights up next to me and I grudgingly look down.

BETTY

Rumi has a new home!

"Looks like a good day for everyone," I say, smiling up at her.

She raises an eyebrow in question. "Oh? Is it a good day, EG?"

"Every day with you is a good day." I wrap my arms around her like a vice and her lips crash into mine.

"You're so corny," she says between kisses.

"You love it." I capture her lip between my teeth and drag it off slowly.

My stomach growls, and we break apart laughing. "I was

actually on my way to see what you wanted for lunch when I got the text."

"Are you on the menu?" I ask sincerely, running my hands along her sides, unable to keep from touching her when she's this close.

"I believe I'm the special on the dessert menu today."

I squeeze her hips, and she automatically jogs them against me, a preview of things to come. "Can I have dessert first?" I ask just as my stomach grumbles again, and I groan. "We still have greenhouse tomatoes, right?" I grit out since my body can't seem to get on the same page.

"There are two left, and George dropped off a loaf of bread yesterday while you were out." George picked up bread baking while we were gone and has proven to be quite good at it.

"Toasted tomato sandwiches?" I ask as Nellie slips off my lap, holding her hands out to me.

"Obviously," she says, leading me inside.

Sitting at the little kitchen table in Betty and Joshua's house, Nellie and I eat the last toasted tomato sandwich of the year, and I savor every bite the way I do every smile Nellie sends my way. The best things in life are worth waiting for.

AUTHOR'S NOTE

My grandmother suffered a ruptured cerebral aneurysm when she was thirty-seven, she was a wife and mother of four with a job and an active social life. The effects of the rupture left her with partial paralysis and the inability to speak – she could say a couple of words and somehow that's all she needed. It was a second rupture twenty-three years later that ended her life. An aneurysm they were told would likely rupture within five to ten years of the first one, so the fact she lived so long was impressive, a true testament to how stubborn she was.

My dad and his siblings found out about the second aneurysm at her funeral but no one had the same reaction as Teddy, thankfully. Aneurysms and strokes hit close to home in my family, on both sides. People talk about being afraid of cancer but I've always been afraid of aneurysms and clots. Teddy and Zoey's fear mirrors my own. A fear that I nearly realized while writing the book. I had gotten some respiratory virus that left me with an aggressive cough for weeks. Into the second week, I started getting awful headaches at the back of my head that would last about twenty minutes and then disappear gradually, the throbbing growing duller. I started doing some research about cough headaches and through reputable sources discovered that they aren't all that common and one at the back of the head may be a sign of an underlying condition vs a symptom of the cough. The consensus was the same across the board, call your doctor. This was all the encouragement I needed to take it seriously. Nineteen days after my doctor's appointment, I had an MRI that showed a healthy brain with beautiful blood vessels. Yay!

Nellie's diagnosis of Von Willebrand Disease as an adult also hits close to home after I was tested for a blood disorder following excessive bleeding during gallbladder surgery. Shockingly, my results showed a high VWD activity factor (clotting), something the doctor attributed to me having had COVID between my surgery and being tested. Please remember my fear of clots. *nervous laughter* After being tested again months later my results showed that I was in a normal range. Another test a few months after that and the same result was achieved, yay me! In the meantime, though I did a lot of research, the body is fascinating and I wanted to share my experiences in a more creative and healthy way than the constant worry I let myself live with.

Above all, let this be a reminder to advocate for yourself if you don't think something is quite right. Only you know your body.

And finally, tomorrow isn't a guarantee, love big for as long as you can.

"To have had them at all is the best part."
- Natasha "Tash" Anderson

ACKNOWLEDGMENTS

This book felt a bit like it was years in the making. Teddy's story was so personal for me and I hope I did it justice.

Cassandra, having you by my side throughout this journey felt extra special this time around as this is a story we share. I am so damn grateful for your continued support throughout every single step of the writing process. I'm also so happy to have someone to sit at a cafe and work with.

Cristina and Jillian, having you beta read was a dream. Your feedback as well as unhinged comments made the process, dare I say, fun. But mostly, thank you for the voice messages and countless texts. I still have to pinch myself that I get to call you two friends.

Jess, Jenn, Whit, Ramona, Ada and Erin, thank you for being willing to read this in its rougher state and providing such valuable feedback. It's no easy task and I am endlessly grateful to you all.

Alex and Jamie, thanks for putting up with my constant ramblings. Your patience with me is commendable.

Jen, Jen's words of encouragement throughout the writing process of books 1 & 2 meant so much to me. It's hard to imagine doing it now without her here to bounce ideas off of. But I keep her words on my desk and refer back to them when I need a reminder to believe in myself.

Mary-Jo and Linda, look at this, a steamier book and I

wasn't even nervous about you reading it this time around. I think that means I'm a seasoned professional now.

Sarah, thank you for pushing me to look deeper into these characters. I can say with certainty that round two of dev edits wasn't nearly as intimidating, but it was just as important. I feel so lucky that I get to call you my editor.

Ally, damn you're talented! Seriously, I am in awe of your ability to bring my characters to life, while balancing a rather hectic life of your own. I adore you!

Readers, thank you for spending time with me and my characters. I know time is precious and I am so honored that you spent some of it here.

My Family. Dad, thank you for all the stories you shared about Grandma, Grandpa and your childhood. I will never get tired of hearing them. Mom, your enthusiasm has been unmatched as I chase this dream. I'm not sure I will ever be able to express how important it has been to me, other than by continuing to chase it.

Kail, how'd I get a sister like you eh? I love you to the moon and back.

My Grandpa, who taught us a great deal about compassion and putting ones needs ahead of our own. I wish I could have thanked him for these lessons before it was too late.

Sean, when people say, "That guy doesn't exist in real life." I can't help but feel a little sorry for them. I know he does because I get to wake up beside him every morning and go to sleep next to him every night. I get to call that guy mine. (Yes I'm crying as I write this.) I cherish every single, "I'm proud of you babe!" and "I love you!" you utter. And you utter them a lot, so that's a helluva lot of cherishing. I love you! Thank you for loving me.

Linda & Leslie, thank you for raising that guy.

ABOUT THE AUTHOR

Megan McSpadden dreads talking about herself almost as much as seeing a snake on a hike. But she knows we all must do hard things so here it goes.

Megan lives in Hamilton, Ontario with her husband, two dogs, two cats and unruly garden. When not writing she can usually be found photographing families (don't worry they pay her to do it), yelling at her beloved Toronto Maple Leafs, dreaming of traveling somewhere else or cooking something her husband will ask her to make again but knows she won't because Megan doesn't do recipes.

Megan enjoys writing romance that will make you laugh one minute only to cry the next. Don't ask why because she doesn't know.

Stay tuned for Sophie & Foster's story, coming 2025!

www.ingramcontent.com/pod-product-compliance
Lightning Source LLC
Chambersburg PA
CBHW021238190726
48289CB00005B/1376